I0654558

GORILLAZ IN THE BAY 3

De'Kari

Lock Down Publications and Ca$h
Presents

Gorillaz in the Bay 3
A Novel by De'Kari

De'Kari

Lock Down Publications
P.O. Box 870494
Mesquite, Tx 75187

Visit our website @
www.lockdownpublications.com

Copyright 2019 by De'Kari
Gorillaz in the Bay 3

All rights reserved. No part of this book may be reproduced in any form or by electronic or mechanical means, including information storage and retrieval systems without permission in writing from the publisher, except by a reviewer who may quote brief passages in review.
First Edition August 2019
Printed in the United States of America

This is a work of fiction. Names, characters, places, and incidents either are products of the author's imagination or are used fictitiously. Any similarity to actual events or locales or persons, living or dead, is entirely coincidental.

Lock Down Publications
Like our page on Facebook: Lock Down Publications @
www.facebook.com/lockdownpublications.ldp
Cover design and layout by: **Dynasty Cover Me**
Book interior design by: **Shawn Walker**
Edited by: **Tam Jernigan**

Stay Connected with Us!

Text **LOCKDOWN** to 22828 to stay up-to-date with new
releases, sneak peaks, contests and more…
Or **CLICK HERE** to sign up.
Thank you.

Like our page on Facebook:

Lock Down Publications: Facebook

Join <u>Lock Down Publications/The New Era Reading
Group</u>

Visit our website @
<u>www.lockdownpublications.com</u>

Follow us on Instagram:

Lock Down Publications: Instagram

Email Us: We want to hear from you!

IN MEMORY OF LIL RELL

This book is dedicated to the memory of a real Neva Die Soldier. Tyrell Demetrius Hayes, a true friend, brother and comrade. We love and miss you, lil' brah. Hold it down for us until we get there.

Sunrise: December 17, 1993
Sunset: September 13, 2015
Immortalized: 2015

Moja upendo. Ninakupenda mwezi!!!
One Aim, One Struggle, One Goal!
Neva Die

Part I
Resurrection of the Dead!

De'Kari

Chapter I

Stanford Hospital

The gurney came bursting through the doors. Paramedics frantically worked on the body that was strapped to it while shouting out information seemingly to no one in particular.

"We've got a multiple GSW (gunshot wound) victim in his late twenties. Victim appears to be a healthy African American male. Blood pressure is 107/65 and dropping. We need ER doctors and surgical doctors in the ER immediately!" One of the paramedics yelled.

As if by magic, a team of doctors and nurses appeared out of nowhere and took control of the gurney. They scrambled and fussed over the male victim with extreme precision as if they've been practicing their entire life for this very moment.

"We've lost him twice in the bus on the way over. The second time, a defibrillator was used to resuscitate." The paramedic called out as she relinquished control of the gurney to the team of doctors and nurses.

As the doctors rushed Jason Voorheeze to the O.R. for surgery, they continued to spew out orders in a language that only they could understand.

"We're gonna need Doctor Butler and five quarts of blood. The chart says the victim is "O" negative! Give me sixty cc's of Demerol, thirty cc's of morphine, two quarts of saline solution...." It went on and on, as the patient was rushed to the operating room.

French Tip refused to let them separate her from her brother. A second ambulance was called for Mama B. who had to be admitted to the hospital. She was suffering from severe distress and shock.

French Tip had to know about her brother. She didn't think he was going to make it. She'd ridden with him in the ambulance and nearly had a heart attack both times when he crashed. But, thank GOD, He bought him back. Now, Tip allowed herself a small glimmer of hope that that he would pull through.

Eight long, grueling hours slowly passed. The waiting room was reminiscent of what it ad been just a couple of months ago, when Voorheeze had been shot the first time; long solemn looks in a sea of black faces. No one dared to voice the fears that settled deep within their hearts. Much like old fables and urban legends, whose power lies solely in those that speak them into existence.

French Tip was beyond numb. She felt death. Murder was nowhere around but death was present. Both of her brothers were gone, stolen from her. They were her protectors. Who would protect her now? Who would help her take care of her mother? The laundry list of questions that she had spun rapidly in her head. They'd built one hell of an empire, but at what cost? She could taste the death that was ever present, like a lingering virus.

Her thoughts were interrupted by the doctor walking in her direction. As he approached the waiting room, his feet dragged slow, like they were weighted down. His smock was disheveled and stained with blood. He looked like he had been to hell and back. It couldn't be good news, n to with the look on his face. His entire demeanor screamed torment.

"Ms. Juniel," he approached French Tip, giving her his sole attention. "Now, we are not out of the woods just yet" he cautioned. "It's been a long and trying day for the all of us ,I'm sure. I'm sorry for the tragedy that has befallen your family. Thankfully, we were able to get your brother stable for now."

French Tip jumped into the doctor's arms; hugging and squeezing him tight. Everyone was loud and celebratory. The doctor had to wave his arms to get everyone's attention. "There were a lot of complications during surgery; all of which were successfully tended to. However, the next twenty-four hours are crucial for him. Your brother still has a hell of a fight ahead of him."

"Okay doctor. I understand about the fight, but for now, my brother is okay though?" she asked him, sounding like a little girl, who'd gotten in trouble and was now standing in front of the school teacher.

"Yes maam, for now he is okay." Doctor Butler didn't want to give the young lady any false hope. From what he'd been told, she'd already been through a great deal.

Cantelope walked over and hugged her cousin. They'd both been through a lot lately, but they were fighters, and fighters pushed on.

Doctor Butler said a few more things to them then retreated to his office. He didn't know how many more seventy two-hour shift's he had in him, but he knew the last one really took a lot out of him.

French Tip stayed in the comfort of Cantelope's arms for a little while longer. She needed to feel a sense of security. True enough, Doctor Butler had made it clear that her brother was not out of the woods just yet. At least she could find momentary ease in knowing her brother had a chance to live. Any fighting odds were good odds given who her brother was. Neva was he the type of person to bow down or to get rolled over. He would always fight and stand for something, so she knew he would fight for his life. The question was, would fighting be enough?

The upper echelon of Neva Die Dragon Gang was obsolete. T'Rida and Clark were dead. Voorheeze was laid up in a hospital bed fighting for his life and Gunz was half way across the country doing only God knew what. French had to decide fast because she knew they could very well be on the brink of a full-fledged coup or even worse a civil war.

She made her way to her mother's room to check on her after telling Cantelope to let the rest of the regime know that there would be a meeting at the War Room in two days. She opened the door figuring her mother would be asleep at that time of night, but felt it was necessary to update her due to the severity of the situation. When French sat down, Mama Beckum's eyes fluttered open. She was trying to focus.

"My My Baby" was all she could get out. She was so drained. Sleep alluded Mama B. due to the amount of stress. She was wondering if the suffering and loss of her children could actually be punishment for her past sins? Could God be that cruel?

"He's okay, Mama!" French Tip took her mother's hand into her own.

"He made it out of surgery okay. It was a long surgery. There were a couple of problems during the surgery, but they took care of them. Due to the level of trauma that his body endured, the doctor felt it was best to put him in a medically induced coma". French Tip took a deep breath. "The induced coma was the best option for recovery. Without doing so, there was a high probability of his body going into shock, which in this stage could prove to be fatal. Now he has time to heal and rest." She made sure to sound confident as she filled her mother in. Heaven knows her mother needed some good news. A ray of sunshine in this dense storm they've been through.

"Thank you, Jesus! Thank you, Jesus!" Mama Beckum cried out, her heart still broken over losing her first born. But, she wouldn't' be ungrateful, she counted the blessings she'd received.

French Tip just held her mother's hand rubbing it. She was lost in her own thoughts. She knew that this was only the beginning of the trouble to come....

**** N. D. ****
11:47 p.m.

BEEP! BEEP!
BEEP!BEEP!

He sits in the dark raging like a body builder in the middle of Roid-Rage. He doesn't know how long he's been in the dark confines of the hospital room.

The devil was a lie and he knew it. But, as he stared at the bandaged body with all the tubes and hoses running out of it, it was hard to ignore the devil and not do his bidding. He remembered reading "Thugs Cry" by Ca$h while he was locked up. A single hot tear slowly traveled down his face as he cursed the irony.

"Voorheeze where did y'all go wrong? We're revolutionaries not gangstas! Brah, all that gangsta shit that was the old us. The new us, were Enlightened Visionaries. Did you forget that? Lil Brah, y'all doing just like them old ones did before us. We were supposed to be the ones to break the cycle. That's why our umbrella didn't fall up under them three letters. We might be up under the oath and the codes, but what we were building wasn't..."

His thoughts were interrupted by the sound of footsteps stopping outside of the door. He quickly opened the door to the bathroom and rushed inside. He didn't know who was getting ready to enter the room, but he was not ready to see anyone. Just to be safe he took his FN off of his waist and held it, ready!

"Okay, just please remember to keep it down and hurry. No one is supposed to be up here, I could lose my job." A female nurse spoke just above a whisper, yet the urgency was evident in her voice.

"Don't trip, babe. You doin' a nigga a favor. I won't get you in any trouble. Dat's my word on dat. I'm in and I'm out". The stranger told her after crossing the threshold. "Here." He told her as he pulled out a large stack of one hundred-dollar bills.

She snatched the knot of money faster than a snapping turtle snatching lettuce. "Okay, thank you! But please hurry." She spun around and left before he asked her for the money back or before something happened.

He looked like trouble and she didn't want any part of it. When he told her, he would give her five thousand dollars, she thought about her sick daughter. She really needed the money and that's the only reason the nurse agreed to break the rules.

BEEP! BEEP!

BEEP!BEEP!

BEEP! BEEP!

He just stood there looking at the broken and bruised body. He could see where the bullets struck from the placements of the bandages.

BEEP! BEEP!

The earie silence was only interrupted by the irritating sound of the machine as it beeped, sent a chill down his spine. Its florescent glow cast an odd hue in the room.

Finally, he slowly approached. Unbeknownst to him, the visitor that was hiding in the bathroom had silently cracked the door open. He was on point, poised ready to let his FN bark at the first sign of foul play.

He stood next to the bed. Shoulders drooped in defeat, head bowed. He couldn't remember the last time he'd cried. He thinks it was at Grandma Beckum's funeral. He's unsure. But as he stands gazing down, tears flow and fall onto the hospital bed freely.

"Look at you. Got me standing here crying like a little bitch. I bet if yo ass could see me, you'd die laughing." He reached out and gently brushed the back of his fingers across Voorheeze's cheek.

The guy in the bathroom was less on guard due to the real tears that he saw the nigga crying, but that banger was still on deck just in case.

"It's all my fault, rogue! I should've told you, but I couldn't, nigga, there wasn't enough time. Fuck!" He smashed his fist in the palm of his other hand. After he taking a deep breath he continued.

"I swear to God though, nigga, I got you. I'ma take care of everything, don't you trip!" He leaned down and kissed Voorheeze on the fore head.

"I love you, rogue." He turns around and quietly walks out of the room closing the door behind him.

The door to the bathroom slowly opened all the way and the first visitor stepped out. It was too dark in the room for him to make out who the other nigga was. There was a brief moment when he had bent down to kiss Voorheeze forehead. The hue of the florescent light illuminated his face a little, still he was unable to make out who the other man was.

So, distracted in his thoughts, he didn't hear the young nurse as she opened the door.

"Oh, um excuse me, who are you? And what are you doing here?" She asked him as she turned the lights on. The nurse was coming to tell the other guy that it was time to go. She didn't expect to see someone else.

"Sistah, please do not be alarmed. I assure you I am not a threat and I don't mean you or brotha any harm." He spoke in his most docile tone while making his posture non-intimidating.

She looked him over. He looked harmless and he was so cute with that smile, those innocent eyes and them gold teeth. "Okay, but you can't be in here you're gonna get me in trouble. I can't afford to get fired. I need this job." She stepped aside making a gesture that he had to leave.

"Thank you, my queen, I won't cause you any grief. "He reached in his jeans, pulled out a knot and handed her half of it. "I just needed to see my brotha and make sure he was okay."

"How many brothers does he have?" She asked as she accepted the money, neva saying thank you.

"What do you mean?" He paused in mid stride as he asked the question.

"There was a guy here not too long ago. He said that he was his brother too." She wasn't paying him no mind. The young woman was focused on trying to guess how much money he'd given her. It was more than the other guy gave, she could tell by its thickness.

De'Kari

**** N. D. ****

Chapter II

The Next Morning

Chief Vieira was in a state if confusion beyond her control. She'd sat at the vanity in her room staring at herself in the mirror for the past three hours, looking at the same face. The same puffy red eyes that ran smeared mascara down her face. The same worry and stress lines. The same runny nose. Most importantly, the same eyes that were sad, lost, frustrated and confused!

The image hasn't changed, and it wasn't going to. She wasn't a drinker. The same glass of Chardonnay that she'd poured hours ago was still sitting untouched. She was supposed to be at work hours ago, but couldn't find the strength to get dressed. She sat in her bra and panties. Her ample breast straining at the material of the bra begging to be freed.

When she'd first met La'Mont, she had no idea of the life he lived. The sex was great. It was the best she ever had. As their affair continued and she got to know him, he was a very nice, caring, giving, and understanding person.

She rubbed her finger around the rim of the glass as she thought. He was an excellent listener. All in all, he was the perfect gentleman, even if he was a little rough around the edges. Since they had only been seeing each other a relatively short time, she'd had no time to think about, let alone realize that she was falling in love with him.

The tears began flowing again. Stopping them was useless. More would just take the place of the ones she wiped away. What was she going to do? The aching of her heart was driving her insane. She was near the point of delirium.

She had to know what happened to him. She couldn't take it any more! She'd nearly had a heart attack when the news got out about the shooting at the church. The initial report was that he had been killed. Then a report came that he may have survived.

Finally, she got up. She decided she would get dressed and go see for herself. Hell, she was the police, he was a high profile suspect out on bond who had been gunned down. She had every right to stop in on him.

As she passed her floor to ceiling mirror, she stopped and looked at herself. She was not fat. Her breast were huge, and her ass was massive, but it looked good. She used to feel self-conscious about the size of her ass. All white girls did. After she met La'Mont, he'd changed that. He pointed out to her that she was perfect.

"God made seven colors in the rainbow so that those colors could produce an endless supply of color, but for every color there was somebody". When he spoke those words, she was breathless. La'Mont told her he thought her big ass was sexy and made her clothes look better. Even if he didn't have her body feening for him, her mind was.

She smacked herself on the ass hard and smiled as it jiggled. Proud of everything her mama gave her! Vieira was going to go see her man!

**** N. D. ****
Sunnyvale, CA

The Brass Rail is a small old strip club in downtown Sunnyvale. If someone's first encounter or at a strip club was the Brass Rail, they would wonder why niggaz went to the strip club at all. It was that bad. The lighting was bullshit, the service busy and the dancers, god damn! We are talking bullet holes and everything else. But it was a good place to conduct business. People minded theirs and stayed the fuck out of yours. Just the way it should be, establishment included.

This was why Gunz was sitting at one of the back tables patiently awaiting his guest. The mothafucka came thru for him in a major way but that still didn't make him legit. If anything popped off, Gunz was ready. This red head chick, who looked like she'd shot half a gram of heroin into her veins just before she came out, approached him and asked him if he wanted a lap dance. He declined the dance but tipped her two hundred dollars anyway. She lit up. Without knowing it, Gunz had given her hope. In a world of shit, where it was "dog eat dog", everyone was out for self. Gunz reminded her that not everybody was corrupt. There were still some good people out there. She felt like crying. Instead she quickly tucked the money away before Hindu or one of his spy snitches noticed it. Shit, she was keeping this for herself. He wanted everything with his fat ass. Shit, he acted like a fucking pimp.

Finally, his guest arrived. Gunz didn't get up. Instead, he gestured for the man to take a seat. Gunz casually took in the man's attire. Cowboy boots, jeans, thin button-down long sleeve shirt and a fucking cowboy hat, the fucking Mexican thought he was a white boy.

Gunz finally picked up the drink that had been sitting untouched at his table. Out of sight of the guest, three men stood up and made their way to the exit.

Gunz waved the server over, "Whata ya drinking, Cowboy? And before you say you ain't drinking." He leaned forward and stared directly into his eyes, "Trust me, you're drinking."

Lt. Urena was definitely nervous. He had been planning and hoping for this for a long time. Still, one couldn't ever get totally ready to break the law. You just did it.

"I'll take a Coors Light." He nervously said as he looked around.

"What can I get for you handsome?" The waitress was probably the best-looking thing in the building and she knew it. Her confidence said so.

"Say, beautiful, let me get four double shots of Hennessy and a bottle of Coors." He reached inside of his pocket "You know what, on second thought just bring me a bottle of chilled Henny, two glasses and a bottle of Coors." Gunz tossed three hundred dollars on her tray. It wasn't that he was a trick or flossing, Gunz was just one of the people who understood and respected every aspect of the game.

Shit, a hustle was a hustle. Who was he to knock someone else's hustle! Some niggaz looked down on stripping and prostitution, not Gunz though. It took a lot of guts, self-will and a lot of other shit to strip and put up with the lame ass niggaz that gawked over them or the wannabe niggaz who felt like the women were pieces of meat or property because they dropped a few dollars on them. Mothafuckas didn't understand that it was just entertainment. Strippers were dancers, like any other dancer. Only they danced butt booty ass naked!

The DJ announced the next dancer. A white girl, who looked like she was fresh from the trailer park, came out. Gunz' attention was drawn to the front door. Two of the three men who'd exited suddenly returned. A sign that there weren't any other police out there. The third one would remain outside just to make sure none popped up expectantly.

"Cop, this is yo rodeo, talk." Gunz leaned back in his chair and waited.

Urena cleared his throat and fought to find his nerve. "It's like this, I've been looking to approach you guys for a long time. Since before Thomas was killed. I just neva knew how nor ever found the opportunity. When I learned about Grear and the case she was compiling on Mr. Harvey, I saw it as my opportunity, my shot." Urena was still feeling nervous, but he'd found his rhythm and he was going to rock with it.

The waitress had other plans.

"Here's your order and your change, sugar." She batted her eyes at Gunz when she spoke.

"I don't ever change sweetheart. Why should I collect it? That's all you, beautiful." It was a two-hundred-dollar tip. Honestly, it was nothing to Gunz.

Urena was using the time to ogle her body. Shit, he was drooling all over himself. He'd neva been with a black woman, but he's fantasized about being with one for years. But, they intimidated him.

"Thank you, baby. Now, if you need or want anything, you make sure you give me a call." Their waitress looked over at Urena, saw how thirsty he was and said, "that goes for your little cute cowboy friend, too!" She walked away shaking her booty.

Urena looked like he was on the verge of having a brain aneurism.

"You alright, cop?" Gunz didn't give a fuck if he was or not. He was getting the man back focused.

Urena took a long swallow of his beer. Gunz cracked the Henny, filled both shot glasses up and pushed one over to Urena. "There you go. That there will help you get your feet back under you."

Urena didn't drink Cognac. He needed something to take the edge off though, so he picked it up and downed all of it. The taste was horrible, but he loved the burn of the alcohol as it flowed down his throat. Gunz poured him another.

"As I was saying, informing you about agent Grear was the golden ticket that I needed…"

"Cop scoot your chair back a little bit." Gunz cut him off before he could finish the sentence.

Although he didn't understand the request, but he did as he was told. He scooted his chair backwards, getting in the way of a man who was walking by. The guy stumbled over the chair. He dropped something in Urena's lap. He did it so quickly and smoothly, no one saw it. The only thing the other patrons saw was a man bumping into someone and apologizing.

As Urena looked down into his lap, a look of confusion clouded his expression and a question burned question burned his tongue.

"That's one hundred thousand dollars, an expression my gratitude for what you did for me. I'm sure that you'll agree that's quite fair." Gunz downed the shot and refilled his glass.

"I think you've misunderstood me. Miss Grear… Agent Grear was a gift, a token of my commitment per-say. I wasn't looking for a one-time payout, I'm looking for a good, cohesive, ongoing relationship." Urena reached for the glass "believe me, I can be very vital."

Gunz wasn't impressed. He'd always been game tight. Fucking wit' Voorheeze on that Safety and Security shit had only laced his boots tighter and made his tools sharper. He waited for Urena to finish the second drink.

"Randy look," calling Urena by his first name definitely got his attention. "I know what you want. I knew your intentions when you called me in Philly. I know about your gambling debts to Big Henry and I know about your immense appetite for the ladies." He downed his drink, not for the taste, but to let the information sink in. Gunz had been drinking Hennessy since high school. He could drink this shit all day.

"See, the money is a warning, Randy. The debt you owed Big Henry is taken care of. You don't owe him shit. As expensive as that was, it, t in itself, was enough payment for that little bit of information you gave. The cash, well it's to let you know that I don't fuck around. I'm very generous with my money. I am just as philanthropic with my bullets. I could give a fuck if it was to some nigga who owed me seventy-five cents, a lieutenant on the police force, or the President of the mothafuckin' United States. I don't like Donald Trump's mothafuckin' ass anyway." Gunz filled both glasses up again and then leaned back.

"Your personal phone is about to ring, Randy, pick it up." Five seconds later Lt. Randy Urena's phone rang. Nervousness swept over him again. His number wasn't listed. He had been communicating with Gunz through a disposable he had.

"Hello?" He hesitantly answered. His eyes remained glued to Gunz.

The caller hung up.

Gunz called the server back over.

"As of right now yo debt is paid and the cash is yours, no strings attached. If you decide you still want to proceed with your original plan, call the number that just called you. Remember, Randy, I'll erase you and everybody you think you love, if you cross me." He stood up from the table.

"What can I do for yo fine ass now, sugar?" Their waitress finally made it over to their table.

Standing face to face with her, Gunz realized she was actually cute. If the owner would fix the cheap ass lighting, maybe niggaz would notice.

"Take care of my man nice and good-like, baby." Gunz told her after counting out a stack ($1000) and handing it to her.

It was money well spent. He already knew what choice Urena would make. People with vices always made the wrong choice. On his way out Gunz walked passed the stage and the redbone that was on it. He couldn't help thinking *Then again if the owner fixed the lights niggaz would get a good look at the rest of the barracudas that worked there."* Outside he climbed into the passenger seat of the black and red BMW X5 Drive 35i. The man that had bumped into Urena was sitting behind the wheel.

"You ready?" AJ asked his big cousin. "Let's head to that meeting, family." Gunz didn't need to say anything else.

Since he'd been back, Gunz loved everything that A.J had done in his absence. AJ had actually grown into one hellavuh leader and commander. Everything he was given, AJ expanded. He'd created some new shit and from what he said, he had other plans in the making. Gunz really was impressed when he learned that AJ was still in communication with Joe, Dame, and the rest of the Case Niggaz that showed true love. Ultimately, Gunz knew that he would have to make a decision. Seeing the "Boss" moves AJ had made once he stepped up in position, there was no way Gunz would just step back in his place.

**** **N. D.** ****

Chapter III

Union City, California

With an eerie feeling, a less confident one than the façade that she put on, French Tip scanned the living room looking into the faces of those present. C-Murda, J. Styles, Johnny, Spitz and Stone Cold were all accounted for. AJ and the Oakland Chapter were M.I.A. She feared the fuckery had begun already. Her eyes met Cantelope's, she couldn't forget her sister. All of the Lieutenants and Capo's were present. All of the Generals were gone and missing like a lost limb. French wondered if they could recover from the devastating blow.

"OK, y'all. We've waited long enough for them. At this point, we must acknowledge the possibility that our Oakland Section might have gone rogue." Again, she locked eyes with Cantelope. She needed strength. "After our meeting, the necessary people will look into that. Whatever the outcome, we'll deal with it accordingly. As for now, a more pressing matter must take precedence. We all know that we are now unfortunately an organization with a governing body that has been crippled." The mood in the living room was grave. Sunken spirits are throughout the room. If Voorheeze pulled through, that would be a blessing, but their body count was irrelevant considering their losses.

Faint music could be heard being played in the back yard. "Everything will be business as usual…." The sound of people coming into the house interrupted her. Everybody whipped out their bangers, ready for whatever!

**** N. D. ****
Union City

He's sitting low in the Dodge Challenger Demon. The windows are tinted, and he is parked a few houses down with a direct line of sight to the house and its occupants. He's been there for close to three hours now. Patience is one virtue that he has more than enough of. He sat and watched each and every person drive up and make their way to the house.

He had to admit that considering the nice sunny day, the music and smell of barbeque is a hellavah guise. No matter how many people showed up, it would just look like they were having a little get together. The music was just loud enough to be noticed, yet nowhere near loud enough to be a nuisance. That was some smart shit.

Platinum Cookies weed smoke filled his lungs as he pulled on the blunt, continuing to observe. It had been far too long. Things have gotten so far out of hand. Sure, money was on point. Any nigga would be more than pleased with the amount of money that has been accumulated. But, he wasn't just "any nigga."

His calm demeanor and soft-spoken voice gave off the perception of an easy target or ordinary "Joe Blow" . The fierce, nerve twitching, soul touching look in his eyes did little to betray the level of destruction that was caged inside of his 5'10" 190lb frame.

He was a vanguard of his people, first and foremost. A god amongst men. He would build and assist with the construction of communities. But, to those who knew and understood what his catalog of tattoos represented and stood for, The Dragon concealed underneath his clothes was a warning of his true nature and intent. A regional commander in position and field General by rank, much like his brotha who has gone astray, his name was widely known and respected within the circles that mattered. He is truly one of the Black Guerilla Family's greatest assets.

Putting the blunt out in the ashtray, he decided it was time. Gunz and A.J. had pulled in about twenty minutes ago. That was more than enough time for things to settle down. He took a deep breath to still his spirit. These were gangstas that he was going to confront, but they were his people first and foremost. So, he needed things to go smoothly. He opened the door and climbed out of the Hell Cat. He loved this damn machine they called a car.

When he'd left brothas were driving scrapers. He had a "94" Buick LaSabre on 24-inch rims. He was young and stupid, just like everyone else. He crossed the street and made his way to the War Room. By the time he made it to the front of the house, so had five other brotha's. Four of the five looked like the starting defensive line for the San Francisco Forty-Niners. All six made their way to the front door.

**** N. D. ****

Meanwhile

The BMW X5 turned onto Santa Elena Way. A.J. was still driving while he and Gunz talked. Things had gone well overall for the family, even with the losses considered. But, it was time for some things to change. One thing both Rida and Voorheeze always preached was evolving with the times. They needed to evolve, or they would surely fall. The tragic misfortunes that they'd experienced made now the perfect opportunity to make those changes.

Gunz knew that the Guerilla Family did well in the area of development and strategic planning along with disciplined structure. Being Oakland born and raised, Gunz had witnessed the Guerilla Family's get down first hand.

But, Gunz was and forever would be Deep East Oakland. After the love Rida and Voorheeze had shown him, he would rep Neva Die Dragon Gang to the fullest! No questions asked. They got out of the SUV and made their way to the front door. There was the sound of music coming from the back, but Gunz knew only one person was in the back on the grill. He took note of the **Dodge Challenger** Demon with the tints a little way down the street, making sure to register it in his head. Any car with tinted windows automatically drew his attention.

The only mothafuckas who sat behind tints were motha-fuckas that didn't want to be seen. Well, the only people that didn't want to be seen were the exact people a nigga needed to see.

They walked in the house. Naturally, Gunz entered first. Gunz had only been to this new location once but knowing that this was a cover for his folks, it felt like he was coming home. Philly had been treating him good, but, damn he missed the Bay.

"We will be business as usual…" He heard someone say as they walked in, but whoever it was stopped in mid-sentence.

They turned the corner after A.J. locked the door and was greeted by a room full of killas all holding bangers pointed at them.

"Well, god damn! If this is how y'all welcome a nigga home, a nigga just might stay out on the East Coast a little longer." Gunz joked with a smile on his face.

A huge smile crossed French's face.

"Boy, don't be walking up in here like dat ass won't get cooked!" Cantelope joked "acting like we ain't Gorillaz in here."

"Shit, you already know dat I know bout them 'Gorillaz in the Bay' but shyyyt when Godzilla in dis bitch King Kong turn monkey real fast." They all laughed at Gunz' joke. The sapphire eyes on his iced-out dragon chain were as blue as the waters in Figi while the rest of the diamonds throughout the body of the dragon reflected on the floor like a strobe light.

French Tip remembered one of her brothers saying, *"and remember one monkey don't stop the show, homeboy."*

A.J. chimed in "Sis, got you wit that one, cuzzo."

The atmosphere in the room was vastly different from the start of the meeting now that Gunz was back. Without question, the Mobb was still intact. They all embraced. Gunz had been gone for two years, so the emotions were strong. They spent a little bit of time catching up.

"Alright, but look y'all, we gotta make some changes." Gunz didn't know how everyone would feel about him being gone for so long and coming back giving orders. At the same time, he couldn't be anything less than himself. "I know some people ain't gone like the changes. Shit some mothafuckas are scared of change. There are only two things you can do to sinking ship. Abandon ship or fix the problem. We gone…

"System disarmed." Sounded on the alarm system.

Gunz came out with a big ass .44 Desert Eagle in his hand faster than the system could finish the alert. He looked directly at A.J., "I thought you locked up?"

A.J.'s .45's was cocked and locked, one in each hand. He didn't know who it was coming through the door, but he felt sorry for them. "I did" was all he replied.

****

Meanwhile

After watching the BMW X5 pull up, the leader waited about five minutes before looking over to his passenger and deciding it was time to move. They double-checked their weapons making sure they were loaded before exiting the **Dodge Challenger Demon.**

The secondary USALAMA (security squad) exited their vehicle as well. The two groups met up directly in front of the War Room. The leader made sure his men fully understood their assignment before approaching the door.

After entering the house, the leader overheard the question about locking up.

"I disarmed it! Now I'm about to come around this wall. Please don't shoot me. We all family so hold your fire." Someone called out from around the corner in the living room.

"Nigga, who the fuck is you?" Gunz called out, his gun trained on the entrance, ready to kill.

His answer came in the form of one man who rounded the corner with five Silver Backs behind him. They entered the room staring down the barrels of twelve different guns and were not phased in the least.

Everyone stared at the nigga who'd barged into their sanctuary uninvited with no-one knowing who the fuck he was! This mothafucka had the heart of a gunslinger. Him and them big ass fucking line backers he had with him. There was nothing special about his look. His height and build were ordinary. His Cavalli jeans and his shirt were as well. Yet, two things held everyone in the room back from filling all them mothafuckas up with slugs. First, the power and respect that his aura commanded was hypnotic. There was something about him, but no-one could figure it out. Part of the reason they couldn't focus on him was the huge fucking Dragon piece hanging off the iced-out chain that was around his neck. It dwarfed Gunz' chain easily. It was covered in black and red diamonds. The chocolate Diamonds covered the entire body except where the scales were, that area was full of blood red diamonds. The Dragons eyes were canary yellow along with the flame that came out of its mouth. The Dragon was about nine and a half inches and the twenty-five -inch chain that it hung on was a chocolate and red one-carat invisible set of diamonds. Even the fucking chain commanded your attention.

French Tip had heard her brother and T'Rida talk about a nigga that had a similar description to the nigga standing in front of them. But, this definitely couldn't be him. That nigga was locked away in Folsom State Penitentiary doing twenty years for murder for hire.

"My brotha, the question isn't who am I. It's what am I," the intruder calmly spoke.

"Nigga, I don't think you're understanding just how real shit is." Gunz recocked the Desert Eagle. A bullet spit out the top of it for emphasis. "If you don't tell me who the fuck you are, I'mma show you what I am."

"And demm mothafuck'n black giant looking mothafuckas behind you gone dance too." A.J. was and always had been trained to go.

His words weren't a threat, but a warning.

The tension in the room was thicker than Cubana Lust in a G-string. He could feel it. He didn't have to look in the faces of the killas. His killas, Gunz knew they were ready.

"You know Leonard, Tommy told me that you was a hot headed brotha, but I thought all of that would've been out of your system by now..."Most people would've relaxed a little bit after hearing the intruder call them by their name and even mention T'Rida, but not Gunz. "So, before this turns ugly and my peoples turn that red dot on your chest into a hole, I'll answer your question." Everyone was so focused on him, no-one had had noticed all the infrared dots on all of them.

"My name is Dok Holliday, but you can call me Dok. I am the father and Chief Commander of what you all call Neva Die Dragon Gang. I was able to disarm the alarm to every property we have from the White House, all the Green houses, the dark room and I even know the locations of the Koffee Shop and Satin Doll." He looked over at French Tip, "But, I don't have the security codes to your personal venues."

French Tip had a look of disbelief on her face. Everyone else had looks of shock on their faces. All except Gunz. After hearing what the nigga said, Gunz knew exactly who he was.

Voorheeze had often spoken highly of blood. Voorheeze would say constantly "I'mma 4-star General. Dok is the 5-star. He's the only nigga I answer to." Gunz could hear Voorheeze voice now. But, the nigga Voorheeze always talked about had dreadlocks all the way down his back.

Dok continued, "Gunz, my brotha, I agree with your as-sessment. It is time for a change." He lifted his hand with his two fingers up like a peace sign, but he had his pinky finger up with it. Instantly, all the red dots disappeared. "My brotha, I'm not your enemy. I'm the brotha that you've neva met. Earlier, I said you guys call what we have Neva Die Dragon Gang. That's neva what it was meant to be, a Gang. The name is Neva Die Dragons because we were all Dragons when this was originally started. All of us were and are members of the Black

Guerilla Family. But we were chosen to make a difference. That's where Neva Die came from, it's an acronym, it stands for:

New
Enlightened
Visionaries
African Decent...
Determined (to)
Increase
Education and Economics"

Everyone stared even more shocked at French Tip as she cut Dok off and continued to quote the rest of the acronym.

She stood up. Mouth wide open, eyes bugged and hands covering her mouth. Her pistol was sitting on her chair. Only she could hear her heart beat, but it sounded so loud to her, she thought everybody could hear it.

"Darrell, I know that's not you." She finally said.

"Nice to finally meet you, Le'Nita or should I say French Tip." They embraced like they've known each other forever.

Dok actually knew everybody. True, he'd just did a twenty-year run in prison, but Neva Die was his idea. He had Voorheeze construct the organization from an idea that Dok had back when they were cell mates in Santa Rita County Jail. Dok was fighting life and Voorheeze was facing 159+ years. They both believed everything that their organization stood for and represented, but now a lot of their comrades had turned sour and lost their way.

T'Rida'd ended up catching a case a few months later. He too was a part of the Guerilla Family and they were all real revolutionary. They truly believed in being vanguards of the people. They'd dreamed of an Urban Utopia for the people. A Black Paradise for the people, by the people. They would hustle to get enough money to buy ten city blocks and it would start from there.

The idea T'Rida had of Gunz and Voorheeze putting their money together after the lick in West Oakland was all Dok's idea. He'd prepared Rida on what to do long before he walked out the gates of DVI. The blue print was sketched, carved and engraved in his head. Once things started going both T'Rida and Voorheeze made sure to give Dok weekly updates. Sometimes they would talk so long Dok could barely get up for his job in the kitchen.

Everyone listened intently while Dok filled them in on information none of them were ready for. All the guns had been tucked away but everyone was still on standby.

Gunz was dissecting everything the nigga said. Only two things could be, as far as he was concerned, either this nigga was the real Dok Holliday or he was a Fed. The question was how to get him to prove who he was. "Look man, niggaz ain't trynna be all disrespectful and shit because if you are who you say you are I ain't trynna go there with you," his gaze was steady and confident "but right now my family done been thru a lot and I gotta make sure our security is on point. Checked and then double checked. So, until I'm able to holla at my big brah, how I'm supposed to know what you saying is real shit?" Gunz was as sincere as he could be.

Dok respected the doubt. Had he been allowed to gain their trust so easily he would've been highly disappointed in the laxness of their security protocol. He would soon learn just how secure that protocol was.

"Young brotha, I expected you to ask me some type of questions or to give me some type of resistance and doubt. I wouldn't respect it any other way." Dok reached his hand out to one of the goons that was behind him and he handed Gunz something.

"Here you go, brotha." Dok handed Gunz a photo. It was a very old photo, although it was still in pretty good shape, like someone took care of it. The corners were still a little frayed and some of the color had faded.

Gunz took the photo. It was of Voorheeze, T'Rida and a third person. They were on the yard at Duel Vocational Institute in Tracy. Gunz had been there before, so he recognized the yard when he saw the photo. It had been taken years ago but you could tell who was who still. The dude with Rida and Voorheeze had dread locks all the way down his back.

There was a commotion towards the front of the house. Everyone turned and looked as a group of six more Guerrilla looking mothafuckas came into view, followed by D.J. and Keak, and a team of wolves. One of the six niggaz was holding his head trying to manage the bleeding from a gash that was there. Embarrassment was written on all of their faces.

"Next time you text me and give me an order to secure the perimeter of confirmed hostiles and tell me not to use lethal force, you might wanna let a nigga know that these hostiles are big Guerilla looking, giant mothafuckas." Keak told Stone Cold.

Dok was fuming that his team had been subdued. It's true they were all family and on the same team, but security was something he didn't take lightly. He'd be sure to take care of it.

"I take it these are the infrared dots?" Gunz asked him with a smirk on his face. No-one saw Stone send the text not even Gunz. But, Gunz knew his people were always on point.

"Yeah, they was holding some good shit too. We relieved them of that shit though." D.J. spoke out, already making plans in his head about the shooting range.

"Like I told you, my brotha, we on the same side." As Dok was finishing his statement, a phone began to ring. "That's for you, brotha." Dok told him even before reaching into his jeans to retrieve the singing phone.

The new intruders brought a tad bit of tension into the room with them, but for the most part, with them stripped for their weapons, shit was all good. Gunz took the phone from him. He was wondering who the fuck wanted to talk to him. His demeanor was calm, yet his eyes betrayed anger. "Yeah hello," was all he said.

"Yo, what's up, young'n?" The caller said into the phone excitedly. The voice sounded vaguely familiar.

"Only one man has ever been able to call me young'n and I ain't heard from him in almost a decade." Whoever the fuck was on the other line would make the mothafucka standing next to him pay for that mistake.

"Young'n, it's me, boy! Damn, has it been that long that you don't remember my voice?" Gunz didn't believe it. He hadn't spoken to Wu since he was in Santa Rita and gotten hit for all that time. Wu was truly a big homie, well-loved and respected. He was Gunz mentor before all the shit happened. Gunz wouldn't be the person he was today were it not for Wu's teachings and guidance.

"Yo, we gotta problem. 5-0 coming and they deep!" J. Styles called out looking out the front window.

He caught everyone's attention. "I guess one of the neighbors saw that little scuffle." DJ was referring to the reason one of the big niggaz had the gash on his head. "Either that or they saw all them damn guns."

Styles neva put the 10 on the 2. This time was no different. It looked like the police cars weren't gonna stop coming.

French Tip kicked into action. "Lock and load and dress the kids for church!" She opened the garage door which led to a mini armory.

"Right, wrong or indifferent, we ride." A.J. sure didn't give a fuck about dying. He lived each day like it was his last.

"Thirty stacks say I kill the most." Cantelope was ready to make her She-Wolves proud.

Dok couldn't believe what he was hearing. On the one hand, he respected their Kevin Gates. They sho-nuff were ready to die bout it. On the other, why go through all the trouble. Why put in all the work to build something just to throw it away so easy? After all they were only looking at weapons charges. What Dok didn't realize was after everything they had been thru they were ready to let somebody feel their pain even if it would cost them their lives.

Gunz was still talking to Wu. Fuck the police, his big homie was on the phone.

"Look, young'n, I'ma let you tend to that situation, but I wanted to let you know that cuzzo is the truth. I been rock'n with Dok Holliday for a while. He good peoples, young'n. Y'all a lot alike." If there is one person whose word Gunz would take hands-down it was Wu's.

"Family, we're not about to shoot it out. None of us are about to die. We're not surrendering either."

"This is the Union City Police Dept...." Someone came over the bull horn. No-one paid attention.

"I estimate we got a couple of hours before they risk making contact if you guys were seen with guns and the assault rifles." He turned toward Gunz, "Lil brotha, have your people focus on wiping down every surface in the house three times. From my experience it's best to split into three groups and hit three rooms at once. Rotate in five minutes."

"French, unlock every cage, drawer, rack and shelf out in the garage that is holding a gun or ammunition. My Ndugu's will start getting rid of them." The calm, quiet, stranger that first walked in was gone. A 5-star General was now directing his troops.

"Troy!" Dok called to one of the brothas that came with him. "Yeah, Mwezi?" His gold teeth shined against his dark skin "master bedroom there's a picture of Angela Davis upside down, turn it ride side up spinning it clock wise, next open the bathroom door all the way. There's a wall safe inside the medicine cabinet. Turn the dial to the number of teeth a dragon has, then open the closet door and turn on the room lights." When he'd finished talking the tall brotha left no questions asked.

Dok looked at Gunz and took a deep breath. He wasn't used to having to repeat himself. "Lil brotha, it's going to take them a minute to thoroughly wipe every surface."

The police were still on the loud speaker talking to nobody.

"Darrell, just where do you think you gonna take all these guns? Even if you are as good as my brotha says, the entire police force is outside?" She really was confused.

"Your brother's house," he simply told her.

He watched Gunz giving orders to wipe everything down. After all, Wu said he was the truth. On the strength of Wu he was listening.

French Tip still didn't understand, but instead of being the one to ask questions, she figured she would just have a mothafucka show her what da business was. She went out to the garage and unlocked everything that was locked. Dok and his men wasted no time removing stuff. She was nosy, but didn't want to appear so or lazy, so she grabbed a duffel bag full of boxes of ammo and followed the line of giants. The first thing she noticed was her mistake. A duffel bag full of boxes of bullets was heavier than a mothafucka. As she struggled with the bag her mind wondered why they were heading towards the master bedroom. She received her answer as soon as she stepped in. The walk-in closet was opened and so was the wall at the back of it. French Tip didn't break her stride. Curiosity wouldn't let her. She struggled to switch the bag to her shoulder and entered the tunnel inside the closet.

The air was dry and the atmosphere catastrophic. There were running lights, so she was able to see. *"Damn, the bag was heavy"* she thought but she toughed it out. She could hear one of the giants walking behind her. She wasn't going to be a punk.

Finally, the end was approaching. She stepped thru the opening and got the shock of her life. She was standing in the closet of her brother's bedroom. Directly ahead of her was the bed where she'd left a picture of her brother posing like someone else was in the picture with him. But it wasn't. The photo was a selfie. It had me and Danika stenciled on it. Only a couple weeks ago she was standing in this exact same spot searching for answers.

"Excuse me, sistah." The huge Gorilla behind her said. "Oh, I'm sorry." She had forgotten he was behind her, she had just stopped shocked at the revelation. As quickly as she could, she made her way deeper into the room.

Once she wrapped her mind around what everything that was standing inside of the room meant, French Tip made her way back through the tunnel. In just under forty-five minutes the War Room was just as clean as it was on the day Voorheeze bought it. All the weapons and ammo were moved into Voorheeze house and the Mobb was ready to leave. After thoroughly inspecting everything and being satisfied, that not one bullet remained, they were ready to go. The punk ass cops were still on the bullhorn with their idle threats. They were making threats to an empty house. Let them have fun figuring that one out.

**** N. D. ****
Voorheeze house

"All y'all know how my brother is about his shit. So, if you ain't gotta touch it, leave it alone." The warning French Tip gave was unnecessary, everybody knew how Voorheeze was about people being in his house.

"Shyyt, you ain't even gotta speak on it. Don't none of us wanna deal wit his crazy ass. I luv Big Brah, but that don't stop him from being crazy as fuck!" Though everyone seconded that shit, nobody else was going to voice it. Fuck that!

First thing Keak did was head to the fridge. He and DJ were both starving. Hell, they were always starving. Opening up the fridge was one of the worst decisions they could have made. The smell of the putrid and rotten food smacked the shit out of their noses.

"God damn!" they both yelled out in unison. The acrid smell was so strong, DJ was actually choking. They came running out of the kitchen like they were being chased by demons.

Everybody was cracking up! "What, y'all didn't find no food?" Cantelope couldn't help herself.

"Shyyt, mo' like we found Jimmie Hoffa!" Keak was able to laugh now. He realized that they came flying up out of the kitchen like two white chicks in a Friday the 13th movie, being chased by Jason Voorheeze!

The smell finally made its way into the living room and they all realized why Keak and DJ ran out of the kitchen so fast.

"Ooh! Ungh! Ungh!" French Tip grabbed her nose and dashed out to look for some air freshener. She came back with three lit incent.

"Why y'all do that?"

"Hell, auntie, we didn't know he was the one who killed Jimmie Hoffa's snitching ass and threw him in the fridge." Finally, DJ could talk.

"Man, how long has it been since Big Brah was here?" C-Murda spoke for the first time.

"Lord only knows." This was the only thing French could say while she placed the incense strategically around the living room and kitchen.

Dok Holliday and even his men had a good laugh out of the situation. Gunz thanked him for getting them out of the jam without casualties or bringing heat to the organization. They all figured it would be best to lay low all day and creep out under the cover of the night. Lady J and the twins were to come at 1:00 o'clock in the morning in three SUV's. An hour later Mike Vegas, Africa and Stunna would pull up to get the rest of the group. They would send people to pick up their own vehicles. French Tip, on the other hand, had different plans. She knew she shouldn't have followed through with her plans, but she said, "fuck it!" She spent the night in her brother's house. In the morning she showered, got dressed and jumped in her brothers Lambo headed for the hospital with a lot of things on her mind.

The hospital ward where they had Voorheeze housed was relatively quiet aside from the nurses assigned to the ward and a doctor or two here and there. There were five of Dragon Gangs beasts outside the room. She greeted Double G. He was 6'9" 325lbs, if he didn't put the fear of God in you, his brother,

Tiny Africa's 6'8" 368lbs of brick solid muscle combined would take care of that. Murda arrived last night or early this morning depending how you looked at it. The Twinz had been there since he came out of surgery.

After briefly greeting and speaking to each one, French stepped in the room. Her heart dropped at the sight of her African Warrior all laid up with tubes and bandages coming from everywhere and taped all over his body. Last night she didn't get the opportunity to check on him.

French Tip wasn't prepared for what she saw. Her feet were so heavy. Each step she took was a mountainous effort. How, Dear God, she wondered. How did this happen to her brother? She cried for what seemed like forever. It was a cry that her spirit needed. Her eldest brother was dead, second brother was flirting with death and her mother was on the verge of a breakdown. Even with the members of the organization around, French Tip felt so alone. She cried some more and prayed. The beeping of the machines was like acoustic tunes in the background noticeable but forgotten.

Outside, Nina was irritated. She wasn't sure why, but something was amiss. Since the first time Voorheeze was laid up in a coma, she had held countless conversations with Pastor Juan for endless hours. She didn't even know what made her pull him aside that fateful day as he was walking out of Voorheeze's room. The pastor was very down to earth. She hadn't expected that. Most of the ministers and pastors she had known growing up were all hellfire and brimstone, death and vengeance. Pastor Juan was different, he was loving and caring in a "Gangsta for God" sort of way. No matter the circumstance or topic of conversation, he always had a funny way of saying "It's that God" and neva once making it seem or sound weird. Hell, he was kind of cute too! Nina found herself saying once "How would that look me hooking up with a pastor and finding God? What a joke!" or was it?

She wanted to tell her best friend and twin about what was going on with her, but she didn't know how. As she stood with her back to the wall next to Voorheeze room door, she finally realized what was wrong with her, why she was irritated. The Pastor had gotten to her. Nina didn't want to kill anymore. She still had the heart. She'd just lost the desire.

Her thoughts were interrupted by French Tip, who finally came out of the room. She looked like the world was thrown at her and she just climbed out from under it.

"Big sis, can I do anything for you?" Nina didn't understand why people would say are you okay? You could look and tell she wasn't okay.

"No, twin." French took a deep breath, straightened her back and threw her shoulders back. "Ain't shit none of us can do but pray to God and see what He decides."

Nina couldn't believe the connection with what she was thinking at that moment. She said a silent prayer asking God to give her a sign if He really wanted her to hang her guns up.

"On second thought, I heard that you have been hanging around Pastor Juan. Give him a call for me and see if he can drop by and say a prayer for my brother and my mother." She told Nina as she turned to go and check on her mother.

Nina didn't know if God answered everybody's prayer, but He'd just answered hers.

French stopped dead in her tracks. It looked like it was shaping up to be a long day. A mothafuck'n cop was walking their way. Both brothers stood to their full heights. Her pale skin already had some color to it, but the moment she saw Tiny and Double G, she turned crimson.

"H...Hello, I'm Chief Vieira of the Milpitas Police Department..." She began to say but Tiny wasn't hearing none of that.

"Trick, I don't care what your rank is. Ain't none of you pigs getting through dis door." Her being a woman didn't matter to him either. She could get it too. He stepped toward her to prove his point.

Chief Vieira took a step back. "H...Ho..Hold on! Wait! I'm a, I'm not here in official capacity."

"Fuck dat 'posed to mean?" Tiny wasn't liking her using all them big ass words. He felt like she was trying to make him look stupid.

Something about the whole situation was off. Women could tell certain things about another woman. French Tip stepped up and placed her small hand on Tiny Africa's back. "It's okay, Tiny."

"You sure, sis?" He just wanted a reason. And if she gave him one...

"Yeah, I'm sure, let her through." French had to see if her woman's intuition was right.

**** N. D. ****

Chapter IV

Redwood City, California
Last night

Sheriff's deputy Horsely was feeling mighty good about himself. He had gotten himself assigned to the Special Task Force in charge of capturing the bastards responsible for all of the cop killings. He'd been transferred to the unit only two weeks ago and already he had gotten the attention of Hedgecock. Although Hedgecock himself was only a rookie, it was his work that drew everyone's attention to the Neva Die Organization.

Though it still was unclear how the organization was connected to the killings, Hedgecock had uncovered enough information for it to be known that the organization was indeed connected somehow.

Deputy Horsely received a text message from Officer Hedgecock himself asking him to meet him on the road under the Dumbarton Bridge. Ravenswood SF Bay National Wildlife Refuge off SR84 was where people could park under the bridge in their cars. Before the Mercury in the water reached toxic levels, fishermen used to come and fish under the bridge for sturgeon and gill sharks. The message he received stated that Hedgecock had found a new solid lead that would bust the case wide open. He was requesting Horsley's assistance in return for sharing the breakthrough and arrest.

It didn't matter to Deputy Horsely that he was coming in on his off time. Hell, he worked so much over time that to him, work was work. Horsely loved the job! He didn't even mind that if was late at night he was called out. The only thing he could think of was if Hedgecock said it was big, then dammit it was going to be big. He pulled off the turn right around the time the call went out from the Dumbarton Bridge Control Booth that there was a malfunction with the camera system on the bridge. Horsely drove all the way down to the end of the lot. He didn't see Hedgecock or anybody for that matter which was okay though because there were two sides to the bridge to the other side. Once he was there he noticed a dark blue Dodge Ram 3200 parked midway down the parking lot.

The windows of the Dodge truck were tinted. Horsely parked on the passenger side of it and got out. He expected Hedgecock to climb out of the truck, when he didn't Horsely knocked on the passenger window.

"Open the door, buddy. It's colder than a witch's tit out here." He was a big guy, but anyone would be cold below the bridge by the bay waters.

When no-one answered he knocked again. The wind picked up, howling like a wild beast. Suddenly he felt uneasy as apprehension washed over him. He noticed a cloud covered the moon, causing the night light to dim.

"*Maybe it was some type of hazing ritual,*" he thought to lessen his concerns. He looked around but didn't see a single soul. Fear motivated his large frame as he made his way over to the driver's side of the truck. He didn't notice the weird drawing of a bat that was drown on the window.

"God Dammit Hedgecock, if this...." He yanked the unlocked driver's door open. What he saw froze the breath in his throat, cutting him off in mid-statement. He almost lost his lunch.

A dead park ranger sat with both hands on the steering wheel with his decapitated head in his lap. The thing was, the head was facing Horsely and there was a gruesome smile on its face.

"What the fuck?" He stumbled backward.

"Here's looking at you kid." He heard over his shoulder. His fear screamed DON'T LOOK! But he ignored the call and spun around, WHACK!

To Batman the saying was true "the bigger they are, the harder they fall." Because his big ass went down like a giant Redwood or a Great California Sequoia. Both massive trees went down with a mighty crash.

When Horsely came to, he didn't know how long he had been out. What he did know was he was stripped butt naked. The whooping wind was biting ferociously at his naked flesh. His hands were cuffed behind his back with his own hand cuffs. When he moved his legs, that's when he felt the discomfort. He lifted his heavy head and looked down. Fear gripped his heart tightly. An industrial vacuum was between his legs. That's not what caused the fear. The aluminum hose that was connected to the Shop-Vac was rammed up his ass. He could only imagine the gruesome shit that was about to happen to him.

"You know, a lot of people are unaware of the fact that I'm from Mississippi...." Horsely could hear the voice, but its owner was standing behind him. He couldn't see him. "You know, the deep south. People wouldn't believe how much 'Klan activity is still going on."

By now Batman had made his way around to the Shop Vac. He had some sort of nozzle apparatus in his hands and a back pack on. It was actually a portable oxyacetylene tank set inside the pack. The long hoses connected to the nozzle in his hand were attached to the tanks.

"My mama and pops had nine kids, of which I'm one of the youngest. When I was... oh I don't know maybe around seven, eight, a white Klansman that looked just like you, raped and killed my oldest sister. The sight of my sisters violated, mutilated and abused body nearly drove my mama crazy." The smile that Batman gave him was so sinister. The look in his eyes tormenting. "It's payback time, cracker! You might not've been the cracker that did it, but you's a cracker and that's good enough for me. Besides you look so much a like him, you's probably his cousin or sum'n." He pulled a flint striker from his pocket, messed with the two valves on the nozzle then held the striker to the tip and struck it.

The flame lit up the night "I saw this shit in a movie once. The mothafucka had two rats on a niggaz' stomach with a metal lid over it..." Horsely had seen the same movie.

"Dear Jesus, don't let it be." He cried. "Don't do this, man!" "You know when I saw the movie I didn't believe it. I always wondered if that shit was real or not..." he adjusted the valves. The flame turned from orange red to a hot whitish blue. "Its eighty hungry rats inside of this Shop Vac cracker. Do they really hate heat like that?"

Batman didn't wait for a reply. He put the torch to the Shop Vac. Neva in his life had Horsely known a fear like he knew now. He didn't even care about shame, as a stream of hot piss shot out his tiny little pink dick. Soon, the Vac began heating up! The *ting* sound metal makes as it expands was shooting off. It sounded like the someone was taking shots at the can with a pellet gun.

"Let me tell you something cracker, September 14, 2013 a young black man named Jonathan Ferrell was on his way home when he crashed his vehicle." Batman looked so evil, Horsely thought he was possessed. "The brotha knocked on a nearby door seeking help. But, the old cracker that lived there called the police. You wanna guess what happened?"

Horsely was so frightened that he couldn't talk.

"Don't worry, I'll tell ya. The cracker pigs shot the brotha ten mothafuckin' times! Ten times! All he wanted was help. Instead, he was murdered in cold blood."

"_Please. Please don't do this, bro! please!" He was literally crying.

"Bro? Cracker don't try to sound cool! Like we friends or something! Just stop crying like a little bitch and be my guinea pig." He placed the nozzle almost directly on the can now. The area where the nozzle was aimed glowed red. You could hear the sound of tiny claws scratching against the can. The sound was only audible because the wind died down briefly.

Batman smelled the stench and smiled. He shook his head, "that was a real mistake, cracker. Rats love shit everybody knows that."

No sooner did he speak than the hose started moving.

"No, no, no, no, no, God! Nooo!" Horsely shook so violently that for a moment Batman thought the hose might fall out his ass.

The nozzle was held in place as more and more rats fought each other, biting and clawing to find safety. The only sanctuary was Horsely's ass hole. The thing about rats, once they started fleeing for safety they didn't stop.

They were now chewing their way through his colon. The screams he made would shake a lesser man's soul, but not Batman. He would make the devil his bitch. Even with the wind slowing down, his victim's screams would neva be heard. There were too many cars racing over the bridge.

"That's for you Robin", Batman said as he hit his fist over his heart. He pounded it a few times before taking one final look and getting out of there.

Sooner or later they would either get the cameras up and running or they were going to send someone for a look especially after not getting a response from Ranger Dave.

The frenzy was well underway, it was a guarantee the rats would finish the job.

**** **N. D.** ****
Stanford Hospital
Today

"So how long have you been sleeping with my brother?" French Tip couldn't believe she was asking the Chief of Police this question. The obvious signs were there loud and clear.

"Excuse me?" the question caught Vieira off guard. She felt her skin get hot as the blood rushed to the surface. "Okay, first off honey, you need to know that we don't bullshit around here. This is our family, so everything is straight forward no beating around the bush. Secondly honey, it's written all over your pretty, white face. You love my brother. I'm just trynna figure out how'd that happen", wasn't no sense beating around the bush.

Chief Vieira took a deep breath. The dam of tears threatening to break. Her pale skin was beet red from embarrassment, guilt and shame. This little girl was young enough to be her daughter, yet she spoke to her like she was her parent. But, who was she kidding, yes, she was in love with him. All of him. From the way he molded and shaped her body, to how he sexed and made love to her mind.

"My Lord, I'm so ashamed." Those words, that admittance broke the dam, the tears flowed.

French didn't have any remorse or sympathy for her. Sure, she was a woman hurt and emotionally wrecked. She still was a fucking cop. French just folded her arms across her chest and waited.

When her cries turned to sniffles, Vieira looked far away and spoke. "We met months back. I was actually at the grocery store shopping…" in fifteen minutes Chief Vieira told French Tip everything. Not that she trusted her or anything. She simply had to share with somebody. Keeping it all in her mind and heart wasn't helping. She had to get it out.

Vieira told her how it began as raw animal lust. She had always had a thing for black men, but was too afraid to test her fantasy. When Voorheeze approached her, not only was he a giant dark hunk of a man, he also had the confidence of someone who knew exactly what he was. It was fun, the sex was amazing, and she was having the time of her life. She loved being around him. He didn't know that she was a police officer. She certainly didn't know that he was connected to the streets. By the time she learned who La'Mont was, it was too late. She was madly in love.

If this wasn't some Hollywood, Netflix shit French Tip didn't know what was. "So, what you plan on doing about everything now?" She needed to know there were no threats to her brother of any kind.

"I don't know," Vieira looked defeated. "I know what I'm supposed to do. But my heart wants me to do something completely different."

"Well, I'mma leave you alone and let you have some more time with my brother. Hopefully you can figure it out…" she stopped with her hand on the door knob. "Just know this, if you cross my brother, you won't have a heart to be crying over." Her beautiful chocolate face did little to cover the evil lingering behind the threat.

French Tip walked out the room. She told her people to give the Captain all the time she needed but not to let anyone else in. No-one questioned her about it, though their faces showed that they wanted to. To her left, French noticed Nina across the hall down aways talking to Pastor Juan. She started to head that way, but figured she was too tired to talk to anyone else. Hell, she still had to see how her mother was doing.

Five minutes later she was walking into her mother's room. The sound coming through the door was enough to give her the answer she wanted.

"I don't wanna hear that shit! You mothafuckas must not know who the fuck I am! I used to work here so I don't wanna hear none of that bull shit!" Mama Beckum was going off. There were three nurses in the room and they all looked terrified "my name is Bernice Delores Beckum, trick! You better ask somebody and go get my shit." She was standing up with a cane in her hand holding it like it was a Billy club.

"Mom! Mom! What the hell is going on?" French Tip yelled trynna get some order in the room.

The nurses looked at her like abused puppies wanting to be saved.

They were scared and didn't know what to do.

"I ordered two Jell-O's and this here heffer only brought me one and when I told her that she made a mistake she gone tell me it don't look like I need two helpings of Jell-O. Trick! I'll fuck you up!" She jumped like she was going to hit them with the cane.

The nurses screamed and hugged themselves. French couldn't help laughing. That was Oscar approved, it was so funny. She turned towards the nurses "ladies, you may go." They started to scurry towards the door. "Oh, and please bring her damn Jell-o."

To the one who made the crack about the Jell-o she got directly in her face. "And if you ever disrespect my mother again, I'mma kick yo fuckin ass before I kill you."

"I....I...I'm..." she tried

"Get the fuck outta here! Hoe!" Mama Beckum shouted.

The last nurse scurried away like a mouse cornered by an alley cat.

"Sit your butt down, Mama!" "In here scaring the shit outta the little white women." She told her mother as she walked over and gave her a kiss on her cheek.

"Shut up. That heffer needs to know who she messing with." No sooner did the words leave her mouth than there was a knock on the door. A new nurse walked in timidly and sat the Jell-O with a spoon on the tray next to the bed and scurried out of the room.

Doctor Butler told Mama Beckum that she really should stay at least a week and rest up, but she would be able to be cleared for release the following day if she wanted.

They sat and talked for two hours. They had a lot to talk about. They still had to bury Clark. Or at least his empty casket. In the end the decision they made was just to have the mothafucka buried. No-one could live through or felt like dealing with the hassle of another funeral. Besides, they could neva say good-bye in their hearts.

**** **N. D.** ****

Chapter V

"So, as you see brother Steve, I've kept abreast of everything that has been going on. When I'm done, we will have a better living for our people and you would've made a substantial amount of money." Dok reached out and grabbed the glass of Chai tea Steven had provided and took a drink. His first sip instantly creating his new favorite drink.

When he first walked into his office Steve didn't know who the brother was, but he knew he meant business. Ten minutes into their meeting, Steve knew he was right with his original assessment. Now, it had been forty-five minutes of Steve listening to the well-dressed man and Steve was outright impressed. Not off the money he stood to make, although that was always a good thing. Steve was impressed with what the brotha had in mind, as well as with the man's intellectual level and business sense.

"Tell me, Mr. Holliday, where would you like me to begin?" This rather unassuming question from Steve would begin something major. He sat in his butter-soft, leather chair behind the Presidential desk he had imported from China. It had belonged to some Ming General during the first Dynasty. It's been years planning, mapping everything out in his mind over and over constantly. Dok knew exactly where he wanted to begin. Where he needed to begin for maximum results.

"First off, we need property big enough to house a Youth Center in the following areas, East Palo Alto, East and West Oakland, Berkeley, Richmond and throughout San Francisco" Dok pulled a card out of his inside jacket pocket of his Michael Jordan suit. "This is one of my colleagues. If you give him a call, he can fill you in on a few locations in each of the areas that I mentioned that we feel would be prime for what we have in mind."

Steve looked at the card which read "Sons of Khatari" the name Little Thomas was underneath C.E.O. He looked up at Dok with a raised eye brow.

"Trust me, my brotha, I tried to get him to use a more professional name. He wasn't having it." Dok smiled remembering the long conversation he had with Lil Thomas about it. If one of the buildings s run down a little, that's okay because one of my brothas has a construction company. As long as it isn't deemed inhabitable we can deal with it. Oh, and Steve, call me Dok, brotha."

Steve reached out and accepted the hand that Dok offered him. He was eager to get started for many reasons. The most important being, he was tired of seeing his community look like shit and the kids being forced to run to the streets because of a lack of things for them to do. He was tired of seeing his people kill themselves and destroy their future. He was ready to help.

Lil Rell and Scooter were waiting for Dok the moment he stepped out of the office. These were not only his sons, but his security. They were little kids when he first went away, now they were full grown men, seasoned and raised in the streets. They'd become advanced in the art of Guerilla Warfare from his teachings and instructions. Both of them were very intelligent and highly lethal. They made their way to meet up with Gunz to discuss the issue with their connect.

Forty-five minutes later they were all sitting inside Gunz office at the back of the Koffee Shop. Gunz, AJ, DeeDee, Dok, Lil Rell and Scooter were all present. It wasn't crowded in the least, given the size of Gunz office.

"Big Brah told me that at the time he had a sit down with the mothafucka, that blood was supposedly, on some way other shit, as far as his security goes." He was looking at Dok, but he was talking to everybody. "We might wanna do a little more planning before we move."

"Are we set with the transition?" Dok asked side stepping the suggestion.

"The transition is good to go." Gunz replied as he lit another blunt of platinum cookies.

"What about the chemist? They good to go?" Dok asked.

A.J. spoke up, "they've been in the lab now for five days. Got it going like a nice little bakery." The blunt that he was smoking was the size of a niggaz thumb.

"What about..." Dok started

"Distribution been ready. I set up a nice system. Shit gone go sweet. Y'all just watch and see." DeeDee cut him off. Proud of his new plan.

The only ones who didn't speak in the room were Lil Rell and Scooter. They were always told to observe ninety percent of the time and speak ten percent. Part of the ninety percent was spent was thinking. So, they just watched and listened.

"Gunz, I'll tell you what, young brotha, I'm going to be focused a lot on building Elesia after we get everything aligned. So, why don't you and your team sit this one out..." Dok wasn't fucking with the cookies. It was pineapple Cush in his blunt. He took a pull. "My brotha, y'all have been through a lot lately. Me and the brothas will deal with Mr. Toure, and don't worry we are very efficient and very convincing."

"Brah, we can't just sit back and let y'all deal wit blood by yourself. What if things get complicated?"

"Won't be any complications!" Everyone looked to Lil Rell. They were shocked to hear the young man speak and amazed at the finality in his voice when he made the statement.

Dok looked at him. They maintained eye contact and Dok nodded his head. Lil Rell pulled out his iPhone and hit a button. The sound of his FaceTime was like some out of space shit. When the caller answered, Lil Rell held the phone up, so his face was visible. (They were only to speak Swahili)

"Habari Gani (How are you) little brotha?" the voice in the phone spoke.

"Habari Gani, wewe aku (I'm fine, how are you)." Lil Rell spoke with a big smile on his face. The face on the other end of the call smiled as well. "Dinners ready my brotha."

The smile on the other side vanished, "I don't understand the language you're speaking, little brotha."

"We we Utayari ni mfalme (are you ready for war)?" The smile that returned to Lil Pooh's face was brighter than the first one.

"Ni Tayan! (I'm ready)" Pooh knew that Lil Rell hated being corrected but you had to iron out all the kinks for the outfit to be sharp.

"Asante (thank you)" Lil Rell told him in voice that was a little strained.

"Sikitu (welcome)" Pooh was always ready for that action.

AJ and DeeDee wanted to know what was said. From the look on Lil Rell's face, Gunz knew it didn't matter. Whatever was said, somebody was about to die. He may not have been able to speak the language, but the look on Rell's face was universal to killas everywhere.

"Brotha, if you're good then we're good." Gunz took another pull on his blunt and then put it out.

**** N. D. ****
Milpitas, California

Officer Hedgecock had just finished the briefing of the new Task Force which consisted of officers from East Palo Alto and Menlo Park, San Mateo Sheriff's Deputies, Santa Clara Sheriff's Deputies and officers from here at the Milpitas office.

The briefing was good. Even though he was nervous, he'd held his composure and did an excellent job. The shit hat happened to the new guy, Horsely was sad. Before Hedgecock transferred over to Milpitas he had worked with Horsley briefly. He was a good guy as far as Hedgecock was concerned.

"So, do you think the tech guys can clean the disc up enough to give as a solid image?" Officer Peters walked up to Hedgecock with a cup of coffee in one hand and a massive Togo's sandwich in the other.

"Lord knows, I surely hope so. We need a solid break right now. Hell, the assholes are way ahead of us on this." Hedgecock walked over to the 85" flat screen that was paused on the suspect from Horsely's murder.

"We wouldn't be as far along as we are if it wasn't for you." Peters wasn't a kiss ass. He was just stating a fact.

Hedgecock loved the praise, yet and still it wasn't enough "We need to get more, Peters, before another one of us dies."

There was no reason for Peters to respond. They both shared the same sentiments. The looks on their faces was proof of the unspoken worry and fear in the heart of all law enforcement throughout the Bay Area.

There was a commotion outside in the hallway. Both officers walked to the doorway to see what was going on. What they saw was all officers worst nightmare. Federal agents were coming down the hallway, which meant they were taking over the case. Peters looked at Hedgecock to gage his response. A bit lip, fire red face and two balled fists was what he saw.

Chief Vieira was storming down the hallway with the agents. It was clear that the Chief was pissed off as well. Hers was the face of someone doing something that they didn't want to do, but she had no choice about it.

"Officer Hedgecock, these are agents Wendell Roberson and Jose Gayton of our great local FBI." Her big breast swelled as she took a deep breath. "Unfortunately, I can't stop them so don't ask, I've been on the phone all day trying to. However, they're not here to steal the show. Or so they say. They're here to lend a hand."

Hedgecock looked at agent Gayton first. He was 5'2" maybe 130lbs with a bald head. He was Mexican. Hedgecock thought two things, first, how the hell did a Mexican get a name like Gayton? Second, he looked more like a weasel gangbanger then a cop. Next, he looked at Roberson who offered his hand to shake. He was a 5'10" 245lbs, fat, bald headed black man. He too looked like a weasel.

"I'll let you guys work your testosterone levels out and see who's bigger or whatever you gotta do to get an understanding. But, we need to see some results. She turned to leave, and everybody looked mighty hard at her big, white ass as it bounced down the hall. Once the Chief and her nice ass was out of view, they ducked back into the conference room to get acquainted.

"You two don't look like cops to me. If you don't mind me saying." Hedgecock had to get that off his mind.

"We didn't start off as cops that's fa'sho" Agent Roberson's comments caused he and Gayton to laugh.

"We're part of a special unit called The Snitch Crime Unit.... "

Hedgecock interrupted him "Come on, guy, let's be for real."

Neither Roberson nor Gayton was laughing or smiling. It didn't take Hedgecock long to get the hint.

The government became fed up seeing criminals constantly beat the system, it grew desperate to find a solution. Although paid informants and snitches were leading to numerous arrests, some high paid, high powered attorney almost always got the criminals off. Most often, they would use the defense tactic saying the witness or (the snitch) was only saying what they were supposed to say in order to get themselves out of trouble. In a jury trial this almost always worked.

A solution to this problem was needed and the SCU was formed. Roberson was the first test subject. Back in 2002, he had been arrested in Hayward for eight robberies and an attempted murder. He snitched on his co-defendant who was sent to prison for nine years. The way the program works once a subject snitched on someone, their record is wiped clean, courtesy of the government.

Next, they were given training and then a badge. To date, the unit turned to be more than just crooks. They were crooks trained to be officers.

Somewhere during this revelation Hedgecock found a chair and sat in it. There was no way he would've ever believed the story he was told had it come out of anyone else's mouth besides the fed himself. Shit! He still didn't believe it, but he knew it was true.

"So, I hear you guys have had something of a breakthrough of sorts." Gayton spoke up for the first time. He was an Ex-Norteno drop out turned snitch. He'd told on so many people the SCU was very proud that they recruited him.

"Yeah, the night of the murder the activity control monitors malfunctioned. We believe the suspect tampered with the system." Hedgecock got up and walked to retrieve the remote control off the DVD player. "One of the park rangers was able to get one of the monitors back up in time to catch this."

The screen came to life. The screams and pleading of Horsely moments before he died relayed his level of fear. With his arms presumably handcuffed behind his back, he flapped around like a beached whale trying to get the vacuum hose out of his ass. The perpetrator stood by lighting the side of the Shop Vac with what appeared to be a portable acetenyl torch.

The footage was heart breaking. Watching a grown man so engrossed in fear, scream and cry like a child having nightmares of the Boogey Man. The footage was very dark. Hedgecock informed them that, that particular night was a rare moonless night. Even so, agent Gayton knew someone who could help out with the video. He thought of a snitch form San Francisco, Russ Coleman, he could help. The SCU had people just about everywhere. The unit had been going for almost fifteen years now and had come a long way.

"You mind if I get a copy of this? I know somebody that might be able to do something with it." He asked Hedgecock hoping there wouldn't be a problem.

"You bet. As I've said we need all the help we can get." These guys didn't seem so bad to Hedgecock. Maybe having the help of the feds would turn out to be a good thing.

De'Kari

The other side of Milpitas

The assortment of aromas mixed and sailed through the air creating a sea of delicious temptations and indulgences. As it was close to closing, most of the hungry patrons had already left full and satisfied with smiles on their faces. The lingering aroma of their meals were the only evidence of their prior existence.

Samori Toure sat in his office going over some books. A glass of Louis the XVIII sat half full on the desk while a lit Cuban sat burning in the ashtray. He could see every inch of his restaurant via the video cameras. This was his nightly routine of course the books he was going over had nothing to do with the restaurant. He could care less if it made one penny. Mr. Toure was satisfied with his chunk of the American Dream. Much like his ancestors of this country, he was getting rich off of the blood, sweat, and tears of others. He was making a fortune off of the backs of Blacks.

Being that his African heritage was linked to the Mandingo tribe, he saw himself as being above the African Americans who would sell their souls for the price of the dollar. They were Akata (cotton pickers) like the village cats of Africa whom he would trample and kick with his sandal as they scattered and scurried away.

A knock on the open door was followed by the head of security sticking his head inside.

"We have company, my brotha." His words drew Samori's attention to his video monitors mounted on the wall.

Three black Suburbans were pulling into the parking lot. Samri Toure wasn't concerned in the least bit. His security was unmatched by the lazy -undisciplined Americans. Nevertheless, he didn't like people dropping in unannounced nor did he like interruptions in his daily schedule.

"Come, Suja. Let us see what this is." He told his security as he stood up from his desk and headed toward the front.

Once the Suburbans came to a stop, all of the men stepped out of the vehicles at the same time. This wasn't some movie or some urban novel. This was real life and they were real Gueril-las. Nobody opened the door since nobody likes little "Yes Men." These were all stone-cold, trained, killers. There was a chain of command, but there were no Big I's and little U's. This was a one-man nuke. A closed iron fist. Dok gave the orders but he could be given an order as well.

The night was chilly but there was no breeze. Dok looked for the moon but his eyes were only rewarded with the shadows of clouds blocking the moon. The door of the restaurant opened as they reached the front. Even if Dok hadn't studied the face of the man he was there to meet, his presence betrayed him.

"Mr. Samori Toure, my name is Dok Holliday. I am aware that you knew my late brotha, T'Rida and you know my little brotha, Voorheeze, as well. I think we have some things to discuss." He directed his comment at the man whom he knew was Samori Toure.

The man spoke to his two subjects briefly in a language foreign to Dok. The one on his left said something back with a look of alarm on his face. The sharp tongue of Toure silenced any doubt that whatever it was that he said would be carried out.

"Mr. Holliday, it is true I knew Mr. Thomas Smith and I too know Mr. Simpson, but you see, my friend, I don't know you…" The tension was thick and anyone could feel it. Toure paid it no mind. "This business that you say we should discuss shall take place. However, if you want a meeting, your men must wait here." As a finality of what he was saying, he smiled.

"Let's go." It didn't bother Dok at all to leave his men. He could take care of himself perfectly well.

Inside the restaurant, seated at a table, Toure offered Dok a drink which he politely declined.

"So, my friend, tell me what you would like to discuss." Toure asked then took a generous swallow of cognac.

The smell of the curry spices and the flavors that mingled in the air was making Dok sick. He didn't know what was worse, the smell of the curry or the arrogance of the leech in front of him that was sucking his people dry. The fucking parasite.

"I'm not one to beat around the bush nor waste time, neither yours or mine." Toure poured himself another healthy glass of the Cognac while Dok talked. "We're undergoing a reshaping in how we are going to conduct our organization in the future. The sales of cocaine and heroin no longer fit our agenda."

This got the Africans attention. "You tell me you no more sell the dope?" This had to be a joke, only the black bitch was not smiling. "You black beetch! You sell the dope till I say!" Toure was outraged.

"Look, man, now I ain't about to be no more black bitches. Now, I came here tonight to give you an option. But, if you call me one more bitch, you can die with the rest of your people."

Some of that arrogance disappeared at hearing of those words. Suddenly, Samori Toure noticed that it had actually gotten a little quieter.

"Sujaa! Sujaa!" he yelled out. Panic now traceably noticeable behind his cockiness.

"There's no sense yelling for anyone, they're all dead." The way he spoke the words was so nonchalant.

Toure still tried to feign toughness even with sweat beading up on his forehead. "You listen to me, you black beech..."

Boca! Boca! Boca!

The 40 caliber Desert Eagle silenced all threats. "We don't play with that bitch word, brotha."

With that, their problem of a connect who wouldn't let them go was over. Cocaine, crack, and heroin had destroyed his people for so long. Dok couldn't see himself continually contributing to the problem. They had way more than enough money to take time to reorganize and come anew. Come fresh.

They could produce fifty kilos of crystal meth and 20pounds of fentanyl a week with the chemistry team they had. In time, that number would spread. The important thing was instead of feeding poison to his own people, they would be selling it in the white communities. For once his people would be able to breathe.

He calmly stood up and exited the restaurant. He hadn't lied when he told Samori Toure that all of his people were dead. The three trucks were just a distraction. The main threat had snuck onto the premises during the serving of dinner. An entire BGF hit squad had taken care of all of Toure's people and employees, except the women. They had been tied up in a storage compartment. The fire would attract the police and fire department. They would hear the women's cries and screams and rescue them. Dok Holliday was old school; no women, no children were to be harmed.

**** N. D. ****

Chapter VI

Missouri City, Texas

The air in the room was humid like the air in the state of Missouri. The loud, wet smacking sounds of skin slapping against skin sounded like a kitchen sink being plunged.

"F...Fuck me d-daddy," Bent over doggy style, she was throwing that ass back at him as he drove into her relentlessly. "Give it to me!"

He watched as sweat dropped from his face onto her huge, golden ass. He was fucking her long, deep, and hard. She had nothing to do with the frustration that he was taking out on her. That was the fault of the other bitch! The sight of his sweat landing on her ass gave him an idea.

He leaned back as he was stroking and spit a glob of saliva directly on her asshole. He took his thumb and started messaging her asshole. "Sssss...ummm do it!" He knew what she was talking about. Slowly he let his thumb slide inside her ass.

"Yes!" she screamed! "Now fuck me, Daddy! Hard! Daddy fuck me!"

She lifted her head in ecstasy. Her eyes closed with a smile on her face. Spiritual was indeed in Heaven. She had already cum twice and could feel another one rapidly building.

"You love this dick, don't you?" He asked as his thumb fucked her ass in rhythm of his dick fucking her hot pussy.

"D...Daddy, yes! I... I love iiiitttt!" She screamed as another explosion ripped through her body. The shock wave of pleasure made her dizzy. She wondered how she could be dizzy with her eyes closed. Yes, indeed the dick was good.

He could feel his nutts tightening as they swelled. He used both hands and grabbed her by the waist. She knew that's when the real fucking would begin, and it did. He was pounding into her pussy so hard that his balls were stinging her clit as they smacked into it.

His thrust was deeper now, more sporadic. "Gimme that fucking pussy!"

"It's yours, Daddy! Ssss…It's yours!"

"Aaargh!" At the sound of her surrendering, he finally gave up his seed.

The two of them collapsed on the bed in a heap of cum, sweat and satisfaction. The sweat was cooling their hot flesh.

As his chest heaved up and down with deep breaths, he told her, "turn on the air conditioner. God damn, a nigga dying in here."

The last thing she wanted to do was move, but after the work that he just put in, how could she tell him no? She gathered the strength to climb her 5'2" body off of the bed to do as he asked. Her ass looked like two old school kick balls were used for her ass cheeks. The vision of such a lovely sight was causing his dick to slowly start rocking-up again.

She made it to the thermostat, finally, on a wobbly knee and still out of breath. God knew that if she died at that very moment, it would be okay by her. Since she was up, she made her way to the bathroom to wash the evidence of their love making off of her. His phone began ringing while she made her way to the bathroom. But she was lost in her own thoughts. She didn't pay him any mind. When he'd first reached out to her, his request had been too bizarre to take seriously. Jump on a plane and fly out to Texas? He was crazy. When he told her that there was a first-class ticket at San Francisco International with her name on it, she new he was serious. All her life, she'd done the norm. Always what was expected of her and it got her nowhere.

So, she'd called her firm and took an immediate leave under vacation time, left a note for the Warden (her no good husband who was holding her hostage) telling him she had to fly to the East Coast on emergency company business and she'd hopped on the plane. That was a few weeks ago and she has been in heaven since. She thought as the sound of him answering his phone brought her out of her thoughts.

"What's up, rogue?" he answered the phone, hating that he had to get up.

"Nigga, I hear that it's so hot out in dat bitch that the lizards be doing pushups. "Gunz joked into the phone.

"Shit, nigga, I don't know bout no lizards, but a nigga damn near died just from fucking." He was serious as a heart attack.

Gunz bust out laughing.

"Nigga, I'm serious, I damn near had a fucking stroke." Although he was as serious as could be, he had to laugh. Plus, that was a good way to cover his uneasiness.

Gunz calling him on an unscheduled call meant either something good transpired or something bad, but something was up. He wanted to come right out and ask, but he was too gangsta to appear eager like a little kid. So, as the air conditioner cooled the room, he cooled his nerves.

"I ain't gone beat around the bush, cuzzo, or keep you waiting on why a nigga called you. You all good, my nigga. Pack yo bags and come home. "Those were the words that Clarkola had been waiting to hear for two months now.

He took a huge risk that night he had flown in to go see his brother at the hospital, but he had to see him. In his heart, it was his fault that his brother had gotten shot. The guilt tore at him until he had no choice but to go see him. Considering that he didn't know if the case Tieka was building on him before he killed her had gone anywhere or died out, he was on the run. Also, add the fact that he had killed a federal agent to his list of issues.

"Not to disrespect your gangsta or nothin, but you sure bout dat?" Hell, checking ain't cheating. Not being cautious is how he found himself in this predicament to begin with.

"Naaw, no disrespect. But, you good homie. Shit's been checked and rechecked. You straight." Gunz didn't take it as disrespect. Whenever you were talking 'federal' all niggaz got nervous. Even the hardest of niggaz.

"I owe you, rogue. If it wasn't for you…" he let the sentence trail off. There wasn't a need to state what they both knew.

"Come on, cuzzo, don't tell me the heat down there is turning you soft." Gunz joked.

"Naa, nigga, I'm just saying thanks." Wasn't nothing soft about being grateful. "I'll see you in a bit."

"Off top, cuzzo, in a bit." Gunz disconnected the line.

Clarks mind drifted back to that day. *He had been tripping off of the wild sex from Spiritual. "L" had gotten locked up for stomping the shit out of the nigga at the club. He was on his way to take care of some business when two SUV's pulled up blocking his path. He'd reached for his banga thinking it was them YNM niggaz until the tinted window rolled down and he saw Gunz face. Clark didn't comprehend it cause Gunz was supposed to be in Philly.*

"Ain't no time to talk, cuzzo. Get in." Gunz voice didn't leave room to talk. Neither did the fact that they were on the middle of a busy intersection.

Considering the fact that Gunz didn't rock like this – jumping out on niggaz in broad day light and it wasn't a move – plus the fact that he was in Cali period made Clarks decision relatively an easy one. He jumped out of his brand-new Challenger and into the Range Rover while one of Gunz goons jumped into his shit.

It was then that he learned that the woman he had been sharing his bed with and was beginning to give his heart to, was a fucking D.E.A. agent who was trying to build a case against him. She was very close to having everything that she needed.

The first move was to fake his death. That had been Gunz' idea. The moment lieutenant Urena filled Gunz in on everything, Gunz began formulating everything. With the help of a young robotic engineer the ambulance was rigged. The day of the shooting, Clark had taken two real slugs. One in the shoulder and the other in his upper thigh. Shit had to look read. Plus, that left real blood at the scene. The construction crew that sent the ambulance into the IKEA parking garage was actually his team.

The moment the ambulance drove into the parking garage, the rigged ambulance, with bodies that they had bought from Jones Mortuary, was ready to go. And go it did, right off of the University overpass and onto the 101 Freeway. The crash caused so much commotion that no-one paid attention to a second ambulance driving off.

Next, against Gunz wishes, Clark had to deal with the treacherous, trifling, skeezer that wanted to end his life as a free man.

As he heard Spiritual turn the shower water off, he thought back to the day he saw her go into the downtown government building. *He'd followed her to San Francisco and watched. After he saw her go into the building he walked back down the street to her car. He'd used a slim Jim to get in and waited for her. She was in such disarray that she didn't see him raise up behind her. Nor did she see the piano wire. She'd felt its bite as he pulled on it around her neck. The recognition, confusion, and fear that he saw in her eyes through the rearview mirror gave him a feeling that was euphoric and sweet as his first kill. Fucking Parasite!*

"I hope it's me that you're thinking about that has got you smiling like that." Spiritual told him as she walked her naked, heavenly body over toward the bed.

"You know you always gone put a smile on a niggaz face, the way you do what you do." He responded as she brought him back to reality. He could neva get enough of how flawless her body was.

"I see you're not lying." Noticing his rock-hard dick that was saluting her physical perfection.

She didn't waste a second covering it with her hot, moist mouth.

"Ungh! We're outta here after this. So, make it good." He laid his head back and got ready for the ride she was about to take him on.

**** N. D. ****
East Palo Alto, California

Dok climbed out of the Challenger feeling proud of such a beautiful day. There were clouds in the sky, a few blocking the sun and there was a slight wind chill, but it still was a beautiful day to Dok Holliday. Somehow, Steve was able to talk the city into selling the infamous Rec Center to the Organization. For decades it had been notorious for the drug trafficking and usage on its grounds. The city desperately tried everything to clean it up, but nothing worked. Even a makeover and name change to YMCA didn't help.

After finding out that the organization had plans for using the facility for children in the community, the city council decided to give the private sector a chance to see if it could achieve what the council couldn't. Naturally, it wasn't going to be a question. Already, the word was out that some BGF mothafuckas bought the center and were guaranteeing it would be safe for the kids at all cost. There was a clear message out that there would be a zero-tolerance mentality towards anyone using the facility or its grounds for anything drug related or illegal for that matter.

Someone had to be there for the kids of the ghetto. They had to have some type of safe haven from the everyday turmoil that was their lives. Dok and the Committee knew this. They had known it for years, yet no-one was able to rise to the occasion. Well a mothafucka was rising and his name was Dok Holliday. He smiled to himself as he walked up to Steve and shook his hand.

"It's good to see you, my brother." Dok's smile was just as genuine as the truth of his words.

"Likewise. I see your people don't waste any time." He said referring to the 'Sons of Khatari' work trucks and crews that were already busy at hand getting the center ready.

The two young brothas stood there and surveyed the work for a moment. Passerby's either slowed to stare at the work or honked the horn in recognition or in appreciation. Shit, the word was out that these brothas meant business. A dopefeind that was in the park getting high early that morning had learned the hard way. The months he would spend in the hospital healing would give him a lot to think about.

"Would you like to take a tour? Have me show you around a little?" Steve asked him after a while.

"Naa, my brotha, I already know what it's going to look like when it's done in my head." He pointed with two fingers to his temple "I've had it all planned and mapped out up here for a long time."

This wasn't some overnight shit that had been thrown to-gether. This movement was years in the making. Voorheeze might have lost sight, but he and T'Rida began this dream by accumulating the capital. This was all their dream and he would pick up where his brothas left off.

Steve could tell that Dok was mentally somewhere else. Wherever that maybe, he wondered if there were more brothas like Dok there.

"So, have you decided on a name?" Steve wondered.

"All our Community Centers will be called Elysian Fields." Dok informed him without having to return from wherever he was.

"Elysian Fields? Steve had neva heard the name before.

"It's Paradise, my brotha, Paradise!"

**** **N. D.** ****

Chapter VII

San Jose, California

He climbed up to the top of the third flight of stairs. Winter was just about over, but his nerves had him so hot. It felt like he was in the middle of summer. He was nervous because he knew when she saw him his mom was going to kick his ass. Being her first-born son, he could only imagine the hell faking his death had put her through. So, before he resurfaced to the world, Clark had to fix things with Mama Beckum first.

His nervousness was evident by how softly he knocked on the door. When no-one answered, he knocked a lot harder. He couldn't stop his heart from pounding. Deep in their heart every Gangsta was still scared of their mama. No matter how tough they were or how many bodies they had, they were always mama's babies.

As he heard the alarm being disarmed and the deadbolts unlocking, he braced himself. He thought he would hear 'Who is it.' His response would lessen the blow. Instead, all of the locks were unlocked then the door swung open. For a moment she just stared at him. Her mind taking time to register. She was wearing her lounge-around gown and some house shoes. The moment passed, and all hell broke loose.

"Aaaaaaaaaah!" She screamed at the top of both lungs while she stood there shaking her head. "Aaaaaaaaaah!"

"Sssssh! Mama, calm down." He was looking around nervously. The last thing he needed right now was for one of her neighbors to call the police.

"Mama, calm down!"

"Clarence! Oh, my gawd!" She rushed into his arms not believing what she was seeing. She had to touch him to make sure he was real!

Once she felt her baby, the dam broke and the river of tears flowed freely from her eyes.

De'Kari

"Oh My God! My baby! My baby!" She just kept repeating over and over while a multitude of emotions swam through her.

Clark couldn't' do anything but hold her. He felt fucked up knowing that he was the cause of her sorrow. Even though faking his death was necessary along with not letting anyone know that it was staged. He still wished whatever pain she endured could be taken away.

Finally, Mama Beckum was able to gather her composure enough to stop crying. She broke free of his embrace and pulled back from him. Then, without warning, *slap*! She hauled off and slapped the shit out of him. The sound resonated through the hallway sounding like a baseball bat connecting with a fastball straight down the middle.

"Mothafucka! Have you lost yo rabid ass mind?" The first slap Clark didn't expect or at least wasn't ready for.

The stinging in his face had him on high alert though. So, when she swung again, he was ready.

"Come on, Mama, damn! You tryna knock my head off." He said while catching her arm in his hand as she tried to smack him again.

"Boy, I should bust your mothafuck'n head open." She swung at him again. This time with less energy and force in her swing.

He stepped into it and hugged her again. He guided her into the apartment, neva breaking their embrace. Mama Beckum was so happy that her baby, her favorite son had returned to her. To God she would forever be grateful because her prayers were answered.

While she was in that hospital bed she'd prayed constantly to a God she hadn't talked to since she was a child and her father was a reverend at Open Bible Baptist Church. That was a lifetime ago, and she had traveled so far away from the church. She hadn't given the church or God a thought since her father was alive. As she lay in that hospital bed, Mama Beckum prayed. She was so desperate due to her pain that she'd told God that she would dedicate the rest of her life to Him and she would do His will if he would just grant her one wish and bring her son back.

"Mama, I'm sorry. I didn't have no choice." She felt his sincerity in her heart.

"Boy, shut up and tell me everything!" As they made their way to the couch she added, "and I mean everything."

Mama Beckum was as gangsta as they come. Back in the day, she did a bid in federal prison and in state. Women in Chowchilla State Prison still told stories about her up until Chowchilla was closed as a women's prison. So, he didn't have a problem with telling her everything.

After all, this was his mama and she deserved to know what would make him break her heart like that. She deserved that much.

"God damn, boy! Ain't no coochie that good to make you that mothafuck'n stupid! Look at me! Forgive me Father for my mouth." What he'd just told her would make a Catholic nun curse.

He couldn't respond. He'd had long enough to reflect on his careless actions and poor decision making.

"So, what are you going to do now?" She asked him as she pulled a cigarette out her pack and lit up.

Clark looked at his mother like she was crazy as fuck. "I'm bout to get this dough! What you mean what am I going to do?"

"Clarence, you don't think God is trynna tell you some-thing?" She asked after blowing out a cloud of smoke.

First, he wrinkled his face then he leaned back. Her question had caught him off guard. "God? What you mean God?" He asked.

She briefly told him about all the praying she had done, her promise and deal with God and how she believed it was all connected somehow.

"Mama, I'ma keep it 100 wit cha. If God is talking to you, I think that is wonderful and you should listen…" he stood up and kissed her on the cheek making sure to get out of her way before saying, "Cause, Mama I been talking to God for a minute now and He told me to get up and get dis money."

"Boy, I'ma slap you." She couldn't help but laugh with him. Inside she was praying for him once again.

"Oh, Mom, listen, I know you. Don't get on the phone letting the world know I'm back. Let me stay low for a while." He knew how his mother was and he didn't need his name ringing.

"Boy, I'm not gone call nobody! Go-on and do yo thang!" She yelled at him as she waved her hand in good riddance at him.

He gave his mom a look like he wasn't playing with her before heading out the door. The air temperature had dropped a full eight degrees by the time he left. The moment her door was closed and locked, Mama Beckum activated her alarm system and sat back on her couch. She said a silent prayer thanking God for bringing her baby home to her and declaring that she would change her life.

That quick she forgot all about La'Mont being in a coma. She picked up her IPhone X and scrolled through her contacts. The moment she found the name she was looking for she pressed send. Her heartbeat raced with anticipation while she listened to it ring.

"Hey Bernie?" Finally, Christine answered.

"Gurl, hut Up! Guess what?" Mama Beckum couldn't wait to spill the tea.

****** N. D. ******

Clark sat inside his Challenger waiting for his phone to ring. He'd only walked down from his mom's apartment five minutes ago, but he hated sitting in cars. He and his brother shared similar paranoias about parked cars. His iPhone rang. He looked at the caller I.D. and answered immediately.

"What's up, rogue?" He spoke into the phone while checking his mirrors.

"What's up, dad. Everything copasetic out there?" The caller asked into the phone.

"I don't know yet, rogue. Gimme a few days to be sure. You know I'ma hit you if I need you." Clark responded to the question while eyeing some nigga who'd just walked out to the dumpster with a garbage bag in one hand and a cellphone in the other up to his face talking.

"A'aight, dad, it's yo play. You know where I'm at if you need me." The caller hung up without hearing a response. There was no need for one, they already knew how each other rocked.

The nigga carrying the garbage bag had already dumped it and was heading back to whichever apartment he came from. Still, Clark kept his .50 on his lap as he started the Challenger and pulled off. One of the things he was doing while he was waiting on that phone call was rolling a blunt of some Platinum Cookies. As he drove down the freeway, he lit that blunt while listening to the new Mozzy.

It took him damn near an hour to reach the Koffee Shop. It was a little past 10 p.m. It was normal for the shop to be open and still doing business at this time of night. After all, the Koffee Shop was the best aftermarket upgrade/detail shop in California. Not to mention, it carried the hottest used cars on the West Coast, both Domestic and Foreign.

Clark pulled into the side gate leading to the back parking lot. There was another door that led to the main building back there. This was the door that Gunz used for late night meetings. Parking the car, he wondered what this place looked like in the daytime, it was so busy now. There were niggaz running all over. He climbed out the car and made his way to the door, only stopping briefly to speak to a couple of guys he knew.

Apparently, there was a new nigga, who was supposed to be somebody important, who Gunz wanted him to meet. Clark wasn't into meeting no new niggaz, important or not. To him a new nigga was just that, a new nigga. At the same time though, had it not been for Gunz, he knew he'd be in Lompoc or

Herlong Federal penitentiary waiting for canteen or some shit. He would've been in the cell with some old Italian mobster wannabe. Just on the strength of that, Clark owed it to Gunz to at least have a talk with the nigga. But that was as far as owing a nigga would go, as far as Clark was concerned.

The door to the office was open, so Clark just walked in. He could hear a conversation going as he approached the office. To his surprise, the conversation didn't stop when he entered. Some light skinned nigga was talking to Gunz. Clark noticed A.J., whom he nodded his head what's up to, as he took a seat on one of the plush, down, stuffed leather chairs that furnished the office. Two young niggaz, who he had neva seen, one standing the other seated, were both over by the nigga who was talking. Something about the little niggaz made Clark feel uneasy. He couldn't tell if it was their demeanor, the way the one that was seated was staring at him or what.

"...and once we've got all of the Elysian Fields up and running, then we can focus on the day care centers and other ventures that will help not only our people and communities, but are going to also help us out tremendously." Dok finished going over some of his plans with Gunz and A.J.

"Clark, what's going on, Cuzzo?" Now that Dok was done, Gunz addressed him.

"Shit, you know me, ready to get to dis money." Clark spoke fruitfully. All the community shit and kumbiyah. shit could be left to niggaz like his brother. Them niggaz were the Martin Luther King "I have A Dream" type niggaz. He was the Malcolm "Get it by any means" type. Thinking bout his brother brought the guilt and hurt again.

"We all ready to get to that money..." Gunz gestured his hand over to the light skinned nigga that was just talking. "But first, let me introduce you to who I wanted you to meet. This is Dok Holliday."

Taking his cue, Dok raised one hand with three fingers up, ring finger down with thumb, in a hood salute, "How you do, brotha," he inquired.

"What's up, rogue?" The tone in which Clark returned the greeting left none in the dark about his feeling towards the nigga.

"Aside from your brother and T'Rida, Dok is the third link in the chain that is Neva Die. Actually, the entire concept of what Neva Die was his idea and dream. So, in a way he's thee founding father out of our three founding fathers..." Gunz was speaking before Clark interrupted him.

"Ok. Him being the founding father and all that's beautiful, rogue, but what that got to do wit me?" He asked sounding like a young, dumb, cocky kid.

"It's got a lot to do with you. Just as we all moved to the cadence of T'Rida's drum or how everyone moved to sound of Voorheeze or my beat. There is a hierarchy within our organization or family. There always has been, always will be. This brotha sits at the head of that hierarchy." Gunz told him, not too much liking his attitude or the fact that he'd rudely cut him off.

Lil Scooter didn't have to question or wonder what page his brother was on. All of their lives they'd been in sync . No doubt, as his right arm went to his waist band, he knew that his brother was doing the same thing. .There wasn't any room for talking when that Dragon reared its ugly head. Just ask Samori Toure and his people. Samori may not be able to attest to these two but his people surely could.

"Peace be still. Let there neva be strife and feuding whenever brothas are gathered. For the betterment of self and one's people is always foremost on the agenda..." Peace be still, to some sounds like a greeting, but to his killas it's a command not to act. "Brotha, Clark I don't come to cause dissention nor cause any controversy. The brotha is right as far as Neva Die being my dream and vision. But, it's our family. But, let it not be lost upon you. Building our community instead of destroying it and our people are upmost and will not be stopped nor hindered by anyone." As the last sentence was spoken, Dok's entire persona and demeanor changed. If Lil Rell and Lil

Scooter made him uneasy, the look Dok was giving Clark, made him think to be sure that he had his banger on him.

"You keep talking dis community and our people, Martin Luther King, Harriet Tubman bullshit. Rogue, I'm Smack Mobb, always have been and always will be. And as far as E.P.A. is concerned, I worry about my city. You can worry about whatever the fuck you want, but not P.A. All you gotta worry about is supplying me with the work and I'll worry about getting you yo money! All that other shit, that shit is for the birds and them BGF niggaz on the prison yard that my brotha fuck wit!" Clark could give a fuck how Dok took what he said. Clarkola wouldn't bow down or tuck tail for nobody!

Fuck hearing a pin drop in a room. It was so quiet in the office you could hear a drunk mouse piss on cotton. A.J. had to respect the size of the balls that this East Palo Alto nigga had on him. Shit, his little brother was just as crazy!

Scooter and Rell were both waiting for the sign to go! A word, a head nod! Fuck! Anything and they would pop off. No matter how deadly the duo was, their discipline came before and above all else. So, they wouldn't move unless given an order to do so. Then the Dragon would surface and breathe fire.

Dok just looked at the fool in front of him. He could tell that the man was scared. What some saw as him showing bravado in the face of fear, Dok knew it was just more fear. A greater fear. This was the fear of being perceived as coward. Unfortunately, every year thousands of brothas are killed because of that "false pride."

When Dok looked at him though, he also saw himself and Voorheeze. They both were filled with that false sense of pride way back when they'd first met. Back in Santa Rita they were the only two Guerrillas in the POD with nine other Kumi niggaz who'd tried bully tactics with the rest of the pod. Against those odds, they'd stood together against the immortality and unfair treatment that was going on. They didn't care. They were ready to "Die Bout It."

It would be too easy to kill him. Dok was sure that every gun in the room would back his play. But, his heart wouldn't back him from the pain he would cause Voorheeze and his family. They had been through enough heartache and grief. Like a father grizzly with his cubs, Dok exercised more patience and spoke again.

"Peace be still my brotha. For the respect I have for your brother, I will excuse the outburst and disrespect, but my brotha, we will not supply you the poison, which you will kill and poison our people with. This family is moving on to greater things than crack and heroine.

I would love to still have you as a part of this because it will be glorious. But if not, then I wish you well." Dok was all diplomacy, no feelings or emotions.

"I just told you, patna, you ain't gone tell me how to eat especially in my city." Clark stood up. He was eye balling the little nigga sitting down when he said, "And if anybody got a problem wit what I do in my city, den it's whatever." After waiting a second to see if anyone had a problem he turned and headed toward the door.

"Clark!" Dok called out.

Clark didn't respond, he just stood there half expecting a bullet to the back of the head.

"The YMCA on Bell street. I don't know if you know or not, but we bought that a little while ago for the kids. I understand that's your City and all, but I would appreciate it if your workers kept a two-block radius away from the center, I would like that to be a drug free zone. After all it's for the kids. Elysian Fields is BGF property. You know them penitentiary niggaz your brother runs with." No matter how subtle he worded, it the threat was understood.

When Dok finished speaking, Clark didn't even honor him with a response, he just walked out of the office.

"Okay, now I'm not one to question shit when it ain't my business, but this is my business cause it's gone bite us all in the ass. So, I gotta ask why we letting this nigga walk outta

here instead of bodying him?" He asked the question to everyone, but A.J. was looking directly at Gunz.

It was Dok who spoke up. "Because his brother is my
brotha which makes him my brotha, and I won't kill my brotha
unless I have to." Dok informed him.

Scoot and Rell hadn't bothered asking because they already
knew the answer.

As Dok thought about Voorheeze, he hoped that it
wouldn't come to that. But, if he had to, he wouldn't hesitate.
Even though he wanted to, A.J. didn't say anything else. He
knew Clark was going to be a problem. He was a street soldier,
made Lieutenant and became a Capo. Now he would resurface
as a General. Damn right, they should've killed him. If he had
been an Oakland nigga, A.J. would've bodied him, no questions asked.

Clark made it to his car, thankful that a hail of bullets
hadn't cut him down. He started that shit up with the quickness
and got the fuck out of dodge. The moment he was on the
street, he picked up his iPhone and scrolled to the last received
number and pressed send.

"Calling kind of late, dad. What's up, everything good?"
The caller asked. You could hear the sleep in his voice. Clark
had awakened him from a good sleep.

"It's time for you to come home, rogue." Clark let him
know.

"So, everything's all good?" he asked sensing there was
something he wasn't being told

"Shyyyt, we ain't even get around to dat. There's some
other shit that we'll discuss when you get here though."

"So, you need me ASAP?" He was wondering if he needed
to drop everything and get there.

"Naa, ain't dat serious, just come home." He told him.

"A'aight, dad, I'll see you in a minute."

"A'aight." Clark clicked the phone off.

When he'd gone on the run, Clark wasn't the only one. He
knew his lil cousin was as worried about the feds as he had

been. He was supposed to get a feel for shit and move around before he made that call. Unfortunately, after tonight he might have another war on his hands!

**** N. D. ****
Milpitas

Urena was in his office with the door closed looking at his new watch. Should he have bought it? No. Was it too much? Absolutely! Did he give a fuck? Hell no! it was a stainless steel Aude mars Piguet that featured a Royal Oak offshore chronograph. At no time in his life would he have a need for an offshore chronograph. At no time in his life would he have a need for an Aude mars Piguet, but he didn't have the worries that someone in his professional capacity had. Hell, he was in bed with the Mobb and life was great at least that's how he saw it.

His very expensive watch was a striking contrast against the dull, pale poverty of his small office. The Dell computer that sat above his old tarnished desk was the only thing remotely of any worth in his office. Everything else was second hand or could've passed for second hand.

"Ah such a lovely watch", he thought. Today would be a good day, he could tell.

A knock on his door took his thoughts away from that good day.

"Come in" his tone reflected his feelings. He didn't really want whoever it was to come in.

The door swung inward and the last person whom he wanted to see, Officer Hedgecock was at his door. His complexion was very pink, standing there in uniform. He had a look on his face like he'd smelled a rotten egg or swallowed it.

"Leu, we got a problem, sir." Hedgecock told him as he walked into the office.

Urena thinks to himself *"there goes that good day"* and then he responded, "What kind of problem?"

He noticed that Hedgecock was carrying his phone. He really doesn't have time for some boyfriend and girlfriend bull shit. Thinking he had girl problems

"You need to see this sir."

Just like he thought, some bull shit.

"Officer, I don't have time for no bullshit!" He barked at Hedgecock.

"I assure you, sir, this isn't bullshit." Hedgecock shoved the phone into his face. As he stood over Urena, he couldn't but notice the expensive looking watch with the diamonds around the face.

When Urena looked down he saw a YouTube screen. He was just about to say something when the video began to play.

"Holy Shit!", was all he could say as he watched in horror.

On the screen was the same video that they had seen in their briefing. Only this video was clearer. A lot clearer. As Lt. Urena watched Officer Horsely die degradingly all over again, *"the poor son of a bitch"*, he thought to himself.

"We don't know who uploaded the video, but it's been up just a couple hours. One of my tech guys found it not too long ago."

Urena bolted up out his chair. "What the hell do you mean only a couple hours? On the internet that might as well be all year!" He did not want to be the one to take this to the Chief, but there was no time for chain of command on something like this.

He snatched Hedgecock's phone and headed toward the Chiefs office. He didn't know how someone had gotten their hands on the video, a better video than their own at that. But, they'd somehow gotten ahold of it and leaked it on the internet. Undoubtedly there was going to be hell to pay. So far, they had been able to keep the police killings under wraps. That was out the window now. The backlash had begun already. Messages and alerts from other sites were popping up and pinging one after another. One message said, "If Black Lives Don't Matter, Neither Should Cop Lives."

Urena didn't notice that Hedgecock was with him until he saw the reflection in the window of an office they were passing.

"Officer, that will be all. I'll make sure and get your phone back to you." He didn't have time to wait on a response.

Hedgecock wanted to argue, but he knew that arguing with a lieutenant, no matter what, he would lose. He turned around and looked to see if anyone had witnessed his embarrassment. Not seeing anyone paying attention to him, he made his way slowly down the hallway, back the way they had just come.

Urena made it to the Chiefs office. Outside her door he readied himself and took a deep breath. He wondered how long it had been since he'd felt nervous while standing outside of someone's office.

"Come on in!" Chief Vieira called out after he knocked on the door.

The Chief was always so nice, he wandered if she would be nice and cheery after this. He opened the door and walked in.

"Lieutenant Urena, how may I help you today?"

In front of her sat a stack of papers. She looked up from them with a smile on her face as she asked the question.

"Forgive me, ma'am, for breaking protocol by coming directly to you" he nervously began.

She waived her hand to say don't worry about it while at the same time telling him, "It's okay, what's the problem?" She knew there had to be a problem for him to be standing in her office at that moment.

The paper she was holding in her hand she laid face down on her desk. He didn't need to see the letter she had just finished writing Simpson.

"Well, Ma'am, somehow someone has gotten a copy of the video showing Deputy Horsely being murdered and has posted it on the internet. A bunch of social media sites have picked it up rather via chat rooms or actual clips of the video." Urena made his way to the desk with the phone in his hand. The video was already playing. "This is spinning into one major cyclone, ma'am."

She watched the video play and couldn't help but see all of the alerts and chats that were being sent.

"Dear Lord, help us." was all she could say.

The decision not to go public about the murders was hers. She was thinking of public safety overall but it wasn't not going to look that way once this got out.

Meanwhile, throughout the station word was spreading like wild fire blown by gusts of the Santa Anna winds of Southern California. Fearful anticipation of an all-out media frenzy loomed over the heads of everyone. It had been nearly four hours since the leak of the video. Currently, the identity of the source of the leak was priority.

The identity of the person who'd leaked the video may have well been on the top of everyone's 'to do list', but as officer Hedgecock was getting ready to find out, that was the least of their worries.

He sat in the conference room which had been turned into a make shift work area/command center for him and his guys. Hedgecock was fuming over Urena's disrespect in shutting him out on presenting the footage to the Chief. It was his team that discovered it, God Damn it! He stood up for the fifth time since Urena had returned his phone five minutes ago. The raging waves in his ear were the sound of blood flow from his heart beat. It didn't allow him to hear his cell phone that was ringing.

Just by chance he happened to glance down it the middle of his tantrum and noticed that the screen was lit up. Reluctantly he snatched it up.

"This is Hedgecock." He more yelled than spoke into the phone.

"Officer Hedgecock, this is Carla Daniels from KTVU Fox News…"

"Look lady, I ain't got time for this shit today." He started to hang up the phone.

Frantically she called out, "You don't have time for murdered police officers!"

He looked at the phone to check the caller ID, "What did you just say?" He questioned, hoping against all hope that he had heard her wrong.

"Sir, I have it from a reliable source that your department is in conspiracy with other departments to cover up a killing spree that's targeting law enforcement personnel throughout the Bay Area." Carla Daniels could not see through the telephone she could she would tell herself that Hedgecock gave the answer away by how big his eyes had gotten and how wide his mouth was open. But even if those were not giveaway signs, his already red face suddenly got two shades darker.

"Listen here lady, any reporter worth their salt would know the difference between a good, news-worthy story and a damn hoax," he tried to bluff.

That's what they were taught at the academy. Lie. Deny. Bluff. Cover-up. These were called the four essentials of police work.

"Right you are sir..." her voice was now condescending as she spoke. "And I will have you know that I have been with Fox News going on fifteen years and I definitely know the difference between a good story and a hellavah story. And this is a hellavah story..."

"Look lady..."

"Furthermore, we are running the story at 5 p.m. with Leslie O'Neil and I'm running a follow up on the 6 p.m. segment. Seeing as how you are the officer in charge of the special task force set up to stop the killer or killers, I just wanted to see if you wanted to defend why the police have decided to keep the public in the dark for so long. The public has a right to know." Carla was far from some rookie. She knew she had a story, but she wasn't going to reveal her hand.

"Well I...I...Uh.......I....Miss Daniels is it?" He finally blurted out.

"Yes, it is" she sounded like a grade school teacher speaking to one of her students.

"I…I'm…uh…I'ma have to get back with you on this Miss Daniels" all bravado and attitude were gone as he sheepishly uttered the words.

"You do that, Hedgecock," addressing him just by his last name now. "Just keep in mind that with or without a comment from the police, we are running the story." She said and hung up the phone

Hedgecock didn't see her bring her right elbow down and right knee up at the same time with her fist balled as she yelled "Yes!" Nor did he hear her when she yelled to her boss Cynthia. "Run it, Cynthia they're as guilty as a mothafucka caught in the middle of a bank robbery with a gun and a bag of money in his hands, running!"

He did however, see the thousand pieces that went flying everywhere as his iPhone shattered like an egg shell from the force of him violently throwing it against the wall. At the same time yelling "FUUUCK!"

He reached for a bottle of Sky Walk Candy Bomb Energy Drink at the same time someone called out to him, "You alright there Hedgecock?" It was Sgt. Andreatta. Out of the group that was gathered outside of the door, she was the only one brave enough to stick her head inside the door.

Hedgecock looked broken and defeated. The man looked like he'd lost his best friend, wife and dog all in the same day.

He looked at Jaran and took a deep breath, as he exhaled he told her. "Naw, Sarg, I'm not okay. Things aren't okay. Hell, we're not okay."

After his next gulp of the sky walk, the bottle was nearly empty. "Fuck it" he said and finished the bottle. He walked past Sergeant Jaran and the rest of the nosey mothafuckas that were standing behind her. The look on his face told mothafuckas not to bother him.

The Chief needed to know exactly what he was just told! She needed to know it now! This time though, she was going to hear it from him directly. Fuck Urena! And Fuck protocol. If the Chief had a problem with it, fuck her too!

He had a god damn job to do and he was going to do it!

**** N. D. ****

De'Kari

Chapter VIII

Tracy, California

She slowly lifted her head off the floor. Because of a raging headache, it took her nearly a whole two minutes to lift her head a mere five inches. The disgustingly putrid smell assaulting her nostrils told her that the thick sticky fluid covering her face and chest had to be vomit. As trifling and disgusting as this sight may be, it wasn't the first time she'd awakened to find herself in this position.

In fact, lately she had found herself passed out in a puddle of her own vomit almost every day. Only to wake up, clean up the mess (not worrying about herself), then grabbing a new bottle of alcohol and do it all over again.

Since the tragic day that she'd lost the love of her life She'd been succumbing to the will crushing power of a broken heart. Her heart wasn't just broken but shattered because her love was pure and true. Her love didn't run away and leave her abuse and mistreat her. No! Her love had been stolen from her.

Finally, after what seemed like forever she was able to stand and slowly make her way to the bathroom. After peeing for what seemed like a life time, she wiped herself and walked to the sink. The taste of old, stale vomit in her mouth made her want to throw up again. She reached for her toothbrush and Colgate and began brushing her teeth.

Without thinking, she looked into the mirror. Her heart broke into a million fragile, tiny, little pieces when she saw her reflection. For months now, she'd done everything she could not to look at her reflection in the mirror. She didn't want to see the truth.

At that moment, the truth of reality socked her in the side of her head like a drunk woman beater swinging a Louisville Slugger.

Monique didn't just give up, she flat out quit! There was no way on God's green earth that anyone would recognize her. She didn't even recognize herself.

Her hair was nappy with food and God only knew what else tangled inside of it! Blood shot, red eyes with Safeway sized grocery bags underneath them stared at her from the mirror. Dried vomit was all over her shirt, her face and even in her hair.

Without warning the tears cascaded down her face. The tears were just one more foreign substance added to many already on her once beautiful face. Yes, she was ashamed of herself! But no one knew the pain that she felt.

T'Rida was her everything, he had been her first and only true love. The fights and infidelity that occurred when they were younger was forgivable because they were only children at that time and that's what children did, act immature. They always had gotten back together because a love like theirs was one for the ages. It was a love for the story books.

The police had stolen a piece of her the day that they killed him. When Voorheeze would call and check up on her, she would fake like everything was okay. She knew that he was going thru it himself, so she put up a front and neva let on that she was really hurting and feeling destroyed.

She picked up the acrylic soap dish and shattered the mirror by slamming the dish into it.

"Arrrgghh!" she yelled as she struck the broken mirror over and over again "you mother fuckers!

Finally, she dropped the dish and stormed out of the bathroom and out of the room with nothing but a filthy t-shirt and even filthier panties on. She hadn't bathed or showered in almost two weeks. She was that hurt and depressed. If she were able to smell herself she would've stormed right back in that bathroom and taken eight or nine bubble baths.

Instead, she marched her filthy ass into the kitchen. The bottom of her feet was so dry and cracked that it sounded like a cat with claws was walking across the marble floor instead of a 38-year-old widow.

She opened the refrigerator and bent down to the bottom shelf looking for a bottle of her pineapple Cîroc. A foul rotten odor invaded her nose.

"Oh, my Gawd! She called out as she forgot about the bottle and began looking for the source of that awful smell.

Five minutes later she still hadn't found it. She checked everything but came up empty. Her mind was so cloudy from all of the alcohol that she didn't realized that the smell was actually coming from between her legs. The not bathing on top of the countless times she'd urinated on herself because she was so drunk, created a smell that would put a corpse to shame.

She found a bottle and cracked it open before even closing the door. She guzzled the cool liquid down just like a nigga. The cool, thick, clear vodka burned its way deliciously down her throat to her empty stomach.

She slammed the refrigerator door and made her way to the living room. As she walked, her right ass cheek itched so she scratched it. The material of her panties was so stiff it felt like she was scratching a pair of painter's overalls.

She sat down on the leather couch in the same exact spot where she always sat. This was her daily routine. A blown-up photo of her and T'Rida was mounted on the wall ten feet in front of her.

The photo itself was a life size picture of her and T'Rida. It was of him proposing to her on stage at club Carsjanae's the night of his 27th and final birthday. He had been violently gunned down shortly after that night by the Milpitas Police. "They killed my innocent husband", she told herself.

Her tears raced the alcohol she gulped down her throat trying to see if they would land on the soiled t-shirt faster than the alcohol landed in the pit of her stomach. The race was too close to call. Every day the race would end in a tie as she passed out in a drunken stupor. Today would be no different.

Three hours later, Titas opened the front door. "Hold up, gimmie like five minutes", he called over his shoulder. Aubrey already knew what was up, so he didn't say shit.

Titas closed the door behind him and made his way to the living room where he knew she would be.

He could smell her way before he got to the living room. The sight broke his heart and made him want to cry. He dropped his back pack and his book bag right where he stood. Anger rose through his body like mercury in a thermometer held next to fire.

Ready to murder somebody he spun around and went back to the door.

"Brah, Brah we can't today man." He told Aubrey once he opened the door.

"Come on T, she's my mom too. We brothers and we can take care of her together," Aubrey sincerely told his best friend.

"Naaw, Sauchi, not this time. It's too bad, cuz." Titas knew that Aubrey was sincere without even having to look at him. He'd helped Titas before, neva bringing it up afterwards.

But this time shit had just gone too far. They dapped each other up and Aubrey left while Titas headed back into the house.

"Come on, Mama." He spoke to her unconscious body as he easily but gently picked her up to take her to the bedroom. She smelled so bad he thought to himself this is not my mother, my protector, my queen. First, he laid her on the bed and then made her a bubble bath. Then he undressed her while holding his nose, so he didn't puke.

He carried her over to the bath tub and put her in. The bath sponge she had was not going to cut it, so he ran to his bathroom and grabbed his Axe body scrubber. Then he ran back to his mom in less than twenty seconds, so she wouldn't drown if she happened to tip over. While he was in his bathroom he snatched his Axe Body Wash as well. He was going to need some strong shit for this, not no Strawberry Essence or any other feminine shit. Finally, he began the chore of washing his mother.

Neva once through all her trials and tribulations had he looked down on her, judged her or thought less of her. And he didn't now. He just bathed her and talked to her gently. At one point she opened her eyes, reached her hand up and touched the side of his face.

"Oh Titas, I love you, Baby.", she was still incoherent when she said it.

He didn't give a fuck. All reserve evaporated, and he began to cry.

"Oh my God what's that smell? Titas?" his sister called out from the front room.

"In mom's room!", he yelled out. It's not like he could wake her up

"What the hell is that smell?" Na'Shay called back

"Mom!" he answered

"What?" She asked in shock

There was no need to respond she was in the room by then. She could put two and two together he figured, and she did. Once she made it to the bathroom. Titas aka Choppa-T stood up and handed his big sister the body scrubber.

Na'Shay couldn't believe how black the water was.

"Uh, uh, here…" she started to resist. She loved her mama, but she felt her mama was grown she could take care of herself.

"Not now Shay Shay, I need your help." He told her as he walked to the door. "Change that water and run her some fresh hot water with some of that girly shit in it while I start on this room and do a good job."

Na'Shay stood there looking down at her mother for a full minute before she budged. All she thought was if the loss of a man could do you like this then she was glad that she liked women and not men. What she was too young to realize was a man didn't cause this nor the loss of a man, it was love! Love wrongfully detached.

Dutifully she did as she was instructed.

She was now seventeen and her brother was sixteen. Both of T'Rida's children had turned out okay despite having to literally raise themselves for the last seven years. Na'Shay was the spitting image of her mother. Beautiful, but she had T'Rida's fire. She was as stubborn as a mule, like him as well. She also inherited his height. She stood nearly six feet. Unfortunately, for her brother and her mother, she'd inherited her mother's body.

Choppa-T stood six foot and weighed 270lbs. The boy was a pure beast. He resembled his mother in the face but got his size and behavior all from his father. He was a gentle giant until those buttons were pushed. He wouldn't know this yet because they hadn't been pushed yet, but they were going to.

Na'Shay finished way before he did, so after she got Monique dressed in the bathroom, her brother carried his mother into Na'Shay's bed. Then he finished taking care of her room. Things needed to change! He knew exactly what he was going to do.

Oakland, California

"Cuzzo, I understand what you're saying and that only adds more leverage on my side of the field. My nigga, you've neva been selfish. For you it's always the team first and that's why you make such a damn good leader." Gunz looked over at Big Rocc "what type of nigga gets an opportunity to be the mothafucka. Do the damn fool when he does, and doesn't have a problem going back to second in command once the boss returns?"

He threw his arms out to the side as if to say, "nigga tell me."

"G, you know niggaz ain't moving like that!" Roc told him after blowing a cloud of Grand Daddy out.

Gunz played off the momentum, "Exactly! If it was anybody else, mothafuckas been tryna figure out how to kill me just to make sure they hold the spot." Gunz words were true in every hood throughout the U.S…the laws of the streets made it that way.

A.J. finally spoke up. "Brah, look man, it's simple, before you left you entrusted me with something valuable. All I did was keep it safe until you returned like you asked. You back nigga, take yo spot."

"You not getting it, Cuzzo, ain't no spot for me to take. Check it out." Gunz decided to take a different approach. He sat down and began rolling a blunt.

"Lil Cousin, a nigga is really feeling this positive shit that Dok is on and I'ma lean my energy more towards that." The blunt was now rolled, he lit it and took a couple pulls before he continued. "You know if you need me, I'm here anytime, but the streets are yours, blood. As a real nigga, I'm honored that you would relinquish the spot for me, but it's yours cuzzo. You and Rocc hold it down."

"Nigga, y'all gotta see this shit!" DeeDee came running into the office shouting like he'd just seen the livest concert ever. "Dis shit been all over the internet all day. Blood, check this shit out!" He yelled as he grabbed the remote to the T.V.

They were all in Gunz back office at the Koffee Shop. The 85" Smart T.V. came to life.

"To recap Jim, our sources tell us that at least thirteen local law enforcement agents have either been murdered or presumed murdered along with a federal D.E.A. agent. Now Jim, all of these murders have in fact, gone unsolved and actually have been covered up by our local law enforcement until now. KTVU Fox 2 has exclusive rights to the footage that you are about to see. A video of the latest killing.

In the rising wake of unpunished police brutality and the so-called justified killings of hundreds of innocent African-Americans through-out the county, it is clearly evident from the footage that someone has said enough is enough!

"We would like to take this time to advise all of you viewers at home that the following footage is extremely graphic. We warn and advise that all children under the age of eighteen be removed from the viewing area!"

"DeeDee what you done turned on the damn screen?" A.J. knew whatever it was had to be some real gangsta shit to have DeeDee so hyped

"Just watch, nigga!" DeeDee called out with a devilish grin on his face.

Right on cue the video came to life on the screen. It was the darkened version that the cops first had.

"Oh shit!" Came from A.J. the moment officer Horsely opened the drivers door and found the dead Ranger. "Yo what the fuck is that on his lap?"

"Now, see dat's some mothafuck'n gangsta shit! Got dat bitch handcuffed, butt ass, fucking naked wit his own cuffs. Now dat's some ole school shit!" Big Rocc's attention and interest was finally peeked.

Just when everyone thought the video was done, a large warning strip rolled across the screen. What followed was a cleaned up, clear version of the video that had just gone off. Vivid and graphic in every detail.

"Nigga, I'm just saying, I bet Black Lives start to matter in this bitch now!" DeeDee yelled out excitedly.

"Brah, did them rats just really eat through his body like that?" A.J. didn't ask anyone in particular.

"Lil Nigga, you saw them bite their way out dat fat mothafuckas stomach, didn't you?" Big Rocc hated dumb ass questions.

The only person not to speak was Gunz and he had good reason. A damn good reason. He paid attention to every single detail. The anchor woman was back talking.

"This video was anonymously sent to our station just a little past ten this morning. The hours that followed were spent researching the allegations.

So far, we are able to confirm the following; Lt. Boots of the San Mateo County Sheriff's Department, Detective Rick Jenson of the Milpitas Police Department, Sergeant Henry

Costa, of the Milpitas Police Department, Detective Diana Richards of the Santa Clara County Sheriff's Department, Officer Henry Peterson of Menlo Park P.D. and an officer from the San Mateo County Sheriffs have all been killed in the past few months while eight other Officers have gone missing and are presumed dead.

I have it on good authority that a Drug Enforcement Agency agent who had gone under cover was also murdered. The same source has informed our station that the Federal Government has sent agents to help solve what appears to be a serial cop killer…"

If what he saw wasn't bad enough, at the mention of the feds Gunz picked up his phone and scrolled to Dok's number in his contacts. His blunt was almost gone. He gestured to Dee-Dee to roll him another. He needed the mothafucka now. The rest of them were busy making up scenarios of what they would do if a cop pulled them over.

"Cuzzo, we got a problem." was all he said when Dok picked up.

"One bigger than you think, my brotha." Was Dok's response before he hung up.

Gunz grabbed the remote control from off the desk where DeeDee placed it.

"Shut down everything in the streets! Everything! I want new phones and new numbers for everybody. No, as a matter of fact I want every last resource we got spent on buying throw-away and go-phones. I want five hundred of them, now!" Gunz tone and speaking pattern was calm, but his raging emotions was evident to all…except one.

"G, what them crazy mothafuckas killing cops got to do with us?" DeeDee was so engrossed in the news he didn't see the fire in Gunz eyes.

"I know my orders ain't being questioned." The calm was still there. A true General didn't need to yell.

"I…N…No….G, I wasn't questioning…"

"Well get to carrying them out." Gunz couldn't help thinking the little nigga needed a lot of discipline.

DeeDee hopped up with the quickness, stumbling over his feet as he made a B-line to the front door to do just what he should've done from the jump.

A.J. couldn't help the laughter that erupted from him, nor did he try to.

"Leave the street shit to me and Rocc. You're moving on to the positive shit." He couldn't stop laughing.

"We got a problem and if we don't solve it, won't be no more street shit or positive shit!" As he hit the blunt DeeDee dropped on the desk when he jumped up. Gunz knew he had their attention then!

**** N. D. ****

Chapter IX

East Palo Alto

"Nigga, I'm just saying the whole hood thought you was gone. First mothafucka hear that you got shot up over by McDonalds. Then, the next thing a mothafucka hears is the fucking paramedics done got airborne, Whoosh," Linell made a gesture with his hand like something flew off a ramp. "They say, Nigga, da ambulance looked like an Olympic high diver. Nigga 101 was shut down like eight hours, bro." With all his excitement and movement, all the weed should've fell out of the blunt Linell was rolling, but this nigga was a pro. He ain't drop one single flake or crumb off the cookies.

"Nigga, the shooting was real! Nigga, I got hit twice once in the shoulder and once in the leg." He lifted his Gucci shirt to show him the bullet wound.

"Nigga, the one that hit a nigga in the leg, got me all fucked up. Had to get a rod and shit, nigga, I can't even bend my leg all the way." Clark grimaced as he remembered the pain he'd felt that night.

"My nigga, you was supposed to be bussin' back!" L took a minute to light the blunt.

"How you gone tell me bout bussin', when you bout to go hit in the yard behind punching on a nigga?"

"Oh, oh, but I beat that mothafucka's ass though." Linell reminded him.

"Hold up." Clark told him as he dug in his pocket for his ringing phone.

This phone didn't have any contacts saved in it. So, the number is foreign to him.

"Hello?" If he didn't recognize the voice, he'd hang up fast.

"Nigga, you got a lot of mothafuck'n nerves." His sisters voice was definitely one he recognized. "I mean here it is a mothafucka's on the verge of a breakdown and I gotta hear it from the streets that I'm crying for nothing! I'm saying though, where they do that at?"

With all that was going on, he had forgotten to hit French Tip and run shit down to her.

Linell could hear her every word as she went in on Clark viciously.

"Sis, look…"

"No, mothafucka, you look. Just mothafuck'n yesterday, I'm sitting my dumb ass over here tryna plan another funeral and guess what, nigga? I could've been preplanning the grand opening for my fashion show that neva happened, guess why?"

She read him his full rights for five minutes. He just sat there and listened. After all, it was his baby sister, plus he knew he was in the wrong. More importantly, he'd had a bitch of a time healing from the first gunshots. He wasn't trying to get shot again, not by his sister.

'L' was trying to maintain a straight face, but the cookies were kicking in and lil sis was going H.A.M. He bust out laughing so hard French Tip could hear him. That only pissed her off more, so she hung up. 'L' didn't stop laughing until Clark reached for his Desert Eagle and drew down.

His laughing stopped in mid "ha" at the sight of the eagle. Noticing that Clark wasn't looking at him but behind him "L" reached inside his jacket and came out with his Glock 50 wit the extended dick hanging from it. He might have acted like a square when it came to his day job, but "L" been bout da life since his days at Paly High.

It was far from summer, but one couldn't tell from how bright the sun was blazing. The two of them were standing in the streets, guns ready, it was like a scene from Bad Boyz II as the trucks came rolling down the street.

There were three Denali HD Super Pickups, two Chevy Durmax Diesels, One super heavy-duty Dodge pickup and two Hummers. One H2 and one H3. Every truck was black with tinted windows, big ass chrome tires and from their sound, Clark could tell that they were supped up. The two Hummers were tricked out with candy paint, rims, the whole nine yards. The shit was crazy.

"Man, you know dese, niggaz?" 'L' asked while cocking his Glock, putting one in the head.

"Naaw, nigga, but I hope brah hurry up! I ain't got enough bullets for all of these mufuckas." He responded while following 'L's lead and putting one in the head.

The H3 was a candy caramel with deep dish peanut butter tan 32-inch rims. The passenger door to it opened.

"Come on, dad! You niggaz standing there all terminator'd the fuck out in the middle of the streets like it ain't white folks in P.A. now or something." Tut called out with a big ass smile on his face. He was standing up on the floor runners. His dreadlocks hung down to his shoulders now. He looked like a smaller version of 'L.'

"My nigga, you almost got lit up out here driving down dis mothafucka like a bunch of Haitians" 'L' joked as he re-tucked his banger.

Tut climbed down from the H3. 'L' couldn't help but wonder why lil niggaz always got big ass vehicles.

"Now, look-a-here, shawty." None of the three saw the passenger door on the candy purple H2 with matching rims open up. "Me and the fellas ain't drive all the way out to Cali to roast in da sun, shawty." Some light skinned, T.I. looking mothafucka was standing up on the floor runner.

"Aww, dad, that's my crazy ass cousin, Man-Man. From the way you was sounding I figured I'd bring some niggaz with me from the 'A', dad." Tut answered. "Plus, I got a lil gift for, blood." He nodded his head at 'L'.

They made their way towards the back of one of the HD Denali's. Man-Man was already in the back of the truck bed by the time they reached the truck.

Clark wanted to know what the gift was as much as 'L' did. Tut had sent a text to him saying to have 'L' with him but he'd neva explained why.

The truck bed was customized with an air tight compartment built in under the truck bed. The compartment was built large enough to hold a thousand kilos. After making sure the correct buttons were pushed in to unlock the hidden compartment, Man-Man lifted the door.

"God damn, Shawty!" Shaking his head and stepping back he looked at Tut. "We got us a problem, Shawty."

"What's up, Man Man?" Tut could tell by the look on Man-Man's face that it was serious.

A breeze picked up and carried a foul odor to them. Tut already knew the answer.

"Shawty dead!" Man Man told him flat out.

"What you mean dead? How'd he die?"

"Wait, hold up, nigga, who dead?" Clark was looking back and forth from Tut to Man Man.

"That Nigga (Tut said while pointing his finger at the body). I told you I was bringing a gift."

It was the bitch ass nigga who'd called the police and pressed charges on 'L' after getting his ass kicked at Club Carsjanae's. He was hiding out at his grandma's house in Atlanta until it was time to testify on a real nigga! Tut had different plans.

"You niggaz rode all the way back from the ATL wit that mothafucka in that box?" Clark couldn't believe this shit. "Did it ever occur to you niggaz to check on him?"

"What da fuck for, there's 'nough wind blowing fo da nigga to breathe." Man Man was wondering if this nigga was joking or crazy.

"Apparently not, nigga." Clark stated flatly. Then he turned to 'L', "well looks like you can pull yo time waiver now and do a speedy trial. Charges will be dropped by the end of the month."

That was as far as the good news was going to go because a police car was pulling up from the other end of the street.

When the car finally came to a stop, a little, fat, short, nigga got out. So, did every other nigga that was sitting in the trucks!

"And the grave shall spit up it's dead! Oh! Shit! It must be the end of the world!" The fat little nigga shouted.

"Where?"

"Fuck you want, Norris?" Clark asked the cop.

"You know faking your own death is illegal?"

"You know I can show how easy it is to do." He shot back at him.

Norris might have been a lot of things, stupid wasn't one.

"Come one now, Clark! You know I'm just playing." He gave a fake laugh, trying to cover his fear.

Man-Man didn't know how they got down in Cali, but he was ready to show 'em just how they did it in the 'A'! His strap was out and ready to start talking. Norris played like he didn't see the strap hangin' in Man Man's hand, but his sudden change in behavior said otherwise.

"Y…you guys gotta get these trucks outta the streets" Norris was reassessing the situation as he was speaking. He didn't like his assessment.

"Yes, Sir! We not tryna get killed, sir. Just reminding them that Black Lives Matter, sir." Tut did his best slave imitation.

"Get the damn trucks out of the street." Norris rushed his little ass back to his car and reversed all the way down the street.

He said fuck the speed limit or any kids who may have been around, considering it was a residential area. Today he must've been feeling his fast and the furious.

Clark turned to look at Man Man, "Nigga you's a crazy mothafucka. We gotta be family."

He embraced Man Man like he was a long-lost cousin, and in a way, he was.

De'Kari

PART ll

A B C G
Any Body Can Get-it!

De'Kari

Chapter X

Sunnyvale
11:15 p.m.

He watched her head as it bobbed up and down. The sight of her sucking his dick like Super Head herself should've held his attention, but it didn't. The only thing he could think of was a nigga trynna tell him how to run his city. Mothafuckin' clowns had him fucked up. He had put up with all that wannabe Mafia shit on the strength of his little brother. That was his thang. But Clarkola was a street nigga! A mothafuckin' E.P.A. nigga!

The magic of Spiritual's mouth went unnoticed along with the slurping sounds she was making as he reached for his phone. On any other day, the way she twisted her head and circled her tongue around his helmet just before devouring him, would've had him curling his toes and grabbing her hair just to hold on. Tonight, it didn't even phase him.

Clark waited patiently for the line to be picked up. No matter what was on his mind, his heart rate still quickened and his dick throbbed in her mouth at the sight of her fifty plus inch ass. It was just the right everything. Size, complexion, firmness to soft ratio, just enough cellulite. Shit, Spiritual was fuckin angelical.

Finally, the other line was picked up "A.B.C.G." Four simple letters were all it took. Not even a phrase, just four simple syllables. One letter uttered in each syllable. That was all he said into the phone.

At 11:15 p.m. on Friday, March 17, 2017, Clarkola uttered four letters that would begin the domino effect for all Hell to break loose!

East Palo Alto
11:56 p.m.

"Even though dis ain't splittin' a niggaz wig Shawty, Mayhem is still Mayhem." Man-Man said to the driver as he hit end on the call he'd just had. "Let's get it, Shawty."

The driver neva spoke. He just put the truck in drive and headed to their destination. That new Gucci Mane was bumping in the speakers. Bone agreed Mayhem was Mayhem, but Murder was Murder. The navigation told him to make a right on University Ave. The sight of a McDonalds reminded him how hungry he was.

At 6'4", 305lbs, Bone was always hungry. Man Man was thinking how nice the area was compared to back home. Cali niggaz had it sweet. He couldn't imagine the city he been seeing being the murder capital for three years. Not with the IKEA and Target and fucking Facebook. Nuh-uh, these niggaz had it sweet.

They made a right onto Bell St. and the navigation said that they'd reached their destination. They weren't' going to stay long, so there was no need to park. Bone stopped in the middle of the street.

Both of them climbed out of the all black Durmax Diesel. Bone had a Mack 11 with an extended clip. Man climbed down holding an AK-47. In the pitch black of night, they were barely visible.

"Well Cali, meet Hotlanta, Shawty." As if those magic words were a wake-up call. The night sky lit up like the skies in Baghdad.

They both aimed their perspective tools of mayhem at the newly finished "Elysian Field Youth Center" and just swept their arms back and forth.

It only took seconds for both guns to click on empty chambers. They were back in the Super Duty truck and pulling off before the red light behind them on University ever turned green. They'd caused a shit load of damage to the building though.

"Well, shawty, that mothafucka won't be open for business on the a.m. and dat's foe damn sho." Bone knew even though it was said seriously that Man Man was joking.

The two of them had grown up together since grade school. They knew each other as well as brothers knew one another, maybe even better. The navigation wasn't needed. The directions were pre-given and were too simple to mess up. At the first corner they made a left. Drove all the way to the corner and the freeway was straight ahead to the left.

Once on the freeway, Man Man typed the address for their next destination in the navigation. Mayhem is Mayhem, he thought as he reloaded the weapons.

"I'ma use the choppa on the next one, Shawty." When Bone said Shawty it was so drawn out it sounded like an old school cassette take getting caught in the player. Plus, his deep baritone voice made the late Barry White sound like Michael Jackson.

Forty-five minutes later they were driving through the streets of East Oakland. Coming down International Blvd., which used to be E14th St., the looks on both of their faces said it all. This was worse than back home. The run-down buildings and filth in the streets were one thing – and boy was it filthy-but here it was almost 1:00 a.m. and the streets were lit up with activity.

On first look, it appeared that these were everyday citizens. Well, at least from a distance it did. These were zombies. The worst of the worst of dope fiends. The kind that spent every second of every minute lurking and scheming on a come up so that they could score their next hit. They were the dope fiends that the legends "will kill you for five dollars" or "will sell their soul for a hit" spoke of. The dope fiends and hookers both looked like night of the living dead. Most looked like they hadn't showered or changed clothes in weeks. Some looked like they hadn't done so in a year.

They reached their destination, but it was on the other side of the street, so they had to drive to the next set of lights and bust a U-turn. Two things about 'Elysian Fields East Oakland', the first was it's located directly, in the middle of the busiest street in all of East Oakland. Second, there were so many crack heads and prostitutes on the porches and around the building, it looked like an early 90's house party.

"Baby, you two fine ass niggaz looking to get into some freaky shit?" A high yellow prostitute as thick as The Body XXX and as ugly as Shanaynay asked. Her breath smelt like some new type of hybrid monkey shit.

Man Man looked over at Bone, "If you could see the ass on shawty den you'd know why I would consider that."

The look Bone gave him said he was wondering if Man Man was crazy or not.

Man Man turned his attention back to the Barewolf that had propositioned him. "Come here, Shawty. Now don't talk ,just listen, okay." She nodded her head up and down. Her disease filled pussy was getting wet from the way he was taking charge.

"If I wasn't here on business, I would love to bend you ova and fuck you in that big ass dinosaur booty you got just to see how tight it is. But, Shawty, you listening?" She licked her cracked lips and eagerly nodded her head again. "If you wanna live, beautiful, I would get outta here fast."

"You o'le bitch ass, no pussy getting, faggot ass n…" she stopped and shut the fuck up while scurrying backwards, the moment she saw him lift the AK off his lap, Bone was already out the truck carrying the Calico.

International Blvd was the complete opposite contrast of Bell St. in East Palo Alto. International was very busy and it was lit up. That didn't stop them.

"Crazy ass country bumpkins!" The prostitute yelled as she was in a full sprint down International.

The rest of her cronies weren't that lucky. Man Man sprayed the left side of the building and swept in, knocking chunks out of the building the glass window and the bodies. They had nowhere to run because Bone did the exact same thing on the right side. It was a slaughter! It took Bone a little longer to run out of bullets because he had a drum on the Calico.

Most people that drove by minded their business. Most of them were hood niggaz doing hood shit. The rest were just so used to this type of shit it was just another night to them.

But, one woman who just happened to be a social worker, almost home after responding to a client who had an emergency that took five hours to finally get resolved. She saw the senseless massacre and began crying as she sped away.

"If Black lives truly mattered, somebody should've told them two fools that." She said out loud frantically speeding away.

As Bone got them the fuck out of dodge, an Man lit a blunt and handed it to Bone. He then lit one for himself. Next, he reloaded all the guns. If the police got on them, they could get it, too. Once that business was taken care of he picked up his phone and sent the following text.

"1236."

1236 or 1.2.3.6 which when translated to the alphabet meaning A.B.C.G.

In the span of roughly an hour and a half, they'd successfully shot up two buildings, prevented the grand opening of two Youth Centers, killed seventeen people and wounded twelve others. Which would make anybody wonder "Do Black Lives Really Matter?"

****** N. D. ******
Milpitas

Batman was sitting on the couch eating a fat turkey, ham and cheese sandwich. It was loaded with the works: lettuce, tomato, pickles, everything. He was watching the news coverage about him killing Deputy Horsely.

"Well, Robin, it looks like I done messed around and fucked up." He said out loud. He was speaking to Voorheeze even though he wasn't there.

For Voorheeze, declaring war on the police had been personal. Their little killing spree was all about revenge for T'Rida's death. But for Batman, it had been something else entirely. It was so much more than the death of one brotha. He'd long since grown tired of the plight that his people were suffering and forced to endure since the death of 12-year-old Tamir Rice, from Cleveland, Ohio. Tamir was shot and killed on Sunday, November 23rd while playing with a BB gun at the park by his house. The police shot the little boy repeatedly and afterward they watched him die instead of giving him medical treatment.

Deep down, Batman was a spiritual man. Though he knew what he was doing was wrong, he convinced himself that Voorheeze's phone call was God's way of telling him to do something that would shine the light on what was being done to his people. He may not have been as crazy as Voorheeze, but he wasn't all the way there either.

He finished his last bite of the sandwich and washed it down with a Heineken that he'd grabbed from the refrigerator. Now that he was nice and full, he would be able to work.

Lieutenant Josephine Sullivan was butt ass naked, just where he left her strapped to a table, before he raided her refrigerator for food and caught the news.

"Now Lt., tell me are you gonna give me what I want or do I gotta get it the hard way?"

"P…please…please don't rape me." She was so scared she could barely beg.

"Rape you?" Batman was offended, "Woman, I ain't gotta take no pussy! Rape you! Na na, what I want is information. But first, I gotta show you that shit is real." He tried to stuff a dish cloth in her mouth. Fear of the unknown made her buck up and resist.

The force of him butting his head against hers as she raised up, made her eyes roll to the back of her head.

"Yeah, I gotta show your stupid ass. Don't rape you." He mumbled to himself as he attempted to gag her with the cloth again. Like most dumb mothafuckas, she learned after pain.

Once the dish cloth was stuffed nice and tight in her mouth, he walked over to the counter and picked up the scalpel he'd placed there earlier.

"If you don't gimme what I want, I promise you that you're gone be begging a mothafucka to rape you." Lt. Josephine Sullivan had no idea just how true his statement was.

"On New Year's 2009, a young 22-year-old black man was enjoying a night out with some friends". As she was talking he grabbed one of her breasts. Fear froze her as she peed on herself. "This young black man was only a child!" In one swift motion he sliced her nipple off with the scalpel.

Her screams and cries were muffled. Her attempts to wiggle out of the straps were humorous.

"I would ask you if you know his name, but I'll just go ahead and tell you." He squeezed her breast harder causing blood to run down the mound.

He pushed the scalpel into the flesh at the base of her breast and sliced his way around the breast as he spoke to her. "His name was Oscar Grant and he was murdered."

The pain was far beyond anything she had ever felt. She was shaking so hard that the table was moving. Her mind was racing, how could she get herself out of this? She needed to get away from this crazy man. She wished her husband could save her. That wish would neva be answered and she knew it. Not with the two bullet holes in his head. He lay on the floor seven feet away staring lifelessly at nothing.

When she finally simmered down enough he removed the gag out her mouth. She was smart enough not to scream. But her sobs and murmurs were uncontrollable. He used the dish cloth from her mouth to wipe the blood off of the scalpel in front of her, fucking with her mental. The violation she felt was worse than the pain.

"You're going to tell me exactly how to get inside of your Police Department. Every key code, every access point, shift rotations, officers on duty, everything! I want you to act like I'm your boss giving you an annual audit. Do you understand what I'm telling you?" When she didn't answer he slapped her so hard he bruised her face.

"Yes. Oh God, why are you doing this?" She cried out. In all her years on the force Sullivan have neva mistreated anyone. She treated everyone fair and equal.

"Why am I doing this? Did you just ask me why I am doing this?" The moment she opened her mouth to speak, he shoved the rag back in her mouth.

"Fucks wrong with you? Asking me some dumb ass shit? Did you ask any of the thousands of cops that killed innocent blacks why they did it, huh?" Losing his temper, he took the scalpel and went to work. Batman started by slicing her other breast off. He took the scalpel and made an incision from one side of her collarbone to the other. Then, he started at the base of her neck and sliced down until he reached her panty line. She was passed out.

When he was done her body looked like she had been in a fight with the X-men and Wolverine had won.

He walked to the kitchen and grabbed another Heineken. Batman woke her up by pouring half of it in her face.

"There's a statewide manhunt for me right now so I ain't got time for games. Ask me another question or don't tell me what I want, I'ma slice your pussy up next." He made cutting gestures with the scalpel. "Lip by lip."

Thirty minutes later Batman realized three things; pain was greater than fear, but the fear of pain was the ultimate. He also realized after everything that she'd told him that his plan would not work. Not with all the cameras and facial recognition. Lastly, he realized it was truly hard to kill a woman. That's not who he was, but he had a job to do and doing his job is what he did. Her naked, dead body still on the table was proof of that!

He thought about cleaning up after himself, his fingerprints and what not, then he remembered they already knew who he was. At least they knew who to look for. They had no idea who he was! They about to learn though!

**** **N. D.** ****

Oakland

"The events of last night may seem pressing, my brotha, but they're not. That's just the street mentality of retaliation trying to take over and cloud your judgement. We know who it was already. What we don't know is exactly what these Weupi's (white people) know. Thus, that takes precedence. As you said, that cat on the screen is brah's peoples. You were gone when they had the funeral for Clark and Big Brah got shot. So, what you don't know is that was that same cat that killed that Sutton kid and saved brah's life. It's only going to be a matter of time before they connect him and then we're all under the radar." Dok was talking to Gunz, who was irate over the stunt Clark pulled with the Rec Centers.

To Gunz it was a personal slap in the face. They'd broken bread together. Neva Die put that ungrateful mothafucka on and this was how he showed his appreciation. Gunz wanted to flat out murder the mothafucka, but he knew Dok was right. Still, his anger wouldn't allow him to verbalize his feelings.

"That decision you made to shut shit down was a wise one. I think the best play right now is to focus on the Elesian project until we get a feel for what's known. It ain't like we're hurting for the money or nothing". Dok shared with him. The two of them were alone in the back office of the Koffee Shop.

"Yeah, that's a good look. But, I'ma check with Hawaii 5.0 and get us some light shed on what's what" Gunz finally replied using the analogy of the early 90's tv. sitcom as a reference to Lt. Urena.

He pulled out his phone and punched Urena's number in. Technically, Gunz didn't take orders from Dok, after all he himself was a founding father. But out of respect for his name and what he'd done, Gunz was willing to listen to the voice of reason and follow logic. When that shit was over and done with Gunz would teach that mothafucka Clark exactly who he was fucking with.

"We need to talk," he spoke into the phone once Urena picked up.

"Uh, now's not really good for me…"

"Listen, be at the spot in an hour. I don't care what you're doing, be there!" All that now's not a good time shit, Gunz wasn't trying to hear none of that.

When he got off the phone he looked at Dok. "Blood, you good? I got some shit I need to take care of before I meet up with this mothafucka." He asked Dok as he got up and prepared to take off.

"I'm straight, my brotha, I'ma finish up these designs, then I'ma check in with the little ones to see how everything is coming along." He answered knowing that Gunz wasn't going to leave the issue alone.

"You know what, I'ma have to link back up with you and go over a couple of ideas."

"What you talking bout?" Gunz was curious

"For the Satin Doll affair. I think I need to bring something new out" The sly grin on his face said Dok already knew what he wanted.

"That's cool hit me. But, I need to let you know something." He tilted his head down and looked down his nose at him. "You might be big brah and all, but I'm not about to let you shit on me in dat whip department.

"Then, my brotha, I advise you to come saucy, cause the kid gonna come wet." Dok was serious as a heart attack.

Gunz left Dok in his office and walked out of the Koffee Shop, wondering what Dok had up his sleeve. He pushed his Austin Martin through the streets of the East thinking about what he wanted to stunt with. It ain't no secret niggaz in the 'Town', Oakland's nickname, were known for their whip game. It was nothing to see a teenage nigga pushing something foreign, just look at them "Stubby Ent." Niggaz. A young nigga in a Porsche or Jag truck was the norm. So, when it came to shutting shit down, a nigga really had to step his game up!

The momentary distraction was good for his mental, but as he was nearing the corner of 85th and E14th. He had to throw his game face back on. The flow of traffic was stupid. When they were selling crack, he clientele was off the hook. 85th was the biggest money-making spot in the East. Once they made the switch from crack to crystal, it was a whole different ballgame. Their chemist had shit so pure and clean that they couldn't burn their bubbles if they tried. While the snorters, every time they snorted a line their nose bled. The shit was that potent. If you held a shard up it looked like pure glass. No fog whatsoever!

When Gunz parked and got out he was wearing a big, shit eating grin. He was proud to see how A.J. had shit going. The spot was running smoothly. Since the reigns had been turned over to A.J., he had opened up quite a few more spots. Over all, this was still the money maker.

One of the little ones that was serving packs was looking at Gunz like he was looking at Michael Jordan. "What's up, Lil Blood?" Gunz called out to him. Lil Sammy couldn't' believe the Legend was talking to him, "W…what's up, big homie!" He proudly called out louder than necessary. Hehe wanted everyone to know that the big homie had spoken to him.

Normally, DeeDee didn't get out of the car. He oversaw all the spots in the East. Since the fall of the A-Team, they had reached out to the Gas Team, so they had West Oakland on lock right along with the East. DeeDee would ride from one spot to the other. He would park for a while and make sure shit was running the way it was supposed to. Gunz was the Big

Homie and he wasn't gone disrespect the Big Homie by making him come to him. So, he put the big thang on the driver seat and climbed out.

"What's up, big brah?" He asked Gunz as the two embraced.

"If what I'm seeing around here is any inclination, then shit is good." Gunz answered, referring to the clientele that was passing through the spot.

They were on the side of the store, so they could see everything going on. DeeDee subconsciously tapped the Glock .40 on his waist. He kept his eyes alert and his head on constant swivel.

"Brah, on the real, switching over to that glass shit was the best move we could've made, the money going dumb ass stupid." DeeDee told him as he pulled out a pre-rolled blunt.

"That's good, cause once they legalize this weed shit, we gone take a loss on our weed spots." Gunz told him as he accepted the blunt from him.

"Trust me when I tell you, from the numbers that we're seeing, we can shut all the weed spots down and our money will still climb." DeeDee explained matter of factly.

"You sound like we done hit an oil field or something." Gunz thought the little nigga was putting the 10 on the 2.

"Brah, we doing sixty bands a day just in this spot!" He told him with pride.

Gunz couldn't believe what he'd heard. The pride in Dee-Dee's voice and the look on his face told Gunz that the youngin' was serious as hell! Gunz was really impressed! When it was his, this same corner did eight thousand a day, some days nine. Sixty thousand a day and they'd just started with the crystal meth. That only meant it had the potential to hit one-hundred thousand a day. AJ had already told him that they served everything from $10 packs up to a whole onion-ounce-out on the blade. They trap spots was where they served their weight.

"What time you expect to hit up wit blood?" Gunz asked referring to A.J.

"I just holler at him before you pulled up. He on his way now. " DeeDee answered while taking a hit off the blunt.

They continued to smoke and chop it up while they waited on A.J. to pull up. Gunz was seeing what DeeDee was talking about. Money was coming hand over fist. He'd neva seen so many white people in East Oakland in all his life. What was fucking him up was the amount of Black people that were coming through buying the shit. He would've neva guessed so many blacks fucked around with the shit.

A.J. pulled up about ten minutes later. Of course, the two of them A.J. and DeeDee had heard about the shooting. The entire Town was talking about it. When Gunz told them about Dok's feelings, they quickly let him know that their sentiments were the same as his. Knowing they felt the same way as he did, gave Gunz the reassurance that his team would be ready if he needed them assembled. He still wasn't ready to make that call, but he knew he would be forced to make it sooner or later.

After talking to them a little while longer, Gunz got back in his whip and jumped on the freeway to go meet up with Urena. Normally, he wouldn't fuck with the radio, but he needed a change of pace, so he could do some thinking. Every station was talking about the police killings. There was all types of speculation, everything from a one-man vigilante to the Black Mafia taking out hits on the police in retaliation to all the killings of blacks. Everyone was searching for Levell Jenkins aka Batman.

From the people calling into the station it was evident that the people were divided. Half believed that he was making matters worse for the people. The other half felt it was about time somebody stood up for the people. Gunz smiled to himself when a cat named Blood James called in and told Sana G that the UBN or United Blood Nation Mobb as well as Piru were one hundred percent behind Batman and what he was doing.

He sent a clear message that if Batman needed any assistance, they would give it to him.

This time Urena arrived at the strip club before Gunz. As Gunz approached the table he shook his head in disgust. A manly looking chick was on top of Urena giving him a lap dance. Urena had a goofy looking smile on his face until he saw Gunz.

"U...Um...ugh. That's it for now sweetheart. Let me take care of some business. We can...uh, finish a little later," he nervously told her while patting her on her ass.

Gunz waited for her to leave before he took his seat. If he had to put his money on it he would've sworn that it was a man.

"Your extracurricular activities can be done on your own time. Keep that shit in check when you're on my time.

"Sorry about that. It won't happen again." Urena was nervous every time he was around Gunz.

Even though he was on duty, he had already had two drinks in hopes that it would calm his nerves.

"Make sure that it doesn't!" Gunz hated this place. The smell of sweat, ass and alcohol were over bearing. "Tell me what you got and what you gone do about it."

"Well so far no-one has connected him with the shooting at the funeral involving La'Mont or to your organization. I only remembered his face because the marksmanship in which he landed all three shots to the kid's forehead from the distance he was at. If someone were to look over the evidence from the shooting and see..."

"Make sure that they don't!" He interrupted him, "In fact, you need to make sure to steer this entire investigation and manhunt away from me and my family. If you do, you'll be rich. If you don't, you and your fat wife gone die." Gunz didn't wait for a response. He stood up, dropped the two manila envelopes on the table and walked out.

Urena greedily picked up one of the envelopes and flipped through the stack of hundred-dollar bills. There had to be twenty, maybe twenty-five thousand in the envelope he thought as he looked up and waived Sparkle back over to the table. He handed her a hundred-dollar bill and leaned back in his chair.

This was going to be easier then he'd thought. All he had to do was get rid of Levell's name from the police report. Since he was neva booked, there was no photograph. Oh, and he would have to destroy the interview. Urena thought that would do away with any connection. No doubt there will be a shoot on sight order after the lives of so many officers were taken. So, it would be a smooth clean-up. With this in mind he enjoyed his lap dance.

**** N. D. ****
East Palo Alto, California
2 weeks later

The day was festive. It was a beautiful day out. There was free Bar-b-q and live music. The weather was nice and sunny, and everyone was enjoying themselves. It was the grand opening of Elysian Fields and the community came out in droves to celebrate the event.

Dok made his rounds through the grounds meeting mothers and fathers who were beyond grateful for what he was doing. Though they were discreet, Scooter and Rell were always in earshot of their father. If something were to pop up, they were ready.

A camera crew approached Dok as he was finishing up the conversation.

"Mister Hayes! Mister Hayes!" the reporter called out making her way to him. "Mister Hayes, Julie Haener for KTVU Fox 2. Is it possible to have a moment of your time to discuss what you are doing across the Bay Area?" When he told her yes, the camera crew kicked into gear and set up on the spot.

"Mister Hayes, so tell our viewers exactly what it is that you and your organization are doing for the black community."

Dok hated cameras of any kind, yet for years while formulating a plan, he had been forced to come to grips with the idea that today would eventually come. Though he'd tried to figure out, he had to admit that there was no way around him getting in front of a camera. That day was finally here. Like every other challenge, he embraced this one.

"Well ,Ms. Haener, it's simple actually. Right now, the Black Community within the urban cities of America are not only dying off and being killed by the police at a rather alarming rate, but we are slaughtering one another. As a by-product, our communities are dying. We, as a people are dying." Dok looked over at the Brand-new community center. Everyone followed his gaze, even the camera man.

"We at Neva Die admit and acknowledge that we contributed to the destruction of our people, The Black Civilization. So, we follow closely to the teachings of Chancellor Williams, Leron Bennett, George Jackson and a few others who not only teach us the truth as to what really happened to our people. But, just as importantly, how to work towards fixing the problem we helped create." The entire time he looked at and spoke to her instead of the camera.

She moved the microphone from his face into her own. "What exactly are some of the ways your organization is doing this?"

"Well, for starters the opening of Elysian Fields Youth Centers in Oakland, San Francisco, Richmond and right here in East Palo Alto. We also have Nubian Rootz, which is our day care center and pre-school. Neva Die's sole mission is to strengthen our communities through love, loyalty and education which will in turn generate an economic means that our people can stand on." The pride of his words was clearly visible on his face. Julie Haener could tell this young man enjoyed helping his community.

"Never Die. That's a rather unique name. Where does one come up with such a name for an activist group?"

"It's not NEVER. It's Neva. N-E-V-A. Neva Die is an acronym. We are the New Enlightened Visionaries of African descent Destined to Increase Education and Economics. That's what the Neva Die Movement is all about. We are all The Brotha's God Forgave and we are giving back." Lil Rell had been checking out a cat who looked out of place. He made eye contact with Scooter and went to go check it out.

"Brothas that God forgave?" The question itself was full of curiosity, but her look was the icing on the cake.

"We all have a past, Ms. Haener. Yet the brothas, we don't run from ours ,we face the future and run towards it. The same energy we put into tearing up the streets, we now use to rebuild those same streets." His tone and the finality of his statements clearly said that the interview was over.

Julie Haener had to admit that the young, black man was both powerful and intriguing. She thanked Dok for his time and asked him would it be ok to contact him for a follow-up should one be needed. He gave her a business card and made his way over to see what was up with Rell.

Dok didn't question his son's ability nor judgment, neither one of them. But, after all the gangsta shit, he was still a father. It turned out to be nothing. The nigga was looking for his son. The fact that he was by himself and looking around is what had caught Rell's attention.

**** **N. D.** ****

Chapter XI

Stanford Hospital

"I don't know if you are able to hear me or if I've just been wasting my time all these weeks. I'm going crazy some days, I don't know which way is up." Vieira wasn't ashamed of the tears that escaped her eyes. She didn't care who saw her vulnerability. As she looked at Voorheeze, she knew that she was in love.

"The Governor is making a big stink out of everything that is going on. It seems that one of the officers killed, a Sergeant Costa was a relative of his. The governor is coming down hard on us to find the suspect or suspects and bring them to justice."

She paused to rub her hand across his forehead and down the side of his face. Her own tears landed freely in her lap. So many tears had landed that the fluid soaked through her pants.

Vieira is grateful to French Tip for allowing her total access regarding visits with him. The instructions were clear and followed. She was allowed access to him at any time, no questions asked. She was also not to be bothered during her visits, which were nearly every day.

"Some are trying to link you to all the murders. I know that they are wrong. My baby is too sweet to be involved in something like that. Hopefully, by the time you come back to me, we will have captured the people behind all of this and you can get by your situation. Then you and I can be a couple. We won't have to hide what we have from anyone!

It'll just be you and I and we will be so happy. La'Mont, you make me so happy! I love you La'Mont Simpson." Chief Vieira stood up and bent down and kissed Voorheeze on the lips. The truth of her words was evident in the tender way she kissed his lip.

The doctors had explained to the family that they could awaken him at any time. The damage to his body was so severe that they felt his body would heal easier and quicker if he remained in the coma. There was no way for Vieira to know it, but Voorheeze heard every single word. It was killing him that he could do nothing but lay there lifelessly and listen. The feeling wasn't foreign to him though. Just a couple of months before he had experienced the same feeling the first time he was in a coma. He'd almost lost his mind that time because the experience was alien to him. This time he knew what it was. That didn't mean that he didn't like it any less.

Vieira looked at her watch. It read 3:00pm. She gave him one more kiss and whispered in his ear, "I'll wait forever."

The knock on the door came right on que It was time for his sponge bath. She didn't need to be told because the nurses were very prompt. At 3:00p.m. every day he received a sponge bath and they moved all his limbs and rolled his body. This was to prevent his blood from clotting and causing bed sores.

"Come in." She called out as she made her way to the door to leave. The two nurses walked in and Vieira walked out.

Redwood City

Knowing that every cop in the state was looking for him, most mothafuckas would get the fuck out of dodge. Batman wasn't most mothafuckas. He and Voorheeze were cut from a different cloth! They didn't run from the fire. They fanned the flames and threw fuel on that shit.

"I would've neva believed it if I hadn't seen the shit with my own fucking eyes." Batman sat inside the stolen Ford F-150 Rosche edition looking out of the tinted windows.

It was a very comfortable truck, with its custom leather seats and smooth soft leather on the steering wheel. The cabin had so much room that even a seven-footer would feel comfortable sitting in the truck. He knew that the mothafucka he stole it from would be highly pissed off to lose such an expensive truck.

He was watching Jose Guadalupe Gayton also known as the 'SCU' Agent Gayton. He'd followed Gayton all the way from the Police Department in Milpitas where he'd stolen the truck. Now they were in the parking lot of El Grullense (El' Greasy), a taco restaurant in Redwood City off El Camino Real.

Agent Gayton pulled into the parking lot and got out to order some food. Batman watched him and seethed internally as Gayton joked with a female who was there before him. Just the sight of the little, faggott ass, snitch made Batman's blood boil.

"No matter how you dress it, you could give it little neon pink lights and all the badges in the world, and a snitch is still going to be a snitch. " He said to himself as he reached for the handle and opened the door.

His plan was to follow agent Gayton to the apartment he shared with his mom. There, he was going to have fun with everyone in the house. But, he couldn't watch this slimy little rat any longer.

He made his way towards them. As he got closer, he took his chrome .45 off his waist and held it down by his leg.

"My, so you are a bold little somebody, aren't you Walo?" She smiled and flirted. Only Batman noticed that she wasn't a she, it was a he. Agent Gayton was trying to pick up a transsexual.

"I'm bold because I know I got what you need." Agent Gayton responded grabbing the crotch of his pants.

"Oh, do you now," the tranny asked as his eyes looked down at what Agent Gayton was grabbing.

"Since you got what mothafuckas need, can you tell me who Alvin Haynes was?" Batman asked the agent with a look of disdain on his face.

They both looked at him with a look of confusion and anger for being disturbed. Agent Gayton's confused look was mixed with irritation.

"No man! Nobody knows who the fuck Alvin Haynes is. And we don't give a fuck either, man! Can't you see we're busy?" He didn't see the big ass .45 in Batman's hand, but Daniella did.

"Look, honey, I don't want no problems. I'm just waiting on my food and I'm gone. Whatever y'all got going on, Mama's, I don't want no part of it." The wig, makeup and fake tits did not fool Batman. He knew it was a dude. Fuck all the bullshit.

"Don't ever address me with your vile, disease filled, dick sucking mouth. "Pure hatred was laced into the words Batman spewed out.

"Hey, man! Watch your mouth around the lady!" Agent Gayton was so enraged by the blatant disrespect. Plus, he didn't need this crazy motherfucker to fuck off his chances of getting laid tonight.

"A lady? Mothafucka, you can't see that, that's a mothafuck'n man!" It was clear to Batman, God and even Stevie Wonder that Daniella was a man.

Daniella may have been a transsexual now but he was also an ex-Norteno and right then all the ex-gangbanger came out in full force. "Now hold the fuck up, homeboy!" His arms still flailed about like Sha-nay-nay or Wanda from In Living Color. "You ain't got to be out here disrespecting…."

The big ass hole that the bullet of the .45 made in his forehead shut that shit up faster than a mothafucka.

Two of the Mexican women that were waiting in line with their husbands began screaming and acting irate. The woman in the window was getting ready to call them to retrieve their order that was done. She too screamed as she left the food on the counter and ducked down.

Batman didn't care about none of that. He pointed the gun at Agent Gayton's head and asked again. "Alvin Haynes! Do – you – know – who – the – fuck – Alvin – Haynes – was?" He spoke each word deliberately slowly, as if he was talking to a real re-re. A certified retard!

Before Agent Gayton could react, Batman sent two missiles directly into his chest. The impact was so strong at such a short distance that it knocked 5'4", 130lb Gayton clear off his feet.

Batman walked the couple of feet that it took to stand over Gayton's shaking body.

"Alvin Haynes was brutally beat to death January twenty-sixth by a bunch of coward-ass, crackers, hiding behind the badge of San Francisco County Jail as Deputies" after he spoke those words Batman pointed the big cannon at Gayton's head and squeezed the trigger three more times, rocking the one-time snitch turned cop to sleep for good.

Sirens could be heard in the distance. Those who were too scared to move looked on in horror as Batman walked up to the pick-up window and grabbed the bag of food. He turned around and walked back over to Daniella's dead body.

"Now you hold the fuck up, homeboy!" He told the corpse, then he shot it four more times. Afterwards he walked back to the stolen truck and got in.

Instead of driving off and getting out of dodge, he opened the bag of food and ate a taco. The little Piesa's were so scared they didn't know what to do. Meanwhile, the sirens got closer and closer. With the delicious taco now gone, he finally pulled off at a normal speed.

As he was exiting the parking lot, a squad car came speeding into the parking lot. It almost sped right into him. Batman glanced over at the Sheriff's Deputy casually and drove off like nothing happened. It wasn't long before he saw the flashing red and blue lights in his rearview. Paying them no mind, Batman continued to eat the second taco. By now the lights had multiplied from one set to three. His nerves were as calm as a pond in the middle of June. Still, he figured it was time to see what the expensive Roush package on the truck could do.

Batman down-shifted and put the pedal to the metal just as he was turning right onto Main Street, heading directly towards Downtown Redwood City. What he didn't know was that he was heading directly towards the police station. Pedestrians stopped and stared at the powerful truck that was now leading five cop cars on a high-speed chase straight through the heart of town. Just as they were passing the All-pro Bail Bondsman,

Batman nearly ran over a short nigga with long dreads who was crossing the street, not paying attention to what the fuck was going on.

At the last minute the nigga finally heard the sirens and looked up. "Ole bitch ass, nigga!" JuJu yelled at the truck as he jumped backwards barely avoiding getting run over. JuJu had just been released from the Maguire Correction Facility Main Jail which is located on Bradford St. and Main St. He'd been having a string of bad luck lately. This was his fourth time being released in one year. Every time he turned around he was getting some type of petty parole violation.

Before getting out this time, he'd made a vow to himself that this time would be the last time. He was determined to get back on his feet and climb back to his rightful spot in the food chain of the underworld. Juju took his last hundred dollars and headed to San Francisco to get a plug on a sack of crystal, so he could get his hustle on. Thoughts of his plans rushed through his mind as he watched the wind selfishly snatch the five $20's he'd dropped jumping out the way of the speeding vehicles and sent them in five different directions almost as fast as the vehicles flying by.

JuJu was too pissed off to give a fuck. Lady luck was too busy fucking him to throw any kind of luck his way. He stood there right in the middle of the street with a dumb ass look on his face tripping off of his bad luck. Finally, he said fuck it! And kept it pushing. Though he was trying do shit differently than before, somebody was about to be food.

Even if Batman had known any of that he would not have given a fuck. He was in his element and couldn't nobody tell him shit. The truck was pushing 95 mph, people were frantically scrambling to get out the way. More police and Sheriff's Deputies joined the pursuit. On Veterans Blvd. he shot thru the red light ,barely missing the back bumper of a Honda Accord that was just passing the intersection. The cops weren't so lucky.

As Batman made the left turn more cars were going through the intersection. The first Deputy that followed him from El Greasy slammed hard into the side of a red Chevy Camaro. The impact sounded like a cannon going off. The second car swerved to the left. That was a fatal mistake. The police cruiser smacked head on into a city bus. Two more cars crashed while the rest navigated the obstacle course of wreckage.

By the time they did, Batman was already swinging the F-150 onto Whipple Avenue jumping onto 101 North. Once he hit the freeway he opened that bitch up and let it do what it do! The police didn't have a chance. By the time he reached highway 280 on-ramp it was a wrap.

As he cruised down 280 North headed for junction 92, the San Mateo Bridge, Batman flashed back to the little, short nigga who had been was crossing the street. Another two seconds and the truck would have no doubt sent the 5-foot 4-inch JuJu flying to his death. Reflecting on that made Batman think about Kevin Garrett from Chicago, Illinois; Bernard Moore from ATL, Tyree Crawford from Newark, NJ; and Christopher Kimble from East Cleveland. Before he knew it, images of Jason Champion and Nuwnah Laroche of Ridgefield Park, New Jersey flowed through his mind. All of whom were struck and killed by speeding police cars. Their only crime had been walking down the street enjoying the day.

Still, today, no one has been called to answer for their deaths.

He was so engrossed in his thoughts that Batman didn't see the Highway Patrol car that just came onto the freeway. He was too busy dwelling on the fact that he'd almost become a part of the very statistic he was fighting. The sirens brought him back from deep thought.

He checked his rearview and then looked in the passenger seat. His instincts told him to floor it, but the reflective moment he'd just had told him not to. Batman pulled over.

"You fucked up today, cop." He spoke to himself as he put the truck in park and reached over to the passenger seat.

The officer was busy looking down at the screen of his laptop. He'd made the tragic mistake of taking his eyes off of the suspect. Right about the time that the bulletin came across the screen, matching the trucks description to that of a homicide and a high-speed chase, batman was walking towards the squad car with a M-16 in his hands.

The last move the patrolman made before all hell broke loose was to reach for the radio to call for backup.

The big 7.62's that spit from the barrel completely shredded the patrol car like cheddar cheese. The bullets causing the siren that was turned off the to come back on only to shut back off permanently. The hood of the Dodge Charger flew up. One of the bullets had caused the latch to release.

Batman causally headed closer to the driver's door. "They might not mean shit to y'all, but believe me, Black Lives Matter!" He fed the rest of the clip into the driver's side door and window. He could see the patrolman's body jump around like he was listening to an old school Busta Rhymes song. Once he emptied the clip he walked back, got into the truck and pulled off. Highway 280 had very light traffic this day, so no-one had witnessed the killing. It still would be accredited by most to the same killers that have been killing all the other cops.

**** N. D. ****

Chapter XII

Fremont, California
2 weeks later

"I'm just saying dad, fuck them niggaz." Tut hit the blunt of the strong Wonder Woman before he continued, "You already know, I'm bout whatever. But it doesn't make no sense focusing our time and energy on them mothafuckas when it's money to be made, dad." Tut looked over at Clark to see if he was paying attention to what he was saying.

They were inside Tut's condo off of Stevenson Blvd. in Fremont watching Gonzaga play Kentucky in the March Madness Sweet 16. Clark had just finished telling Tut about plans to keep fucking with Neva Die through the Youth Center. In the past few weeks Bone and Man Man have been on a terror trip.

Vandalism wasn't cutting it any more. They'd jumped the night janitor, and two of the employees. Workers got robbed at gun point and they even paid the smokers to linger around the center getting high and causing a nuisance. Any way they could find to fuck with the workings of the center, they did.

Ignoring Tuts comment, Clark spoke up, "Rogue, can you believe that the bitch ass nigga had the nerve to have French Tip call me and ask me to fall back?" He took a bite of the hot wings he was eating. With a mouth full of chicken parmesan, he asked, "Me take orders from my little sister. Nigga, where they do that at?"

"Clark, think about it though. Them niggaz ain't fucking wit us at all. But, terrorizing a youth center? Come on, dad, dat shit ain't gangsta." Tut further tried to reason with him.

Everyone thought Gonzaga finally had a chance at making it to the final four. But Kentucky was doing their thang and it didn't look like it was going to happen this year.

"Fuck you mean, nigga! That mothafucka tried to tell me how to do shit in my city. Nigga, that was fucking with me enough!" Clark was fuming. Every time he thought about that night, he saw nothing but blood.

"All I'm saying, dad, is if you feel that niggaz violated that severely, then why we not taking it to them niggaz instead of bullying the worker ants? Blood, where the fuck they do that?" Clark's outburst didn't phase Tut at all. He had too many bodies under his belt to be phased by a mothafucka raising his voice.

Gonzaga was on an eight-point run trying desperately to mount on attack. Although Clark was engrossed in the game, Tuts comment made a lot of sense and drew his attention. He thought about it for a minute while he bit into another wing.

"You know what nigga, you right. I don't know why I'm playing around wit these niggaz. If a nigga disrespect you, get at that motha fucka in a real way. He grabbed his desert eagle and tucked it on his waist before snatching up the rest of the Wing Stop.

"Come on rogue" he told Tut as he headed for the door. "Hold up, dad. Even if Jesus is on his way back he gone have to wait till we put this shit away. You know I don't fuck wit no messy ass house." While he was talking Tut began picking up all the food bags and shit that was on the coffee table.

To make shit go faster, Clark helped him. It only took a few minutes and they were out the door. They jumped in Tuts H3 and headed for the Dumbarton Bridge. Talking wasn't needed so they rode in silence.

Thirty minutes later they were driving down University Blvd.

"What's the play, dad?" Tut questioned as he pulled up to the light on Bay Road. He could see all the smokers congregating at the bus top in front of McDonalds.

"Just pull right on in front of that mothafucka." The plan was to send a mothafucking message and there was only one way to do that.

Ever since the attacks began, Dok made sure that there was a guerilla on sight in case things went any further. Today

Kiumba was doing security. Kiumba was a good solid soldier. He was too old to be out in the streets, but he always wanted to be on the front line. Besides he was good at bussin heads.

Tut turned right onto Bell Street and pulled over. There was no way to be incognito in the truck with the $6,000 paint job. But, they weren't trynna hide or blend in. For a moment they sat and scanned the area looking for their target. The center was doing food give away today so there weren't any kids out. Still, it was relatively busy. Finally, Clark made out who he was looking for. He pointed him out to Tut and the two killas climbed out of the truck and crossed the street.

The moment they made it to the other side of the street them hammers came out. People looked at the two of them and got the fuck out of the way! Death walked towards the parking lot.

Mrs. Johnson was a nice old widow who played the piano at Born Again Christian Center. She also volunteered at the Boys and Girls club over in Menlo Park. Ever since her husband, Gerald passed, she'd been struggling to make ends meet, but somehow God always made a way. She was worried about not having enough food to last until she got her SSI check on the first. Mrs. Bell had told her about Elysian Fields passing out food boxes. There weren't passing out the regular "welfare recipient" food like most of the centers were doing. Elysian Fields was passing out nice, wholesome food like they did over at the Ecumenical Hunger Program. And they had the nicest young men to assist you out to your vehicle and load it for you. Even though she didn't have the money to spare she thought about giving the young man that was helping her a tip. He reminded her so much of her late Gerald, so quiet and mild mannered.

For the fifth time she began thanking him again.

"This is so nice of you sweetheart, out here helping us little old ladies who are..." The sight of the two men with guns in their hands caused the statement to get caught in her throat.

****

135

Why do I always get stuck helping the ones who wouldn't stop running their mouths? Kiumba thought to himself as he loaded the food into the old 2005 Suburban. He wasn't even supposed to be doing this bullshit but one of the niggaz that was needed to take a shit so Kiumba was filling in just to help out. As he was placing the last box into the back of the Suburban, she started yapping her gums again when she stopped mid-sentence. Kiumba knew something was wrong.

****

Clark was a man of a mission. Nothing and no one would stop or detour him. Tut strolled right along with him, his eyes on a constant swivel, surveying the area for any potential danger. Any movement whatsoever Tut was squeezing. Their target was directly ten feet in front of them. Some old hag was so busy talking his ear off that ole' boy wasn't paying attention at all.

As they passed the car next to the Suburban they were loading the old lady looked up at them and shut up faster than a fat broad eating a cheese burger. The abrupt silence caused the target to look up.

"Welcome to East Palo Alto, nigga!" The words left Clarks mouth a split second before the missile left the Desert Eagle.

At point blank range, the 50-caliber Desert Eagle bullet literally made Kiumba's head explode. Blood and brain matter flew everywhere. The majority of it covered poor Mrs. Johnson. She just stood there horrified, stunned into utter silence. The body lay jerking on the pavement.

Together they turned and walked back to the truck with their eyes on full alert for anybody who thought they might want to retaliate.

Magically, Mrs. Johnson became unfrozen from her trance. Her loud screams could be heard all the way at the 76-gas station across University. Other people were screaming and running frantically as well. Tut and Clark climbed back inside the H2 and drove off. They headed back across the bridge to Tuts condo.

**** N. D. ****
Stanford Hospital

Once again Chief Vieira sat alone in the hospital room crying her heart out and talking to Voorheeze. Things were really heating up and she needed to be at work, but her love came first. She had to be there for him. Her cell phone started ringing.

Gently, she place his hand back down on his side and reached for the cell phone. It was Dominique Diaz. She's the Mayor's personal assistant.

The Chief answered right away. "Hello, Miss Diaz."

"Hello, Chief Vieira, how are you today?" Dominique Diaz was a very beautiful woman with a very raspy voice.

"Miss Diaz, I'm fine thank you. How may I help you today?" Whenever the cigarette smoke scratched voice of Dominique Diaz was heard on your telephone, it was to bring you bad news.

Chief Vieira braced herself for the inevitable. A bad storm was certainly coming her way.

"Well, Mayor Skillskowsky just received a call from the governor's office informing her that Governor Costa is scheduling a press conference for the evening to discuss the recent deaths in law enforcement. After the press conference the Mayor wants to have a meeting with you and your top brass." Her words cut just as much as her voice scratched.

Vieira knew what this meant. Somebody needed to take the blame for the shit storm that was sure to come from the press conference. The old adage was true, *shit always ran down hill*.

"I see. And Miss Diaz, where exactly would the Mayor like for us to meet?" Vieira admired the Mayor and all that she's done so far. Nevertheless, she wouldn't look forward to the meeting.

"She's expecting to see you at nine p.m. sharp." Diaz informed her. "Thank you, Miss Diaz." Chief Vieira hung up. She didn't have a problem with the Mayors assistant. However, she was just that, an assistant and Vieira was the Chief of Police.

****** N. D. ******
Oakland

"I ain't wit the I told you so's. I just wanna know how you wanna handle this shit. Niggaz gotta do something after this!", Gunz was beyond irate! Way passed pissed off. As he paced the office, the rage inside of him was evident.

Dok looked at the young man who was no doubt ready for war. Gunz was only a few years younger than Dok and a little more seasoned. After all, Dok had been away from the streets since 2002.

Lil Rell and Scooter was positioned, as always, next to their father. Always on standby for security, A.J. and Big Rocc were also present. The six men were discussing the latest plight to the harassment Clark has been causing over at Elysian Fields.

This latest fiasco, the killing of Kiumba, had everybody fuming. Kiumba wasn't just some employee or volunteer. Kiumba was a comrade. He was cut from the cloth of George Jackson and Fati. A Guerrilla had been touched.

It was time for the Dragon to surface.

"Peace be still, my brotha. Your feelings are both understood and mirrored. Brotha Kiumba was a solid soldier, an even better brotha! So, believe me, although I may seem calm, the fire deep within me is raging and burning." Dok paused and took a moment to tell Lil Rell to step outside and keep Usalama (security) on the door.

Normally, when they met in the back office of the Koffee Shop, the door remained open. For this discussion, it needed to be closed. A.J. and Big Rocc both just sat quietly listening while smoking blunts. To A.J. it was whatever! Anybody could get it! Anywhere, any time. Big Rocc had an inner pain, one he was silently nursing.

"Once the door was closed, Dok continued, "I neva thought this day would come. Infact I promised myself that it wouldn't eva come to this, but it has." Everyone in the office including Lil Scooter was shocked when Dok walked over to the mini oak bar and poured himself a drink. None of them had ever seen him drink. He poured himself a double shot of Pineapple Cîroc.

"Gunz, my brotha, there's no doubt in my mind or my heart that you and your team can do your thang. But, I'm going to need you to fall back..." those words almost sent Gunz overboard. He stopped directly in Dok's face with his nose flaring and eyes blazing. "Fuck you mean, fall back? A nigga just touched somebody on our side, ain't no fucking falling back! Now if you niggaz is scared, nigga, just get out the way we got this shit!"

His movements where slow and smooth but no one lost the meaning when Lil Scooter stood calmly to his feet.

"Peace be still. My brotha, I don't think you quite understand what I'm telling you." Dok turned to pour himself another drink, he wasn't backing down to a challenge. He was merely defusing the situation.

"A Gaid (Guerrilla) was touched. So, the Dragon will surface. Even if I wanted to allow you to take care of this I can't. Gunz this is family business. Family will take care of it."

Gunz had been around enough Jamaa (family) niggaz while growing up in Oakland to know there are politics and antics involved. Deep down, he knew the rules and he knew the game. It still didn't sit easy with him.

"Fuck you saying, brah? Me and my team supposed to sit back and watch while y'all let them thangs bang?" Though he

139

was still livid, the fire in his eyes and the steam coming off of him had died down.

"My brotha, you already know what time it is. I'm not telling a gangsta not to get on some gangsta shit. I'm telling my brotha to let family handle family business."

Before Gunz could respond, it was Big Rocc's turn to shock the room.

"I guarantee you little-big homie, your entire team won't be sitting on the sidelines."

"What is that supposed to mean, my brotha?" The big man's statement caught Dok off guard.

"It means that I arise from the center of the earth to spit fire out of frustration and anger because there is a hatred against greater than those the same color as me." His words silenced the room. Gunz and A.J. didn't know that he was saying something that only the upper echelon of the Guerilla family would know and understand.

Over the years Dok had seen so much that nothing really shocked or stunned him. Big Rocc's revelation didn't either.

Scooter was still standing with his hand on his waistline. He didn't give a fuck about niggaz being calm and collected. Scooter was staying on his shit.

Dok looked Gunz in the eyes "Well, my brotha, it seems that you will have someone in on the activities." The smile that Dok gave Gunz made him feel uneasy, but he waved it off.

They spent the next hour discussing everyday operations and a personnel shift. Gunz was going to need to lend assistance with the further development of Nubian Roots and the rest of the positive community development programs that they were orchestrating. A.J. and DeeDee would need to take on a bigger load making sure the rest of the organization was taken care of. The She-Wolves would be used to assist them in getting things done.

The revelation of Big Rocc being Jamaa, a sleeper, meant that he was fully in the beef and ready for a war if necessary. He'd made it known to Dok that no matter what he would be bringing his right hand D.J. He might not be family, but he was a strong sympathizer and a part of Big Rocc's Civilian Cadre.

After the meeting, Dok made sure to make the necessary calls to follow protocol. The Central Committee had to be informed of what was about to transpire. The news of Kiumba's death had already been sent to them a couple of days ago. So, they should already be expecting the news he was sending. It was simple, NO ONE touches a Guerilla if it's not sanctioned! NO ONE!

**** N. D. ****

De'Kari

Chapter XIII

After handling his business in the streets, Dok headed home to Berkley. His heart was heavy. It was weighed down by his forced decision. He had tried avoiding a confrontation with Clark as best he could. Because of his love for Voorheeze, he didn't want to sick the Dragon on Clark. The ignorant motha-fucka gave him no choice when he took Kiumba.

Janette was in the bed sleeping when he walked into the room. He hesitated at the door then walked over to her side of the bed, leaned down and kissed her on her cheek. He loved his wife unconditionally and took a little pleasure in seeing her sleep so peacefully. He walked over to his side of the bed and sat down to take off his shoes.

"You wanna talk about it, baby?" Janette asked without opening up her eyes.

Dok looked back at his Queen and smiled before he reached around and stroked her back. "Hello, my Queen, what are you doing up?"

"How could I sleep when my spirit senses the presence of my King?" Now she rolled over and took his hand inside of hers. He gently caressed her face with his hand.

"My presence should make you feel safe, so you should sleep peacefully, not wake up." Now Dok was caressing her face with his own. "What makes you think that something's on my mind that I might wanna discuss?? Janette was always so intuitive. Dok was often impressed by the things she could sense and feel.

"You've been sitting over there for five minutes now and haven't made one single attempt to take your shoes off."

There was no sense playing with her intelligence by acting like nothing was wrong, so he told her.

"Tomorrow, I need you to go stay with your mother for a little while" he braced himself for the tongue lashing he knew he would receive. Instead she asked him, "And what about the boys?" She wasn't asleep when he walked in. All night she had been having a bad feeling. By now, she was wide awake. She sat up and looked at her husband.

"The boys are going to stay with me, except PeeWee, he will accompany you." Dok couldn't understand why the explosion hadn't come yet, But he was ready.

"The fact that I waited for you twenty long years while I was forced to raise your sons on my own without their father should keep you from making whatever decision it is that you're about to make. I know you well enough to know if it's got to be done, you are going to do it." Silently she wiped away the tear that slid down her face.

"Darrell, I'm not going to get in your way or have you not focused on whatever you have to do by stressing you out. I am going to tell you this because I've earned that much. If you go back to prison, I won't do another bid. I love you with all my heart, but I can't do it. if something happens to one of my boys, I'ma kill you."

Dok could hear the tears in her voice, he didn't have to turn around. What Janette didn't know was he was crying too. His tears were because he had to bring this to her. He hadn't even been home a year yet and it was back to a body count.

"Nette, you know I did all that I could to avoid this." Her words were truer than any he had ever heard. The twenty years that he was down, Janette was there right by his side. Every visit, every commissary, every phone call, the whole nine yards. She had been through it all with him. It had been difficult, but she'd found the strength. A second time around would literally kill her.

"I know, that's why I can't argue. I knew who you were and what I was signing up for when I did it. That's why I won't say nothing, just be careful, babe." The tears ran freely down her face now. He leaned down to kiss the tears away. He felt so bad.

"I will, my love" was all he could manage in between kisses.

"Just shut up and hold me, babe." Fear had such a tight hold on her. Janette loved him and didn't know what would happen to her if he was taken away from her again.

Dok laid down with his clothes on and held her for a while. Janette broke his embrace and turned around in his arms. It started as a kiss and ended up with the two of them making love for the better part of the night.

****

The following morning Dok watched with a heavy heart as Janette and Pee Wee drove off, leaving Berkeley headed for her mothers. He didn't want to send his Queen away, but he knew it was the best choice. Do couldn't under estimate his adversary. He didn't think anyone knew where he laid his head, but he couldn't take the chance. Not with Janette's life. The silver two door Mercedes following her helped set his mind at ease. With that worry now out of his mind, he climbed in his Challenger ready to take care of business.

About thirty minutes later he was pulling into the yard of 'Sons of Khatari (sons of the Dragon) Construction Company.' The company is located off of Industrial Boulevard in Hayward, roughly twenty minutes south of Oakland. The family met up here every morning for a meeting before starting the day. Due to seeing Janette off this morning he was running a little late, but it couldn't be helped.

Dok was surprised to see the yard bustling with activity instead of everyone inside for the meeting. (Everyone who worked at Khatari was family) Suddenly, a loud call went up. It sounded somewhere between a shriek and a whistle. Everyone stopped and looked towards the gate as his vehicle drove thru. Dok parked and got out. He was immediately greeted by Lil Rell.

"It's not like you to go off the grid." He stated as soon as he reached Dok.

"Off the grid? I'm a little late because I had to see your mom off this morning." By now Scooter had made it over to them.

"How did that go?" Scooter asked with a look of humor and slight fear on his face.

"Better than I thought."

Rell cut him off "Why is your phone off?" For the first time Dok caught the slight irritation in his son's voice.

"My phone's neva off." He reached in his pocket to solidify his statement. His IPhone was black when he pulled it out. Immediately he tried powering it up to see if his battery had died.

When the phone powered up and he saw seven missed calls from Rell, he knew two things. First, he knew Janette turned his phone off sometime during the night. Secondly the scrambling activity he saw as he pulled into the yard was the Usalama Squad getting ready to go out and find him. They must've assumed something happened to him.

Rell saw the look of recollection on his father's face. Yet he still couldn't let up so easily. That's not how he had been trained. "We're at war and you chose now to be the first time you slip on your security."

Scooter knew his brother and where he was going, so he quickly tried to defuse the situation. "He's here now Rell, and we know he's safe so everything's good, brah."

"Naa, he ain't good. Safety and security is always to be of the utmost significance and importance." Rell spit the first line of the safety protocol at him.

Dok smirked to calm his anger as he stared his son in the eyes. He could see there was something else below the surface. As soon as he glimpsed it, Rell tucked it away.

"No, your brother is absolutely correct. We have our safety procedures in place for a reason. A noble reason at that." He looked both of his sons in the eyes and then stated flatly, "It won't happen again."

146

Dok Holliday may very well be the overseer or Chief and Commander of Ground Force Troops East Bay. But as Lieutenants of his personal usalama squad (or security squad) the boys could make a call about his safety or counter an order he gave if it was to protect his safety or the security of the Cadre (chain or unit)

Somewhat satisfied, Rell turned on his heels and together the three made their way to the conference room. When Rell wasn't looking, Dok made a face to Scooter like a kid mocking getting a scolding. Scooter tried to hide his snickering, but it was useless. Rell turned around and gave both of them a look that would scare one of the twelve disciples of Jesus. They sobered up and made their way inside the conference room.

The atmosphere in the room was the same as it was on any given day. Dok had no doubt everyone knew of the pending war, but you would neva tell by the looks on their faces. These were trained Guerillas, to them this was just another day.

Once Dok assumed his position at the head of the room, he began.

"Mjemwa Usabui (good morning)", he called out.

"Mjemwa Usabui Ndugu." Their response was uniformed and crisp.

"If ever my word proves untrue..." Dok began reciting the first line of their oath and the next person at the command picked up where he left off and so on until everyone had recited what they were supposed to recite.

"This morning, we will begin this baraza a little different. Pressing matters will be saved until the end. Instead, we will open up with this quarters economics report." He looked at Akili, who took his cue and spoke up.

The normal components of day-to-day operations only took fifteen minutes to go over.

"Does anyone have any pressing issues other than the issue that we all know is on the table?" Dok didn't' think anyone did, yet protocol was protocol. So, his eyes scanned the room.

"Word was sent to the Central Committee in regard to the death of our beloved Kiumba." He took a momentary pause out of respect for their fallen comrade. "I've also sent word of my plan of action against those responsible for one of our comrades being touched without a sanction.

"Protocol states that I bring the issue before the governing body for a vote to go to war. So, I call to vote all of those in support of a military strike against those who killed our brotha."

"Will the war council be needed for this military strike that you are suggesting?" Pendasi asked before the vote was called. She was Minister of Education and Liaison to Military Intelligence.

Dok glanced over towards Zair, his Minister of Justice and head of the War Council before answering. "The war council has been informed of the situation and it has been agreed upon by me and the Commanding War General that the council may not be needed for this campaign, but he will be advised and kept abreast, nevertheless. "

Pendasi looked as if she was pondering this information. Then she nodded her head in acceptance. The vote was taken, and the approval was given. Dok didn't have to wait on the Central Committee's response. True, he needed their blessings in order to go to war, but had no doubt in his mind that they would give the green light. Besides, it wouldn't be a full out war per se. Dok wanted Clark, not the rest of his team.

Hours Later

They'd been riding around for three hours without any sign of Clark or anyone from his team for that matter. The night was dark and Dok was getting pissed off. Rell was driving, Scooter was in the back and he was in the passenger seat. They were in an all-black Nissan Camry. He was ready to call it a night as they pulled into the Chevron gas station on University Ave. A black Denali HD Super Pickup truck was at the pump. Their intel had told them that he had a team of country niggaz that drove those big ass trucks.

Dok had Rell pulled up to the pump on the other side and behind the truck. Scooter got out and put $10 on the pump. The nigga that was driving the truck was so busy yapping away Scooter could've easily slumped him right there. But, they were after big fish not tadpoles. Scooter was on a low-key scrimmage paying full attention to the nigga while pretending he was in his own zone.

He heard the country mothafucka tell the girl he was talking to, to hold on. As he finished pumping the motha fucka said "Man tell Bone I'm on my way."

Scooter walked back to the window and bought a POM juice. By the time he made it back to the Nissan and got in , the Denali was just pulling out from the pump. Ten minutes later they were driving down Camellia Ave. Rell pulled over and parked three houses down from the Denali. They watched the dude as he entered the house with a black gate. They were right behind him.

If the shit in their hands didn't say that they weren't playing, the way that they walked up to the house said it loud and clear. Dok was carrying on SKS, Rell had a M-1 Carbine and Scooter had a Calico. They did not come to play.

As all three approached the porch, the door opened. Dok froze and lifted the SKS aiming at the chest of the nigga they had followed.

"Hold up, let me get my phone." He was talking to someone over his shoulder. When he turned around and saw the three niggaz with military type weapons, he froze. Scooter rushed up the three steps followed by Rell, pushing the nigga back into the house. Dok calmly followed behind like a military commander following behind his trained troops. When they crossed over the threshold they saw one nigga with his back to them watching T.V.

"Damn, nigga, you gone let all that hawk in here. Close the door, Shawty." Bone called over his shoulder.

When Biscuit didn't answer, Bone finally looked over his shoulder ready to call out again. Whatever he was thinking about saying froze right in his fucking throat when he laid eyes on the three big ass barrels that were facing him.

Dok made a small clicking sound with his mouth. Immediately, Rell and Scooter took off with precision to go search the rest of the house. Bone looked at the brotha with the long dread locks, calculating his chances as he sized him up. The read he was getting was conflicting, so he decided to try another route.

"Hey, what it is, Shawty? What ch'all want wit us?" While he spoke, his eyes darted from Dok to his black berretta that lay under a magazine on the table five feet away from where he was sitting.

"If you open your mouth one more time, I'ma feed you some hot shit." The easy going, smooth and laid back Dok was gone. Standing in the living room of a house in the heart of the Gardens was a stone-cold killer. His name was Dok Holliday.

Bone was far from stupid, so he shut the fuck up quick, fast and in a hurry. He was beyond nervous, but he would neva show fear. To show fear would be a disrespect to his gangsta.

Rell and Scooter came from the back forcing a third nigga stumbling in front of them. As they entered the room, Bone made eye contact with June. The look on June's face as the two men forced him into the living room told him everything that he needed to know.

"Found this one in one of the back rooms counting money." Scooter looked to his pops to catch his reaction when he told him "it's at least four or five hundred back there."

The amount didn't faze Dok in the least. He wasn't there for money, he was there for his pint of blood. Initially he only wanted Clark, but from the moment he stepped foot onto the porch he was fully back in goon mode. His mind was back on War Mentality.

"Fuck that money. We ain't come for money." Dok's response put the fear of God into June and Lil Joe. Bone was spooked too, but he wasn't going to let it show. He wasn't going to let some Cali mothafucka punk him. Fuck that!

"If you ain't come for the money, what the fuck y'all here foe?" Bone did his best to mask all fear when he spit the question out. Doing his best to sound gangsta.

Unfortunately, he wouldn't receive an answer to his question. With two quick taps of the trigger of the SKS, Dok sent a barrage of bullets into Bone's upper torso. The silencer on the barrel suppressing all sound. June looked on terrified at the gun as smoke rose up out of the barrel. Lil Joe was so close to Bone that his body bumped up against him while the slugs made his body dance.

Dok shook his head from side to side then spoke to no-one particular "I told his dumb ass not to say another word!"

Rell looked over at Scooter. The expression on Scooter's face said that he was un-phased.

"Now fellas, I don't have time for no games or no bullshit. I came here for Clark, but if his life means more that your own, then I will gladly take yours and move on.

June couldn't believe this shit. Fighting with his baby mama is what lead to him being here. They were in a feud over child support and visitation rights when her new nigga decided he would step in and play Captain Save-a-Hoe. June tried telling the nigga that it wasn't any of his business, but the nigga wouldn't listen. One thing led to another and things got physical.

June was only 5'7" and weighing 157 pounds it was a given that he would lose to the 6'2" 215-pound Lonzo. June wasn't a fighter, he was a shooter, but it didn't stop him from giving it his all. After the ass whooping, June crawled and walked to his car where his Glock .40 was.

Lonzo answered the door by jerking it open when June banged on it. The shocked expression on his face when June filled him wit hot shit gave June a hard-on. His snitching ass baby mama told the police everything. So, when Tut talked to him about California he was all game.

What he wasn't game for was dying for some nigga that he didn't know. Fuck Clark, he didn't have no loyalties to that nigga, and he damn sure wasn't dying for him.

"I'm only going to ask you one time so don't play with me. Where is Clark or how can I find him? The barrel of the SKS was pointed directly at Lil Joe. He blinked his eyes rapidly and squirmed around on the couch like he had to shit.

"L-l-l-look m-man, I swear on my kids' soul I don't know where that nigga is. If I did, I would tell you, brah, that's on my kids." Lil Joe was so terrified that the truth dripped off the works that came from his mouth.

Dok took a step closer and aimed at Lil Joe's head, "Brah, I swear man, I don't know! Man, I don't know!" Tears began falling out of his eyes as he thought about his children.

"You know what, brotha, I believe you." Dok's words caused Lil Joe to exhale a sign of relief. For a minute there he had a thought that God had abandoned him.

He closed his eyes to say a quick prayer thanking God for being there at his time of need. As he lifted his head to the sky, blood and brain matter erupted from the back of his dome as Dok squeezed the trigger, blowing the back of his skull off.

Rell had been hearing stories all his life about his 'father's gangsta and the things he's done. This was the first time that he would witness the cold heart of the man he called father. He stole a quick glance at his brother and he could tell from the expression on his face that similar thoughts were running through the mind of his brother.

June may have been a shooter, but he was far from a cold-blooded killer. So, seeing his two homeboys die so close to him, with such ease, had all of the bitch coming out of him. It was easy to stand behind a gun and pull the trigger. It didn't take heart to do that. Any coward could shoot somebody. But to calmly and methodically kill two people all close and personal like that, it took the heart of a gangsta! A heart that June didn't have.

"Look here, man, I ain't trynna die over whatever beef you got going on with Shawty, you heard me. I don't know where dude lay his head at, but I got his number. I can call him for you." June was seconds away from pissing on himself. His face was covered with sweat and his heart raced a thousand miles an hour.

"Then get to calling him." Dok looked at his two sons as if he was seeing them for the first time. "Find something to bag that money up in."

They moved with quickness, thinking that it was about time he saw shit the way that they saw it in regard to the money. Scooter quickly found some garbage bags in the kitchen and he and Rell went to handle that.

June reached into his pocket to grab his cell phone. He was so nervous that he dropped the cell twice, fumbling with it. He nervously looked up at Dok, scared that the crazy nigga with the long dreads might grow inpatient with him and blow the back of his head off. Finally, he was able to get a hold of himself and dial the number. The line rung forever. June's heart was racing so fast he thought he would have a heart attack.

"Hello?" By the time Clark answered the phone, fear had such a tight grip on June that he couldn't talk.

"Hello?' Clark repeated into the phone.

"Uh s-say man w-we got an issue." June finally managed to get out. He said it so low that it was just above a whisper.

"June is that you? Nigga, what the fuck you mumbling into the phone for like a little ass girl?" Clark thought the country mothafucka had lost his mind or was drunk or something.

"June ,rogue, you know I ain't for no bullshit at my spot. Nigga where Bone at?" He was going to get to the bottom of shit. If them niggaz was counting and guarding his money while being drunk or high there was going to be hell to pay!

"D-dead.", Was all June could muster.

"Nigga, what you say?" June had Clark's full attention then, but he neva got the opportunity to hear June's response.

153

Dok took a step forward and grabbed the phone out of June's hand. Fuck the pleasantries! This mothafucka wanted to take it there, so Dok was taking it there.

"I tried being reasonable with you on the strength of my brotha, but you continued assaulting the people. You are a leech sucking the life out of our community. I gave you peace and you returned it with genocide. So now you've awakened the Dragon…"

"Nigga, you think I give a fuck 'bout yo threats!" Clark cut Dok off. He was heated. Hearing that Bone was dead and knowing that Dok was in his stash spot had Clark seeing red.

"I don't make threats, my brotha, but I assure you that tonight was only an example of power. A million miles of barb wire won't protect you from the face of the Dragon." Before Clark could respond, Dok hung up the cell phone and placed it inside his pocket. He couldn't leave it behind with his finger prints on it.

At that moment Rell and Scooter came out the back carrying two big ass Hefty garbage bags filled to capacity. They were just making it to the living room when Dok raised the SKS and sent June on his way to meet up with his comrades.

He neva looked over his shoulder. He knew that they were there because he felt their presence coming from the back.

"Let's go" Dok told the two boys his plan. Needless to say, they didn't like it, but they wouldn't dare voice their opinions, not after the shit that they'd just witnessed. Now they understood all the stories that they'd heard. What they didn't know is that they hadn't seen anything yet.

Dok pulled the Nissan away from the curb and drove to the corner. The night was quiet and peaceful. He made a U-turn and pressed his hand down on the horn. He held it there as he drove down the block. The loud horn attracted everyone's attention. This being the hood, people weren't afraid to come outside to see what was going on. The loud horn constantly roaring was becoming a nuisance.

What they saw when they came out of their houses was a dark four-door Camry with all the windows down. Two dudes were in the backseat holding garbage bags out the window with paper flying out of them. One of the neighbor's curiosity got the best of him and he walked to the sidewalk to investigate it. As he bent down to get a closer look, he couldn't believe his eyes. Quickly he began snatching up as much of it as he could. People seeing his behavior decided to investigate to satisfy their curiosity. Before long, it was clear that the paper was $100 bills that was flying out of the car and pandemonium broke out.

Once the boys informed him that all of the money was gone, Dok pulled down the block and drove off. They hadn't come for Clark's money, but Dok figured instead of letting the police have it, it would do better for the brothas and sistas struggling in the hood. At all times Dok put the people first.

They drove in silence, each man lost in his own thoughts. Dok was wondering if he should say something to the boys or not. This was their first time ever witnessing him body some shit. He rationalized that they had to see it sooner or later. This is what they've been training for. They would have their time to shine but he needed them to see that he wasn't a dictator. He was 'bout dat action. Or 'bout that life' as they called it. So, instead he cut the stereo on and let that Mozzy skip.

"I got some shotta's out in Stockton and we fully rocking /Don't try to pull up in Vallejo cause they get it popping/ I love the City all my San Francisco niggaz get me/ Oakland Raiders function with it we been in the locker"

By the time they made it to the freeway Dok was fully engrossed in the song and deep into his own thoughts. He took 101 North instead of using the San Mateo Bridge, he decided to ride all the way to the Bay Bridge while he thought about Kiumba. The brotha was A good Soldier who fell behind nothing. If the sacrifice was for a cause, Dok could take it a little easier, but it wasn't. It was a senseless act at the hands of a coward, a dead coward.

"And I ain't passing out no xanny unless you finna pop'em/ I ain't passing out no blammy unless you finna pop'em/ Teary eyed about my patna when I think about him/ Get teary eyed about my daughter when I think about her."

**** N. D. ****

Chapter XIV

Irate didn't describe Clarks state of mind. He was well beyond pissed off. When he'd gotten the phone call and heard the sucka ass niggaz' voice, he knew that he would take the loss. Fuck it, he could bounce back from that. He wasn't ready for the report that Tut gave him. They were able to recover ten kilos from the house that Dok and them didn't take. What threw Tut for a loop was how many people were out at that time of the night. It seemed like the entire block was out gathering something. After pulling up to the house he soon learned that the money from the stash house had been poured out all along the street.

Hearing that Dok had poured all of his money out in the streets was like a slap in the face. It was intended as blatant disrespect and Clark was taking it as such. He lit a blunt that he'd grabbed out of the ashtray. Hanging up his IPhone, he began thinking about how he would respond to the disrespect. East Palo Alto was his city and if he didn't respond, the streets would talk. The only issue was Elysian Fields was the only thing in East Palo Alto that was connected to Dok and Neva Die. It would be futile to attack the Center again. He would have to do better than that, and he was going to do it now. Fuck waiting for later.

A knock at the door came just as he was lighting another blunt. He didn't need his Glock because the video monitors clearly showed Tut and Man. Clark went to go let them in. When the phone call first came thru he was lounging in the bed watching his favorite movie "Shottas." Young Marley was a beast! Clark had seen the movie over thirty times and could neva get tired of it. He had thrown on a pair of black, army fatigue, sweatpants and a wife beater along with a pair of Jordan's. This is how he opened the door.

"What's up, dad?" Tut greeted his big cousin as he stepped inside the town house.

"Murda, nigga." Clark responded after their one arm embrace. Man Man stepped in the house without uttering a word. Bone was his right hand and a mothafucka had touched him. There wasn't shit to talk about. Mothafuckas had to pay for that shit.

They walked into the living room all taking seats on the butter soft leather inside the room. Clark took a long pull on the blunt he was smoking. When he exhaled the smoke thru his nose he resembled a red eyed demon. The anger shadowing his face made it a tone darker.

"Are you good to go, rogue?" Clark finally asked Tut once his lungs were empty of all the smoke.

Tut leaned over and grabbed one of the pre-rolled blunts out of the ashtray on the coffee table. He lit it and took a couple drags off of it before answering.

"Shit, dad, as soon as you give the green light it's good." The taste of the weed was so good Tut had to look at the blunt. "The shit them niggaz pulled was crazy, dad. When we pulled up to the block that mothafucka looked like Halloween! Mothafuckas were running all over the place like they lost their mothafuck'n minds or something. I'm telling you, dad, if I hadn't seen that shit with my own eyes I wouldn't have believed it. Nigga it was money stuck in bushes, in the trees. Mothafuckas were even crawling under cars and shit."

Clark looked over at Man Man. He started to say something to him but thought differently. The look on Man Man's face spoke volumes. Clark knew the language all too well.

Revenge!

"Now it's our turn to get their attention." Clark stood up from the leather recliner "Gimme a minute to get dressed and we can roll out." He told them as he turned to walk out.

"I thought you were going to sit this one out?" Tut asked. He was shocked that Clark had changed his mind.

Clark paused and turned back around to face his second in command and little cousin. He blew the weed smoke out of his mouth and spoke, "That sideline shit foe niggaz dat ain't in the game. I'ma coach, I walk the field." With that being said, he spun back around and went into his bedroom.

Ten minutes later, dressed in a black pair of True Religions, all black J's (Jordans) and a black hoodie covering his bullet proof Kevlar vest, Clark was almost ready to go. He walked over to his dresser and opened the bottom drawer. He removed two black 9mm P89s and placed them on top of the dresser. Next, he bent down and grabbed six clips. Two for the P89s and two extra for each. Lastly, he grabbed two silencers. Clark tucked one of the guns into his waistband and slid the other into the front pocket of the hoodie. The extra clips went into the pocket of his jeans. Now he was ready to go!

The three walked out of Clark's town house with death in their hearts and murder on their minds. They climbed into the black Tahoe with tinted windows and drove off in silence.

They pulled up to the single-story house a little after 4:35 a.m. as the Tahoe pulled up to the curb a sinister smile crossed Clarks lips.

"These mothafuckas must really think shit sweet. Mothafucka laid up nice and comfy like niggaz wasn't gone get that ass." He chambered a round into the P89 and then screwed a silencer on it while the other two checked their guns.

Man Man was just rocking back and forth with the most sinister look on his face. He actually didn't know how to cry, his life had been so fucked up for so long. He neva, not once, shed a tear. But if he did know how to cry, he would be crying for Bone.

"Let's get it." Clark told them once everything was in order.

**** N. D. ****

Gunz looked over at the clock, 4:29 a.m. He was dead tired. He'd wanted to call it a night over an hour ago, but he needed to make sure that he finished going over the books. They hadn't been done in a while and he neva allowed the books to get behind. He was almost done. Maybe another twenty or thirty minutes was all it would take.

He wanted to get home to Nastasia. Since meeting her at the San Jose Airport all those years ago, Gunz had fallen madly in love with her and the feeling was mutual. When he went out to Philadelphia the two had gotten together and quickly became inseparable. Nastasia really didn't approve of his life style but by the time Gunz trusted her enough to tell her about it, she had already fallen madly in love with him.

When Gunz first received the call from Urena he rushed back out to Cali. Once that business was settled he'd sent for his woman. The week before Clark popped back on the scene, Gunz had made Nastasia's dreams come true when he proposed to her. But that wasn't it. He had given her his word that he would give it all up for her and raise a family. He'd just asked her to give him six months to get all his affairs in order and give Dok time to make the transitions.

Gunz snapped his mind back from day dreaming about his woman. He needed to finish up and get home to his future queen. Just as he picked the pen back up to fill in the last page of the ledger, his phone began going off. He picked it up off of the desk and made a strange expression with his face. It was his ring app letting him know that someone was approaching his front door. He touched the screen to pull the live feed up on display and bolted out of his seat!

**** N. D. ****

It only took him thirty seconds to pick both locks and have the door open. Tut stood up off his knees and put his lock picking kit back into its case as Clark and Man Man stepped past him with guns in hand. Once his lock kit was back in his pocket, Tut pulled out his Desert Eagle and followed them into the house, quietly closing the door behind them.

The house was dark and as quiet as a cemetery. Suddenly, the faint sound of a cell phone ringing could be heard coming from somewhere in the back of the house. Clark looked to Man Man and nodded his head in the direction of the noise, but there was no need to because Man Man was already heading that direction.

Tut followed Man Man down the hall while Clark walked in the other direction checking out the kitchen, the second living room and the guest room. All the rooms were empty, but Clark couldn't shake the feeling of being watched. He stood still and tried to hone into his senses, but nothing happened. He gripped the handle of his P89 tighter and retraced his steps.

By the time he made it back to the living room, Man Man was pushing a fine ass Mulato broad into the living room. The silk nightgown that she was wearing hugged her body like a midnight lover would. Her body wasn't as thick as Spirituals but to Clark she was by far one of the top five most beautiful women he had ever seen. Watching the tears disrespect such a beautiful face as they escaped her eyes, he briefly became angered that he was the cause of the fluid ruining such a gorgeous face.

Fuck feelings! This was war, and in war you had casualties. All military strategist knew that! He couldn't be soft, not at a time like this.

"Always expect the unexpected." Clark said to himself looking at the beautiful sacrifice.

"Who are you?" He asked her.

She was too afraid to answer. Although she wanted to, her fear would not allow her vocal cords to work. Her chest felt like a bowling ball was attempting to rise out of it.

When Clark looked at Man Man he raised his hand all the way back to backhand her in the mouth, but he was too slow. Before anyone knew what happened, her head violently snapped back from the force of Tut punching her dead in the mouth. The punch knocked her backwards sending her crashing to the floor. The speed of the punch was so fast that it wasn't until she was already crashing onto the ground that she realized she had been struck. Man Man just stared at Tut like he was stupid. He was mad that Tut had robbed him of the moment of violence. Clark took two steps, stopping once he was standing over her. Blood was pouring onto the floor from her broken nose and busted lips. Nastasia lay on the ground in a fetal position sobbing violently.

Clark leaned down like a loving, concerned friend and gently asked "Are you okay?"

A whimper escaping her mouth was the best she could do to answer him.

"Come on sweetheart don't cry. Come here. Let me help you."

Fear of being struck again overpowered her previous paralysis. Shaking and feeling helpless, she slowly extended her hand to him.

Nastasia didn't know who these men were or what they wanted. She had been awakened by her phone with Gunz hysterically telling her to get up and run to their safety room. The panic in his voice caused her to immediately respond without question. In her haste to get out of the bed she dropped her phone. Yet she was still too late.

Man Man came thru the bedroom door just as she was crossing the threshold of the walk-in closet. As she was punching in the 6-digit code to open the safety room, he snatched her by her long hair and violently threw her to the floor. After kicking her a couple of times, he forced her to get up and walk to the living room.

"Lord God, please help me! Don't forsake me heavenly Father! Oh Baby, where are you? Who are these men?"

Nastasia asked Gunz in her mind.

Clark helped her stand to her feet then said in a caring voice, "I'm sorry about that. Are you okay, sweetheart?" She was still shaking and whimpering as tears flowed down her face. She couldn't speak so Nastasia just nodded her head up and down eagerly.

"Okay, Okay, you don't want him to do it again do you?" Clark asked her as he pointed at Tut.

Vigorously, she shook her head no! When he'd punched her, it hurt like no pain she had ever felt before. The tears just continued to spill over her eyelids and down her face.

"Then answer the mothafuck'n questions then, nigga!" When he yelled she jumped backwards, he was so close to her face that his words vibrated off of her face.

"If I ask you a mothafuck'n question you fuckin answer me! You understand." He grabbed her by her shoulders and shook her as he shouted for emphasis.

She once again nodded her head vigorously while bringing her two hands to her mouth. Nastasia looked like a child holding the bed sheets to their mouth while waiting for the boogey man to jump out of the closet.

"I can't hear you." He tapped his earlobe.

"Y-yes, I u-understand." She managed.

"Good. Now I asked you, who are you?" His tone was back to being calm and mellow.

"M-My... My name is Nastasia." It was barely above a whisper her voice was so soft.

"Okay Nastasia... tell me... who you are?" Clark sounded like he was talking to a grammar school child.

Man Man was standing there watching, smiling with a satanic look on his face. Seeing the woman quiver in fear was turning him on. Tut on the other hand, wasn't receiving any pleasure from the situation. When he'd punched her in the face, he only did so because it had to be done. As a rule, he hated harming women and children.

"I-I'm Leonard's fiancé." Even thru the fear Clark could see the pride in her eyes as she'd spoken her title.

All the men looked at each other, shocked by her revolution.

"And where is Mr. Leonard at this time of morning?" Clark asked with a warm smile on his face.

"He's at the office." She weighed her options in her head wondering if it would be to her advantage to tell them about the security monitors." He knows you're here so I'm sure he is on his way by now."

"And how would he know that we are here?" Clark figured she was lying, trying to work an angle.

"There are security monitors all over the property." Nastasia saw that the information made them feel some kind of way, so she spilled all the information, thinking it would help. "The camera from the doorbell ringing alerted him of you approaching the porch."

Clark had heard of the app from his nephew, D.J. who was a computer engineer, thought that was some futuristic computer geek crap. Now he realized apparently not. Clark was wondering if Gunz had called the cops.

"We gotta get outta here, dad. Them people might be on the way." Tut gave voice to his thoughts while drawing his Desert Eagle.

**** N. D. ****

He couldn't press his foot down any harder on the pedal if he wanted to. The Aston Martin fish tailed as he took the Fallon Road exit because of how fast he was going. It's a good thing the light had been green because he would've blown right thru it had it been red, with no regard to his own safety.

The moment he saw Clark and Tut walking up to his house he'd rushed to his car while calling Nastasia. He couldn't imagine the fear he felt if he were to lose her from his life. While the phone rang he said a prayer to God, hoping she would make it to the safety room before they got to her. She responded to him with actions instead of words after hearing the warning. He was thankful and thought that God just might do him that favor.

When he realized she'd dropped the phone he brought up the video monitoring app. A smile crossed his face when he saw her race into the closet. Only to have his heart drop at the sight of some yellow nigga speeding into the room behind her.

He'd almost crashed into a Dodge Durango as he ran the red light by the plaza.

When Tut punched his baby in the face, Gunz exploded! His Mack-II was sitting on his lap and he was ready to get off on some Denzel Washington shit, fuck Man On Fire, Gunz was the Equalizer.

"Come on God Dammit!" He shouted in frustration. The fact that he'd gotten from Oakland to San Ramon which was about fifty miles in less than twenty minutes was a miracle in itself. His heart was telling him that he wasn't moving fast enough! He was just a few miles away. The road was relatively empty, he might just make it.

"No! No! No! No! No!" Gunz yelled as he pounded his fist against the steering wheel.

The cause of this reaction was Tut pulling out the two-foot long Desert Eagle.

"Come on Baby! Keep'm talking, Mama, I'm almost there." Tears began rolling down Gunz face. Although his mind had him wishful thinking his heart told him what was coming.

He wanted to close his eyes, but he couldn't. Wanted the sports car to go faster but it wouldn't! Why didn't he buy the Lotus like he originally planned? The Lotus was a faster car! He cursed himself!

"Fuck you! Fuck you! You bitch ass niggaz! I'ma fucking kill you! I'ma kill you all you niggaz!" Now, only a mile and a half away, Gunz was watching as Tut raised the Desert Eagle and pointed at Nastasia's chest while Clark turned to walk away.

"Please God, Please Father, I'm so sorry for all my sins, please don't let this......Nooooooo!" The loud roar of pain erupted through the quiet night.

The force of the bullets slamming into her chest knocked her three feet backwards. Her body was sent airborne, then came crashing down on top of the coffee table, ending it toppling over and landing on top of her as she hit the ground.

With his vision blurred by tears, Gunz helplessly watched as Tut walked up to the love of his life who laid defenselessly bleeding on the floor of their living room. He pointed the canon down at her bleeding body and shot her four more times.

Gunz felt like his entire soul was ripped out of his chest. It was as if his life line was cut off from his body. He took the corner of Pine Tree Ave. doing sixty-eight miles per hour. The back tires of the Aston Martin skidded against the pavement as they fought to gain traction.

Nastasia was his breath of fresh air, his oxygen. She'd made it possible for him to breathe again. It was supposed to be a surprise, so she didn't know that he had sped their wedding date up by three months. He was going to trick her by saying that they were going on a yacht cruise. The yacht would pull up to Monterey Beach where their friends and family would be waiting to surprise her with the marriage ceremony at sunset. Afterwards everybody would board the 250 ft. yacht where they would party the remainder of the night for the reception.

The tears flowed freely. The back left tires smacked against the cement of the center island. The Aston Martin threatened to lose control but Gunz wouldn't let it. He knew that praying to a white Jesus wouldn't help. What kind of God would allow a man to witness the spark of his life being snubbed out? Gunz thought to himself *"fuck all that God shit! God didn't care about niggaz in the hood!"*

When Gunz turned onto his street he could see headlights approaching him. It looked to be an SUV. Instincts told Gunz that the headlights were them niggaz. He grabbed the handle of the Mack-II sitting on his lap. He wanted to cut them off and rain bullets down on the bitch-ass niggaz. What kind of pussy-ass, hoe-ass nigga would shoot an unarmed, helpless woman? The mere thought of it shot fire thought the veins in his body.

He needed to get to his baby though. She needed him. Something in his heart told him that even though he'd watched her get shot seven times, she was still alive. As the Black SUV approached he could make out Tut in the passenger seat with the nigga that chased her into his room driving. Which only meant that Clark was in the backseat.

Death was Gunz comforter. Blood for blood was his only option. He was getting ready to yank the steering wheel and ram into the SUV. He would follow up by jumping out of the Aston Martin with the Mack-II-barrel singing. He could hear Nastasia's voice in his heart! She wasn't dead, and she needed him!

At the last possible fraction of a second, he changed his mind about ramming the truck. However, he did raise the Mack-II, with one hand and squeezed the trigger. The night sky lit up with fire and sound as the bullets left an eerie streak through the air, as they flew from the barrel looking like a trail of fire flies in the night, shattering glass and piercing metal.

The action caught Man Man off guard. The hot piercing sensation that he felt in his left shoulder caused him to swerve the Tahoe a little. Clark tried to return the fire, but it was futile, Gunz had already driven by. Besides sirens could be heard in the distance as police and emergency medical crews responded to the reports of gun shots and a woman screaming.

As the Aston Martin came skidding almost to a complete stop, Gunz jumped out. The sound of the Aston Martin crashing into the tree in his front yard didn't faze him at all. He raced into the house and damn near collapsed as he saw his world laying on the floor helplessly with the coffee table laying on top of her. Gunz was so enraged he snatched the table off her with one hand and sent it soaring across the living room. He dropped to his knees and gently lifted Nastasia's onto his lap

"No, No, No! Baby, I'm so sorry! Please Stasia, Baby don't leave me." The tears flowed like an open faucet. Foamy blood ran out of her mouth and down her cheek. Though barely, Nastasia was still alive. She was holding on.

Their love was so pure that even in her weakened state she could sense Leonard's presence. She knew that she was in the arms of the love of her life. Gunz pulled his phone out and called the police hoping that they made it in time. He was told by the dispatcher that help was already on the way and should arrive shortly. The woman tried to keep Gunz on the phone while she continued to talk to him, but that shit was dead.

Moments later the police and paramedics arrived. It took some work, but they were able to get Gunz to let them tend to Nastasia. Gunz didn't know why but at some point, he thought that maybe White Jesus might look out for one ghetto nigga. It seemed that Gunz patience would continue to be tested that early morning as some white boy cop continued to try to question him. At one point he asked Gunz if he knew who was responsible for the attack. When Gunz looked at the cop and responded, "Dead Men!" The look on his face told the cop to leave him the fuck alone, unless he wanted to be one of those dead men.

It's a good thing that the Aston Martin crashing into the tree caused the Mack-II to fall out of the passenger seat and slide under the dashboard. Had they found the Mack-II there surely would've been hell to pay.

Newark, California
5:00am

Batman was sitting in the recliner in his living room on Magnolia Way in Newark, California eating a bowl of chitlins and drinking a nice cold Samuel Adams. The 85inch Samsung T.V. was on but he wasn't paying attention to the television. His attention was focused on the coffee table in front of him that was covered with folders and newspaper clippings. He had notes and internet printouts spread all over the living room of the town house. This is where Batman's attention was. He was going over the paperwork to plan his next strike.

Batman was felling real good about himself. For far too long, blacks had been abused and victimized without anyone lending a hand or giving a fuck. He used to cringe in anger every time he heard a report about some white dude killing one of his people in cold blooded murder and getting away with it. He was tired of the punk ass police slaughtering his people and getting away Scott-free. Not no more, though! Now he was watching reports of cops being killed by him and he was getting away with it Scott-free.

A beeping sound in his earpiece alerted him one second before the 85" screen blinked off of the news station and was replaced with a split screen of four multiple monitors. The cameras showed the front of the complex, the back of the garages which was behind the main building, the front view from his porch and his get-a-way route. Every monitor except his get-a-way route was swarming with S.W.A.T., S.C.U. and F.B.I.

Batman was neva one to give up. One of the things he'd learned from Voorheeze was safety and security. One of the most important rules to Safety and Security was keeping your composure. If you were level-headed and composed, there was always a way out of any circumstance. Looking at the monitors again, Batman smiled. He just had to stay calm and wait patiently until it presented itself.

Although he didn't expect them, at his front door Batman was prepared for them. There wasn't time to grab all of his material, so, he swiftly just snatched up everything for his next strike. He didn't want them to figure out his next move before it was time.

Next, he snatched up the keys to the truck and headed for the back-sliding glass door. Already pre-packed and waiting for him were two Army Surplus duffel bags loaded with stuff, a backpack and an M-16. As he threw all the gear over his shoulders, Batman was thankful for the many hours he and Voorheeze spent inside of 24-hour Fitness.

Just as the S.W.A.T. team had the battering ram in position to knock down the front door, Batman was walking through the back, sliding glass door. On his way out, he flipped the switch on the wall by the door. Instantly, a sulfuric nitrate fuse ignited.

The fuse burned in two separate directions running the entire length of forty-eight hundred square feet of the town house. Within seconds the entire place erupted in flames.

**** N. D. ***

Chapter XV

Newark
4:33am

Hedgecock was checking his weapon for the third time already. While the rest of the teams around him focused diligently on their safety gear, he only gave a fuck about his weapon. To him, safety gear was for those on the defensive. This was an offensive play through and through.

The hottest ticket in town for law enforcement was the joint agency raid on the suspected location of the notorious cop killer everybody and everyone wanted in on this one. Only the best were selected Hedgecock told himself, as he stared down the sights of the M-16. Since he was part of the team, rubbing elbows with the big dogs, he had brought out the big toys.

Hedgecock was eager to show these government boys just who he was. The cool, brisk air almost guaranteed he was fully awake and alert as they had met up around the corner from the targeted location thirty minutes ago to have a last-minute meeting with everyone. Then they broke into their perspective infiltration teams, where each team leader held a second meeting.

The signal to move out was given and everyone climbed inside and on top of their perspective vehicle. Naturally the Feds wanted to be the first inside the habitat, but it would be Hedgecock and his team who would lead the initial breech. As he prepared himself, he thought how they had found the suspect. An anonymous tip was called in with the possible sighting. The detective unit that was sent to investigate spotted Lt. Urena's brand new truck which had been stolen from the precinct and driven by the suspect at the time of the killing of Federal Snitch, Agent Jose-Walo-Gayton.

Upon further recon a lone African-American was seen going to and from the unit. There were four units on either side of a courtyard with three units in the back. After the intel was gathered, a strike team was assembled for this morning's raid on the unit.

Two teams would penetrate. One would cover the back and a team would roam the perimeter keeping it sealed tight. Alpha teams would consist of the FBI's Tactical S.W.A.T. unit and Hedgecock's team. Bravo was the team covering the back of the unit and Delta was the team covering the perimeter.

4:58a.m.

"All teams deploy cautiously to get into position." One of the Delta Team members scouted the entire area two hours ago for any possible barking dogs. The area was secure.

Coms (communications) were checked earlier but the double click inside of Hedgecock's ear was a last-minute confirmation that all systems were a go. Just before entry, one of the neighbors across the courtyard opened their door and stepped out on her way to work. Quickly members of the Delta Team rushed her, secured her and removed her from the Hot Zone.

5:01a.m.

"Alpha Leader Team One breech on my go. Five, four..." Hedgecock watched with anticipation as he listened to Alpha Leader count down in his ear.

"...three, two..." all the members waited for the sigh to go. The green light.

Alpha Breech One stood poised with the Battle Ram ready. The shit hit the fan!

"One! Breech! Breech! Breech!" All precisely on the signal of Breech.

Flash bangs and stun grenades went crashing through the front and back windows along with smoke grenades. The sound of the grenades going off were like m-80's and M-160 cherry bombs going off on the 4th of July.

The moment the bangs of the grenades were heard the Battering Ram crashed into the front door right where the dead bolt was. The entire door hinge splintered apart in a thousand little pieces as the front door violently tore free. Members of

Alpha One and Alpha Two stormed inside of the Town House, all alert and on the ready!

The first thing Hedgecock picked up on was the emptiness of the unit. There was sparse furniture in the front room, but the place was too clean. There was no feel of a presence inside of the unit. Still he proceeded to lead up the stairs that were directly in front of him to his left.

From the layout obtained from the leasing office, they were aware ahead of time that it was a 3-bedroom, 2 bath unit. All of the bedrooms were located upstairs. Hedgecock headed up the stairs headed towards the farthest room on the left.

Lt. Urena was two people behind Hedgecock. Urena's job was to secure the master bedroom while the next team secured the last room.

Without breaking stride, Hedgecock kicked the room door in. The door swung open to a completely empty room. There was not a single thing inside the room, not even in the closet. As if on cue, he began hearing everyone inside of his earpiece sounding off that their area was secure.

"Alpha leader two. Area secure." Hedgecock spoke into his coms also letting everyone else know that his designated area was clear.

On his way back down the stairs he was trying to figure out what happened. The intel had been verified and checked out. The suspect had been seen entering the unit last night and presumably neva came back out. So, where was he?

Downstairs everyone was walking around with lost looks on their faces. No doubt thinking the same thing. Delta One came over the coms informing them all that no-one has breached the perimeter. The answer had to be here somewhere.

Ten minutes of searching turned up absolutely nothing. Hedgecock just couldn't accept that. He decided to head out towards the garage and see if he could find something there. Across the horizon it looked like the sun was getting ready to make its appearance.

Outside in the back, Hedgecock made his way towards the garage. He stopped in mid-stride when he heard something over by the gate. With his breath held, he spun, aiming his rifle in the direction of the noise. Fuck alerting somebody on comms, he was ready to light some shit up.

"Come on motherfucker." He whispered to himself as he approached the wooden fence.

He heart was beating so loud that he couldn't hear his own breathing. Still he proceeded. Just as he got close to the fence he heard a scurry directly towards his left. He swung his rifle around as fast as he could, ready to squeeze the trigger. Right before he pulled the trigger he saw an alley cat sprint away from the fence, race to the other fence and hop over it. Hedgecock out a sigh of relief. He would neva admit to himself, let alone anyone else, but he was scared shitless.

As he was turning to leave he noticed that a door had been cut into the fence.

Federal informant Wendell Roberson came over the comms unit, "hey guys, it looks like we have activity next door." Hedgecock pushed on the door of the fence and it opened. He stepped in and noticed through the glass sliding door the unit next door was ablaze. What caught his attention was the fact that both the sliding door and the garage door were wide open.

"Alpha Leader Two, there was a passageway cut into the fence that leads into the next-door backyard. Repeat we have a possible breech in the backyard, Alpha Leader Two proceeding to further investigate.

"Alpha Leader Two, this is Alpha Leader Three. In route to your location. Me and a couple of my guys are on you six." Lt. Urena was already through the sliding glass door when he sent the transmission.

"10-4,"Hedgecock whispered into his coms. He already crossed the threshold of the walk-through garage door. It was dark and musky inside of the garage. The only light source was the light coming into the door he'd just crossed and another walkthrough door on the other side of the garage that was open.

He paused for a second once he stepped in to give his eyes a chance to adjust to the darkness. Once his eyes adjusted, Hedgecock noticed that the garage was bare. Making one sweep with the rifle to confirm his thought, he headed towards the open door.

He heard Urena and his men enter the garage the moment he reached the other door. Hedgecock took a deep breath and then stepped through the door.

"Officer down! Officer down! I repeat Officer down! This is Alpha Leader Two, I'm outside of the back of the garage to the adjoining unit. We have an officer down!" As Hedgecock dropped to his knees to assist the fallen officer, he could hear Urena and his men approaching. "Be advised it appears that the suspect has taken the officers clothes. I repeat suspect is dressed like a member of the Delta Team!"

**** N. D. ****

Batman laughed so hard that tears rolled down his face.

"I repeat the suspect is dressed like a member of the Delta Team!" He called out in a mockery of the cop he just heard over the radio.

He couldn't help but wonder how they were going to respond once they realized that he had also taken one of the FBI's tactical S.W.A.T. vehicles. They were really going to shit their pants then. It was all so easy. He had seen it in a movie played by Denzel Washington. He had motion sensors and cameras wired and rigged around unit six and unit seven. Both were leased by him under separate names. Batman would always enter and exit out of unit six. Once he entered unit six, he would use his secret door in the fence to walk into unit seven where he resided.

When he saw the S.W.A.T. units getting ready to bust the door down, he knew that they were at unit six. Batman made his way through the garage. He could hear the pig talking to someone on his radio through the door. He looked through the peep hole that he'd installed and saw that the pig had his back to the door.

Batman slowly opened the door and stepped out as silently as he could. Knowing what he was already going to do, thoughts of Eric Garner a 43-year-old brother from New York who the police murdered by choking him out, crossed into Batman's mind.

"This is for Eric." The fraction of a second that it took for the officer's brain to register what he had just heard was too late.

In the blink of an eye, Batman reached out his hands and snapped the cops' neck like a dry twig left out in the Death Valley heat. In just a matter of minutes Batman stripped the dead body of its uniform, put it on and was climbing inside of the Tactical Assault Vehicle.

Law enforcement always left their keys inside of their vehicles, especially the feds. They were cocky and arrogant. They left their keys inside of their vehicles because they figured no-one would fuck with their shit.

Batman drove off without a care in the world while listening to all the chatter on the police radio. By the time they discovered the body of the dead officer, he was already on the 880-freeway heading south. He got on the freeway at the Thornton exit and was already passing the Mowry exit when the transmission came across the radio about the stolen assault vehicle.

"*Fuck the police! They will learn that they are not superior to the same laws that they are supposed to uphold. The feds too. Even our so-called government for the people are corrupt and racially biased. But I'll make them pay attention to what's going on. I'll remind them that everybody answers to somebody and they must answer to me!*" He thought to himself as he continued listening to the APB that went out over the radio and the rest of the radio chatter.

**** N. D. ****
Milpitas

Chief Vieira was fuming. She'd just hung up her office phone after receiving the news of the botched raid on the suspected cop killer. She knew that letting the feds get involved was a bad idea. However, after the Governors little speech, the decision was far out of her hands.

After the Governors little speech about public safety and the safety of law enforcement, the heat had really come down on the Mayor who in turn came down pretty hard on the Chief. She was really wanting the raid to be a success so that at least she could show that she had apprehended the suspect. That was the main reason she didn't want outside agencies involved in the raid. Yet, the Mayor all but told her that the feds would be running point.

Vieira was a veteran. She knew all too well neva to count your chickens before they hatch. Which is why she was telling the Mayor that she was strongly against informing the Governor about locating the suspect at least until they apprehended the suspect. *A hard head really does make a soft ass she* thought, but at least she wasn't the one that the Governor was about to rip a new hole.

She picked up her phone to see if she had received a response to her text message yet. Her screen was blank indicating the answer to her question was no. She knew that it was too early, but she still had to try.

Over the course of her frequent visits to the hospital, she and French Tip had held several conversations and had gotten to know one another. Vieira learned early on that French Tip loved her brother very much and was extremely protective of him. She admired and respected that. The two ladies had exchanged phone numbers and continued with their getting to know one another.

French Tip had told Vieira at their second meeting that Voorheeze coma was medically induced. Countless times over the past few months, Vieira had desperately wanted French Tip to make the decision to wake her baby up. That moment neva came. When word came down from the District Attorneys office that the charges against him where being dismissed, Vieira was so happy, she nearly cheered openly in her office while reading the report.

She acted purely on impulse when she had picked up her cell phone and sent French Tip a text message informing her of the news. Her reasoning was just maybe this information would give French Tip reason enough to make the decision. Vieira knew that what she did could get her fired, yet she did it anyway. She just hoped to God that it wasn't a wasted risk. She was lost without him. She needed him back.

Vieira put the cell phone back on her desk and decided to get up and make her morning rounds. She needed something to take her mind off French Tip responding to her.

**** N. D. ****

He sat all alone in the crowded hallways shedding more tears than Tupac rapped about on the song "Shed So Many Tears". It's as if he was on his very own metal chair island, lost in a storm of misery and tragedy that no one could feel but him.

Thoughts sped through his mind like Danika Patrick. The one thought that continued to come back around like it was on its very own conveyor belt was how is it even possible. Gunz wouldn't dare tempt God but he couldn't fathom that his baby could still be alive. But she was. He'd lost track of how long he had been there. Hell, in his mind state, he couldn't keep track of anything. Though he had neva in his life been religious, he prayed to God whole heartedly and continually. His baby was still here! He knew she was a fighter. That went without question, but he couldn't help but ask himself could there possibly be a God. If so, did He care enough to answer his prayers?

Everyone couldn't help but to stare at the black man that didn't look as if he should be crying. Yet, all who looked at him could tell that his anguish and pain was real. The white woman who looked at him with open lust thought it beautiful for someone who looked so rough and dangerous to be so weak and vulnerable.

There weren't but a handful of blacks in Dublin or San Ramon. The upscale wealthy neighborhoods were predominately white and Indian. Dublin and San Ramon were filled with the wealthy. When a mob of angry black niggaz came storming into the hallways of the E. R. everyone nearly shit themselves from fear.

Gunz knew something was wrong. Hospitals are very noisy all the time. All of a sudden, you could hear a cricket fart it had gotten so quiet. The only thing he could hear before he lifted his head up was the sound of marching feet. He didn't know how they found out but Gunz knew who was coming before he looked up.

Cantelope was the first to reach Gunz. He could hear the sound of her Manalo heels echoing off the walls. She didn't feel his slight hesitation when she hugged him.

"Gunz, I'm so sorry, baby", she whispered into his ear just before letting him go.

French Tip, on the other hand, picked up on his hesitation and reluctance to embrace her, yet she decided not to say anything. After all she couldn't begin to imagine the state of mind that he must be in. It was French Tip who had seen the story on the early morning news.

Gunz had asked French Tip to keep an eye on Nastasia to make sure she didn't find out about the early wedding. Using the Satin Doll Fashion Show as an excuse, French had gotten close to Nastasia. She had been to the house several times. So, when she saw it on the news, she immediately left out of her house. Speeding through the streets, she called Dok.

After hugging French Tip, Gunz turned to face Dok. The pain on his face was evident. The two warriors embraced like brothers. Dok couldn't find the words to console his brotha. The anguish he would feel if something were to happen to Jeanette would crush his entire world. He could only imagine Gunz' pain. As they embraced, Dok silently thanked God that Jeanette was safe.

"May the spirit of the Khatari be with you, my brotha." Dok gave Gunz a firm grip, reassuring him that the family was there for him.

Gunz took a step back and shook his head. His legs gave out and he plopped down into the chair. How could the family be there for him? It was too late. They weren't there when he needed them to be, just as he wasn't there when Nastasia needed him to be. He looked at Dok and tried to speak but couldn't. The pain that gripped his chest was unbearable. With every heartbeat Gunz felt like someone was beating on his chest with a sledge hammer.

Everyone stood around taking up most of that section of the hallway waiting on Gunz to speak. Just then, two security guards came around the corner. They were answering a call of concern regarding the group. As the frail Opie Taylor looking rent-a-cop took one look at the group of hardened killas, they turned back around just as fast and decided that now would be a good time to take lunch.

Gunz couldn't blame nobody but himself. He knew in his heart that he should've dealt with Clarks bitch ass himself. Clark was a street nigga like he was. He wasn't some revolutionary. He had to be got at like a street nigga! Gunz had ignored that the moment he decided to allow Dok to take care of the situation. Gunz had made the mistake! He wouldn't make another!

He looked at Cantelope again and then at French Tip. They both had been loyal and solid soldiers. Just how far would that loyalty go, he wondered. After all blood was thicker then water. It was times like this that he missed Chiba! Anne was beyond loyal, she was tested and proven, and died for her loyalty.

"My brotha, talk to me. I can see the storm clouds brewing in your eyes." Dok's voice brought him out his mind and back to reality.

It only takes a split second in time to alter the course of one's life. Well in the split second that Gunz snapped back into reality the course of numerous lives was altered. When Gunz stood up, the weak and grieving fiancé that was just wallowing in his sorrows disappeared. A General and East Oakland legend stood up.

He looked at French Tip first.

"I'm sorry little sis, you should've been told what was going on in the beginning. Now, it's too late. You're guilty by association so I can't trust you." As he hugged and kissed her, his words struck her in the face like an iron fist.

She stumbled backwards with a shocked look on her face. No, he didn't just disrespect her like that. She was about to address the situation, but something in her soul told her not to.

Next, Gunz addressed Johnny Spitz, "J-Spitta, I want your best to guard my queen. I'm placing my world into your hands. I don't want no one let in. If you see a She-Wolf kill her on site...."

"Hold the fuck up, Gunz." Both Cantelope and French Tip spoke up at the same time interrupting him, but Gunz didn't waiver.

"That woman is all I have in this world and if something happens to her, no-one will know peace." The entire time he spoke Gunz stared deep into Johnny Spitz eyes. His look sent chills down Johnny's spine. He needed to know that his response was sealed with conviction.

"Say no moe, Big Homie, I got you, my nigga." Johnny knew that he wasn't staring at a man. He was seeing Death's Demon.

The energy level in the hallway intensified with so much electricity you could power a small generator.

"Get ahold of A.J. and DeeDee and tell them to dress the kids for church." He was instructing Big Rocc.

Suddenly he heard A.J.'s voice. "We already right here, family. Sorry it took us so long, that 580 traffic is a mothafucka. And we already locked and loaded!" A.J. spoke as he and DeeDee walked up to the group.

A.J. made his way through the group to give his big cousin a hug.

"Peace be still, my brotha. I know your pain…"

"You don't know my pain, Dok! No-one does." When he turned to face Dok, Gunz had tears in his eyes. He wasn't ashamed to let them fall freely down his cheeks.

He bit down on his lip and took a deep breath then spoke. "Now the first time you asked me to fall back cause one of yours got touched. I didn't want to, but I did out of respect. Regardless of what happened or how, that shit just landed on my door step." Gunz paused so that shit could sink in because his next words were meant for all. "Dis Town Bizness now and Anybody Can Get it!"

Gunz saw the way Scooter and Rell tensed up at his comment, but he didn't give a fuck! They could get it too!

Dok knew the look that he saw in Gunz eyes. He recognized it all too well because he himself had the very same look in his eyes when he lost the love of his life, the boys mother. So, he knew there was no talking or reasoning with Gunz, so he didn't try. Instead, he nodded his head in agreement.

A stunned and angry French Tip looked confused as Gunz turned towards Big Rocc and his team and said, "Let's do what we do!" and marched out of the hospital on a mission. She didn't know who it was with, but she knew it was war!

**** N. D. ****

She didn't know what to think, let alone know what to do. The shit that she had just heard was beyond believable. They were all family. The bad times were supposed to be over, but it seems that things just kept getting fucked up. She needed her brother. If Voorheeze was woke, everything would be okay.

Again, she had to ask herself could it be possible? Was what she heard true? She couldn't believe that Clark had tried to kill Nastasia. Hearing that he was the one responsible for shooting up the youth centers and harassing the workers, was just as unbelievable. Not her big brother.

She had heard the rumors in the street about someone robbing one of his stash spots and throwing the money all out in the streets. Is this what all of this is behind? Money! She pounded her fist on the steering wheel out of frustration while the tears fell. Mothafuckas had the nerve to keep this away from her, but fuck that! She was going to get some muthafuckin' answers and she was going to get them right fucking now!

The tires of her pink and black Challenger screeched loudly as they skidded across the paved street when she slammed on her brakes. French Tip could give a fuck about the neighbors or disturbing the peace. In her anger she grabbed her pistol and tucked it inside of the holster clipped on the back of her pants once she stood up.

"This mothafucka done clearly lost his mothafucking mind!" she mumbled to herself as her Louboutin's clicked and clacked against the concrete and carried her to his front door. French Tip didn't knock on the door once she got to it. She banged on it like she'd lost her mothafucking mind.

It took a full two minutes for him to answer the front door and she'd banged on it the entire time.

"God damn, sis! Is you crazy? Banging on the door like you done lost your mind." Clark asked her when he finally opened the door a crack.

He had a robe on and his gun in his left hand. Wasn't no telling who it was banging on his door that time of night.

From the smell of incense and sex that drifted to her nose, French Tip knew he had company. *"Oh well!"* She thought.

"Naw, nigga, but apparently you're not only crazy but you done went and lost your natural mind too." She told him as she pushed her way past him and into the house.

"French, now ain't the time." He hurried up and closed the door and followed her into the living room.

"Now's the only time!" She wasn't hearing his bullshit. She was too fired up.

The girl that was laying under the covers by the fire quickly sat up and covered her naked breast as best she could with the comforter when French Tip stormed into the room.

"I'm sorry to interrupt yo groove honey, but you got ta go!" her head and hand both snapped in sequence as she told the girl to leave.

"H-Huh?" Spirit fearfully stuttered. The woman standing over her looked like she was on the verge of a break down.

"Don't stutter, honey, get up and go." The conviction in French Tips voice told Spirit not to ask another question.

When she stood up, French Tip did a double take. The girl had the biggest ass she had ever seen in her life. No wonder her brother didn't want to be interrupted.

"Baby gone into the other room for a minute while I talk to my lil sister." Spirit could breathe a little easier at the revelation that it was his little sister and not some crazed lover.

"Okay this mothafucka think I'm playing." French Tip mumbled to herself as she reached behind her back and pulled out her 9mm.

"Now, I didn't say shit bout hiding in no room. I said get the fuck out! Now she could leave this mothafucka, (she cocked the nine back putting one in the head) or she could leave this mothafucka! Clark, try me if you want to."

He didn't know what was bothering his little sister, but this wasn't her. Not wanting to see just how far she was willing to go, Clark wrapped his arms around a trembling Spirit and looked into her frightened eyes. She was innocent, a square, so he could only imagine her fright.

He kissed her deeply and passionately telling her all the things that he couldn't say. When he finally broke the kiss he said to her, "Baby get dressed in the room and head home. As soon as I'm done with my sis, I'll call you."

Feeling like a little girl after that kiss, Spirit sashayed her way down the hall to do as she was told. Neither sibling spoke a word while she was in the room. Clark did take that opportunity to walk over to his bar to roll a blunt. Just as he sparked the blunt, Spirit came down the hall. After one more deep and passionate kiss, she was gone, not before saying goodbye to French Tip, who didn't respond.

Once he heard Spirit's truck pull off he turned his attention to his sister. "Alright, so tell me what's the emergency?"

"You gone play me like I'm some dumb bitch, huh?" She couldn't believe the audacity of this nigga.

"Look you came over here with something on your mind, so talk." She was his sister and all, but Clark still didn't like being questioned.

"Clark, how could you? We're family." She began to cry. "Nastasia…" was all she could get out.

Realizing now what this was about he corrected her. "No! We!" He pointed back and forth between them, "Are Family! They're outsiders. I tried to tell brah that shit, but he wouldn't listen." She knew her ears were hearing him clearly, but she still couldn't accept what he was saying.

"Mothafucka, are you crazy? It may have been Voorheeze that brought you in to the fold, but it was the family as a whole that made this shit possible! You wouldn't be shit without us!" She spat out, full off hurt and anger, as she pounded on her chest trying to get him to understand her reasoning. "Whether you choose to accept it or not, mothafucka, we are family."

Clark walked over to the couch and sat down. He took a few drags off the blunt, giving himself time to formulate his next statement.

"Them mothafuckas that you are siding with drew first blood when they drew their imaginary line telling me what to do in my city and where I can and can't do it at. I didn't cause nor start this war, but I'll be damned if I'ma fall back from it. They sent you over here thinking our bond will cause me to fold. Now that, that niggaz slut was touched, mothafuckas want to talk? Ain't shit to talk about!" There was the truth. Even without saying it, he just admitted that it was him that got at Nastasia.

She knew it all along but just didn't want to accept it. Now she didn't have a choice. The pain trapped her voice in her chest preventing her from being able to speak.

"You're my little sister and I love you." He took a hit off of the blunt and blew the smoke out through his nose. "But since you riding with them, you gotta go! And the next time you see me, I advise you to squeeze." When the words left his mouth, his demeanor was so laid back and relaxed that it sent chills through her body.

This mothafucka had to have lost his natural, mothafucking mind, she thought to herself. French Tip couldn't believe the level of disrespect that he was issuing. The pressure that she felt pressed up against the small of her back reminded her of her pistol. For a minute, she contemplated blowing his mothafucking head off right then and there. But she'd delivered the news.

Now she didn't trust herself to speak. If she were to verbalize her feelings, her words would betray her emotions. The results, no doubt, would be catastrophic! Instead she just glared at him for a second. French could see that the money had gone to his head. She wasn't seeing her brother. She was looking at a mothafucking problem! This mothafucka had actually threatened her!

With that in mind, she took a deep breath and slowly stood up. He didn't even look at her. He didn't have to. Clark knew that underneath her killer exterior, his sister had a big heart. She wouldn't do anything unless she was pushed.

French Tip walked out of the house with her aura so calm, it spoke volumes of the storm that was brewing inside of her!

By the way she walked back to her car and drove off, no-one could have guessed that she was using all her restraint not to murder some shit.

De'Kari

Part III
My Brotha's Keeper

De'Kari

Chapter XVI

East Oakland

Dok sat in the leather office chair fuming. The half empty glass of Hennessey Privilege resting on top of the desk in front of him was evidence of his level of anger. He reached for the glass. This time downing it completely before setting the empty glass back down and reflecting on the orders again for the umpteenth time.

Word came down from the Central Committee by way of the Military Intelligence. The Committee had given the Green Light on a surgical Military strike against Clark and his forces just as Dok figured they would. They also delivered a blow to his strategic plans that he was not contemplating. As Commanding Officer of Ground Forces, it was deemed that the risk and setbacks, of his involvement by the police, or worse, his untimely demise by the hands of opposing forces. Would present too great of a blow to the forward goal of the collective.

Long story short, Dok was ordered by the committee to step aside and allow Mtambo, Executive Commanding Officer of the "Elite Guerilla Unit" full access of ground forces and command of military personnel.

Elite Guerilla Unit, better known as EGU, was made up of Cadres of forces all highly trained in the arts and practices of Guerilla Warfare, they specialized in everything in weaponry from knives and small arms to machine gun fire and heavy artillery. Each Cadre and member were specialist in multiple forms of hand to hand combat, explosives, demolition as well as poisons.

While Dok and his Cadre of Ground Troop Forces had been overseeing the fruition of Elysian Fields and Nu Africa, the rest of Military and Cadre personnel were doing their parts in getting the People's Army ready. An army of New African Revolutionary Nationalist.

Elysian Fields was just one part in a massive movement to bring about a new government of, by and for the people. As much as Dok didn't' like the order, he had no choice but to follow it. The refusal or disobeying of a direct order or mandate passed down by the committee was an automatic neutralization of one's self. Dok wasn't about to sign his own death certificate.

Under normal circumstances no general or senior commander would ever allow his men to be under the leadership and command of another general or commander. Due to the circumstances, Dok didn't have any choice but to allow some of his personnel to be apart of the detachment. There was a possibility that there would be hostile friendlies in the combat zone.

No-one had heard from Gunz and his team since they stormed out of the hospital. Considering there was no doubt that Gunz was hell bent on destruction and death, the possibility that they would find themselves in the middle of the designated target zone, for that reason members of Dok's Cadre would be needed for identification purposes. No-one wanted any self-inflicted casualties.

For their own security measures one brother wouldn't allow the other to go alone even though they were all Guerillas. Because of this, both of his sons ended up going on the strike with EGU. Dok's nerves were working overtime as he listened to the mission unfold. A micro Electronic Radio Transmitting Device or ERTD was attached to the outside lapel of Scoots black camouflage army fatigues. It was transmitting via blue tooth to the Echo speaker that was next to the empty glass of Hennessey.

**** N. D. ****
East Palo Alto

"Alpha, Bravo. This is Charlie. Everything is quiet. We are a go." The voice came over everyone's earpiece. It was

Cuana, second in command of the Usalama Squad and a member of military intelligence.

Cuana was leading the Recon Cadre and was responsible for the extraction of the Strike Unit. Given that the New African Revolutionaries primary and principle enemy was the United States government, their level of sophistication in all aspects was way beyond anything that anybody in the ghetto was used to or capable of dealing with.

Cuana was positioned on the roof of the house on the corner of Jervis and Alberni, looking at the targeted house which was located a third of the way up Jervis. She was watching the house through a pair of HD-1 High Resolution Night Vision Binoculars, equipped with infrared and thermo-nuclear lenses. They were the newest in advanced military special operations vision ware.

Aside from Cuana, members of the Usalama Squad were positioned on the corner of Bay Road and Jervis and behind the target house on Westminster. The triangular position of the team would ensure the hot-zone was secure.

Outside of the targeted house two niggaz dressed in all black were on point keeping security. Due to the night chill, they both had on thick jackets. The shorter of the two niggaz was smoking a cigarette while facing the street telling the second nigga a story about some chick he took home the other night from the strip club.

The taller of the two niggaz had his back to the streets, hands in his pockets, listening to the story with his head buried inside of his jacket. They were waiting on Mann Blac and Avery to pull up with the new shipment of product. The house on Jervis was only a cook house but with the situation that happened over in the Gardens, Clark wasn't taking any chances whatsoever.

The two niggaz on security standing in front of the house were so engrossed in each others company that they didn't see the black Harley Davis truck pulling up with a Yukon Denali XL right behind it. Both vehicles pulled up to the house on the

1200 block of Jervis. Once both cars came to complete stops, Manny Blac climbed out of the driver's seat of the Harley truck with his little cousin climbing out of the passenger seat.

Cuana waited for Avery to climb out of the Yukon. The intelligence report informed everyone that the kilos of cocaine were in the back of the Yukon. With the patience of a Venus fly trap, she waited.

On cue, a burgundy Dodge Caravan came silently rolling down Alberni unseen by the group that was now congregating on the sidewalk in front of the house. Though they couldn't make out the words that were being spoken, it was evident that Manny Blac was giving instructions on what was to be done with the product.

Just when the caravan made it to the corner of Jervis and Alberni, an all black 2016 Porsche Cayenne turned onto Jervis off Bay Road heading in the direction of the hot-zone.

The Usalama Squad (security & safety squad) was able to see everything play out from their positions on the rooftops.

"U'Tayari (ready)...." A few seconds ticked away ever so slowly "Ansa! (go)." Cuana spoke into her mouthpiece as she squeezed the trigger of her sniper rifle. The sound suppressor on the powerful rifle muffled the sound as the deadly projectile was sent soaring through the night sky.

The nigga that was telling the story when the vehicles pulled up was still smoking his cigarette as Manny was finishing his instructions. He pulled out the Newport 100. The cherry glowed bright red and then all of a sudden not only did the cherry disappear, but the entire cigarette vanished. A fraction of a second later, blood and brain matter burst out the back of his head as the projectile fired by Cuana slammed into his mouth where the cigarette used to be and tore thru his medulla oblongata and out the back of his head. He was dead long before the blood landed on the pavement.

No-one noticed the cherry or cigarette disappear, nor heard a gunshot, but all of them saw his body fly backwards violently from the force of the bullet crashing into his head. Niggaz immediately dropped for cover and grabbed for their weapons. Two of the niggaz that rode in the Yukon with Avery ran and hid behind the truck.

Manny Blac was the only one to realize the shooter was on the roof and was looking up while a figure in black army fatigues and a fatigue beanie jumped out of the caravan.

Immediately he opened-up with an M-16 mowing down everything in his path ,beginning with Manny Blac. The remaining three niggaz began returning fire as best they could. The speed in which the 223's where flying thru the air was shutting that shit down.

The niggaz were so busy focusing on the nigga in the fatigues that they didn't hear the Porsche pull up or see Rell jump out of it with a subcompact Chinese AK-47. When he opened fire, it was like shooting crabs in a bucket.

While that was going on Mtambo walked to the back of the Caravan to retrieve a black canvas Coleman camping carrying bag.

"The call just went out over the wire. Normal units responding, however, we have a bogey less than one minute away coming from the south east." Mtambo heard Cuana's report come through his earpiece, but he was not worried about it. He had one hundred percent faith in his Usalama Squad.

Carrying the canvas bag, he made his way to the front door. Reaching the door, he was able to kick it in with one mighty thrust from his size sixteen Steele toe boots. At six foot six, two hundred and ninety-two pounds of muscle, Mtambo was strong as an ox. Inside the house, he unzipped the canvas bag and removed three incendiary devices which he quickly placed throughout the house.

Scooter and Rell both took up positions outside in front of the house keeping Usalama (security). Standing in a crouched position they resembled two delta force sentries with their black fatigues and M-16's.

"Bogey has just entered the hot-zone. Initiating contact and neutralization." Kipaka's soft voice sounded metallic as it crackled over the earpieces.

She was positioned on top of a roof on the west side of the 1100 block of Jervis. The house was on the corner which gave her a clear view down Bay Rd. The black and white Dodge Charger came racing up 1100 block of Laurel Ave. It's flashing lights and loud siren's inconsiderately disturbing the night's dark peace.

The 5K high power clear resolution scope gave Kipaka a crystal-clear view of the bourgeois

middle class African American who was dead set in a rush to save the day and continue making a name for himself on the Police Force,

Officer Johnson was just coming out of the parking lot of Oakwood Market when the call of multiple shots fired came out over the radio. Unbeknownst to any of his colleagues on the force, Officer Johnson abused the authority of the badge every chance he got. He thought he was better than the low-life, ghetto, welfare niggaz that were from the run-down city. He got his rocks off by making the known prostitutes in the city preform sexual favors whenever he got the urge, or he would run them in on as many charges as he could make up.

As Officer Johnson made it to the intersection of Laurel Ave. and Bay Road, he paused briefly while he turned his head to the right to check on-coming traffic. When he turned to the left a sound like an icepick striking ice was made but Johnson neva heard the sound.

The mini projectile missel that Kipaka sent from her high-powered rifle burrowed into his bootlicking, ass head causing it to explode like a watermelon hit by a baseball bat.

When Johnson's head exploded his nerves caused the right foot to press down on the gas. With the flashing red lights, the Charger flew across the intersection, jumped the curb and crashed into the house on the northeast side of the corner of

Laurel and Bay Rd. The crash caused the siren to make a weird noise before shutting down.

"Bogey neutralized." Kipaka reported.

"Two more units approaching fast. One coming up Alberni, from the east. The second, Bay Rd from the same direction." Cuana's voice was clear and authoritative.

Mtambo was crossing the threshold as Ndege's voice came across the earpieces, "I got the unit on Alberni."

Scooter and Rell were a few feet in front of Mtambo as they escorted him to the Caravan. Afterwards, Rell hustled back to the Porsche where Damu was waiting on guard. As one, they both jumped into the Porsche and both vehicles began to drive off.

The incendiary devices planted inside of the house had already gone off and the house was engulfed by the hungry fire flames.

"Ladies move out." Mtambo ordered.

"There's still a unit approaching your location." Kipaka wasn't disobeying the order, he was reminding the Commander of the fact.

"I'm well aware of that." He looked at Scooter, a nonverbal command was given. "We'll dispense of the unit. Everyone move-out and meet back at the spot."

By the time the Caravan had made it to Bay Rd., Scooter had climbed over the seat into the back row. The all white police Dodge Charger pulled up to the corner at the same time. Mtambo looked over to the officer and smiled.

The white officer knew from instinct that the black mothafucka driving the van was somehow connected to the disturbance. He had been on the force ten years and had learned to follow his instincts. He reached for his radio to call it in when the side door of the Caravan slid open. Instinctively, the officer reached for his service weapon. When the door fully opened and revealed what was behind it, his hand froze right on the weapon.

Just before the bullets went hunting for a target, the white officer shit his pants out of fear. Just as he knew the van was connected, instinctively he knew that he was about to die.

Scooter let off all seventy-five rounds that were in the clip, making sure to only aim at the driver's side windshield. The carnage that was left was unbelievable.

The amount of blood all over the front interior was proof of the kill. Scooter had been trained for guaranteed results. So, he calmly walked over to the car. After confirming his successful kill, he hustled back to the Caravan and they disappeared into the night while responding officers were zeroing in on the location.

**** **N. D.** ****

The loud sounds of a female being sexed good were coming out of the back room, down the hallway. She was moaning and screaming so loud it almost sounded like she was being attacked instead of fucked.

The trio made their way silently down the hallway to the back room. There were two other doors in the hallway, which they checked. From experience, they knew not to pass a door without knowing what was on the other side. Each room housed only a small child. They left the kids alone, safe in their beds.

When they got to the back room the first man opened the door. The other two followed the first man into the room. There was a Philippina woman riding the nigga they came for. She was riding him reverse cowgirl. Her eyes were shut tight, so she couldn't see the three niggaz staring at her massive breast as they knocked all over the place from the force of her bouncing up and down on his dick.

She grabbed one of her giant breasts, put it in her mouth and sucked on it. Then she started bouncing up and down even faster, they just watched. The two were waiting on a que from the first and he was patiently anticipating his next move in his head.

Finally, she climaxed, but she continued riding him until she opened her eyes and saw the intruders for the first time. She let out a scream until the first man pointed a big ass gun at her.

At the sound of her scream, Tut was startled and opened his eyes. The pussy was so good it made a mothafucka close his eyes and savor that shit. At the sight of the intruders, he realized that he'd fucked up. All he could think about was his babies. Considering Gunz and them didn't bother covering their faces, he knew his babies were dead and he was about to die.

Tut weighed his chances in his head. He knew against three niggaz he didn't stand a chance. He would've tried his luck against one mothafucka, but against three it was suicide. Finally, he figured he was going to die anyway so fuck it!

"I see you looking like you're getting ready to try something stupid. Before you do, let me talk to you." Gunz walked over to the left side of the bed so he could have a better view of Tuts hands.

"For what was done to mine, you're a dead man, no questions asked. But, you've got a chance to save your kids and ol' girl." Dok pointed at the woman still on top of Tut cowering away, silently crying.

"Be a man and face what you got coming. Get dressed and let's go. If you try some dumb shit, all of you are dying."

Tut had neva been the type of nigga to let somebody bitch him out or punk him, hearing that his sons were alive changed everything. He would gladly trade his life for theirs in a heartbeat! He didn't hesitate to tell his baby mama to get off of him.

While she sniffled and cried A.J., Big Rocc and Gunz all watched Tut get dressed. It had been Big Rocc that tracked him down. When Tut was finally fully dressed the reality of the situation smacked his baby mama in the face like a back hand from a pimp.

She jumped up letting the covers drop from her naked body. She didn't think about her exposure. She loved her baby daddy. Yeah, they fought and had their issues, but she loved him and couldn't accept losing him for good. No matter how much she held him and cried, it wasn't going to change anything and Tut knew it.

He gave her one long, deep kiss "Babe, I gotta go. I love you. We knew nothing lasts forever, so it is what it is." He wiped the tears off of her cheeks. "You know where the money at, so you and the boys gone be straight…"

"I don't want the money." She cried while shaking her head defiantly from side to side.

"I know…shh…I gotta go, blood." He kissed her one more time then pulled away. He headed towards the door. AJ was the first one out the room followed by Tut.

"What if she calls the police?" Big Rocc asked Gunz.

"Fuck the police! Let her call 'em." Gunz followed Tut out of the room and down the hallway.

They left Tuts kids sleep and his baby mama naked, crying miserably on the floor of the bedroom as they drove off.

**** N. D. ****
Fremont

Cantelope knew she was hearing shit. She hit the blunt again doing her best to try and digest the shit she was just told. Fresh off a flight from Tennessee she had just walked in the house when she received a call from French Tip telling her that she was on her way over.

When she got there, French Tip quickly filled Cantelope in on what was going on. After her confrontation with Clark, French Tip went and had a sit down with Dok where she learned everything.

"I'm not going to even lie to you, Frenchie, that's some real messed up shit" as she blew that smoke out she shook her head, "I can't tell you what to do on this one, cousin. But, no matter what you choose to do I'm rocking with you one hundred percent."

"Thanks girl. But that really ain't saying shit cause I don't know what the fuck I'm gone do." French Tip was just grateful that her cousin was there to listen to her. Since they were kids they had always been there for each other.

French Tip leaned over to ash her blunt inside the ash tray. It had been a while since she had smoked and this new shit Cantelope had wasn't no punk.

"Guuurl, I'm higher than a crack head on the first of the month." Cantelope burst out laughing at her cousin. "What the hell did you say this was?" French Tip felt like she wanted to fall down and float away.

"This that real white bitch, nigga! That Wonder Woman. I got some other shit too called Aurora Indica, it's smooth as hell and taste sweet." Cantelope wasn't in no mellow mood though. After what her cousin just told her, she was trying to take it there!

If nobody got a handle on this shit fast, it could potentially blow up big enough to destroy them all, one way or another.

"If it means anything, you know I'ma die hard loyalist. Neva Die is our family, but shit Clark is my Family! Flesh of my flesh and blood of my blood! I ain't trynna rock against that really. And you know the She-Wolves are loyal to us. They move how we move." French Tip already knew all of this, but hearing it made her feel so much better. She looked up to her big cousin tremendously and needed to know that she would have her back.

"What's your take on Nissa finding God?" French Tip tried to lighten the mood with the change of subject.

"I mean, hell, living the way we live, a mothafucka gotta find something eventually, either Heaven or Hell. Shit might as well be heaven. But, fuck that! What about her being with Pastor Juan? He's the one got her needing Jesus. Little, pretty mothafucka, must got that Holy Dick!" As French Tip erupted in laughter, Cantelope jumped up imitating one of the old ladies in church "Jesus! Oh! Jesus!" Her arms were spread out at sides with her head tilted backwards while she hooped and hollered.

The ringing of French Tip's cell phone spoiled the party. She dug the phone out of her MK bag and checked the caller id. Cantelope was still doing her antics when French Tip answered her cell. The laughter felt good.

All the laughter ceased, and her chocolate skin got darker as her face turned to stone. Cantelope saw the serious look on her face and instantly grew concerned.

Lady J was on the phone telling French Tip what just happened in East Palo Alto not too long ago.

"Hurry up, turn on the news!" She yelled at Cantelope while still listening to Lady J.

"Which one?" Cantelope rushed over to the island counter that the remote was sitting on.

"It don't matter." French Tip ended her call and waited eagerly for her cousin to get the news on. "We might be too late." Was all she said.

Finally, she found the correct channel and hey both watched the carnage from the mayhem in shocked silence. The segment was a full eleven minutes long. When it was over French Tip looked like she just walked in on her nigga fucking her best friend.

"What type of mothafuckas are we dealing with?" From the news report and what she saw. Cantelope knew these mothafuckas were on some next level, Black Ops type shit.

"I don't know, but the shit just hit the fan." French Tip leaned back and lit the half of blunt that had gone out.

Tomorrow would be a nightmare, but tonight she would enjoy what was left of her peace. Or at least that's what she thought.

**** N. D. ****
Earlier that day

The meeting was being convened in the conference room at the Federal Building in Downtown Oakland. The only people present in the room were those already in the loop and those who needed to know.

The meeting had been called to address the current crisis and wave of violence that has plagued the Bay Area. Chief Vieira of the Milpitas Police Department sat at the six o'clock position of the table. To her left was Special Agent Finnegan and sitting beside him was Agent Garcia. On the right side of Chief Vieira sat officer Hedgecock and Special Services Unit or SSU Lieutenant Wynn.

Special Agent in Charge Andreatta sat at the head of the table. Everyone was tired. Individually they all had been working very hard around the clock to try and find some type of lead that would bring an end to the chaos. Tired as they were ,this was the job and they'd all signed up for it. What they didn't know was things were only beginning.

Special Agent in charge Andreatta slowly stood up to address the room.

"Everyone knows why we are here, so I'll skip the formalities and get right to the heart of the problem. Approximately eight months ago law enforcement officers and personnel either started coming up missing or were murdered. Chief Vieira's department is credited for the diligence that ultimately paid off in providing us with the identity of the suspect."

"We now know that a one, Levell Benjamin Jenkins aka Batman is the primary suspect in the disappearances and homicides. A joint effort on behalf of Chief Vieira's department as well as our own, to bring him in, unfortunately resulted in a failed attempt at bringing the suspect to justice. Our efforts will not be in vain. We will get our man. The bureau is working on leads that will give us the suspects current location. Briefing on that will commence immediately following this meeting." She used this break in her briefing to take a drink from the Voss water she had sitting on the table.

Chief Vieira sat patiently waiting for the ball to drop. She was already well aware of everything that had just been said because it was her guys who had made all the process. There had to be more or something new in the case for her to be present. Patiently waiting through all the jibber-jabber was easy for her because her mind was half on La'Mont.

She hadn't even realized that she had dazed off in thought, until Agent Andreatta begin talking again.

"Shortly after our original events, Officer Hedgecock you somehow found your way with front row seats to a shoot out involving two rival gangs. An up and coming gang, calling themselves Young Nigga Mafia waged war on the reigning power, the Neva Die Dragon Gang. Sometime before our shoot out, your police work put you right smack in the middle of the shoot out.

Not only did it land you in the shoot out but unbeknownst to you, you stumbled across an open FBI and SSU investigation. It was the bureau that convinced Lead District Attorney to drop the murder charges against La'Mont Simpson in the interest of justice." Chief Vieira was surprised to hear this but she neva let on.

"This brings us to our next guest whom I'm sure you are all interested in. Ladies and gentlemen, I turn the floor over to Special Security Unit's Lieutenant Christine Wynn." Special Agent in charge Adreatta took her seat.

"Thank you, SSA Andreatta. Ladies and gentlemen, I'm sure that most if not all of you have neva heard of the SSU. So, I'll open by telling you just what SSU is."

"The Special Services Unit or SSU is a federal liaison unit of the California Department of Corrections. It was created in the seventies as a means and way to counter the criminal activities of the prison gangs and organizations. Over the years there have been numerous gangs created on the yards of California's prisons. However, one group in particular grew and evolved so much over the years that a great deal of our time and efforts were focused on them."

"The group in question is the Black Guerilla Family. They began as a group of rough hooligans who pirated the prison yards. They were involved in everything from robbery and extortion to murder for hire. But under the guidance of George Lester Jackson they became educated, motivated and organized. The teachings of Mr. Jackson and a few others gave birth to the New African Revolutionary Nationalist." Finally, she stood up and walked towards a video projector.

"Ladies and gentlemen do not be misunderstood, these are not your typical urban, ghetto gangsters. These are highly sophisticated a committed people to their cause. A cause that quite simply is the overthrowing of the united states government. They are very well trained in military principals and tactics."

This right here," the lens on the projector clicked once she pressed a button on the adjacent Apple notebook. A picture of a gentleman appeared on the wall. "Is Darrell Haynee aka Dok Holliday. He's from Berkeley, California. In his early 20's he was sentenced to twenty years for murder for hire. It is our belief that it was actually a sanctioned execution ordered by the higher ups that went wrong."

"During his twenty-year stint Mr. Haynee is suspected of leaving a trail of bodies all over California. Needless to say, our shining young revolutionary slash killer rose through the ranks. Going from enforcer to leader of the most powerful and dangerous domestic terrorist organization our nation has ever seen. The agency has been watching not only him but a list of his associates and comrades."

"The late Thomas "T'Rida" Smith, La'Mont D. Simpson, Dwayne "DJ" Wilson..." Chief Vieria no longer heard anything else. The revelation of La'Mont being connected to such a dangerous organization hit her right in the face.

Chief Vieira had heard of the notorious Black Guerilla Family. They were often called B.G.F. or Jamaa which was Swahili for Family. The few she'd come across or heard of were indeed dangerous. They were very well disciplined, quiet and secretive. Yet they were connected or charged with being connected to some very heinous crimes.

"…which brings us to Neva Die and our current wave of violence. We believe internal strife has caused a split and a civil war is brewing" Lieutenant Wynn turned towards the room to see if everyone was following her.

"Uh, excuse me. What is the connection with this Organization and our serial killer?" Hedgecock took her momentary paused to ease what was on his mind.

"Yes, well Mr. Levell Jenkins, our serial killer just happens to be E.G.U. ,which stands for Elite Guerilla Unit. It is a highly trained special forces within the organization. He and Mr. Simpson or Jason Voorheeze as he is known, were both apart of the same cadre which is an individualized cell operating independently of the group but still within the group.

"Jason Voorheeze was the commanding officer and Jenkins was his first lieutenant. Hence the name, Batman and Robin was given to the two of them. Their combined suspected body count is more than Dommer, Manson, Tim McVey and Zeno Kowinski all combined. After a botched attempt on a wealthy, racist, Texas oil baron running for State Senate, the cadre was disassembled. Robin ended up in prison on a drug trafficking charge and Batman simply disappeared."

"We suspect Simpson tracked down Jenkins and together they decided to rebirth their old antics by waging war on the police in retaliation of one of their fallen comrades, T'Rida ,Thomas Smith."

The room was silent. Aside from the Bureau, no-one knew what to expect from the meeting. They damn sure weren't expecting this.

Special Agent Andreatta took her cue "Our proposal is simple. We step up surveillance to extend to every member of the organization including the ex-members that have split off. Eventually, someone in the organization will lead us to Mr. Batman."

Chapter XVII

San Leandro, California

When Tut came to his body was shaking involuntary from the cold. He was stripped butt-ass naked and hanging from a steel plumbing pipe that was thirty-four inches in diameter with an old rusted chain that was bound tightly around his hands and wrist.

Aches and pains shot through his body like aftershocks on miniature fault lines after a major earthquake. Or like the spidery cracks that form on a damaged egg shell. His lips had two different gashes in them. One of his eyes was swollen shut. The other had a gash above it.

He had no clue how long he had been there, but he knew it was a few days at least. He could only imagine that he had passed out again from the excruciating pain caused by what they were doing to him. His head felt like it was in a vice grip, pressure compounded, ready to burst from the many blows to it with the brass knuckles.

Tut was a true gangsta through and through! He was the epitome of Blood Gang, the finest product of the Piru nation. Though he was indeed Blood Gang, anybody claiming red period, would be proud of him cause bitch was not in his blood!

He looked around as best he could, trying to find a means of escape out of the cold, dark room. Best he could tell, he was in some type of large freezer or meat locker. His head pounded as he strained for a look, yet still he tried.

A light scrape from behind him caught his attention. He hadn't sensed a presence in the room before, but he knew someone was behind him. The faint scraping sound was barely audible, but he had heard it.

"I'll give it to your fat ass, you got heart and I respect that. But I promised you, blood, I'll either break you or you'll break.

"The emphasis that Gunz put on the word blood was evidence that he was taunting Tut.

Tut didn't know it, but four of his ribs were already broken. Still, after two beatings he hadn't uttered a sound.

Gunz walked from behind Tut so he could face him. His shirt was off and even though they were in an industrial meat storage container, his torso was completely covered in sweat from exertion. The beatings had been literal. Gunz had used his two fists to pummel Tut, at least up until now.

In his hands Gunz was holding a 2ft long steel sailors pipe wrench. The menacing tool had the desired effect on Tut. He tried not to let it show, but fear engulfed his entire body like fog. There was no mistaking the damage it could cause.

"This shit is real simple, cuzzo. You didn't give my baby an option but I'm giving you one. Where Clark lay his head?" When Tut didn't respond, Gunz lifted the massive wrench onto his shoulder.

Tut didn't know what to think. Time slowed down, and it felt like his senses were heightened. He could hear a trickle of water off in the distance from a leaky pipe. He tried to take a deep breath and winced from the pain of the broken ribs.

Before he knew it, a blinding white light expanded in his head as pain like he had neva felt before originated in his left leg and soared through his body to his brain.

Even if Gunz wouldn't have swung the pipe wrench with all of his might, it would've done damage. As it was the moment the bulky metal collided with his thigh, the bone snapped like a bread stick.

Tut bit down so hard on his bottom lip to keep from crying out, that a fresh stream of blood flowed from it.

"Damn, nigga! You's a tough mothafucka. Not one peep huh?"

Gunz swung the pipe wrench back to his shoulder again "let's just see what the fuck we can do about that."

Without hesitation he swung the pipe wrench like a professional baseball player, level and strong. This time it was inevitable. He connected on the same side that Tut had the four broken ribs. The rest gave away like a house made out of a deck of cards blown over. Tut let out a bone shattering, deep animalistic roar! The pain caused by all his ribs breaking simultaneously was like none other.

"That's what I'm talking about! Bitch you came into my castle and violated my Queen!" He swung again. This time he connected to the other side of Tuts upper torso. No sound emitted from his mouth this time for Tut simply blacked out.

The bucket of ice-cold water splashed in his face brought Tut back to consciousness. His body was beyond pain. So much so that he could no longer feel the pain. Gunz had put the pipe wrench down and used Tuts broken body for a punching bag. Nothing on earth ever felt so excruciating. This was the fourth time Gunz had woke him back up.

Tut could barely see. Both eyes were swollen beyond vision, but he could just barely make out Gunz' silhouette with the glock .47 in his hand.

"Had y'all succeeded in killing my Queen, your torment and pain would be ongoing. But she's alive. I won't be able to say the same for you though." Gunz raised his hand ready to blow this niggaz' head off.

Tut was straining with every ounce of his soul to say something. His lungs couldn't suck in enough air to talk. Gunz lowered the gun in humor to see what the nigga would say.

"B-Bl-Blood..." just to talk felt like he had gotten hit by a Mack Truck. Gunz waited.

"B-Blood Gang, C-Street B-Bitch!" He laughed maniacally. Fuck the pain it was worth it to see the look on Gunz face.

He didn't hesitate to put five slugs into Tut's swollen head. It burst like a piñata.

Silently Gunz was happy Tut didn't bitch out. He had always respected the little niggaz gangsta. It's too bad Clark split the family they could've been a dynasty.

**** N. D. ****

San Jose

"No, she really is a nice girl. He brought her by here the other day, so I could meet her." Mama B was on the phone with one of her sisters just gossiping away.

"Tell me B, is she cute?" Her sister asked feeding into the gossiping.

"Huh, cute doesn't begin to describe it. Girl, she is gorgeous! With that kind of body you got to workout ten hours a day to get it." Mama B pictured the girl in her head then added, "I'm telling you that girl has got the biggest ass I have ever seen!"

"How you gone say that Bernie, when you got that big ol' booty you got."

"Shit, compared to her, my booty is flat as an ironing board. "Her sister started cracking up laughing. Growing up mama B, always got teased about how big her butt was. For her to tell her sister that, the girls butt must have been outrageous.

"I'm telling you girl and she has the sweetest name…" just then there was a knock at the door "Hold on girl, someone's at my door."

Even though she was going to look in the peephole, Mama B still yelled out who is it. Her eyes confirmed what she had heard.

The UPS delivery man was standing in front of her door with his all brown shorts suit on. She disengaged her alarm then opened the door.

"Afternoon Ma'am. I have a package for Ms. B." The little fat brotha barely stated. He was out of breath from climbing up the three flights of stairs. She signed for the box then accepted.

Would you like a bottle of water, honey?" He nodded his head yes looking like she asked if he wanted a million dollars.

After she closed the door, she walked and sat the box on her dining room table.

"Girl shut up. Somebody done sent me a nice big ol' box." She told her sister as she retrieved a bottle of crystal geyser out of the refrigerator.

"What is it?"

"I don't know, I'm giving the man a water first."

"Well, who is it from?" Her sister needed to know something, the suspense was killing her.

"I didn't look. Shit, all I did was sign for it, so he could gimme my shit. I only offered him a water cause it looked like his fat ass was gone drop dead on my doorstep." They both laughed at that.

She cut through the tape with a pair of scissors. She moved some of the popcorn filler out of the way then stuck her hands in and picked up what was in the box. She thought it was odd that it was circular and cold. Once it came out the box and she realized what it was. She dropped it and screamed at the top of her lungs. She screamed for so long that her sister began to worry. It was a full five minutes before she was able to pick up the phone and tell her sister that she would have to call her back. Even though she could hear her sister yelling in the background wanting to know what was wrong, she didn't bother answering. Right then she needed to make a call!

Forty-eight minutes later a pounding came on the door. She didn't bother asking who it was or looking through the peephole. She opened the door and let her first-born in. Clark rushed right to her and took his mother into his arms.

Feeling the warmth and security of her baby's embrace, she broke down like a little girl. As all the fear she'd been holding back was finally let go. The tears rocked her body as Clark held her firmly in his embrace. As she cried he guided her into the apartment.

He felt bad. His heart was heavy because he knew that the responsibility was his. He didn't know how mothafuckas found her address, but unmistakably the package was meant for him.

"Mama, where's it at?" He didn't want to seem uncompassionate, but he had business to attend to. He had to get rid of it. It couldn't be found here.

Mama B just cried and pointed over to her dining room table. He let her go and walked over to the table. The box was sitting alone atop the table with it's flaps open. Mama B hadn't bothered trying to close it back. Clark looked inside the box and then removed the contents. Anger boiled through his blood as rage shot through his body. He knew he needed to control his composure for the sake of his mom.

He held in his hands the lifeless decapitated head of Tut, whose eyes were still wide open. Also, in the box were both of his severed hands. The message was sent, and it was loud and clear! They could be touched too!

Clark pulled out his phone and dialed a number. "Get up here" was all he said.

Moments later there was another knock on the door. Clark walked over and let Man Man in. He pointed to the box and told Man Man to get rid of it. Man Man didn't hesitate in doing what was told to him.

Tut's baby mama called Clark that night after Gunz and them had taken him. He did as much damage control as he could but in the end, he wouldn't sugar coat it. He told her to go buy a new black dress. It was only a matter of time before the evidence of his prediction surfaced.

If things couldn't get any more fucked up, French Tip came through the front door.

"Oh, Mami." Mama B left out of her sons arms and into her daughters. Clark may have been the first born, but French Tip was her only daughter, her baby girl.

Clark didn't feel like being in the same room as his sister. It was her people that were fucking with his. She was a traitor in his eyes. Lines were crossed, and sides chosen, and she had picked the wrong side.

French Tip looked over at Clark, "Who was it?" She asked. (She was on her way to the hospital to see Voorheeze when her mother had called her).

Who was it? Like she gives a fuck! He thought to himself. He had to be the bigger person for his mom.

"It was Tut." Their cousin. His second in command. They hadn't touched a foot soldier, they got his second in command. Not to mention the cook house.

French Tip's mind was racing, she had too much going on. She didn't even think before she spoke. "I tried to tell you to dead it." The moment she spoke she realized her mistake.

Mama B tensed up at her baby girls' words. She broke away from her daughters' arms.

"What you mean you tried to tell him?" Mama B's head swiveled back and forth between her two children. "Clark, what is she talking about?"

Clark just stood there glaring at his sister wanting to punch her right in her big mouth.

When she realized he wouldn't speak, Mama B yelled out "God damn it! I'm you guy's mother! What the hell do you got going on?" She looked over at French Tip and the tears started falling again.

"It's nothing mami, I was just talking." She hated to see her mother cry.

"You know what, I'm sixty-three years old. I can't take this shit no more. I'm tired! I've done it all and I'm tired. Both of you need to get out." Her tears had miraculously dried up.

They both felt bad. Clark felt the worst. He tried to walk over to his mother and give her a hug.

"Get out!!" She yelled at the top of her lungs while pointing at the door. "Get the hell out of my house!"

**** **N. D.** ****

Lt. Urena sat nervously in his car fidgeting with his fingers, shakily he reached for another piece of gum and popped it in his mouth. He was trying to take the edge off.

When Gunz came around the back of the abandoned warehouse, Lt. Urena grew a little relaxed but he was still a nervous wreck. It didn't make matters any better when he saw that Gunz wasn't alone. Urena climbed out of his truck which was recovered from the town house Batman was using.

"I thought we agreed that no-one would ever accompany us at any of these meetings?" Urena didn't even let Gunz fully climb out of the Infinity truck.

A.J. and Big Rocc were sitting in the truck along with D.J. Gunz waved the question off. Shit was way too crazy for him to be riding anywhere solo right now.

"Look, shit's kind of hot right now. So, my niggaz move when I move and where I move. Tell me what's so urgent that you insisted on us meeting right now?" The nervousness and worry on Urena's face didn't bother Gunz. The crooked pig was probably worried because somebody had gotten hip to him.

Urena looked around for a minute. He could feel eyes on him. He's been a cop too long not to know the feeling.

"Somebody's watching us." He told a nonchalant Gunz' who laughed at him. "Look, I'm telling you somebody is watching us."

"Shit, they done seen us now. If they're coming, let 'em come. Until they do, why don't you start talking." Gunz didn't have time for no paranoid shit. Hell, he had shit to do.

Urena looked around one more time. Then, he looked at Gunz with a puzzled look as if he had neva seen him before.

"Shit's about to get just a little hotter, homie." Urena told him before he went on to explain to him everything the Captain had briefed all of the department on a few hours ago regarding her meeting with the FBI and the SSU.

It took about ten minutes for him to tell Gunz everything. When Urena was finished, he was surprised Gunz stood before

214

him like he didn't just get told that not one, but two federal agencies were investigating and potentially hunting them.

"Are you just going to stand there? You're not going to say nothing!" Urena couldn't understand it. He, himself would be shitting bricks if he had been told what he told Gunz.

"Fuck I'm supposed to say? Mothafucka, you still the police! I ain't about to say shit to you." Gunz reached into his pockets to retrieve two fat envelopes and handed them to Urena. "Except your salary just doubled, so you better keep us ahead of the curve."

Gunz turned around and walked back to the truck. He had felt the same thing that Urena felt. Someone was watching them. But, he figured if it was some niggaz, they would've come lighting shit up. He knew that meant it was the police or the feds. Since a nigga couldn't get in trouble talking, he figured they were there for the lieutenant. More reason to learn what he had wanted to tell him.

When he climbed into the truck he was behind tinted windows. For the first time he looked around. He knew he was wasting his time. If it was the feds they'd be using some of the best binoculars there was.

"Drive around awhile. We had unwanted guests at this meeting, so I wanna make sure ain't nobody following us." He instructed as he reached for one of the blunts that were already rolled in the ashtray.

"Aight, brah brah." A.J. knew the routine. If a mothafucka was following, them he would be dizzy by the time A.J. finished taking them on turns, curves and circles.

"You think it's some funk or them people?" Big Rocc asked Gunz while looking at him through the rear view.

In response, Gunz told them everything that was just told to him.

**** N. D. ****
War Room

The room was quiet. Everyone sat around the table, lost in a thousand thoughts, trying to decipher and digest what they were just told.

Murda and Styles, T'Rida's first and second in command were busy analyzing the situation and weighing out options. Gunz looked over at Cantelope and French Tip. True, they had been there from the jump, but Clark was their blood. Because of that, he didn't trust them. He hadn't wanted them present at all, but the She-Wolves only listened to them. With that being the case, Dok insisted on their presence. Gunz let his hand trace over his Desert Eagle just for reassurances.

"Look, I know that I know my niggaz well enough that I can speak for us without question. We don't give a fuck about da police, State of Federal. My nigga we rock one-man nuke, but we ride till da wheels fall off. Wolf Pack ain't scared of shit." Finally, Stone Cold spoke up breaking the silence and getting everybody's attention

Next to him, Johnny Spitz just sat nodding his head in agreement. At first, he wasn't going to talk, there was no need. Johnny Spitz didn't talk. His .50 cal talked for him. But, he figured this shit needed to be solidified.

"Rogue, when niggaz signed up to smack shit, mothafuckas ain't make no exception foe the police. Dem mothafuckas can get it, too! Matter of fact, nigga , anybody can get it!"

"The question ain't do we fuck wit it still or not. The question is, how do we go about doing it from here?" There was neva a question of whether. would be there with his big cousin or not. He would follow Gunz to hell and back. His team of wolves would do the same thing.

"What about you two? Y'all awfully quiet over there." Everyone followed his gaze over to French Tip and Cantelope, who were sitting there looking like they were waiting for their laundry to dry.

"That's because there ain't shit to talk about. You lead, and we'll follow." the smile on French Tips face and soothing tone of her voice were a contradiction to the fire blazing behind her pupils.

"Just like that?" Gunz was thrown off by her comment, he had expected her to go against him.

A confrontation of some sort was bound to happen. It was expected. Everyone just sat or stood back and let it unfold. "One thing you ain't got to question or worry about is my loyalty. You, T'Rida and my brother started this. I pledged allegiance and loyalty to this and to you three. Regardless of what's going on now, that pledge supersedes it. You have my loyalty as long as you don't cross the line." She leaned forward, placing her elbows on the table so Gunz could get a better look at her before she said the rest.

"Tut knew the rules of the game just like we know them. That's just how it is. Believe me, somebody will answer for that shit that y'all did to my mother! Other than that, we're good."

Dok took that as his que to step in. Some progress was better than none. He didn't know what transpired with her mother, but he would find out. Judging from the look the sistah was giving Gunz, Dok sure didn't want to be the one who did whatever it was when she came to collect that debt.

"Everyone's sentiments and potions are appreciated and understood. But this is not a test of loyalty and honor. Nor is this something that any of you need to feel the need to stand up for.

My organization and family have one struggle and that is the plight of our people, One Aim. That's the liberation of any and all Afrikans from the concentration camps throughout the United States.

And we only have One Goal and that's over throw the United States fascists government. This is a fight that has been going on since our people were kidnapped and brought to this God forsaken country. But, the war of the new Afrikan Revolutionaries has been waging since the seventies."

"We are not the terrorist or communist that they label us. Although, we do believe in some of the same theories and ideological practices of the late Chinese Communist Revolution up under chairman Mao-Tse Tung. We are the Black underclass of America.

We are the chosen ones to be a part of the New Afrikan Revolutionary Army, fighting to install and bring to power the New Afrikan Democratic Revolution. A government of the people, for the people and by the people." Dok looked over at his two sons with admiration and pride. They had grown into two fine young men.

He pointed at them and continued addressing the group.

"To understand our struggle is to understand us. We were bred to do what we do with an understanding that our very own life sentence inside of one of these concentration camps or even death in our struggle is our end..."

Stone Cold cut him off, "And what do you think we got to look forward to, a white house with a picket fence?"

"I do not aim to ridicule you, my young brother. I only point out that we've taken an oath of death for what we believe in. Most of you signed on to Neva Die knowing that death was a possibility, but the number one motivator was money. Money for whatever reason and I respect that. Before I became a revolutionary, I was a street nigga too.

"I'm sure that by now you guys have accumulated fortunes. If you wanted to walk away and live life, you could with that right now. Even if we wanted to, we don't have that luxury. For us, money is only a tool to aid us in the war and we will fight until the battle is won or until we die." Dok continued to make an excuse for them.

No one in the room looked phased by Dok's address. A few did hone looks of respect. To most of them, the Black Guerilla Family was just some old prison gang. Mostly made up of old washed up dope fiends. The streets didn't talk about the B.G.F. in admirable terms.

The thing that Dok was overlooking was the fact that before the birth of Neva Die, most of these niggaz didn't have a hope in life, let alone a future. They were bastards of the ghetto that the world turned their back on and forgot about. Fucking with Neva Die, they'd become somebody. They became legends! This was their family. This was all they knew.

"Ain't no sense debating what it is and what it ain't. We already know what it is. It's Neva Die! The only question is how are we about to go about doing this? Cause WE…" Gunz emphasized by swinging his arms around the room, "gone do this!"

**** N. D. ****

Chapter XVIII

Union Landing Square, Union City

It was taking the bartender a little too long to bring their drinks, but it was understandable because the place was packed. The start of pre-season had just begun, and the football fanatics were clearly enjoying themselves.

The bartender finally arrived with their drinks. Once he placed each drink in front of the right person, he went to fill the next order and they picked up their glasses. "I'd like to make a toast." SA Finnegan stated as he held his glass of Samuel Adams in his right hand. "To a wonderful start to an investigation. To a good partner and a hell of a boss."

"Yeah! Yeah! Yeah! Kissing my ass Finnegan isn't going to get you anywhere anytime soon." S.A.C. Andreatta joked as she elbowed Finnegan in the side. Then she re-raised her glass in salute "Here's to losing a bet and paying up without a hassle."

"Oooh!" S.A. Garcia teasingly instigated.

"Hold up! Hold up!" Finnegan raised his hands in mock surrender.

"Come on Finnegan you know you take forever to pay your bets." Andreatta jabbed at him.

"Yeah, but at least I pay. A mans got to take time to make sure that everything was on the up and up." Finnegan finally dropped his other hand while defending his actions.

"More like wait until you get some more money after taking care of all your ladies. Salute!" All three held their glasses in salute then took a drink after Andreatta's stab at him.

After she took her drink she did her famous Tommy Lee Jones impersonation. "Neva doubt the big dog…" Garcia and Finnegan both joined in "Cause the big dog is always right."

It was a bit from the movie U.S. Marshalls, which was Andreatta's favorite movie. Secretly, she had a crush on Tommy Lee Jones, but she would neva admit it. Unbeknownst to her, everybody already knew. When she wasn't around, everyone would jokingly refer to her as S.A.C. Andreatta Jones.

"Yeah, big dog you're always right." Finnegan reluctantly admitted. It was all in fun, but he still hated being wrong.

When the Director assigned the case to them, the first thing Andreatta told them was there had to be a dirty cop, maybe even two. Finnegan didn't see it. He thought she was grasping at straws. Like so often the two made their normal bet. Loser buys the first two rounds. Garcia was the smart one. He always stayed out of it and let the two of them bet. He got free drinks out of the deal either way,

The three sat and discussed their game plan and what they were planning to do with the information they had learned. Considering the threat to security, they were given lead way with working this case. Going a little off book was okay if it brought results.

Andreatta had made the call not only to bug every service vehicle and personal vehicle of everyone with ties to the case. She also tapped their phones and placed high tech GPS tracking on their vehicles as well.

It wasn't long before someone monitoring the wire taps inside of the Tech Department intercepted a call from an unidentified man and Lt. Urena discussing sensitive information.

Andreatta's unit quickly deployed and set up a triangular tail on Lt. Urena. Not even two hours after the tail was in place, Urena lead them to an abandoned warehouse in the back of San Leandro.

With the long-range digital audio receivers, they were able to hear the entire conversation between Lt. Urena and the black man that got out of the truck. Even though they were positioned roughly a mile and a half away, the conversation came across loud and clear as if they were only a few feet away from the conversation.

Whoever the guy was, Andreatta assumed he was very smart. Nothing in the conversation was ever incriminating towards him. That was coupled with the fact that although he didn't let one that he thought someone was there watching them. His driver sure did drive evasively enough to lose the tail that was on them.

"The best course of action for us at this point will be to assign a constant surveillance detail on the Lieutenant. In lieu of the facts that we have thus far, I would say it's only a matter of time before he slips and leads us somewhere we would otherwise not have gone.

Meanwhile we continue hitting the grind and do what it is we do best. This Neva Die fiasco, I guarantee you it's dirty. I don't buy the community services, group homes or anything else they are doing. It's all a cover-up. I guarantee." Even with two martinis already down in her system, Andrea was still alert and sharp as a tack.

At thirty-eight years old, saying that she was attractive would be an understatement. Andrea was flat out gorgeous. She was five foot six, one hundred twenty pounds. She was very athletic. Her B-cup breast sat high and perky and her auburn hair was midway down her back with blonde highlights. To top it off, she had the perfect, little round ass.

Her strong mind was still by far her greatest attribute. Which is why there was a strong rumor going around the Bureau that she was next in line for the Assistant Director spot due to open at the beginning of next year.

"Should we keep surveillance strictly on Darrell and his two sons or do you want us to mobilize more units and expand surveillance to cover some of the lesser subjects?" Garcia's question was a good one indeed. They didn't want to waste manpower.

"Let's break into three mobilized recon and surveillance only units. We will target the upper echelon of this organization. Remember, that we survey only unless instructed or at the point of hostile engagement.

Our primary objective is still the cop killer, though we will aid and assist as much as needed. The terrorist theory and component are the burden of the SSU. Unless said threat is deemed real and active." Andrea still didn't' know yet if she was convinced that Levell Jenkins was linked to the Black Guerilla Family and if he was, did that mean the organization was backing his play or was this a solitary mission. Time would reveal all though.

**** N. D. ****
Dublin, California

The Dublin Police Department was busy with movement. It was a little after three p.m. which meant it was shift exchange. No-one paid any attention to the older black man sitting in the lobby. His respectable, but badly worn-down attire and his slouched over, beat down posture spoke of an honest man finally worn down by the heavy ills of life. Ills that were undoubtedly made worst by the fact that he was born a black man.

He'd already been sitting in the lobby nearly thirty minutes before he made his way up to the clerks desk.

The officer of the day was an elderly, grumpy white Sergeant. He'd long ago been taken off of the streets for his continued racial antics, Internal Affairs investigations and the numerous write-ups for insubordination. After twenty-eight years he was now actually two days from retirement. In his mind this God forsaken job and his idiotic superiors could kiss his wrinkled old white ass.

"Excuse me officer…" the elder gentleman begun

"That's Sergeant, boy! Don't you see these stripes on my damn uniform?" The racist sergeant interrupted.

"Ah, oh, oh. Yes, I'm so sorry, sir. Ah, Sergeant, my grandson Freddie Gray was brought in here I don't know what for, that boy never bothers a soul. But, anyhow, he was brought in here. I've been waiting on him, but he hasn't come out yet." The old man spoke while shaking his head.

The sergeant smiled at seeing the mental anguish taking its toll on the old nigger. He thought to himself that the old niggerz grandpa was probably a cotton picker.

"Boy, what chu mean you waiting on him?" He squinched up his nose from the acrid smell of the silent fart he let out. The egg and sardine sandwich tasted good, but it was a deadly combination on his stomach. Especially, given the cheese and sauerkraut he added on it.

"I posted his bond with that company. That one with the logo of the white man on it." The old timer was desperately trying to remember the name.

"Oh well, you old fool. If you posted his bond that means he was already processed and is over at Santa Rita. Your ass is supposed to pick him up there, you old dupe." The Sergeant was really having a good time now.

"Santa Rita?" He looked confused and lost. "W-where's that at?"

"It's in Dublin, now get on out of here. I ain't a map stand, and yo kind can't be taking up all my time." The Sergeant went back to doing what he was doing before he finished talking. He couldn't waste time on some colored, he was looking at porn on the computer.

The old man shuffled his way out of the precinct and down the street to his waiting car.

Five minutes after the old man bothered the Sergeant, one of the deputies called the desk Sergeant. Something about an old briefcase that was left on the ground next to one of the chairs. The Sergeant figured it belonged to the old timer given the condition of the case and the old timer.

Laughing to himself, the sergeant instructed the officer to put the case in the storage closet next to his desk where the lost and found was. He was amused at the thought of the old nigger having to come all the way back over here just to pick up the case. What a hell of a day the little old nigger was having. The sergeant decided that he would make his day even worse by feigning like he couldn't find the case for a while.

"Well I'm sorry to tell you, Mr. Nigger…" Those hateful ugly words would be the last words that the fat racist cop would ever mumble.

Just a couple days away from retirement.

**** **N. D.** ****

Two blocks away from the Dublin Police Department, Batman stopped for the red light. He pulled the little small device from his pocket and smiled.

"I neva knew you, Freddy. But I honor you, young brotha." With a sincere smile on his face, Batman's head was looking up towards Heaven.

He looked at the Electric Remote Detonator in his hand. Just as the traffic light turned green, he pushed the button. In the rear-view mirror, he watched as two blocks back the Dublin Police Department blew sky high. As debris, rubble and body parts rained down on drivers and nearby pedestrians, Batman drove off with a smile on his face a lot bigger.

Hopefully, he thought Freddie Gray would be looking down from Heaven smiling. Batman wasn't in Baltimore, MD on April 19, 2015 when the police kidnapped Freddie and took him on a prolonged ride, shackled and handcuffed to the floor of the van while they savagely beat him to death. He knew if he had been there things would have gone completely different and the young brotha would be alive.

The burden of a vanguard is a heavy one and Batman continued to carry it as he drove the Chrysler 200 down Main St. disguised as a sixty-three-year-old man with old run-down clothes.

**** **N. D.** ****

"Thank you for taking me, Daddy." Little Olivia told her father as she gave him a great big ol' hug and a kiss.

The two were just getting in from Daddy Daughter Day. Today was Special Agent Finnegan's day off. One of his rare, but much needed days off. As always, he began every day with his little eight-year-old angel, Olivia. It was their Daddy Daughter Day.

S.A. Finnegan was a lot of things. At the top of the list he was awesome father. His wife of fourteen years passed away giving birth to Olivia. It took him years to get over the loss of his wife. When he did, he decided to just date rather then to get in a serious relationship again. His wife's death nearly destroyed him. Olivia was the only thing that kept him together. For her, he bounced out of the slump that he was in.

Though he was not quite the ladies' man, Finnegan neva brought his lady friends around Olivia. Susan was the only woman to come around Olivia. Susan has been little Olivia's nanny all her life. The three of them were more like family, they were so close.

"Susan! Susan! Guess what me and daddy did!" Olivia bolted through the door, the aroma of roasted lamb chops, wild rice and garlic asparagus wafted to his nose. Just as he began to call out to Susan, his work cell phone began to ring.

Reaching into his pocket, he retrieved it and answered without bothering to look at the caller I.D., "Finnegan."

"Level 1 crisis, you need to head over to Dublin A.S.A.P." It was SAC Andreatta. She was neva for the pleasantries, just straight to the topic.

"Do I dare ask what happen?" Finneagan asked as he was heading towards the den, so he could put his personal weapon up and grab his service weapon.

"Our guy struck again and this time he's made a statement." Was her response.

"A statement?" Finnegan couldn't imagine a bigger statement than killing police officers.

"He's blown up the Dublin Police Department!"

"Garcia and I are already headed to the scene. Get there as soon as you can. Lord knows it's going to be a circus."

"I'm on my way!" He couldn't believe his ears. A police station? These damn assholes were getting more brazed each day.

He rushed into the kitchen to break the news to Susan that he would be missing dinner. Briefly he told her what was going on and asked that she inform Olivia about dinner. She would be crushed, but she understood that her daddy was a Super Hero who fought the bad guys. She was proud of him.

Even with his emergency lights on and driving like a bat out of hell, i still took S.A. Finnegan over an hour to finally reach the crime scene. When he, did the block looked like a disaster relief zone. The surrounding buildings on either side of the police station were halfway blown apart. The station itself was all but decimated. The entire front of the structure was gone, along with two-thirds of the roof. Finnegan noticed pylon markers all over the street. He could only imagine that they were marking body parts.

A nostalgic feeling rushed over him as he finally found somewhere to park and made his way to find Andreatta and Garcia. At five foot six, fair skin and natural reddish hair, Finnegan looked more like a movie star with his boyish looks, than a police officer. Surely, he didn't resemble an officer of the Federal Bureau of Investigations. He was normally stopped and harassed at crime scenes when he tried to enter. Everyone was so busy today, no-one paid him too much attention. The badge handing on his neck that everyone saw at a glance was good enough for them.

Garcia and Andreatta were found in what used to be the lobby, talking to one of the bomb experts and the head forensic analyst. Noticing their gear Finnegan quickly backed out of the area. Whenever you saw the chemical suites and one-way breathing masks, he knew to back the fuck up quick and asked no questions.

Fifty feet back, he figured would be a safe distance considering there was no wind blowing. For safe measure he backed up ten more feet. Looking around he felt like he had teleported to the remains of a warzone. Finnegan was lost in his thoughts for seven or eight minutes before Andreatta and Garcia came walking over in his direction.

She took the breathing mask off her face and let out a nice, "Wheew!" Even in a full containment chem suit she looked sexy.

"What do we got Big Dawg?" Finnegan was looking for the specifics not the logistics.

"A real shit storm! That's what we got." She scratched the top of her head wondering where to begin.

"You can say that again." Garcia came to the Bureau after the Marine Corps. He had seen action overseas, so he was used to destruction. He just wasn't used to seeing it at home.

"For starters we have what you could only be some type of explosive component. Probably a portable bomb either on a timer or a remote detonator of some kind. Problem is, given the circumference of the blast radius, the explosive guys are wondering if we have some type of mutant bomb. Which I just learned means when you have a bomb made of separate components and ingredients, like C-4 and nitro mixed together.

"Unfortunately, we don't have any survivors. So far, the body count is at 94, but it is expected to continue to rise. The son of a bitch set the explosive right in the middle of shift change. That means we could be potentially looking at the death of nearly two hundred plus officers. Any surveillance we may have had in the area was destroyed in the blast. But, considering this is Dublin , there weren't many surveillance cameras to begin with. The only thing that they have somewhat of an idea on at the moment is a general location of where the devise was set off at. It appears to be off to the left of the Desk Sergeants desk. The specs on the building shows some type of storage closet there.

All things considered, the agency is coming to handle the investigation. I don't know who's getting assigned just yet, but no matter, we will work our own independent investigation since this is tied to our other investigation…" She was cut off by a young agent running up to them.

"Special Agent Andreatta, Deputy Director Mota is on the phone for you." The young agent whose name was Purtle was out of breath from running a full block with the cell phone.

Andreatta took the cell phone from her, spoke for a minute and did a lot of listening. Afterwards, she hung up the phone. Passed it back to Purtle and concluded.

"The Deputy Director has just informed me that the SSU Department may have something for us. Also, one of his contacts inside of the White House got in touch with him and told him that the President was notified of the situation and maybe taking a vested interest in what's going on." They all knew what it would mean to have the President shed national attention on what was going on. It would really be Ringling Brothers and Barnum and Bailey. So much bureaucratic red tape would be drawn anyone could potentially be arrested just so the President could say that law enforcement did its job.

"Until then, what do you want us to do?" Garcia already knew the answer. He just wanted to get the ball rolling.

"Do what you do. Just do it quicker." Andreatta chuckled when she said it but caught the undertone. If this turned into a circus it would be hell.

****** N. D. ******
(Stanford Hospital)

"In truth Ms. Juniel, there would be virtually no harm in reversing the procedure at this point. Our initial concern was the body's response to the overwhelming amount of damage and stress brought on by your brothers' injuries. Simply put, had we left him conscious right after the surgery, there was a chance that his body would've gone into shock which would have caused his body to shut down. Thereby, further damaging and destroying his organs."

230

French Tip fully understood everything that Dr. Butler was telling her. She wanted to make sure that she didn't miss a thing.

"The time that he has been comatose has been quite long enough to allow both his external as well as his internal body parts to heal extensively. He should be fine."

"Thank you, Dr. Butler. I just want to make sure that I'm not selfishly causing my brother more harm. But doctor, I desperately need my brother." Dr. Butler could tell that the poor young lady had the world on her pretty little shoulders, "If you would like I could start the procedure immediately." He hoped that would take some of her ills away.

"Please do. And doctor, how long does the process take?" She hoped it wouldn't be long.

"Well, I can start the procedure now. In a couple of hours he will be woke and able to communicate slowly. It will take a few more hours before all systems are functioning accordingly for him to have pertinent or drawn out discussions. The body will gradually wake itself up a little slower, but let's say forty-eight to seventy-eight hours he should be up and running." The smile that came across her face made the doctor feel good. The hug and kiss on the cheek was an added bonus.

"Thank you, Doctor." French Tip needed her brother. Things were getting out of hand. She knew only he could bring an end to all the madness. At least she hoped so.

She walked over to Chief Vieira to fill her in. The two had such a long conversation after the Chief called her telling her that they needed to talk. She confirmed everything that Lt. Urena told Gunz and added a few more details. Their conversations told French Tip two things. First, she knew without a doubt that Vieira indeed was in love with her brother and wasn't beyond breaking the law and bending the rules for him. The second thing that the conversation told her was that there was no room for debate or wasted time. She needed to have Dr. Butler wake up Voorheeze.

Due to everything that was going on French Tip removed all of her brothers' details and replaced them with she-wolves. The only person other then a she-wolf was D.J. Even more then she trusted her own girls, she trusted D.J. Dwayne would neva allow anything to happen to her brother. Unbeknownst to everyone DJ had always been silent security for Voorheeze.

Ever since Gunz and Voorheeze had conflict at the War Room when Gunz had the Twinz on a secret detail following the nigga Wendell, who was following Voorheeze and T'Rida.

In the heated argument Gunz had pulled his gun on Voorheeze even though Voorheeze was wrong a threat was a threat, and Voorheeze eliminated all threats!

Gunz was the one and only exception. D.J. was dispatched as a weapon of espionage to gather information and seek a weak link Voorheeze could use if the situation ever arose that he would have to eliminate Gunz.

No-one would know of her decision not even her own mother. There was no telling how things would play out and her mother talked too much. She couldn't help thinking that it shouldn't be this way. A tear nearly fell from her eye until she thought about the threat that Clark had made. She hoped that nigga wouldn't force her hand because he'd fuck around and find out the hard way that she didn't give a fuck about him being her oldest brother. She would knock his punk ass down.

****

Vieira told French Tip that she didn't care if everything she had heard about her brother was true, she would be willing to help him beat any charges he may receive or give him enough information to avoid capture. She loved him and would do whatever she could to help.

She'd gone long enough without happiness. Her first marriage was a failure. She was married to a Sheriff's Deputy in San Mateo County. Back then, it was just a paycheck. She'd looked forward to coming home to her husband everyday. After her divorce she gave all her time and energy to her career. She dreaded going home to an empty and lonely house. Still she wasn't desperate, she wasn't out looking for a man that night at Whole Foods when she met Voorheeze. But, it was the best thing that ever happened to her. The entire night had been magical.

From the beginning there was something about him that sent electricity through her body. The sex was phenomenal, but it was more than that. It was all of him. Vieira saw the softer side of him. The side that most neva saw. The hurt and pain, the things he refused to acknowledge but couldn't get over. All the things that he thought made him weak, made her want him even more. She was totally head over heels for Voorheeze.

****

As French Tip went about giving her orders, no doubt to people more dangerous than Vieira could ever imagine, the police Chief couldn't help but admire the young fierce leader. She was beautiful beyond belief with her midnight chocolate rich skin, and her high cheek bones. Both of which complimented her voluptuous body. Although she didn't hide her beauty, she used her strong mind and her courageous heart to obtain the things that she wanted. The Chief could tell that about her.

French Tip made sure to pass strict instructions to everyone. They were to be followed to the tee! No one was to know that Voorheeze was waking up, point blank period. Only Vieira was allowed to see him. French Tip was to be notified the moment he woke up.

After giving out her directives, she walked out. French Tip had work to do.

Chapter XIX

(Oakland)

A person would have to be blind to miss DeeDee. Standing six-foot-seven with dreadlocks that hung all the way down to his mid-section on a frame that held up two-hundred and thirty-pounds, DeeDee could neva blend in with any crowd, less it was a crowd of black dreadlock wearing giants. Having people gawk at him was something he had gotten used to a long time ago.

The little old church ladies in their seventies, had probably neva seen anyone the likes of DeeDee before. His long dread-locks were almost as tall as them. He smiled as he pictured holding one of his Issy Miyachi smelling up next to one of the little old ladies. The tallest in the group couldn't be any taller than five feet.

DeeDee couldn't wait to get his food, so he could get home and sink his teeth into the fried pork chops, macaroni and cheese, collard greens, yams and cornbread. Hands down Souls was the best food in Oakland. Not to mention the sweet tea that would make a nigga run three miles just to be thirsty enough to drink a gallon of it.

DeeDee didn't believe in God, but if some imaginary, white mothafucka in the sky got people cooking this damn good then he believed that was alright by him.

"Here's your order sweetheart." The little chocolate cutie pie that brought his food was breath taking.

She had the sexiest set of eyes that were locked-in on him. She held the bags as he looked over a body that belonged on a stripper pole. Although her smile got brighter as he looked her up and down, DeeDee reminded himself that she was in love with God and he wasn't tryna fuck with that.

Souls was owned by Acts Full Gospel Church and its em-ployees were members of the church.

"I'm everything you learned in church to stay away from." DeeDee figured there was no reason to beat around the bush.

He knew the lifestyle he lived put him on Gods' shit list. A good nutt wasn't a good reason to put a good soul on that same list.

"Jesus said he came to save the lost for the righteous already knew the way." She wasn't trying to hear that mess he was talking. She couldn't help from thinking he had to have a big ass dick, as huge as he was.

DeeDee heard her talking that good Christian talk, but her body language was talking that R. Kelly, 2 Live Crew shit.

"You might get lost yourself tryna help me find the way. I'm telling you, lil mama, the Devil gone cheer when I finally get there." He grabbed the bags out of her hands and bit his lower lip.

The little old bats were making all kinds of grunts and smirks under their breaths. They couldn't believe the hatemongering going on so blatantly out in the open for all to witness.

"Even the Devil once graced the gates of Heaven. If he got a pass, I'm sure you can be given a break. Besides," she stepped close enough for him to smell the Dolce Gabbana perfume that she was wearing as she did her best to stare into his eyes "there's no need to play games, I am a grown woman. I already put my number in the bag. It'll be your loss if you don't use it." When she turned and walked away, DeeDee saw how big her ass was and told himself "white Jesus could get it too if he gets in the way of me getting this."

"Lord have mercy! I've neva in all my life seen the likes of that." One of the little old bats called out.

DeeDee turned to leave and looked at the one that just made the comment, "you can say that again, sistah. I'll make sure to get a good enough look for the both of us." He burst out laughing as he walked through the door.

He jumped in the Benz and made sure to sit the bag on top of the mat that he had on the passenger side floor. The pearl paint job by far wasn't the only thing that made his Benz the cleanest whip in Oakland. The ostrich skin seats and crocodile steering wheel played their parts along with the Persian carpet that sat on top of warming pads. He had a feature that made Vanilla Hazelnut come out of the air vents.

Once the food was properly secure, he turned on the car and left the parking lot. Turning right ,he was thinking just how good it was going to feel bending her over and fucking the shit out of that holy pussy. When he got to the stop sign, he decided to dig the paper with the number written on it out. He didn't want the grease from the food to get on the pater and cause the ink to bleed.

The pork chops were smelling too good. He couldn't resist stealing a bite off of one. Melissa told him he wouldn't be able to get back to the house without messing with the food. Oh well! That shit was good. He was about to steal another bite, but a car honking its horn spoiled that.

He lifted back up from the bag and was getting ready to make his turn when

BOCA! BOCA! BOCA!

The drivers side window shattered. DeeDee didn't waste no fucking time! He put the pedal to the metal and got the fuck up outta there.

A silver Hyundai Sonata had pulled up on his driver's side and a nigga on the passenger side of the Sonata thought he was one of the Dukes of Hazard. He was hanging so far out of the window he was practically touching DeeDee. It's a wonder how he missed him.

DeeDee swung the Benz to the left. He pulled away from the Sonata long enough for him to reach over and snatch his 9mm off the passenger seat. It was times like this he thanked his lucky stars that he'd listened to himself and not everybody else. His 9mm had fifty in the dick.

BOC! BOC! BOC!

DeeDee traded shots with the little nigga. He had to let 'em know that them shits fly both ways.

The Sonata was going back on him. *BOCA! BOCA!*

DeeDee had to think of something. He was at a complete disadvantage, so the odds were against him.

BOCA! BOCA! BOCA!

He didn't know who the niggaz was but they weren't letting up.

Up ahead on the right side, a dope fiend was standing next to a parked car. It looked like she was arguing with the driver. Probably some type of negotiation for some dope. The way she was swinging her hips it was must likely was a sexual favor.

BOCA! BOCA!

The dope fiend let out a loud scream as one of the stray bullets burrowed into her shoulder. She fell forward against the car. People mingling about dropped for cover, pulled their own strap, or got the fuck out of dodge. Shoot outs in Oakland were as common as the pizza delivery man. Actually, on any given Sunday it probably was more common to see a shoot out than it was to see a pizza delivery man.

DeeDee came mere inches away from running the dope fiend over. After falling on the car she flapped to the street hollering bloody murda.

BOC! BOC! BOC! BOC!

After that burst of four, DeeDee risked turning around to take aim and fired three more shots. His first found its mark as he hit the shooter in the arm.

The risky move cost him. When he turned back straight he barely had time to correct. He yanked the steering wheel hard to the left. This stopped him from a head on crash, but he still side-swiped three parked cars. The first car dented in the right fender and cracked the wheel axel.

The right tire was wobbling bad. He either had to slow down or he was going to crash.

BOCA! BOCA!

"Fuck!" DeeDee yelled out. This was fucking great. How was the nigga still able to shoot? He wondered.

BAM!

Focusing on the car and the nigga inside, DeeDee neva saw the Toyota Tacoma coming on the right side. The truck slammed into the front passenger side of the Benz. The force of the crash sent the Benz sideways crashing into a parked car on the street.

DeeDee was fucked. He was pinned up against the parked car on the driver's side. It prevented him from opening the door. The truck was wrecked up against the passenger side. There was no way for him to get out. He wasn't neva no bitch nigga. He was a Neva Die Dragon, so he would accept his fate and greet death with both arms. Too bad he neva got the chance to fuck ol' girl. He burst out laughing. Maybe white Jesus didn't too much like him saying he could get it too.

The moment that thought entered his mind DeeDee saw Clark walking up to the Benz.

BOC! BOC! BOC! BOC! BOC!

Just because he'd accepted death didn't mean he was just gonna lay down.

Pedestrians watched in awe, wondering how the scene before them would play out. Silently, some rooted for the niggaz in the silver car. Some wanted the under dog to win. Sadly, some didn't give a fuck, they just wanted to see somebody get it.

Oddly enough, no-one felt sorry for the nigga in the Benz. In Oakland everyone realized that there aren't any victims. Even in the worst of situations one would realize the mothafucka did something.

Clark dodged the bullets thrown at him. Methodically, he sent a few of his own shots back at DeeDee while he still advanced.

DeeDee hit the button to open the stash box. He didn't know how many shots he'd fucked off, but he'd have that other stick ready just in case. He lifted his hand ready to send a few more shots at Clark, who had gotten dangerously close. His arm stopped halfway when DeeDee remembered something.

BOOM!

The pretty, expensive interior that cost more than ten thousand dollars was ruined as DeeDee's blood and brain matter rained down al over it.

BOOM! BOOM!

DeeDee had made the worst mistake a gangsta could ever make in a gun battle. He forgot about all players. The entire time that DeeDee was focusing on Clark, Man Man had walked around and snuck up on the Benz from the back-passenger side. The truck allowed for the perfect cover for the movement.

Opening up the stash box caused DeeDee to think about where his bullets went, so he could guess how many he had left. That was when he remembered the second shooter. It was just too late.

Clark walked up to the Benz and emptied his clip into DeeDee's already lifeless body. Then' he and Man Man jumped in the stolen Sonata and disappeared. He had to let them mothafuckas know that this shit was not a game. There were real killas in the field, and he was one of them.

****** N. D. ******
(San Francisco)

The surveillance detail was outside and they were Frustrated that they had lost visualization of the target. It was your standard two-unit surveillance detail consisting of four field agents trained in stationary and mobile surveillance. All agents were wearing clothes of the local fashion with two changes of clothes each in the vehicles in case they needed to change their appearance or blend in.

Officer Hedgecock had gone into The House of Prime Rib off of Van Ness, almost forty-five minutes ago. It was believed at first that the young officer was cheating on his wife. That assumption was shot down when Agent Matthews attempted to gain entrance to the establishment. Though he was denied a table due to his dress., Agent Mathews did get a glimpse of

Officer Hedgecock, who was seated in a booth with a black San Mateo County Sheriff's Deputy.

Matthews couldn't get a description of the Deputy because his back was to him, but from a glance, he could tell that the man was both taller and huskier than Hedgecock.

"I'm telling you, this damn detail is a complete fucking waste of time. If it wasn't for this guy and his hard work, the local guys would have neva connected the dots on this case. We should be honoring this guy's work ethic, not detailing him." Agent Maehr wasn't complaining. He was just stating pure facts.

In his book, Hedgecock was a good, old fashioned ,True Blue American.

"You know, Mike, on the surface it looks like I would have to agree with you on that. But, trust me, instinct and experience will beat out surface looks every time. If the S.A.C says that she has a hunch about him, then my money is on the S.A.C." Agent Daly had been around S.A.C. Andreatta too long not to know better then to question her hunches.

There had even been a couple of times when one of her hunches saved his life. They say some people had a sixth sense. Agent Daly believed that S.A.C. Adreatta was definitely one of those people.

"If you two ladies are done with your tea time quarrel, look alive because our target and his mystery guest are exiting the restaurant." Agent Mathews baritone voice came through their earpiece.

Both Maehr and Daly looked alive and focused on their in-dividual equipment. They watched as Hedgecock and the Deputy made a right out of the restaurant and began walking.

Maehr and Daly were in a non-descript white van parked across the street and down a ways. Agent Rivera was seated at a patio lounge two doors down in the opposite direction the two walked in. He was nursing a coke that had long since gone warm. Agent Mathews on the other hand was sitting down at a bus stop. Reading a Time Magazine while waiting on the bus.

"Rivera, I think it's time to let that Coke go and reposition yourself. Daly, you and Maehr hold your position for now. If they stay on foot, we will leap frog using both backward and forward tailing. And if they mobilize, then you guys can assume the following." Mathews was discreetly speaking into the mini microphone hidden on his tie clip. He just looked like he was reading an article. "No matter what, I want the net loose. I don't want to jeopardize the tail, nor do I want anyone compromised."

While Agent Mathews was instructing and repositioning his team. Officer Hedgecock and the Deputy that he was with turned off into an alley way. There was too much noise coming off of the busy street for audio to pick up anything.

"Subject just turned off into an alley way. I've lost visualization. Rivera where are you at?" Mathews wanted to get up and walked towards the alley way, but he knew that he had to maintain his position or risk compromising the assignment and detail.

"Don't worry your ugly, little head, Roger. I'm right behind you, taking tourist pictures of our lovely city." Agent Rivera was only a couple footsteps away from the entrance of the alley way as he spoke.

"Okay Jose. Just make sure to keep it natural and believable." No matter what the assignment, Mathews was always the worry wart. Sort of like a mother hen. But he was damn good at what he did.

Agent Rivera smiled innocently at a couple that passed by him.

"What you mean natural? Matter of fact, Rog. I'm about as natural as they come just ask your wii…."

"Ho-ly shit!" The sight before his eyes was the last thing he expected to see.

Immediately Mathews was heard in the earpiece. "What is it, Jose?"

"You ain't gone believe me if I told you. But what is that old saying, "a picture is worth a thousand words." Rivera had hit the zoom function on his digital camera, as well as auto settings for lighting and video quality. He was recording everything.

Half way down the alley way, the Sheriffs Deputy had Officer Hedgecock pinned up against the wall. Oblivious to anything going on around them, they were locked passionately in a rough embrace, French kissing as if their lives depended on it. Clearly the Sheriff's Deputy was the aggressor, the way he was groping all over Hedgecock. Rivera thought they might actually start screwing right there in the alley way, in broad daylight.

"Soooo, it turns out that our little rendezvous is indeed actually a date." Rivera couldn't wait to hear what responses he got back on that comment.

"What do you mean it's a date?" Mathews almost lost his grip on the magazine.

"What he means is our boy likes beans on his taco." Maehr joked which he followed with laughter.

"Spot check." Mathews called into the microphone.

"Approximately thirty-five yards deep into the alley on the eastern side, leaned up against a building." Rivera looked for some sort of camouflage or object which he could hide behind. As he gave his response to Mathews spot check.

The couple broke their lip lock for a moment only to discuss something briefly. Whatever it was excited Hedgecock, because he attacked his lover's lips again.

A few feet next to them was a garbage dumpster that was full of trash. There was trash that spilled over from the dumpster all around it. The alley way itself was the typical San Francisco alley way. It was fucked up. Trash and old furniture were everywhere.

They moved towards the dumpster and the big Deputy who was easily six foot four, two hundred sixty-five pounds, took his huge French coat off.

"Aw fuck me, I know they not about to..." Rivera couldn't even finish the statement. He was so grossed out. Just think,

243

only moments ago he'd agreed with Maehr about praising this mothafucka.

"About to what?" Daly knew what he was about to say. He just didn't think that two honest representatives of law enforcement would do such a shameful and dumb ass thing in public.

"Rivera what's going on?" Mathews hated being clueless about anything. It made him feel out of control. Helpless."

"Trust me, Rog, you don't wanna know." Jose Rivera meant every single ward.

"Trust you, my ass! Jose, what are they doing? I want a complete response to my question." A passerby turned and stared at the young muscle-bound black man sitting on the bench arguing with himself, like the basket case he naturally had to be.

Agent Roger Mathews paid the fat worn down white woman no mind.

"Currently, Officer Hedgecock is behind a dumpster on his knees with his pants down taking it up the ass very powerfully by the black Deputy that he had lunch with. Even with them being behind the dumpster, I have a hellavah angle and view. There's no mistaking what's going on, Rog. Clearly, Hedgecock has a bigger secret then anyone realized. I'm not gay or nothing but judging by what I see, I'd say that secret is at least eleven inches." He figured that was a very complete response.

"God Damn! This is going on right now?" Agent Daly didn't believe Rivera was mistaken just couldn't believe what he heard.

"Right this very minute." Rivera didn't want to witness the shit that he was seeing, but he knew how important the video was.

"Do you have it on video?", Agent Mathews asked.

"Time stamped and recording, sir." He responded

"Excellent." Mathews was weighing the potential leverage of such intriguing and damaging evidence.

"Rog. Sir, what are our orders while our friend is getting his back blown out?" Agent Maehr despised homosexuals and wanted to get as far away from the ordeal as possible.

"Unfortunately, boys, we're gonna have to wait this one out. Rivera hold your position. Daiy, Maehr as quick as you can change clothes and be ready to go mobile. I want you on the east and west side of the alley. When our two love birds are done, which ever direction Hedgecock heads, that person will replace Rivera and pick up the tail.

"The other will switch positions with myself. Rivera and I will hold an owl view and be ready to pick up the vehicle's trail. I have no doubt that they will be wanting to get away from the area as soon as they finish their business." Mathews gave out the new orders while deciding to get ahold of S.A.C. Andreatta.

The one thing he was sure of was that she needed to know this bit of information.

**** N. D. ****
Location Unknown

After considering the things that had transpired on the streets and couple of situations that took place behind the walls of two California Prisons, he Central Committee of the Black Guerilla Family held council and came to the decision to pass down a few orders and a couple of sanctions. The orders came down the proper channels until they made their way to Dok's desk.

Immediately, Dok had his Minister of Education call a meeting with his complete cadre. There the orders of the Committee were read out loud and discussed to make sure all understood the new orders. The disobeying of a direct order from the Central Committee was an automatic death sentence. Because of this, it was always ensured that all parties that the order pertained to fully understood the order.

The meeting lasted just shy of two hours. Everything from personnel changes and faculty restricting to theoretic Military procedure and the course of action dealing with Clark's team was discussed.

Needless to say, all were in agreement that the situation with Clark had gone on too long. Military Command was directed to strategize a final scenario for the Demise of Clark and his personnel, by utilizing the E.G.U. cadre.

Although Dok was still the commanding General of Ground Force Troops, he was instructed to relinquish authority of all Military personnel over to Mtambo and continue focusing on the growth and development aspect of the organization. Mtambo would give a full disclosure brief in the form of a report each and every night.

Before the meeting ended, the sanctions passed down by the Council were read out loud. There wasn't a need to discuss sanctions at any length. It was simply a matter of carrying them out. In the swiftest possible means as not to endanger or jeopardize the cadre. Sanctions were severe discipline handed down by the Supreme Council, which is the highest level of the Central Committee.

Most often a sanction was a death sentence. Each Cadre had its own Minister of Justice for the hexing of smaller matters and methods of discipline for its members. Even when such matters carried the sanction of death, the committee only got involved when the issue at hand involved the entire Cadre or Organization as a whole, or when the individual is of a certain rank or above was killed, because only the committee can sanction the life of someone with the rank equivalent to a General.

Dok had just finished a conversation with Zair when Cuana walked up to him.

"What's going on, Afrikan?" Her question and tone were innocent enough, but her eyes spoke of genuine concern and care.

"Just carrying out orders while trying to make sure our people are given effective leadership to the causes that we strive for." The response was generic at best and he knew it.

"Come on ,brah. I didn't ask a politician for a summary. I asked my Baba (father) how he was doing. I know you don't like the order. All of us know this. You've taught me so much over the years. One of the most important things you've taught me is that we all need some sort of an outlet. I'm a listening ear." This time the care came across in her voice.

"Aw, Lil One." Dok closed his eyes and took a deep breath, she was right. He hated the decision that the Committee made, but voicing his dislike wouldn't change a thing.

What field combatant would like to be taken out of the field?

Regardless of whether it be a foot soldia or a commanding General, we are warriors at heart and killas at best. It's what we do, it's what we love.

"Now, of course, my fight to further the party and improve our standings in the community and nation as a whole, is as strong today as it was twenty years ago when I first drank from the cup. However, there is a war going on and I'm being told to sit back in the comforts of safety while my men risk their lives. Not just my men, but my boys. Sons who were forced to grow up without me due to my choices and my dedication for the cause. What if..." Dok choked up. For the first time since she'd known him. Cuana witnessed what she thought would be the first time she would see him cry.

She took his arm and guided him to sit down. Cuana wasn't that much older then Scooter and Rell, but she's been around their father more then either of them. Before he went to prison he'd found Cuana in an abandoned crack house one day. She was nine years old, scared, lonely hungry and alone. He took her with him and had been a father to her ever since. As he had grown and developed so had she.

"First of all, don't think like that cause it's not going to happen. You've trained us all efficiently enough to take care of ourselves. Not to mention we've all going thru and graduated both Urban Assault Guerilla Warfare training as well as the Advance Training of the Elite Guerilla.

"They indeed are your sons, but they both are highly trained and sophisticated war tacticians. So, you've got to let them utilize the tools that they've received." Cuana loved this man so much that his pain was her pain. His struggle was her struggle.

"As for you being removed the Field Military as a Combat General, I am sure you have an issue with that. As a tactically trained revolutionary, I am more than sure that you know that this is not only the most logical move, but it is the best move for the entire organization as a whole.

"At a time when all leadership was opposed to your ideas and theories, you held steadfast to what you believed was for the betterment of our organization. You foresaw the change in the war before anyone else. So, it's only natural, now the others have been forced to admit you were right, that you be chosen to be the face of this new above ground cadre." Cuana's words sounded foreign to his ears, coming out her mouth. The words sounded so much like his own, instead of hers.

"Daughter, I don't have the slightest idea on how to be a spokesperson. Do I look like the kind of brotha that you want to meet at your local YMCA or on tv. talking about stop the violence?" They both got a good laugh out of that one.

"Well, you should have thought about that before you let that girl get an interview. And actually, you looked very handsome to me." If only he knew.

To her he was much more than a father figure. He was a big brother, best friend and ideal of what a man was supposed to be.

"You're telling me that because you have to." Dok teased, but then he got serious "You need to know that when I thin of what I have to lose in the field. It's not only the boys. Cuana, you are my little flower ,my daughter and my heart and I love you." He leaned over and gave her a kiss on the check and a big hug.

"Okay now you see why I be feeling jealous all the time." Scooter jokingly interrupted their moment.

He knew his father didn't like the order that the Committee had sent down. Even though he hadn't told him, there was no need for Dok to voice it. Scooter knew his father all too well. He was a warrior at heart. All he knew was the struggle.

"Naaw, little brother, you're jealous because I'm a better shot than you." Cuana loved poking at Scooter over their shooting. Scooter was one hellavah shot, but Cuana was by far the best shot in the Cadre. As Lieutenant Commander of E.G.U. she was in charge of the Usalama Squad.

"For one, I was sick when we took our shooting test. That's the only reason you won. Secondly that long distance sniper shit, that ain't the way to do it. I need to be up close and personal with mine." Scooter and Cuana acted like this all of the time. It was just their nature.

The two of them have been behaving like this since they were kids. To see them, you would neva believe that that they were not biological brothers and sister.

"What's going on, Afrikan?" It always made Dok warm in the heart that his three children always had gotten along so well.

"First, I wanted to check up on you and make sure you're straight." Scooter turned towards his father and gave him his attention, after sticking his tongue out at Cuana.

"Well, you might as well tell me what the second thing is, because I'm good." He really was. Hell, he didn't like the call but he would follow the orders. He picked up on it when Scooter said "first of all" which meant there was something else.

"That reporter called Elesia looking for you. From what I gather, she wants to do a report on you or interview. The message isn't too clear on that part." Scooter informed him, as he took a seat in one of the empty chairs.

"What reporter? What are you talking about?" Dok was confused.

"That sistah, Ms. Daniels. The one that asked you a few questions at Elesia's Grand Opening.

He recalled the sistah that was so ambitious and beaming with pride.

"I don't know about this." Dok reluctantly took the piece of paper out of his son's hand.

"You ain't gotta know about it, pop. Just follow your heart. The rest will follow you." That was one of his fathers' favorite quotes.

Dok smiled at his son, proud of the man before him.

"Where's your brother?" He wanted to change the subject. He didn't want to appear weak in the eyes of the members of the cadre that were still around.

"Security Detail, though not always in sight, shall always be around." Rell stepped out of the shadows behind his father, quoting another of his father's sayings.

"For their job is to be felt but neva seen." Dok completed the second half of the saying.

"And for the record, that might just be a good idea, the interview or whatever. We've been in negative light for so long. It's time something and someone shed some positive light on our cause. This is more than just a fight with the American Government to establish the government of the New Afrikan Revolutionary Nationalist. It's more than building self pride and self worth, it's about giving a lost people hope again. This woman is presenting you with the appropriate platform. You should not only take it but utilize it as you would any other material or informational asset." Everything young Darrel told him was accurate and he knew it.

Dok looked at his children prouder than any father who ever stood in front of his children. Though they were killers, trained and specialized militants were revolutionaries taking up for a cause. They were vanguards for a people who had lost the

250

will to fight. Most importantly they were his little children. His precious seeds.

The four of them stayed and talked for almost thirty minutes. The conversation touched on quite a few subjects. By the time they were done, Dok's mind was made up. He would be an advocate for the cause. He would give Carla Daniels her interview.

De'Kari

Chapter XX

Brian Pickett, 1/6/15 killed by Los Angeles, CA. Deputy

Denzel Brown, 3/23/15 Bayshore, NY shot and killed by officers

Brandon Jones, 3/19/15 Cleveland, OH shot and killed by officers

Askari Roberts, 3/17/15 Rome, GA tased by police three times

Eric Harris, 4/2/15 Tulsa, OK shot and killed by a 73-year-old part-time reserve deputy

Walter Scott, 4/4/15 North Charleston, SC shot and killed by officer

De'Angelo Stallworth, 5/12/15 Jacksonville, FL shot and killed by an officer

Brandon Glenn, 5/6/15 Los Angeles, CA shot and killed by LAPD

Lorenzo Hayes, 5/13/15 Spokane, WA died in jail in the hands of Deputy, no one knows how

Kris Jackson, 5/15/15 South Lake Tahoe, CA shot by police in the back while climbing through window

Kevin Higgenbotham, 6/15/15 Trenton, NJ beaten to death by officers

As name after name rolled up the screen the deep, powerful voice could be heard speaking. The video was made less than nine hours ago, and it has already become the topic of discussion in every conversation across the United States.

"These atrocities that have plagued the fearful hearts of my people, have gone on far too long. Innocent lives lost at the hands of those chosen and sworn to protect and serve the citizens that they are and have been slaughtering at will for the longest. This fascist infrastructure they call a so-called Government has simply turned a blind eye on the crisis at hand. They are the ones who've orchestrated and helped facilitate this modern-day race driven genocide.

"If this injustice were just going on in one area or one region, then perhaps one could argue that it was a singular incident. But, this is happening in almost every state across the map. These weren't gangstas or killas or hardened convicts. These were simply unarmed citizens. Jonathan Sanders who died July 8, 2015 was in a horse buggy when officers spooked his horse and as the brotha attempted to calm the horses, he was choked from behind until his death."

The names of innocent unarmed blacks who were murdered by law enforcement officers continued to roll u-p the screen while the voice talked. The video was on every social media sight that played video. It was also on YouTube, Twitter and Facebook. Though his face is not seen, it is evident to the world that the cat they are calling Batman is the man behind the video.

Victa Larosa III, 7/2/15 Jacksonville, FL – shot and killed by Deputy

Asshams Manley, 8/14/15 Spauldings, MD – tased with taser, shot with gun and beaten

India Kager, 9/5/15 Virginia Beach, VA – shot and killed by officers

Lavarte Biggs, 9/5/15 Durham, NC – shot and killed by officer

LJames Carney III, 8/31/15 Cincinnati, OH – died due to police taser

Junior Prosper, 9/28/15 North Miami, FL. – shot and killed by officer

Keith McLeod, 9/23/15 Reistertown, MD – shot and killed by police

The names continued to scroll up the screen. These were only the blacks murdered by the police in 2015.

"David Felix was living at home dealing with mental health issues when he was murdered by the police. India Kager was a mother and a Navy Veteran. These were not monsters, yet they were gunned down and murdered like wild animals! Fuck that! They think that they can just kill our loved ones, gun them down in the streets like dogs! Like this shit is a game. Like no body gone do shit. Well this is only the beginning! I promise you mothafuckas, the Dragon has reared its ugly head and the face is upon all Law Enforcement! I give a fuck about race, color or creed. If you wear that shield you have made yourself a target."

"Now the Government and police want you to fudge the numbers. I assure you that the individual body count is over thirty slimy pigs. Once you include the Dublin Police Department that got blown up, then were at around 300 dead pigs and I'm just gettin' started!

"Sandra Bland was only twenty-eight years old when we all saw her forcefully pulled out her car like a common thief. She was beat and dragged across the pavement, only to be murdered in the county jail in Walker County, Texas on July 13, 2015. I dedicate my next act of eradication in my quest to eradicate the corrupt and poisonous law enforcement to Sandra Bland, may you rest in Heaven, sistah!"

The video quit playing. He laid there in the bed for a moment to gather his thoughts. He handed the phone back to his sister then finally spoke.

"From the sound of things, you probably should have woke me up sooner." He told her with a sincere concerned look on his face.

Her emotions got the best of her and French Tip jumped up out of the chair and gave her brother a big hug.

"La'Mont, I love you so much, brother." She told him as a tear slid down her face.

She didn't know what brought about the rush of emotions, but suddenly she wasn't a stone-cold assassin. She was a little girl finding safety and security in the warm comfort of her older brothers' arms.

"I love you too, Booger. Don't cry, little sis. It ain't as bad as it seems." What Voorheeze had no way of knowing was that his words were the furthest thing from the truth. Shit was real bad and they were about to get fucked up!

Voorheeze had been fully awake and alert for a few days. When the doctors first brought him out of the coma, he felt groggy and very tired. As time and days progressed he slowly regained control of himself.

Captain Vieira had been there for him the entire way. Yesterday, she'd had no choice but inform him of her occupation, which was a shock to him. A bigger shock was her filling him in on everything regarding law enforcement and the federal agents and Batman.

Today, French Tip brought the news of everything that had transpired with the Family. Learning that Dok Holliday was out of prison and at war with Clark fucked him up. Learning that Clark had threatened his sister was the worst of the news. That blow vibrated to his soul. It was an unforgiveable sin, one he had to deal with.

He was and had always been a natural leader and a leader had to comfort his wolves. Silently he chastised himself for succumbing to his emotions when T'Rida died and not maintaining his discipline. His vendetta against the police would neva be regretted.

Voorheeze hated police for what they did to his brotha and what they've done to his people. For so long, that war would continue but first he had to take care of home.

He decided to lighten the mood. "How was your fashion show?"

Satin Doll was his sisters' heart and soul, so he knew talking about the fashion show would cheer her up.

"I didn't do it." She whispered as the tears flowed. He held her at arms distance and stared into her face, trying to read her pain.

"I wasn't going to have it without you. I kept putting it off until you woke up and could come." Her words touched his soul. This was his little sister, his booger, his little daughter.

Images of when they were younger flooded into his mind. The many lonely, cold nights when all they had was each other because both their parents were out running the streets, somewhere getting high, or tryna get high. The countless days and nights they'd starved because he was unable to steal them something to eat.

He couldn't let the nightmares of his past fuck with him. Not now!

"Then I guess you need to get up. You got a lot of work to do because it's time for the world to be introduced to Satin Doll."

As a smile formed on her lips, the tears stopped flowing down her face.

"How much work needs to be done for you to be ready?" He asked her.

"Just need to get the word out again and get the venue. Everything else has been ready for a while. You know this was the third time I had to cancel the show, so I don't know if the promoter is going to take me seriously." The last time she'd spoken with the promoter, she had gotten the impression that would be the last.

"Call her and tell her you'll triple her salary and pay her in advance. That'll motivate her." He was touched by the fact that she had waited for him. It meant the world to him.

"You want me to give her triple what she charges? Boy, are you crazy?", she asked with a "what the fuck" look on her face.

"Naaw, I want you to tell her you will give her triple what she made last year. In order for her to make sure everything goes exactly how you want it to go, I'm paying for it." The money wasn't nothing, but what it was going to do was every-thing.

"Thank you, brother." She couldn't conceal her excitement as she hugged him again.

They sat and talked for a little while more. Mostly about the revealing of Satin Doll, but also about a few other things.

Yesterday, Vieira had tried her hardest to convince him to straighten up, especially with the feds lurking. Voorheeze wasn't listening to none of that shit. His family needed him. Batman needed him. Mentally he'd been gone long enough fucking with the coke. Now it was time for him to be himself, that nigga he was born to be.

He still hadn't wrapped his head all the way around the fact that she was the police. Not just the police, but the Chief of Police. One thing he hated was a cop.

The two of them had met and hit it off a little while before the shooting. Their chemistry was fire, but there were many things that they didn't know about each other still.

As he got up to get ready to start his exercise routine, his thoughts were on the many things that needed to be done. The many fires that were burning.

In order to combat all the flames, he needed his head in the game. He also needed to prioritize.

****** N. D. ******
Oakland, California

Most people's tempers would be seething, to say the least, right now, but not SAC Andreatta. She was poised, cool, calm and collected. Allowing her temper and emotions to run wild was not her style.

If she allowed the two videos that she had just watched to get the best of her, then she would be allowing the videos and the perpetrators in them to be one-upping her in this battle of the wits.

The video of officer Hedgecock getting reamed by his lover was sickening and appalling. Looking at it from a professional standpoint, that was just his personal life. Him being a freak was his business. His professional behavior and conduct were impeccable as far as she could tell.

The second video, the one that the cop killer posted on social media, deserved her attention and further analysis. She played it again as she thought of the ramifications a video of this magnitude could have. (Andreatta was a graduate of Harvard Law. She held her criminal Law Degree from Yale University graduating Suma-Cum-Lade. She was approached by the Bureau her last year of undergrad school only to turn it down. She wanted to focus on her studies and get her degree). She drew so much attention, that her last year of grad school, the bureau came calling again. This time it was successful in recruiting her.

Her analytical mind was second to none. This talent allowed her to rise quickly through the ranks and earning the respect of her colleagues. She didn't doubt that her opinion was not taken lightly, which was good.

If this video was allowed to grow into full blossom, the ramifications could very well put the country in an uproar. It was not a hidden fact that the number of African Americans being killed by law enforcement across the country was completely unacceptable. If this video were to bloom, there was no telling what the blacks would do.

Immediately after watching the video, she sent word to her superiors of her analysis of the situation and her recommendation. Federal blockage of the video.

It would be a hard fight to get it done due to the first amendment. The freedom of speech would sit in their way. However, the Patriot Act post 911 would give them leverage. After all Jenkins ties with the Black Guerilla Family, which has long since been classified as a domestic terrorist cell would give them the authority to enact the Patriot Act and supersede the First Amendment.

Meanwhile something that they were able to do now was monitor all the sites such as Hood Videos, World Star and track the people that are watching and sharing the video on their social media sites.

Those that viewed the video more than once or shared the video would be tagged and a background analysis would be done on them. The information would be stored in their database until needed. The order had already given to begin the operation.

The problem was, so far, they have been on the defensive dealing with this entire situation. Always one step behind, chasing the culprit. They needed to get ahead of the ball and take the offensive.

Andreatta knew this. It was time for her team to hit the ground rolling. She reached for her Galaxy S8 and dialed a number…

**** N. D. ****
Santa Rosa, California

Agent Finnegan couldn't wait to get out of the stuffy chemical suite. He felt closed in and his range of motion was limited. He hated the feeling.

Five minutes later he was done with the decontamination process and out of the chem-suit. The knowledge gained would be useful, yet he wouldn't want to repeat the experience.

As he was putting his jacket back on, he thought of how much he would hate life if he were one of the lab-techs that worked at the Redwood Toxicology Laboratory.

His thoughts were interrupted by the sound of the tunes of Kid Rock & Sheryl Crow "Picture Away" on his ring tone. Digging inside of his duffle bag, he received his iPhone answering without checking the caller I.D.

"Finnegan."

"Hey, Finnegan. What do we got?" Andreatta's voice had a slight edge to it.

"Hey boss. Your radar must've been going off because we actually just finished up."

"Do we have anything?" Her gut was telling her not only did they have something, but she didn't want to hear it.

"I'm afraid we do." Agent Finnegan took a deep breath and sat down on the bench in front of the locker he was standing in front of. "The Techs have found that the explosive device components were dual flux, or two part. The first and major component being C-4 plastic explosives.

"However, trace analysis found traces of both fertilizer and diesel fuel. Both ingredients found in Imodium Nitrate. Also, there were traces of potassium nitrate, sulfur, and charcoal. Commonly known as gun powder.

"The sophistication of the compounds used to construct the device shows a level of training and expertise that we hadn't seen on our analysis of the suspect…" Andreatta was listening with one ear while thinking.

Her instincts were correct. She didn't want to know the answer to her question. As Finnegan continued talking, her mind was running. The terrorist having advance explosive training was not a good thing at all, for anyone.

"…this new element added with our knowledge of his other training, in fact makes this a level 1 threat. "Finnegan concluded.

"Well, the fact that he is operating alone still at this point in time keeps that threat level down. However, I do agree with your assessment and I concur with your sentiments in regard to the new dynamics that this information adds to the case."

"In fact, I was just thinking to myself that we need to take a more aggressive approach to finding Mr. Jenkins." SAC Andreatta ran off a few ideas she had in her head to Finnegan.

They continued to talk for another ten minutes before hanging up.

Finnegan and Daly were meeting up after he finished at the lab. He told Andreatta there was no need for her to call Daly and fill him in. Finnegan would take care of it.

It took another fifteen minutes to receive a folder of the schematics of the work ups that the lad had available so far. After retrieving this, Finnegan was on his way to meet Agent Daly who had been working on a lead.

**** N. D. ****

Chapter XXI Tracy

San Joaquin County Sheriff's Deputy Purtle was having a rough day and was wondering if it could possibly get any worse. As she sat down in the driver's seat of her Hyundai Elantra, she thought over her day.

She'd woke up at 4:00am and began her morning thirty-minute aerobics. She had started this routine last week after gaining sixty-eight pounds this past summer, not to mention the big saggy fat ass that came with it.

Not more then ten minutes into the routine she over did a move and pulled a muscle in the hamstring in her left leg. The fucking pain bothered her still. She extended her leg involuntarily just thinking about it.

Later on, at the San Joaquin County Jail where she worked, she and one of her many lovers thought it would be hot to sneak into the Lieutenants office during his morning meeting and fuck around. As he sat in the lieutenants chair she had given him a blow job.

Ordinarily she would've gotten the job done in under five minutes. However, she kept concentrating on her leg because of the pain. It was over ten minutes when the Lieutenant walked into his office.

She was placed on leave and sent home. To make shit even worse, on her way home she decided to stop by the grocery store to grab a few things. She caught a flat tire in the parking lot of Safeway.

She dug around the bag until she found what she was looking for her Mr. Good Bar. After the day she'd had, she didn't give a fuck about her diet. She ripped into the wrapper and devoured the candy bar.

After sucking the milk chocolate off her fingers, she started her car and pulled out of the parking lot. Her air conditioner was blowing nice and hard, so the valley heat that was outside didn't bother her one bit.

She slowed and stopped at the red light. She used this time to dig into the bag and grab her blueberry and nut yogurt parfait and a spoon. The light was still red, so she turned on her radio.

Her favorite CD automatically came to life. She opened her parfait and took a bite. It was only 10:30am, but the temperature was already a scorching ninety degrees. The light finally turned green and she drove on, turning left and merging onto highway 4 she began singing along to her favorite song with a mouth full of yogurt parfait.

"Living my life in a slow hell/a different girl every night in the motel/I ain't seen the sun shine in 3 damn days/ been fueling up on cocaine and whiskey/ wish I had a good girl who missed me/ Lord I wonder if I ever change my ways/"

The music was blaring through the speakers. As she sped down an empty highway 4 singing at the top of her twenty-nine-year-old lungs, she slowly began to forget about the shitty start to her morning.

She was so lost in herself that she neva paid attention to the black SUV approaching in her rearview. Kid Rock was singing about putting her picture away and in her mind, he was right in the car singing to her instead of Sheryl Crow.

The more she got in tune with the song, the faster she drove. When the parfait was empty she just tossed the container into the passenger seat. She sucked and licked every inch of the spoon, cleaning it completely of any residue. She turned it into a little microphone just as Sheryl Crow began.

"Living my life in a slow hell/everyone knows but they wont tell/But their half ass smiles tells me something just ain't right/…"

The lights in her rearview mirror drew her attention causing her to stop singing. She reached over and turned the music down. With the volume down, she was able to hear the sirens that went along with the flashing lights. "What the fuck? Come on. Gimme a break." She mumbled to herself. This had to be a day from hell."

Only then did she notice how fast she was going. The speedometer read 88mph. Grateful that she was still in her Deputy uniform, the last thing she needed was a ticket. Usually Deputies gave one another a break. That was part of the unwritten code.

She eased her foot off the gas pedal and began to slow down, in preparation to pulling over and stopping. She even made sure to use her signal light.

After pulling over she placed the Elantra in park. Pure self-consciousness made her check herself in the mirror. Silently she said a quick prayer begging God to keep her from getting a ticket.

She watched as a black Deputy climbed out of the SUV. He made his way to her car with even, confident strides. The hat he was wearing prevented her from being able to see his face, so she was clueless as to what his mood was.

As he approached the driver's side, she let the window down. Throwing her chest out. She whipped her hair out of her face and smiled as friendly as she could.

"Hello, Buddy. Heyy I'm so sorry about that. I just got off work and got caught up thinking about the job." She was trying her best since they were colleagues, she figured she would be okay.

"License and registration, ma'am, and can you please turn that music off." He spoke cleanly and crisply. He paid her story just about as much attention as he did her chest. None!

"Uh, turn the radio off?" She was confused since she had it turned down low enough for them to hear each other.

"Bitch, I said turn the fucking radio off! And gimme yo fucking license and registration!" The bass in which he yelled at her scared her so much she jumped in the seat.

Fearfully and frantically, she turned the radio off and reached for her purse. She was so fearful, she was having trouble pulling her drivers license out of her wallet. Her frustration with the plastic I.D. holder brought all of the bad shit from today to the surface. She was fuming when she finally turned around with the driver's license and registration in her hand.

"You didn't have to be so damn rude about it." She was busy looking at the registration when she spoke those words. She neva saw the fist that came through her window.

BLAM!

The force of the blow was so powerful, that it broke her jaw. The moment Deputy Purtle began talking, the man outside her window swung with his left arm punching her in the face through the driver's window.

Deputy Purtle didn't know what had happened to her. Her vision wavered from the blow. She blinked trying to clear her vision.

BLAM!

Another blow crashed into her jaw. This blow shattered the bone to pieces. The drivers side door was forcefully yanked open. The deputy tried to scream, but the pain in her jaw only allowed a strange sound to emit.

Deputy Purtle was terrified as she was violently snatched out of her car. Kicking and trying to scream, she was dragged across the pavement to the back of the SUV.

A single motorist passed by as this was happening. At first the driver was alarmed by what he was seeing, until he saw the letters F.B.I. T.A.C.T. Unit stenciled across the sides of the black S.U.V.

Purtle didn't have a clue as to what was going on. From the response she received the first time she opened her mouth, there was no way she was going to speak again.

She laid curled up on the floor of the SUV numb and in a traumatic state. Fear gripped and in a world of pain, she prayed through her fears.

As the vehicle sped down the highway, for the first time she began wondering what if this man was not a member of law enforcement at all. That horrifying thought was so unbearably frightening that she urinated on herself.

Retracing her day in her mind, she couldn't help but to think that if she was neva sent home this wouldn't not have happened. Had she not foolishly gone into the lieutenant's office to give Deputy Adela a blow job she would not have gotten sent home. Thus, she would not be in this predicament.

Her head was really throbbing. The head ache she had felt like it would split her head in two. The throbbing started in her jaw and went up to the side of her left face until it met her head ache and the two became one enormous pain. The last thing she remembered was asking God was she going to die today.

They had been driving for too long for her to believe that they were headed for the San Joaquin County Jail, or any jail for that matter.

She wondered if this was her punishment for being so promiscuous. Payback for all the times she'd committed adultery. After her prayer she passed out from the pain.

Deputy Purtle awoke when her head smacked into the wall of the make-shift metal cage. The first thing she noticed was that it was getting dark.

The road they were traveling on was very bumpy. Purtle was only a jail guard and not a full patrol deputy. The training that a street deputy has to pay attention to certain things like sounds and smells to get a grasp of location, she didn't possess.

The S.U.V. came to a sudden stop. Purtle tried her best to sit up and look out of the windows. When she heard the ignition cut off the fear returned.

Her heart beat rapidly and beads of sweat appeared on her clammy forehead.

"God please. I'm so sorry for the way that I've been living. Lord, just protect me and get me through this. I promise I'll change." The sound of her muffled voice was alien in her ears.

Over the hours since her jaw was shattered, and she was abducted the side of her face had swollen up bigger then a grapefruit. Just to opening her mouth caused her so much pain that her eyes watered.

She could hear his footprints crunching on the gravel as he made his way to the back of the vehicle. Every time one of his feet landed she would hear a loud BOOM inside of her head.

Could this really be happening to her? She wondered. He whistled as he walked, which only added to her torment.

When the back doors came open, Purtle whimpered like an injured animal.

"Let's go." His tone said he was zero tolerance for the bullshit.

She climbed down out of the back of the stolen FBI Tactical Assault Vehicle with wobbly legs. Once her feet were on the ground, he slammed the door and snatched her by the back of her neck.

The frightened woman didn't have any idea where they were. All she could see were trees. There was a single old shack looking house in front of them about fifty yards . Her captor roughly guided her towards it by the back of her neck.

The stairs that they climbed up to the porch were just about as old as the house, if not older. They creaked loudly as they stepped on them. The moment she crossed over the threshold a bone wrenching chill traveled down her spine causing her to hesitate. He squeezed the back of her neck and forced her on.

He guided her by the back of her neck through the dust and mold smelling house towards the back of the house. The dust and mold spores were so thick in the air, they caused her to gag and choke.

A large rat, about the size of a college football, scurried away from them with a piece of only God knows what in its mouth.

Stopping at the last door, he reached in the pocket of his pants for another set of keys. The door and the frame were the only new looking things she saw. Both looked to be made of a dark heavy metal. Purtle didn't even realize that she was holding her breath until he managed to get the heavy door open and she gasped out loud.

The room looked like it was a photo or video studio. There were all types of big lights positioned in different places around the room. There was a laptop and some other electronic gear all centered around a grotesque looking chair.

It looked like something out of a horror movie. A chair from the forgotten scenes of Texas Chainsaw Massacre. There were chains and manacles all over it ,with some type of cords or wires hanging from it. The whole setup screamed torture.

"I'm not going repeat myself and I'm not going to raise my voice." He began as he shoved her into the room. "If I tell you to do something and if you don't, you're gonna wish that you had." He took a step towards her and looked into her eyes. "Do you understand me?"

Once again, the chill went down her spine causing goose bumps to appear all over her body. She shivered and subconsciously took one step backwards while nodding her head up and down saying "yes."

"I'm glad we understand each other. Now strip! Take every last stitch off." There was no emotion in his voice as he ordered her to get butt naked.

**** **N. D.** ****

De'Kari

Chapter XXII

Mountain View, California

It was a night like no other. The entire place was jam packed with everybody from everywhere. The guests ranged from people in the music and fashion industries to the Underworld Elite. This was the first red carpet event of its kind in Northern California and it was set off right.

Mozzy blazed the stage with "Peres Calling," "Bladadah" and "Afraid." Young Ma came through and did her famous "freestyle" and killed the building with "Ooui."

The moment Nikki Minaj came out, it set the record straight on what type of event this really was. The Shoreline Amphitheatre looked like mini Hollywood.

The prior cancellations and rescheduling help to make it one of the most anticipated and talked about events of the year. T.V. stations and media from everywhere came out to take part of the World Premier of Satin Doll.

French Tip wasn't smiling, she was cheesing. It was the night she'd dreamed of forever and it was amazing. No drug or aphrodisiac could compare. She was truly happy.

The organizer, a short, gay, black man, who was as hyper as an eight-year-old after eating a bag full of candy, me speed walking right up to her.

"Miss French Tip, girl you need to listen to me. Now I know you said you wanted to just sit and watch the show from the sideline. Hmph, but look, girl, I've been doing this for nearly fifteen years and girl I am telling you, you need to be on the stage for the next segment." His mouth was running a mile a minute.

French Tip opened her mouth to say something, but he cut her off and held his hand up in the air like he wasn't trying to hear it.

"Unh Unh! Now, girl, don't you try arguing with me. Now, you done hired me to make sure that your show was a

success. No, not a success girl, the bomb! So, don't try stopping me from doing what I do. You need to gone and get yo
pretty, black ass to changing and get ready to go on stage."
French Tip had a look of pure shock on her face like he had
just slapped her.

"Ooh, unh unh! No, you didn't look at me like that when
I'm just doing my job. Honey, I know all about yo gun play.
Boo Boo, the streets ain't the only thang that talk. But, listen to
this ,Boo Boo, and listen to it good. You ain't the only one
from the hood, girl, so go and get changed. You going on in
ten." He didn't wait for a response. He spun around, snapped
his head back and raised a hand and stormed off.

French didn't know what just happened. All she was gone
tell him was okay, she would do it. She wanted to laugh but the
nigga had just threatened her. She was still French Tip, sister of
Jason Voorheeze and he had her completely fucked up.

Just the thought started to piss her off, then she saw the
size of his ass and it took all of her reserve not to burst out
laughing.

"Damn, threatened by a bubble butt homosexual on your
fashion premier. How fucked up is that!" French Tip turned
around to see Cantelope looking like a million dollars in a pink
and black body cat suit. Her black Chloe eyeglasses covered
her eyes but French Tip knew they were sparkling with laughter.

Cantelope took her glasses off. The look on her face broke
the dam and French Tip burst out with laughter.

"Oh my God! Did you hear that little mothafucka? Talking
faster than Speedy Gonzales!" She was laughing so hard that a
tear slid down her face.

Instead of replying, Cantelope mimicked the organizer saying every word and syllable just like he did. Her antics caused
French Tip to erupt in more laughter. Cantelope followed.

They walked to the dressing room laughing and talking
about the incident. They did more laughing than talking. There
was no need to go to changing. She stayed ready and neva had

to get ready. Inside of her dressing room were seven different extra outfits that she had on deck.

Fuck what they are talking bout, French Tip was Satin Doll. She was wearing a long pearl colored sheer spaghetti strapped dress, six-inch Louboutin's heels. The sheer dress clung to her curves like painted on skin. She topped things off with a ten carat Paul Morelli four tier hanging diamond necklace with matching drop diamond earrings.

She finished getting her make up touched up and made it to the curtains leading to the stage, with twenty seconds to spare. Even the organizer had to stop and do a double take when he saw her.

"Whatever, Miss Thang! So, you clean up well. So, what? Come on and show the world the Queen." Before she could respond, French Tip was ushered through the curtains and onto the stage.

As he ushered her he placed an earpiece into her ear. The bright lights were the first thing to hit her. She had to stop and blink her eyes until they adjusted to the light.

French gazed out into an ocean of smiling faces surrounding the stage. Flashes were going off all across the arena. Some people applauded, some whistled while others called out shouts and cheers.

"Good evening, French. There's no need to get nervous. Just listen to my voice and I'll guide you through everything. You'll feel like a pro." The voice in the earpiece told her as she smiled and turned towards everyone.

Looking at her, no-one who didn't know her could tell that she was a stone-cold killer. Following the instructions given to her, she made her way to a throne that was sitting left of center stage. Smoke started covering the stage by the time she climbed on the throne.

"Ladies and gentlemen. No Kingdom has ever existed without a Queen, either to rule or to help rule. Many have existed and flourished at the hands of just a Queen with no King.

Some Queens have carried their kingdoms beyond the realm any King could ever dream of reaching. Satin Doll will be held in the likes such as these." The music began to play in the background as the voice addressed the audience. The lights began to dim.

"Along with the interior design firm or our magazine, Satin Doll Fashionista, the Queen is creating and building regimes within her Kingdom so that her kingdom would be the cornerstone of her Empire. Satin Doll fashion is the first brick used to building her empire."

Right on cue Alicia Keys voice came over the speakers as she sang out loud her song "Empire State of Mind." The lyrics were specialized for the occasion. Instead of New York she sung out that she was from Men-lo.

The audience went crazy when the lights brightened back up. There, on opposite side of the stage in her very own throne was Alicia Keys herself.

Models begin walking out unto the stage and down the center of the stage doing her thang. It was beautiful. French Tip was breathless at the thought of Alicia Keys being that close to her.

"Look alive, love because this is a moment that's only happens once in a lifetime." She had forgotten about the earpiece in her ear.

"Look alive for what?", she asked herself.

It wasn't herself that answered the question though. It was the sound of Jay-Z's voice coming through the speakers as he performed his verse. He came strolling down the center of the stage with a model on each arm. They dropped him off directly in front of the throne French Tip was sitting on.

The audience went bonkers when he reached his arm out to take her hand. He helped her stand and rapped to her. She was in a world all alone. It was magical.

As if things couldn't get no better, he gave her a kiss on the cheek when he was done spitting and the house went Ape Shyt Crazy!

**** N. D. ****
Meanwhile

With a black nylon carrying bag strapped on her back. She made her way quickly and silently down the long dark corridor. Her black and gray fatigues concealing her shadowy form as she made her way. Only the very silent pitter-patter of her bare feet striking the floor could barely be heard.

She'd already picked through two locked and sealed doors. As she approached the third she slowed down. Controlling her breathing, she manipulated her heart beat as well and placed the cardio pulmonary listening device to the door.

The silicon encased, high frequency speaker within the device was designed to detect heart beats. Once confirmation was made, she quickly placed the listening device in her nylon and Velcro belt and retrieved the lock picking tools.

Silently she picked the lock. The pulmonary device picked up a single heart beat on the other side of the door. The door slowly swung open without a sound.

The target was standing less than six-feet in front of her, his back facing her. With the grace of a gazelle, she covered the distance in two strides while pulling out her fourteen-inch razor sharp blade.

She was so silent not even the friction of the fatigues made a sound. The nigga on security was clueless to the threat approaching. At the last moment before impact, his instincts from years in combat screamed out danger.

He spun around dropping to one knee while bringing his arms up. The left arm came up with the forearm horizontally in a knife block. His right arm came up powerfully, punching her in the midsection.

As powerful as it was, the blow was not strong enough to phase Kipaka. She retracted the knife while swinging a closed right over hand and connecting cleanly with his jaw. The speed in which the blow came and caught him off guard forced him to stumble backwards. She followed the blow up with a left knee to the solar plexus. It was over that quick! The moment he toppled over Kipaka, brought her right hand up like she was going to upper cut him.

Throwing her elbow up in the punch caused the knife swipe up in a perfect line of course with his jugular vein. For good measure, she brought the blade back down jamming it into the base of his skull. He was dead before the body dropped.

Quickly, she went about the business of wiping the blood off of her neck, changing her clothes and taking down the black wrap that she had covering her head.

The ocean blue, mid-thigh CoCo Chanel dress, matching heels and hand bag were quite the ensemble. When she let her hair loose, it hung down three inches past her shoulders, complementing the sleeveless dress.

The earrings, necklace and bracelet were all by David Webb. She put them on while walking to her destination. She also slipped in her earpiece.

"Alpha, Bravo, Charlie this is Echo requesting comms check", she spoke into the hidden microphone just before reaching the last door.

"Loud and clear." Echoed the members of the EGU.

"Echo, are you in position?" The voice of Alpha-one came over the earpiece.

The lock picked, Kipaka placed the pick set into her hand bag and got ready to open the door.

"Ten seconds out, zero resistance ahead, four neutralized." She told him as she stepped into one of the hallways that lead to the restrooms.

"Alright I want everybody to look alive and stay alert! All of us know the target so I don't want no mistakes. There's a price to pay for harming a Guerilla, and the dragon is here to collect." No-one acknowledged Mtambo's directive. There was no need to.

"Alpha. I am in position." Even though she addressed Mtambo, Kipaka was talking to her entire team.

She'd made her way into the auditorium. It was jam packed and dark down in the audience, but she already knew where she was headed. They wouldn't be elite if they weren't the best that the organization had.

Mtambo was behind an HD Digital video recorder in another part of the auditorium. Also present were Scooter and Rell, blended nicely in the sea of bodies. Ndege was hidden away in a high vantage point, making sure that there were no problems during the exit.

This would be a risky move no doubt. Even for the best, it would prove to be difficult. However, military command decided that this would be the best strategic move. So, the order was sanctioned. Now, it was being carried out.

It was almost guaranteed that Clark would be here today. The beef had gone on for too long. Neva Die wasn't a street gang or the Mafia. It was a branch of the family. The family were Guerillas, and Guerilla's killed. They didn't beef!

He would die here at the Satin Doll Fashion Show. Locating him was difficult, but they had done that. Killing him wouldn't prove to be the problem. Doing so and not getting caught or having anything captured on video or by the thousands of cameras there, that was their problem. The matter was so sensitive that Zair himself, who was the General of the War Council was overseeing the operation.

The War Council wanted to avoid any contact or publicity that could lead back to the organization. With the feds already watching this Cadre, they couldn't afford to be seen. Clandestine was the only way this operation could be carried out.

**** N. D. ****
Meanwhile

So far, the night had gone off without a hitch. The models were fabulous, the performances fantastic! So many big-name sponsors had approached her about backing the label. Even the promoter found time to come up to her and tell French Tip that she needed to do another immediate venue.

She literally was having the time of her life. Satin Doll was a huge success which would only take her higher in life. She would now have a purpose in life that wasn't taking life.

What would she tell her brother? What would he say to her? They had always been there for one another; would he feel like she'd abandoned him?

These thoughts were quickly trying to steal her light and turn the night dark. French Tip had to catch herself by reminding herself that the time would come for her to deal with all of that. Now was not it.

When her name was announced, she walked thru the curtains and took center stage. The night was almost over. She had one last treat for every one who came out, before it came to an end.

"Good evening." She waited while everyone applauded and cheered. "Thank you. Thank you. Honestly, from the bottom of my heart I need to thank each and every single one of you for coming out tonight and helping me share what has been so far the greatest night of my life. I've received a lot of positive feedback as well as potential investors and more.

"However, I could not have enjoyed the greatest night of my life unless my biggest supporter and best friend were here with me to enjoy it. Now I need you to give your greatest effort and help me welcome him to the stage. I give to you, ladies and gentlemen, my best friend," she turned stretching her arm out towards the back curtains with a huge smile on her face.

The audience applauded and cheered on instinct. But the moment they laid eyes on French Tip's best friend, the applause became genuine. The flashes of the cameras immediately went off the moment his Albino white and beige Mauri Alligators stepped on stage.

The vanilla crème colored tailor-made Armani suit dripped of new money. His freshly waxed bald head shined under the bright lights. 285lbs of pampered down and polished Guerilla strolled across the stage with enough confidence and swag to fill the entire auditorium and then some.

Once he reached her, he gave her the strongest, warmest hug that he could, along with an emotional filled kiss on the cheeks. After they exchanged words, he turned and swept his gaze across the crowd.

Everyone in attendance gawked at the giant of a man that stood center stage looking like the 'God of Africa, waiting to hear his first words.

When the applause stopped he spoke, his voice a lot softer than expected.

"The only reason she called me her best friend is because she is my best friend." "But everyone knows our cousin Cantelope is her best friend." He turned his head and looked back at his little sister, "For years everyone including her wondered why I call her Booger, I would neva tell anyone why, not even her."

"We've all heard the term, 'cute as a booger.' Well I used to wonder why people said that. I thought about it. Boogers are so nasty and disgusting and yet kids love them." Murmurs went throughout the audience. "I know, I know. But you can tell a kid a thousand times not to dig in their nose or play with them. No matter what, they do. Kids just love boogers." Everyone burst out laughing. He waited for the noise to die down before continuing.

"That's some kind of love. A special love is what it takes to love something so gross, that everybody else hates. That is truly "unconditional love." That's the kind of love I have for my sister. That unbreakable, she can't do nothing wrong, in my eyes, kind of love. That's why she's my Booger. It's not that she's disgusting, it's that I love her no matter what!" There was not a full seat in the house, there were only standing ovations.

French Tip rushed into her brothers arms when he turned around. The hugged one another like they hadn't seen each other in thirty years.

"I love you, brother!" She told him in his ear with tears rolling down her cheeks.

In the crowd, members of Neva Die were shocked to see their overseer out of his coma and on the stage. French Tip had stuck by her decision for no-one to know he was awake. Not even Clarkola, who was in attendance with his team, knew about it. Voorheeze agreed with secret because it gave him time to dissect the problems they faced and find the solutions at his own pace.

He broke their embrace and turned back towards the podium.

"Many of you don't know this because you don't know me. But, I've just spent the better part of the past year in a coma. That gap in time, the momentary suspension in nowhere showed me that I neva knew what was important. All my life I've chased the things that weren't. Well, I'm don't with that!

"The only other person whom I've always loved like this has neva even known. Lisa! I love you. I've always loved you. It's time that you knew it because I'm coming for you!" With that said, together hand in hand, the siblings walked off the stage.

Shortly after Keri Hilson and Little Wayne took the stage and preformed their hit *Turning Me On*.

**** N. D. ****

Chapter XXIII

Meanwhile

The bottles of Rose were finally starting to make their self known. Clark and his team were definitely doing the most. At first, he was going to skip the event. French Tip told him that she'd invited the Neva Die Family and he didn't want to be nowhere in the same vicinity as them bitch ass niggaz unless shit was popping.

His little sister had made sure to let the organizer know to seat the two groups on completely opposite sides if the auditorium. She knew if they bumped into one another, shit would pop off.

Jay-Z and Alicia Keyes did their thang hands down. But fuck the dumb shit, Clark was gone have to make his way back stage and snatch up one of them thick ass model chicks for the night. Shit if he ran into Alicia, she could get it too, with her thick ass. He didn't want to get up, but he couldn't take it any more. He had to piss like fuck! When he stood up on wobbly legs Man-Man and Banga looked over his way.

"What it is, shorty? You straight?" Man-Man called over the music.

Back home he had partied some and even had his lil times he stunted, but he had neva experienced no shit like this. Neither of them had. There were celebrities all over the place.

"I'm Gucci, rogue. Just gotta piss like a mothafucka!" He called back," You niggaz enjoy the show, I'll be back."

Clark wasn't worried bout no problems, he had the cannon on his hip. He wished a mothafucka would. He'd light this bitch up, fuck some cameras. "Rather be judged by twelve then carried by six" was the motto he lived by.

With those thoughts on his mind, he smiled at a sexy little, fine ass, redbone as he passed her. If he didn't have to piss so bad she probably could'a got hollered at.

**** N. D. ****
Meanwhile

"Echo-One this is Alpha. What's your visualization like?" Everyone had been in position for twenty-minutes. Mtambo was only doing a check to make sure everybody was on point.

"It's not perfect, but I do have a direct visual. I was thinking about possibly moving for a better angle." She responded.

"No need Echo. Halo One is in position less then ten yards away. I got a direct visual from behind the target…" As Scooter was speaking, the target stood up. "Alpha-Team, we have movement. Target just stood up and is possibly on the move."

"Considering how many bottles of that Rose they were popping, he's more than likely heading toward the restrooms. Alpha-One request repositioning?" The voice of Rell filled the earpieces.

"Halo-Two I have to agree with your assessment. Relocate a course to intercept and eliminate if possible. Halo-One. Proceed course for rear tail. Should you acquire the ideal circumstances for elimination, proceed without prejudice and execute elimination. Charlie and Echo maintain positions." Mtambo gave the orders to his cadre to carry out.

The Halo moniker was designated for the specific strike unit of the Hit Detail, those designated to make the kill. If for some reason they couldn't, any member of the detail could execute the hit with approval from Alpha-One, but Halo didn't need approval.

Scooter stood up and kept his distance. He made sure to give Clark his space. He didn't want to draw attention to himself. Following him would be easy. Not too many people came dressed to the event wearing hood shit.

As he was moving, a sexy ass light-skinned sistah stood up in front of him.

"Hello there, handsome." She had the sexiest eyes he had ever seen. "I hope you're not leaving. I've been watching you all night hoping that I would get the chance to speak with you." She was 5'6" with a body like Yadi Da Body.

On any given Sunday, she could get the business, but not today. Today he was on some mob shyt and nothing got in the way of that.

"Damn, beautiful. I'm sorry, but I'm happily married. In fact, I am on my way to meet my wife now. She was running a little late." Scooter side stepped her without waiting for a reply. He had a nigga to smack.

He neva saw the disappointment on her face nor the spark of fire inside of her beautiful eyes.

****** N. D. ******
Richmond, California

The room looked like a mini command center for Nasa. Ten twenty-five-inch T.V. monitors covered the entire wall. There was a table in front of the wall that resembled a huge mixing board in a music studio. Speakers were mounted in various places throughout the room.

The man seated in a chair monitoring it wasn't worried about any sound escaping because the entire room was sound proofed. Even if any sound did escape the room, he was the only one in the entire building.

Young Zair was only twenty-five years old. However, his gun play in the streets was legendary. Within the organization it became clear when he was just a young pup, how extraordinary his analytical mind was. It was clear that he would be a military strategist.

He was currently Active Commanding General of the War Council. He was in charge of every single Military Cadre and oversaw all military operations.

He watched intently as the EGU Forces carried out one of the most controversial operations he's ever overseen. He was at odds over the committee's decision to execute Clark because he was Voorheeze older brother. Voorheeze was Zair's big brotha. He felt that he was betraying his brother by overseeing operation to kill Clark.

Zair had always been loyal to two things. The first being, The Family and the second was Voorheeze.

For over two hours he'd watched the monitors. He listened and followed closely to the communications of Mtambo and his Cadre. The time was drawing near for the execution. If Clark didn't give them the opportunity to carry it out before the designated moment, they would take it then.

It seemed like the opportunity presented itself when he watched Clark get up and walk towards what he agreed would no doubt be the bathroom.

He watched the Cadre move strategically in stealth towards the target. Rell was already in the bathroom taking up his position. Scooter followed Clark.

Zair still kept his eyes divided amongst the other monitors. French Tip was on stage looking so elegant. She looked the opposite of the true killer she really was.

"...Now, I need you to give your greatest effort and help me..." She was saying up on the stage.

Zair turned his head just in time to see Clark enter the bathroom. Scooter wasn't that far behind him. Just as something else stood out to him, her words grabbed his focus.

"...I give to you ladies and gentlemen...My best friend."

The cameras left French Tip and showed the curtains as he stepped through looking like the god Zair remembered.

"God Damn!" He couldn't believe what he was seeing. But now was not the time to question, he had to act!

****** N. D. ******
Meanwhile

Scooter made his way for a middle-aged white man who was exiting the restroom as he approached. Quietly, he opened the door preparing to enter. He noticed two things when the door opened. His brother stood at the sink in his disguise washing his hands, while Clark was at the urinal taking a piss.

Rell gave Scooter a signal to seal off the restroom, which he did.

"Halo-One to Alpha-Team. Halo-Two is in position. Execution in less than ten seconds." Scooter informed everyone just as he noticed the little honey coming his way.

The moment Scooter backed out the door, Rell spun on his toes. Pulling out the garrote, he silently made his way towards Clark, who was so busy concentrating on what he was doing he was clueless to the enemy behind him.

Five more steps…four…Rell brought his arms up ready to loop the garrote around his neck! Three…..held his breath. Two….

"Dragon to EGU stand down! I repeat this is Dragon to EGU Command stand down. Abort the operation." An unexpected Zair's voice came over the earpiece.

The moment Rell put the garrote in his pocket, Clark noticed a reflection in the stainless-steel handle of the urinal. He spun around with fire in his eyes and his hand on his banga which was already coming up off his hip.

Immediately improvising, Rell hung his head and faked like he was drunk. Swaying side to side.

"Me bad my bredrin! 'Cuse me. The blood clot spirits done ran threw me, bredrin." The Jamaican accent was on point. Along with the dreads, it got the job done.

"Nigga, I ain't wit dat faggot shit! Next time watch where the fuck you going or de blood clot bullet gone run through ya!" He mocked the Jamaican accent as he pushed his way past the nigga.

Rell was raging on the inside. He was there! He could taste the niggaz death on his lips. Stand down? What the fuck Zair had meant, stand down? Rell was so furious t spun backwards kicking and breaking one of the mirrors, but he would neva question a command.

Outside the bathroom, Scooter was wondering what he was going to say to the little sexy thang who had followed him from where they were seated. She must've been thirsty to still push even after he told her wifey was here.

As she approached he started to speak, but she kept gesturing with her eyes for him to look down. When he did in her hand was a paper that said "We're being watched."

This caught his attention. Just then the bathroom door opened up and Clark walked out. He was so pissed he didn't pay any attention to Scooter who wasn't in disguise.

"Where's that wife that you were on your way to go get?" She asked once Clark was out of ear shot.

"Oh…I…uh…" Scooter fumbled over his words , with a confused look on his face.

"Look, sweetheart, there's no need to try making up excuses. I know she's not here. Look just take my number and call me. Trust me, you won't be sorry." She handed Scooter a folded piece of paper while removing the black scorpion diamond pin she was wearing.

Next, she gave Scooter a big bear hug and a kiss on the cheek. "Zair, I stand firm in the spirit of George Lester Jackson…" she recited something for five seconds. When she was done reciting it she continued to speak. "The entire auditorium is under surveillance. Abort your mission and leave. There are over one hundred Federal Agents here." She released her hug and bent down. When she stood up she had the pin in her hand.

"Oh look! My pin came off. Trust me, honey. Give me a call. I'll teach you a few things." And with that she turned and left.

"Who in the hell was that?" Rell asked his brother he came out of the bathroom.

From what she just said, getting the fuck out of there was more important then learning who in the fuck she was.

"Alpha-Team this is Dragon. Execute immediate evacuation orders. Again, I repeat evacuate immediately." Zair had terminated the mission and given new orders.

Rell and Scooter just looked at each other before carrying out the order.

**** N. D. ****

De'Kari

Chapter XXIV

#880 N. passing Dixon Landing

Driving felt foreign to Voorheeze as he cruised down 880 headed to the war room. He was glad that he chose to the drive the 300 instead of the Lambo. That was just too much power right now for Voorheeze to be trying to wrestle with.

He'd just left his mom's house. He had to spend some time with her before taking care of business. He wanted to go straight to Lisa once and for all, but he knew this bullshit that was going on had to be taken care of before things got too out of hand.

Clark was his blood brother, but Jama was what he believed in and represented. Neva Die was his life, what he ate, slept and drank. His brother was going to have to respect it. By the same token, Dok needed to slow his fucking roll! Voorheeze didn't know what Dok was thinking, a nigga ain't gone come in regulating shit. No nigga!

Being in the coma this time around had a completely different effect on him. His fire had been reignited and shit was gone burn! The battery pack was fully charged.

Learning that Sutton and Young Nigga Mafia had been erased really pissed him off. He couldn't slide for himself. Knowing that Batman slid for him and did the damn thang was cool though. Somebody needed to feel his fire. Somebody needed to burn.

His phone started vibrating just as he was passing the Tennyson exit. The caller I.D. told him that it was Vieria. She'd been blowing him up since the fashion show. How was he to know it was televised? Better yet how in the fuck was he to know that she was watching it?

"Yeah, Babe." He answered praying she wasn't looking for a fight.

"How could youuuu!" she cried through the phone.

"Vieira. Look ma, I'm sorry, I really am, but the truth is the truth. You and I had beautiful moments, but I've loved this woman since I was a child. I neva knew where you stood. You neva put nothing on the table. So how was I to know you were catching feelings?"

She couldn't answer that question. Not only was she too caught up in her emotions, but she knew his words were true. She just didn't want to accept them.

"Vieira. I care about you a lot, but we're going to have to have this conversation face to face in a little bit. Right now, I'm about to have a serious meeting." He didn't' like seeing any woman hurt, especially one who was by his side like she had been. It stemmed from seeing his mom hurt so much as a child.

"So, you are going to break my heart and run? You really expect me to believe you're going to call me back?" She asked through the tears.

"I've neva lied to you and I'm not gone start now."

Reluctantly she said "okay"

"Bye."

"Bye." He placed the phone back down inside of the cup holder.

He turned on the radio trynna take his mind off the bullshit.

Lil Boosie and Webbie came to life thru the speakers. The custom speakers beat hard while Boosie asked niggaz "Do you got a problem?" This song was the prelude to what was coming.

He pulled up to the War Room twelve minutes later. In True Religion jeans, throw back Jerry Rice Forty-Niner jersey and all black Timberland boots, he looked nothing like the smooth well-dressed gangsta everyone was' used to. The twin chrome 45's with extended clips on his waist said otherwise.

This was his first time at this location. Before the coma, the house on Santa Elana was the War Room. He took a moment to look around and check his security, then made his way up the walkway.

Inside of the house everyone was present. The room got quiet as all idle chatter stopped. Everyone's head turned and faced the natural leader of the Family. The moment was surreal.

"Brother!" French Tip rushed into his arms.

Voorheeze hugged his baby sister all the while keeping an eye on Dok Holliday. He noticed a few faces that he didn't recognize and assumed they could only be apart of Dok's Cadre.

Scooter and Rell he recognized. Although they were grown, he could still see the kids they were when he and Dok were cellmates in Santa Rita so many years ago.

He broke off his embrace with his sister and walked straight towards Dok. The way Scooter's body tensed up didn't go unnoticed by Voorheeze.

"Bredren!"

"What's up, big brah!" The two embraced in a might bear hug. It had been nearly twenty years since they'd last seen each other face to face.

"You look healthy, young god." Dok told him as they stared at each other.

"What happened to the mane?" Voorheeze was referring to Dok's signature dreadlocks that were gone.

"As the times and the enemy evolve..." Dok began "so must we too evolve." They both finished Jonathan Jackson's quote to his brother George together. Soledad Brother's was a mandatory read for them.

The next fifteen minutes were spent getting reacquainted with and introduced to everyone. Almost a year is a long time not to be around someone. Especially in the street life.

After the reintroductionss were out of the way, Voorheeze turned back to face Dok.

"Big Brah, let's address the elephant in the room and get this shit out of the way. Brah, how could you go to war with my brother? My mama's son?" From the moment he heard about it, Voorheeze couldn't believe that shit.

"Peace be still, Bredren. It wasn't like that. I tried to avoid this as much as possible. Clark continued to push our hand." Dok knew this was coming. Years ago, they'd sworn an oath to each other. They were family till the death. So, their family was family.

"Push your hand? A child will always challenge his parent that's why we discipline. You don't try to kill yo child! Or your brother's child!" Voorheeze temper was escalating.

The room was completely quiet. This wasn't what everybody expected. Scooter slowly eased his way into position to have a better shot, in case things went bad. No-one saw DJ do the exact same thing on the other side of the room.

"Gloved hands were used with your brother. I tried to prevent blood shed. Then he killed Kiumba. The Central Committee gave the order. I'm sorry, bredrin, the Dinosaurs made the call."

"Fuck you mean, the Dinosaurs made the call? Nigga dis is Neva Die! We make the fucking call!" Voorheeze was seething. "Or have you forgotten that?"

No-one knew the shit he had been through and why he felt the way he did about "The Dinosaurs".

"Again, Peace, be still, Bredren. Watch your tone and have respect for the "Old Ones." Dok could tell his brotha was hurt so he overlooked the outburst. But everything had it's limit especially disrespect.

"Fuck is you saying, Dok?" Voorheeze hands went to his waist line. "You might be big brah but, nigga, don't forget who you're talking to. My gun play is bar none ,nigga, and my body count is official. Remember that next time you wanna give me a warning!"

The room was divided. If things ended badly, shit was going to get ugly. There was no illusion as to where the lines were drawn. Dok had been leading them this year, but Voorheeze was their leader.

The members of Dok's Cadre were indeed Neva Die, but they were still loyal to the Guerilla Family. Voorheeze's Dragons were loyal to each other.

"As far as them 'Old Ones,' nigga I don't march to the beat of their drums. Them mothafuckas don't know shit about loyalty unless it's to each other." Voorheeze finished.

"Brah ,what you talkin 'bout?" Dok was lost. Where was all of this coming from?

So Voorheeze filled him in. *It all started in Solano. Voorheeze had just become a level II and was up for transfer. Rico was appointed temporary overseer of the yard. 14 comrades were removed off the yard by Inmate Gang Investigation Unit or I.G.I.*

A nigga who was no good dropped a kit to the police saying Voorheeze has given the order to kill officer Jones. The validation process began. Five people were given validation packets. When it was all said and done, it was discovered that Rico was debriefing (snitching by dropping out) and planned it all Voorheeze beat Validation and was ordered to give a detailed report to the committee which he did.

A year and a half later, Voorheeze would find himself at San Quentin. Once there here he would learn not only did the Central Committee not deal with Rico, but Rico had ordered Red and DM to spread lies about Voorheeze saying he was debriefing."

From Folsom to San Quentin, Voorheeze name was drug through the mud. Needless to say, he reached out once again to the Central Committee who ordered him not to indulge in any act of violence as a method in dealing with the civilian population adhering to the rumors. The Committee said that they would deal with it.

Months later, the Committee hadn't done a thing. When he called his committee contact the number was disconnected. He was left hung out to dry all on his own.

Right then he began to hate all that he represented, all that he had stood for. These niggaz or his brothers that turned their

De'Kari

backs on him. These were his teachers, his elders. The ones he idolized.

They had broken the very oath they'd created and sworn to. They had faltered at his side. So, fuck them! ,he decided. And fuck everybody with them.

Three days later he was four days to the house and stabbed a nigga fourteen times. He sat in the hole nine months waiting to see if the D.A. was going to pick up the case.

His brotha from another, Mike Vegas, got on some gangsta shit with the snitch to make sure they didn't. If it wasn't for a Brookefield soldia, Voorheeze would be doing life.

Guilt tore thru Dok like a Ginsu thru a banana. He was at Folsom when he heard the story. Instead of giving Voorheeze the benefit of the doubt, he listened to Red and DM. Worse than that, he himself had cut Voorheeze off and they had been closer than brothers. They dreamed up Neva Die together.

In a rare moment of emotional display Dok began "V., Bredren, I didn't kn…"

"Nigga, fuck yo apology! I don't want yo mothafucking sympathy. You needed to know the truth, so you'll understand." Voorheeze spoke thru clenched teeth.

"Understand what?" Dok looked lost and perplexed.

With the speed of a cheetah, both 45's were out of his waistband and aimed. One was pointed directly in Dok's face. The one in the other hand was pointed at Mtambo.

"You got a choice to make right here, right mothafucking now!" His hand gripped the butt of the four nickels tighter. "You're either B.G.F. or you're Neva Die. Ain't no in between."

Scooter's hands began slowly creeping toward his waist. The Oakland Cadre would no doubt rock, however, Gunz decided to rock. Gunz was a founder of Neva Die too. It was natural for him to rock with Voorheeze. The movement and ideology Gunz had picked up over the year from Dok had his mind thinking differently. As his hand rested on the handle of his Desert Eagle, he knew he would rock with Dok.

294

"Lil Scooter, I guarantee if you pull dat banger you'll be dead before you raise it. That goes for you too, Rell." Voorheeze neva took his eyes off Dok. "What that Oakland shit look like?"

Instantly, little red lights crisscrossed the room. The infrared beams only marked Dok's Cadre.

"East Oakland in the house." Mike Vegas sung out as he came strolling in the room with a big ass 357 in his hand.

When Big Rocc heard his name mentioned earlier, it brought back memories. To see him come strolling into the room sent chills down Big Rocc's back. Magic's son was a more cold-blooded son of a bitch then the devil. Them long ass dreadlocks made him look like the devil.

It got under Dok's skin that he'd allowed himself to get distracted. He had to smile inwardly at how Voorheeze used the same method he had used.

"Peace be still bredren. There's no need for bloodshed. We're all Afrikans and we are still family." Dok attempted to calm things, but Voorheeze wasn't hearing that shit. "Dok what's it gone be? Are you with us or against us?"

"Brah, I'll always be Neva Die. But I'ma Black Guerilla till the death." Those words split the most powerful organization the Bay Area ever witnessed the moment they were spoken.

"Well, I'ma Neva Die Dragon and all I bang is Dragon Gang! If you ain't Dragon Gang, get the fuck out!" Voorheeze shouted.

Mtambo was the first to move. Afterwards Dok's entire Cadre stood up. Gunz stood up as well shocking Voorheeze but fuck it! AJ and DeeDee followed suit. Though they stood, they were all waiting for Dok to make a move. The red lights on their chests didn't mean shit to any of them. They were all killers and not afraid of death.

DeeDee looked at DJ, who was still seated. The look said, "Nigga what's up."

D.J. stood up slowly pulling out a big ass 45 magnum, the automatic was bigger then the Desert Eagle.

"Y'all heard my father. Get the fuck out before I pop off in this bitch!" Everybody looked at D.J. shocked.

Cantelope and French Tip were the only ones that knew D.J. was Voorheeze son. That was why he'd watched him at the hospital.

"Take care, brotha." Those were the last words Dok would ever speak to Voorheeze, or so he thought.

When Dok walked out of the War Room that day, more than half of Neva Die left with him.

****** N. D. ******
East Palo Alto

"Man, I'm telling you, that broad had an ass so gawd damn phat, shawty, I literally had to bend my knees and angle my shit in order to get up in it!" Banga bent his open legs then dipped down trynna illustrate what he was talking bout.

They were sitting around at O.G. Peppi Hanks 'house discussing the women they'd took home from the fashion show the other night.

"Naw, shawty, her donkey probably wasn't even phat, yo soldia probably just a toy soldia." Everyone burst out laughing as Man-Man made a visual by holding his thumb and forefinger two inches apart.

"Ain't no gardner snakes here, shawty. All python." Banga grabbed the crotch of his Sean John jeans and shaking it at Man-Man.

Everyone was deeply engrossed in the conversation except for JuJu. His attention was glued to Peppi's sixty-five-inch flat screen. Peppi had the new Samsung Smart T.V. JuJu was currently fucking wit social media. A live station on Facebook had caught his attention.

On the screen some white chick was asshole butt naked, strapped down to some type of execution chair. The white broad had a bull shit body so that wasn't what caught his attention. It was her eyes.

At first JuJu thought it was some bull-ass-shit. But he'd witnessed real life fear in people's eyes up close and personal too many times. He knew the fear he saw in her eyes was real.

When JuJu saw the nigga that's been all over the T.V. and shit, he knew shit was about to get real.

"Oh shit! Y'all check this shit out! He called getting everyone's attention.

"JuJu, what kinda sick shit you watching?" Banga called out, after seeing the naked white chick and the nigga.

Before JuJu could answer Sam said, "Rogue, ain't that the nigga dats been murking all them cops!"

"Yeah, dat's, blood." JuJu answered

Batman was looking the woman up and down, all over. He was bending down low enough to smell the fear coming out of her pores with perspiration. Every time he would get in her face, she would shiver under the restraints from the terror she felt.

Suddenly he began to talk. "For the next thirty seconds we will unfortunately relive what happened to Sandra Bland that day in Waller County, Texas on July 13th. Then you will see justice. You will watch while San Joaquin Deputy Sheriff Purtle and I remind the Government and their law enforcement attack dogs that this shit is not a game."

The screen went black. Then the famous clip of Sandra Bland being forcefully restrained and drug from her car by trooper Bria Encina whom to this date was neva held accountable, was played

After the clip of Sandra played, the film of Deputy Purtle being abducted by Batman the same way played.

"Deputy Purtle here hasn't had the misfortune of being with the Sheriff's Department long enough to become corrupted by the fascist bourgeois puppet masters that sign her paychecks. She just happens to be collateral damage. She's on the wrong fucking side of a wall!

297

"She must now pay the price for her superiors. We must teach them that 'Black Lives Matter!' I must teach them!" He removed the rag out of Deputy Purtle's mouth.

"Aarrghh! Aarrghh! Somebody please help me!" Through the pain of her shattered and swollen jaw, she screamed as loud as she could.

The entire left side of her face was freakishly swollen and had turned a blackish purple. Her once cute, pudgy face was hideously disfigured.

Without warning he back handed the shit out of her. The pain was unbearable. Her scream was bone chilling.

"If I ain't tell you to talk, you best shut the fuck up!" He was inches away from her face when he yelled his directive. Spittle flew out his mouth onto her face.

He stood erect and adjusted some knobs on the sound board. Then he walked over to his work station behind her. If the big black plastic apron that he had on didn't tell you this shit was about to get fucked up, the scalpel with the pristine blade that he picked up did.

"Naaw, shawty, he ain't gone slice up the snow like that." Man-Man just knew this shit was fake.

"Nigga, it's bout to get real!" JuJu excitedly called out.

"Dat nigga there ,boi, now dat's a lil nigga I can fuck with." Peppi called out.

Peppi was an old head. He'd done it all from shit to shine, smoke to ball. There are so many different rumors about his body count ,the shit was crazy. Now he had found a chef and was eating with the crystal meth and fentanyl.

On the T.V. screen Batman stood behind Purtle whose head was held in place by stainless steele clamps. He checked the angle of the camera, Deputy Purtle was trying her best to see what was going on, but she couldn't move her head a smidge.

Batman took the scalpel and proceeded to scalp her like the Indians used to. He focused on the cut making sure it was as precise as possible. He wasn't worried about her loud screams. They were miles away from anyone.

"We don't know what happened to Sandra Bland, but we know what's gone happen to officer Purtle." During the next five minutes he cut and sliced off various parts of her body, from her ears to her fingers.

The Facebook Live Blackkk Lives Matter page had twenty thousand people watching.

He took the scalpel and removed all of the skin from around her left breast, on down past her navel. She passed out when he removed the skin from the right side. Batman woke her back up by slapping her swollen jaw.

Deputy Purtle couldn't prevent the tears from rolling down her face. In her mind she hated God for not answering her prayers. Where was He now that she needed Him? She didn't know why she'd wasted so much time trying to live the way she was told a good Christian should live. She should have done more fun shit. Sucked more cocks. God was a joke.

The pain of the scalpel slicing into her flesh brought her out of her thoughts. Blackkk Lives Matter was carved across her chest.

By the time he finally killed her, there were two hundred and fifteen million people watching. It was a Facebook record.

"That nigga there ain't no joke rogue." Everyone agreed with Clark, hands down.

Clark stood up off the sofa. "Y'all niggaz make sure this shit goes off with no problems. I gotta take care of some family shit. When I'm done we gone deal with them niggaz once and for all." What he had in mind for Dok and Gunz was no doubt going to show mothafucka's what dat Smack Mobb was like.

It was Friday and Clark was on his way to meet his brother and sister for their weekly dinner. Due to all the shit wit Young Nigga Mafia and then Voorheeze getting shot. They hadn't had their dinner in over a year.

Voorheeze picked a little spot in Berkely called Skates On The Bay. Clark really didn't like fuckin' with it like that. Being so far away from his comfort zone. But he figured fuck it! They were three killas if shit popped off they could handle it.

Voorheeze and French Tip were already seated at the table when he walked in. The restaurant was small but nice. It resembled the kind of spot you would go to and have a home cooked meal.

Uncharacteristically, Voorheeze was dressed in all black. He had on a pair of black Cavali jeans, Black button-down Gucci shirt with a pair of black Gucci shoes. French Tip was dressed in a casual black Fendi dinner dress. A three-quarter length black Fendi jacket set on the back of her chair.

"I see you fuckin' wit the Cavali now." Clark pointed out as the two brothers embrace. "Nigga woke outta the coma feeling like O'Dawg."

"Naaw brah, a nigga just relaxing a lil bit." Voorheeze took his seat. "Shit, still kinda feels weird you know? Like a nigga woke up to a foggy dream, or in this case, a foggy nightmare."

"Shit, speakin' on it, yo niggaz gotta go rogue. I done been far to lenient wit mothafuckas as it is out of respect for you. But that shit they pulled wit Tut, Rogue mothafuckas gotta answer for that shit." The conversation stopped as the waitress came to take their orders.

When she left, Voorheeze picked up the conversation.

"That's what I wanted to talk to you about. It's like this plain and simple, you're my big brother nigga and I'll neva side with an outsider over you. I don't care who was wrong or who was right. You my brother, that's all that matters." Voorheeze told him before taking a sip of his drank.

Nigga, I thought you was all about yo banner and shit? Neva Die over everything!" Clark looked at his little brother suspiciously.

"Don't get shit fucked up. It'll always be Neva Die." He finished his glass then told his brotha what was what.

French Tip sat and watched as her two brothers talked. Voorheeze filled Clark in on everything that transpired at the War Room the other day. Leaving out nothing.

Liking what he was hearing, Clark shared with Voorheeze what he had planned for Dok and Gunz over dinner they all discussed ways to go about doing what Clark had in mind. An hour later they had knocked down two big bottles of Hennessy Privilege, finished their meals and devised the perfect plan to knock down Dok and Gunz.

Out in the parking lot the night air was cool and crisp. Both Voorheeze and Clark had on thick leather Gucci jackets. Clark had on a three-quarter length, Voorheeze had on a full length.

Sliding on his leather gloves, Voorheeze looks over at French Tip.

"What you about to do brother?" She asks as she slid on her on gloves.

"I got a bottle of Privy in the car. I was thinking about driving over to the Marina, kicking it out by the water for a minute." He answered her question while lighting a New Port 100.

"You want some company? It's too young to be trynna call it night. And since you got da Henny, I'm like what it do?" She tried to emulate a thug nigga as she talked.

"What it do, is what it don't do. You know you good." He playfully gave her a hug. "You ain't neva gotta ask.

Clark was already feeling tipsy from the Hennessy they'd drank in the restaurant. Yet he wasn't about to be left out of the fun.

"Shyyt, nigga I know I ain't gotta ask either. Lead the way, I'm right behind you." He was already heading towards his new Champagne BMW 750I without waiting for a response.

Voorheeze was still in the Chrysler so following him was no problem. French Tip was pulling up the rear in her Challenger.

The light on his screen light up drawing Clark's attention to his cell phone. He picked it up and noticed he had a few missed calls. He tapped the screen, bringing it up and notifications menu. Man-Man was two of the missed calls. He tapped Man-Man's number and hit him back.

"Shawty, for a minute I thought I was gone have to bring da cavalry." Man-Man joked into the phone when he picked up.

"Naw Rogue, it's good. Shit wit the fam just running a little longer then I though." He switched lanes following behind his brother. J-Stalins "10 Feet Deep" played in the background. "What's up wit dat other thang though, we Gucci?" He was referring to the play he left them and Peppi Hank's to run.

"Right as rain Shawty." Man-Man responded. Peppi Hanks had come thru for them with twenty pounds of Meth as a tester. If everything was everything, they were about to do some big shit!

"Aight, well look, I'ma be wit my folks for a little longer. I'll hit you up at the spot first thing in the morning." They were pulling up to the marina as he was getting off the phone.

The night was cold and pitch black.

"I don't know how I let y'all talk me into this." Clark complained as he came walking up buttoning up his jacket.

"Talk you into it? Nigga you invited you mothafuck'n self. Fuck you mean, talked you into it." Voorheeze jokingly responded. "Come on o'le cry baby ass nigga, let's go." The three siblings made their way out to the long pier that goes out three miles into the ocean.

The wind factor out on the pier was something to respect. French Tip had traded her Fendi coat for an all black mink that she had in her car.

The three kicked it smoking blunt after blunt and hitting the bottle of Hennessy. The alcohol doing wonders warming them up. They laughed and joked about a lot of shit. Each one taking turns telling stories about when they were kids.

Voorheeze wasn't as big a smoker as his brother was. Neither was French Tip. So most of the weed that was consumed was done so by Clark. As was the alcohol. Two hours later Clark was really fucked up.

"Nigga, m-member when we use watch Naw Yak City?" He was slurring so bad it was hard to make out New Jack City.

302

"Am I my brotha's keeper!" Both men shouted out loud.

When they were kids, New Jack City was the most gangsta movie out. They used to love it. Being that they were brothers, the line that Nino and G-Money used to say to one another became their little saying.

"God damn, rogue, I gotta piss hella bad." Clark suddenly spun towards the outter edge of the pier.

"Yeah, it's bout time to get the fuck up outta here." Voorheeze agreed as he looked over at French Tip.

She'd been enjoying memory lane with her brothers, but her heart was heavy. She understood Voorheeze better than anybody, so she understood his thought process. It didn't make things any easier.

Clark was too worried about taking a piss than to think about his little sister standing right there behind him. If he wasn't so drunk he would have walked down the pier some.

The wind started to pick up some as it rolled across the water. Whistling against the pillars in the heavy pier.

Voorheeze looked over to French Tip. Tears were in her eyes as she looked him dead in his soulless eyes. "I love you" he mouthed the words to her just as the tears escaped her eyes and made a course down her face.

The time was now. It was do or die. Now or neva! Voorheeze slowly pulled one of his Dragons off his hip. A tear escaped his eye as well. He loved his big brother! Clark was his idol. But rules where rules and they were put in place for a reason.

He screwed the silencer on. Clark was oblivious. His body slightly swayed with the breeze.

Drunkenly he shouted, "Am I my brother's keeper?"

Voorheeze raised the Black Dragon pointing it at the back of his brother's head.

"Yes, I am." He recited Nino's words to G-Money before he killed him.

Closing his eyes for one second. He opened them and pulled the trigger. The Dragon spit fire.

Clark's body moved forward. The entire front of his face blew off. Time stood still for Voorheeze and French Tip as the body collapsed in slow motion.

Voorheeze hung his head low.

"If I lie to you, I will lie on you. If I lie on you, I will tell on you!

If I threaten you, I will turn on you. If I turn on you, I will kill you."

They were raised by and lived by this mantra. If somebody broke it, kill them. That was the rule. Clark knew the rule!

Next, he went into Clarks pockets and pulled out his bag of weed. "You ain't gone need this, rogue." He stated and then threw the headless body of his big brother off the pier like a sack of potatoes.

There was no need to worry about the body washing up because he didn't tie it down. With all the sharks in the Pacific waters around the Berkeley Marina, Clark would be long gone in less than an hour.

"He brought it on himself the moment he threatened you, Booger. I wouldn't let God get away with that." When French Tip told Voorheeze in the hospital about her encounter with Clark after Nastasia was killed. He made his mind up then he would kill him.

They sat down on one of the wooden benches and smoked a blunt in silence thinking about their older brother. This wasn't like when he and Gunz faked his death. There was no coming back from this!

After that last blunt they got up and walked to their whips. Voorheeze followed her before heading to the Hayward Hills.

Follow the Saga...
Gorillaz in the Bay 4
Coming Soon

Submission Guideline

Submit the first three chapters of your completed manuscript to ldpsubmissions@gmail.com, subject line: Your book's title. The manuscript must be in a .doc file and sent as an attachment. Document should be in Times New Roman, double spaced and in size 12 font. Also, provide your synopsis and full contact information. If sending multiple submissions, they must each be in a separate email.

Have a story but no way to send it electronically? You can still submit to LDP/Ca$h Presents. Send in the first three chapters, written or typed, of your completed manuscript to:

LDP: Submissions Dept
Po Box 870494
Mesquite, Tx 75187

DO NOT send original manuscript. Must be a duplicate.

Provide your synopsis and a cover letter containing your full contact information.

Thanks for considering LDP and Ca$h Presents.

De'Kari

<u>Coming Soon from Lock Down Publications/Ca$h Presents</u>

BOW DOWN TO MY GANGSTA
By **Ca$h**
TORN BETWEEN TWO
By **Coffee**
BLOOD STAINS OF A SHOTTA **III**
By **Jamaica**
STEADY MOBBIN **III**
By **Marcellus Allen**
BLOOD OF A BOSS **VI**
By **Askari**
LOYAL TO THE GAME **IV**
LIFE OF SIN **III**
By **T.J. & Jelissa**
A DOPEBOY'S PRAYER **II**
By **Eddie "Wolf" Lee**
IF LOVING YOU IS WRONG… **III**
LOVE ME EVEN WHEN IT HURTS **III**
By **Jelissa**
TRUE SAVAGE **VII**
By **Chris Green**
BLAST FOR ME **III**
DUFFLE BAG CARTEL **IV**
By **Ghost**
ADDICTIED TO THE DRAMA **III**
By **Jamila Mathis**
A HUSTLER'S DECEIT 3
KILL ZONE **II**
BAE BELONGS TO ME III

SOUL OF A MONSTER II
By **Aryanna**
THE COST OF LOYALTY **III**
By **Kweli**
SHE FELL IN LOVE WITH A REAL ONE **II**
By **Tamara Butler**
RENEGADE BOYS **III**
By **Meesha**
A GANGSTER'S SYN II
By **J-Blunt**
KING OF NEW YORK V
RISE TO POWER III
COKE KINGS III
By **T.J. Edwards**
GORILLAZ IN THE BAY IV
De'Kari
THE STREETS ARE CALLING II
Duquie Wilson
KINGPIN KILLAZ IV
STREET KINGS 2
PAID IN BLOOD 2
Hood Rich
SINS OF A HUSTLA II
ASAD
TRIGGADALE III
Elijah R. Freeman
MARRIED TO A BOSS III
By Destiny Skai & Chris Green
KINGZ OF THE GAME III
Playa Ray

SLAUGHTER GANG II

By Willie Slaughter

THE HEART OF A SAVAGE II

By Jibril Williams

FUK SHYT II

By Blakk Diamond

THE DOPEMAN'S BODYGAURD II

By Tranay Adams

Available Now

RESTRAINING ORDER **I & II**

By **CA$H & Coffee**

LOVE KNOWS NO BOUNDARIES **I II & III**

By **Coffee**

RAISED AS A GOON I, II, III & IV

BRED BY THE SLUMS I, II, III

BLAST FOR ME I & II

ROTTEN TO THE CORE I II III

A BRONX TALE I, II, III

DUFFEL BAG CARTEL I II III

By **Ghost**

LAY IT DOWN **I & II**

LAST OF A DYING BREED

BLOOD STAINS OF A SHOTTA I & II

By **Jamaica**

LOYAL TO THE GAME

LOYAL TO THE GAME II

LOYAL TO THE GAME III

LIFE OF SIN I, II

By **TJ & Jelissa**

BLOODY COMMAS I & II

SKI MASK CARTEL I II & III

KING OF NEW YORK I II,III IV

RISE TO POWER I II

COKE KINGS I II

By **T.J. Edwards**

IF LOVING HIM IS WRONG…I & II

LOVE ME EVEN WHEN IT HURTS I II

By **Jelissa**

WHEN THE STREETS CLAP BACK I & II III

By **Jibril Williams**

A DISTINGUISHED THUG STOLE MY HEART I II & III

LOVE SHOULDN'T HURT I II III IV

RENEGADE BOYS I & II

By **Meesha**

A GANGSTER'S CODE I &, II III

A GANGSTER'S SYN

By J-Blunt

PUSH IT TO THE LIMIT

By **Bre' Hayes**

BLOOD OF A BOSS **I, II, III, IV, V**

By **Askari**

THE STREETS BLEED MURDER **I, II & III**

THE HEART OF A GANGSTA I II& III

By **Jerry Jackson**

CUM FOR ME

CUM FOR ME 2

CUM FOR ME 3

CUM FOR ME 4

CUM FOR ME 5

An **LDP Erotica Collaboration**

BRIDE OF A HUSTLA **I II & II**

THE FETTI GIRLS **I, II& III**

CORRUPTED BY A GANGSTA I, II III, IV

By **Destiny Skai**

WHEN A GOOD GIRL GOES BAD

By **Adrienne**

THE COST OF LOYALTY

By Kweli

A GANGSTER'S REVENGE **I II III & IV**

THE BOSS MAN'S DAUGHTERS

THE BOSS MAN'S DAUGHTERS II

THE BOSSMAN'S DAUGHTERS III

THE BOSSMAN'S DAUGHTERS IV

THE BOSS MAN'S DAUGHTERS **V**

A SAVAGE LOVE **I & II**

BAE BELONGS TO ME I II

A HUSTLER'S DECEIT I, II, III

WHAT BAD BITCHES DO I, II, III

SOUL OF A MONSTER

By **Aryanna**

A KINGPIN'S AMBITON

A KINGPIN'S AMBITION **II**

I MURDER FOR THE DOUGH

By **Ambitious**

TRUE SAVAGE

TRUE SAVAGE II

TRUE SAVAGE **III**

TRUE SAVAGE **IV**

TRUE SAVAGE **V**

TRUE SAVAGE **VI**

By **Chris Green**

A DOPEBOY'S PRAYER

By **Eddie "Wolf" Lee**

THE KING CARTEL **I, II & III**

By **Frank Gresham**

THESE NIGGAS AIN'T LOYAL **I, II & III**

By **Nikki Tee**

GANGSTA SHYT **I II &III**

By **CATO**

THE ULTIMATE BETRAYAL

By **Phoenix**

BOSS'N UP **I , II & III**

By **Royal Nicole**

I LOVE YOU TO DEATH

By Destiny J

I RIDE FOR MY HITTA

I STILL RIDE FOR MY HITTA

By **Misty Holt**

LOVE & CHASIN' PAPER

By **Qay Crockett**

TO DIE IN VAIN

SINS OF A HUSTLA

By **ASAD**

BROOKLYN HUSTLAZ

By **Boogsy Morina**

BROOKLYN ON LOCK I & II

By **Sonovia**

GANGSTA CITY

By **Teddy Duke**

A DRUG KING AND HIS DIAMOND I & II III

A DOPEMAN'S RICHES

HER MAN, MINE'S TOO I, II

CASH MONEY HO'S

By Nicole Goosby

TRAPHOUSE KING **I II & III**

KINGPIN KILLAZ I II III

STREET KINGS

PAID IN BLOOD

By **Hood Rich**

LIPSTICK KILLAH **I, II, III**

CRIME OF PASSION I & II

By **Mimi**

STEADY MOBBN' **I, II, III**

By **Marcellus Allen**

WHO SHOT YA **I, II, III**

Renta

GORILLAZ IN THE BAY **I II III**

DE'KARI

TRIGGADALE I II

Elijah R. Freeman

GOD BLESS THE TRAPPERS I, II, III

THESE SCANDALOUS STREETS I, II, III

FEAR MY GANGSTA I, II, III

THESE STREETS DON'T LOVE NOBODY I, II

BURY ME A G I, II, III, IV, V

A GANGSTA'S EMPIRE I, II, III, IV

THE DOPEMAN'S BODYGAURD

Tranay Adams

THE STREETS ARE CALLING

Duquie Wilson

MARRIED TO A BOSS... I II

By Destiny Skai & Chris Green

KINGZ OF THE GAME I II

Playa Ray

SLAUGHTER GANG II

By Willie Slaughter

THE HEART OF A SAVAGE

By Jibril Williams

FUK SHYT

By Blakk Diamond

<u>BOOKS BY LDP'S CEO, CA$H</u>

<u>TRUST IN NO MAN</u>

<u>TRUST IN NO MAN 2</u>

<u>TRUST IN NO MAN 3</u>

<u>BONDED BY BLOOD</u>

<u>SHORTY GOT A THUG</u>

<u>THUGS CRY</u>

<u>THUGS CRY 2</u>

<u>THUGS CRY 3</u>

<u>TRUST NO BITCH</u>

<u>TRUST NO BITCH 2</u>

<u>TRUST NO BITCH 3</u>

<u>TIL MY CASKET DROPS</u>

<u>RESTRAINING ORDER</u>

<u>RESTRAINING ORDER 2</u>

<u>IN LOVE WITH A CONVICT</u>

<u>Coming Soon</u>

BONDED BY BLOOD 2

BOW DOWN TO MY GANGSTA

Gorillaz in the Bay 3

www.ingramcontent.com/pod-product-compliance
Lightning Source LLC
Chambersburg PA
CBHW070550260626
47161CB00002B/557